BEYOND THE RIVER OF SHAME

Ken Czech

ALL THINGS
THAT MATTER
PRESS

ISBN: 97809980717-5-6

Library of Congress Control Number: 2017934584

Map of Sam and Florie's routes courtesy of Ken Czech.
Baker, Samuel W. -- Albert Nynaza Great Basin of the Nile and the Exploration of the Nile Tributaries, London: Macmillan 1866

Acknowledgments

I would like to thank my readers Libbie Hawker, Pat Horgan, Brenda Foy, and Mary Czech for their keen eyes and suggestions. My wife, Mary, receives additional note of thanks for her patience and support during the long process of researching, writing, and re-writing.

I would also like to thank Deb and Phil Harris of All Things That Matter Press for seeing my book to its fruition.

THE BASIN OF
THE NILE
to illustrate
SIR S.W. BAKER'S ROUTES
AND DISCOVERIES

SCALE GEOG. MILES

Sir S.W. Baker's Routes

Chapter One

Wallachia, Southern Romania
Autumn 1858

Florie von Sass shaded her eyes against the tawny glare of the setting sun. The sultry wind rippling through the fields of ripe wheat stirred her hair, lifelike, until she tied a threadbare scarf over her golden tresses. She sniffed the air, its taint oddly metallic, reminding her of melted copper at a smithy's forge. Storm brewing, she thought as she glanced at the pewter-colored clouds building beyond the village's hilltop cemetery. Sudden movement along the hill's crest drew her gaze. Odd. No one should be out there among the headstones, especially at this time of day. She rubbed her hands nervously over her frayed apron. Should she tell someone?

"Aren't you done taking those sacks of turnips into the cellar? They want you in the wheat field."

Florie's mouth tightened, her study of the boneyard and its interlopers broken. She hadn't noticed the two women staring at her. Stela, with the mocking voice, wore a haughty smirk. Corinna, her companion, had pinched cheeks and bad teeth. In contrast to their olive complexions, dark hair, and equally dark eyes, Florie looked—and felt—out of place.

"Look at Florie's face, Corinna. Can't you tell she's in love?" Stela jeered. "Tamas Comanasti has been hangin' around her for weeks, cooin' and makin' eyes. You know what's on his mind."

Corinna whistled a low note. "Tamas Comanasti? He'll inherit the biggest farm some day and he'll be rich. I'd like to wrap my legs around him, that's for sure."

Florie's cheeks reddened as she tried to keep the image of a naked Tamas from bruising her thoughts.

Stela appraised Florie from head to toe, as though seeing her for the first time. "Can't say what he sees in a Hungarian wench like you with your pasty skin, pale hair, and what not all. I'll admit, you've got hips and titties the envy of any, but you're almost past your prime. What are you now, nineteen?"

Florie faced both women, her blue eyes flashing. "Almost eighteen," she retorted testily. "Not Tamas, nor anyone else, has a claim on me."

Stela clucked her tongue teasingly. "Pretty soon you'll end up a dried old prune with flat paps no man will look at. By then, I'll have a brood of kids and a husband who takes care of me. So will Corinna. No cold winter nights for us. And when Tamas is tired of playing with you, you'll still have nothing. You'll always be an outsider."

"You should stop trying to steal our men and just leave," Corinna piped scornfully. "You're not one of us. You really don't belong in Mehadia. Why don't you go someplace else?"

Florie clenched her fists to keep from snapping back. Her cheeks puffed with a sigh of relief when the two women, arm in arm, ambled away to attend to other chores. When she'd first arrived in the village of Mehadia ten years earlier, girls like Stela and Corinna had bullied her because of her foreign mannerisms and odd accent. No family in Mehadia or any of the other farming villages in the region could afford to take in an orphaned refugee from the Hungarian rebellion, let alone a wisp of a girl. To survive, she wandered from one hamlet to the next, mucking animal stalls, emptying the slops, and helping with the harvests. Payment usually consisted of supper, secondhand clothes, a few coins, and a dry barn to sleep in. It was easier to rely on herself than the likes of Stela or the other villagers.

Brow knitted in agitation, Florie glanced at the cemetery hill. Now all seemed quiet there. "Just my imagination," she mumbled, chewing on her lip.

Still muttering, she drew the cord tight around the neck of a coarsely woven sack stuffed with turnips. She hefted the sack to her shoulder, grunting as its weight settled, before carefully easing down the creaking steps of the root cellar to tuck the turnips next to other sacks of vegetables. Pausing, she leaned against one of the timbers supporting the low ceiling. Above her head, a draft of air caressed a gauzy film of cobwebs. A soothing quiet permeated the cellar. In the semi-darkness, she breathed in the fusty scent of earth packed around pale stones that formed its walls. The floor felt hard and cool under her bare feet. Mounds of cucumbers and beets had been pickled and jammed into kegs filled with tangy brine, while the pumpkins, as yellow-orange as a glowing moon face, had had their meat and seeds dried and stored in earthenware jars. Baskets of apples nearly filled another storage bin. The memory of the smell of apple tarts bubbling and crisping on the stove made her mouth water. But these vittles were reserved for the time when winter winds blew from the lofty Carpathians and cruel snow shrouded the earth, a time drawing near despite the sweltering mugginess of this late afternoon.

Four more sacks of turnips waited. Beastly heat! Florie mopped her brow and neck with her scarf. Blowing out her breath in a whoosh, she draped the square of cloth over a nail protruding from the cellar's doorframe to let it dry. Then, with a grimace of determination, she finished storing the remaining sacks, stomped up the stairs into daylight, slammed the door to the cellar shut, and lowered its locking bar into place. Without hesitation, she turned and strode toward the wheat fields. Although most of the cutting was done for the day and many of the farmers were trudging home with their curve-bladed scythes balanced on their shoulders, wheat remained to be bundled into sheaves. Women's work, she thought glumly, always women's work. While they viewed her as an outsider, the villagers welcomed her strong back easily enough.

As her palm strayed across her sweat-wet brow, Florie realized she had left her scarf in the cellar. Pursing her lips in exasperation, she pivoted on her heel to retrace her steps to retrieve it. As she did so, her gaze drifted to the graveyard on its lonely, dreary hill. Again, someone — or something — moved along its crest. A thousand times she had gazed at the mound beyond Mehadia's outskirts and never seen anyone there except during burials. But no one in the village had died recently. She gulped.

"What are you looking at, gypsy girl?" drawled a voice from behind her.

Startled, Florie jumped. "I'm not a gypsy," she replied, thrusting her chin defiantly. Tamas Comanasti had a way of flustering her. Sweat matted his mop of black hair, and his brown eyes glittered mischievously. He looked almost handsome in his dusty, round-faced, broad-shouldered way as he leaned on the long shaft of his scythe.

"Well, what did you see out there?"

She pointed toward the hill. "I'm not sure. Somebody moving about the tombstones, I think. Now they've stopped."

"It's ghosts you saw," he warbled in a tremulous voice.

"Don't make fun of me," she said crossly.

Tamas chuckled and squinted toward the gray bluff beyond the wheat fields. "There's nothin' out there 'cept graves, rocks, and ravines. Past those, the steppe is as flat as Mama Oldau's pan-fried blinis — until you cross the Danube, that is. Then you're in Bulgaria on Turkish land."

Florie shuddered and sketched the sign of the cross. The Turks were slave raiders. It was unlucky to even mention them.

"I only know what I saw," she replied stubbornly. "Anyway, I have to help bind the sheaves."

"And I'm here to help you so you can join in the celebration," Tamas said, bending in an exaggerated bow. "There will be a feast and dance after the winnowing. I'd like it if you joined me."

Florie's gaze flitted nervously toward the wheat fields. The village women continued binding and stacking while the men tromped toward the village. She hoped none were watching her and Tamas.

"I don't need help with chores," she said. "You know your father doesn't like it when you talk to me. I have no kin, no dowry. I can offer nothing to your family."

Tamas gently brushed a strand of hair curling over her forehead with his finger. To his surprise, she drew back a step. "What my father thinks is his business, Florence. I don't care that you're an orphan, or that you're Hungarian, not Wallachian. All I know is that I like you and want to spend more time with you."

Her mouth formed a strained line. Tamas' family was the wealthiest in the village. His father, Simeon, reported the harvest's outcome directly to the *voivode* in Bucharest. If she married into the Comanasti clan ... the notion startled her. Tamas was beginning to make things more complicated. Maybe it was time to really take notice of him. It would be wonderful to finally have someone she could love.

"People are beginning to stare at us," she said tensely.

Tamas moved closer and cupped her chin in his hands, tilting her face to his. "I don't care," he whispered. "Please, think how I feel about you." His lips brushed hers. She wondered at his touch, gentle and warm although his fingers were hard and calloused. Dizziness swept over her. Her head throbbed. With Tamas so near, she felt her protective barriers of isolation crumbling.

A thunderclap echoed sharply. Something hissed over their heads, followed by more loud booms.

With her heart pounding, Florie spun toward the booming sounds. Shadowy horsemen galloped toward them from the cover of the cemetery, as ragged explosions of orange and yellow flared in the darkness. Peasant women screamed and fled.

"Turks," Tamas cried. "Slave catchers! Run, Florie!"

As she hesitated, his hand slapped her between her shoulders, urging her on. Another musket ball whistled near. Hooves pounded in pursuit.

"The town hall," Tamas shouted desperately. "You've a chance if you reach the town hall. It's strong like a fort!" He stepped toward the invaders, the scythe clutched in his strong hands, its wicked blade swinging.

Florie staggered, kept her feet, and cast a hurried glance over her shoulder. A slave catcher wearing a chain mail shirt and mounted on a chestnut-colored horse lumbered toward them, the bell-shaped muzzle of his pistol raised. Flame belched, followed by the dull *thwack* of a bullet striking flesh. Tamas pirouetted drunkenly and collapsed, blood bubbling from his shattered throat.

Choking back her horror, Florie skidded to a stop and pivoted in different directions. Horsemen fanned in a wide arc, cutting off escape routes. She swerved again. The slaver in the mail shirt wheeled his steed about and leapt down. He waved toward several wagons just emerging from beyond the curve of the burial hill.

Noise thumped about Florie's ears. She realized part of the sound roared from her throat as she steeled herself, her stomach churning, to stoop and retrieve Tamas' scythe, and another part wrenched from the shrieking women gathered up by the Turks and lashed across their saddles. Horses snorted. Guns crashed. Strutting toward her, the mail-clad slave catcher waved his finger, scolding, and clucked his tongue. He drew his sword. With a grunt of effort, she swung the scythe from her hips, slashing its blade toward his chest. He raised his sword, turned his wrist, and deflected her clumsy lunge. Jolted, she dropped the scythe. Before she could recover, he seized her by her hair and jabbered excitedly.

"No," Florie screamed, raking her nails across his face. He yelped in surprise and released her. As she skipped back, she stumbled against Tamas' body and fell, her skull thudding against the ground. Dazed, she tried to squirm away. With a growl, the slave catcher seized her legs and hoisted her long apron and skirt above her hips. He ripped away her undergarment and undid his belt.

"Help!" She tried to kick him. "Help me!"

Panic clotted Florie's throat as his weight pressed her down, his sour stink flooding her nostrils. His metal shirt grated against her belly. She sucked her breath in a long, agonizing gasp, willing her body to ignore the pain, praying she could dissolve under his thrusting and wash away like a house of sand before angry waves.

After the slave catcher finished, she drew her legs under her, trying to lever herself away from him. She nudged against Tamas and huddled next to him, staring into his dead eyes. The remembered taste of his lips on hers faded with the twilight. She whispered his name. The slave catcher laughed, dragged her to her feet, and lashed her wrists behind her with her apron. She swayed, senses reeling sickeningly, a sob of humiliation bursting free as he lifted her and threw her over his saddle.

***

On the day after the raid on Mehadia, Florie lay motionless in the back of a slave catchers' wagon, curled in a fetal position. Daylight peeked through gaps in its sideboards. More boards formed the wagon's roof. Strange, she didn't remember being dumped into the wagon. She didn't care. The shock of what had happened tumbled her into a bottomless well of black despair. Tamas was dead. She might just as well be dead, too.

***

On the second day after the raid, someone lifting her head woke Florie from a troubled sleep. Two or three shadowy faces loomed over her. "You have to drink," one of the faces mumbled. A woman's voice, she thought. A metal cup touched her lips. She sucked greedily.

"Will she live?" another face asked.

"I think so," said the one tilting the cup. "She's had a rough time."

"It's only going to get worse for all of us."

"I know. We'll get her to eat something and she'll get over it."

***

Oxen bellowed as they strained to pull the heavy wagons through ruts cut deeply into the road. Florie winced as the wagon jolted from side to side, slamming her shoulders against its sideboards. Had it been three days or four since Mehadia was attacked? It didn't matter. She fought past the wretchedness that gripped her. Her hand stole to her belly, gingerly touching flesh bruised by a metal shirt. She didn't want to explore her other hurts further. Better to try to ignore those.

Her nose wrinkled against the biting odors of urine and vomit. Through the dim, grayish light inside the wagon, she could distinguish her fellow captives, all women, slumped against the boards across from her. Like her, they had been wrenched from their homes and now faced slavery. Several had given her water and food, had helped her out of the wagon to pee. If they could survive, she thought determinedly, she could, too.

"I'm glad you're feeling better," one of the women said softly. A girl of about ten quietly sobbed on her lap. The woman mechanically patted her daughter's head as if to comfort her, but the blank expression on her face conveyed neither grief nor comfort.

Florie offered a wan smile. "Thank you for helping me." Her smile faded to a look of concern. "Is your daughter sick?"

"No, just scared. We're all scared."

A blast of wind rocked the wagon. Ice pellets drummed on its roof. Florie glanced through a gap between the sideboards. Slush coated the grass and trees, and the slate-colored sky spat ice and snow. She remembered the unseasonable warmth of Mehadia and wished for a glimpse of the sun. The wagon rumbled across a stone bridge. Drab, wet buildings appeared. A few bedraggled people scuttled across the streets.

"We've come to a town," she said, her voice a dry croak. "Do you know what this place is?"

The woman with the child raised her head and answered, "It's probably Vidin in Bulgaria. I overheard those animals that captured us say that a slave seller named Emile Zeb owns a big market there."

Slave seller. Florie shuddered. She recalled angry parents warning naughty children they'd be sold to an evil Turk in Vidin if they didn't behave.

The wagon caravan filled with captured women creaked to a stop in front of a squat, gray-stone tower. Water dripped incessantly from its dome and puddled in front of a massive gate flecked with rust. A slave catcher wearing a fur-trimmed cape around his shoulders pounded on the gate. Hinges grated as the ponderous portal swung open to reveal a dark maw sloping downward. Guards clad in leather jerkins and metal caps poured out of the tunnel. Wagon doors clanged open and the guards dragged the women out, by the hair if they moved too slowly, and propelled them into the darkness.

Florie hopped from the wagon and skidded through the mud, trying to keep her balance as she entered the tunnel. Her outstretched fingers glided over stones thick with slimy moss. Something gray-black scuttled along a trough cut into the floor, tiny claws clicking on stone close to her feet. Instinctively, she shrank back. God, don't let there be rats! A powerful hand splayed across her back and pushed her. "Keep moving," a voice commanded.

The throng of sobbing captives formed a ragged column that shuffled past barred cells containing imprisoned women. In twos and threes, the jailers shoved the newcomers into various cells.

Florie yelped in pain as one of the guards seized her arm in a pincer-like grip. "You go in here," he growled as he turned a key in the lock of an ironbound door. The hinges screeched. With a grunt, he pushed her inside.

The few candles lighting the cell guttered when the door slammed shut. Nine grimy faces stared at her. Florie shivered, looking for a friendly face, but she read only fear. One of the young women began weeping; another sank to her knees and prayed. She sat down near them, cross-legged, forcing herself to breathe deeply, to not succumb to pure terror. Her gaze roved over her cellmates. All were younger, dark-haired women plucked from Wallachian and Serbian villages. She was the only fair-haired prisoner among them.

The day wore on. No one spoke to her. A few of the women dozed. Her mind wandered to more pleasant thoughts. The year before, she had helped the people of Mehadia cut wheat, joining them in a harvesting dance she knew well: step, gather with the hay crook, swish with the sickle, step. After hours of sweat, a granny, her wrinkled face seemingly cut from folds of stone, pounded a heavy spoon against the bottom of a dishpan until all of the workers had gathered for lunch. There were flagons of cider and water, barrels of pickled vegetables, and fat loaves of black bread. That's when Tamas had first approached her, shyly. He sipped from the same cup as she. Tamas.

A key skittering against the cell door's lock plate broke her reverie. The heavy panel creaked open. A guard appeared and waved in two crones wearing dingy, threadbare shifts. The old women tottered to the cell's center carrying a pitcher of water, a few crockery bowls, and a black kettle filled with soup. Bits of vegetables floated in the thin, grayish-brown broth.

"Share the soup and the bowls," the burly guardsman ordered.

"But there are no spoons," Florie sputtered.

The guard's eyes widened with surprise, then he threw back his head and laughed. He was still laughing after the crones had departed and he had locked the door.

Florie's brow wrinkled with confusion. "Why was that funny?"

Another of the prisoners, a sloe-eyed Serbian woman, her dark hair tied into a tail, shook her head. "They're afraid we'll use the spoons to cut ourselves, you know, let out our blood. Rob them of their share of the money we'll fetch. I'm sure it's happened before."

The Serbian dipped a bowl into the kettle and handed it to Florie. "My name is Zora. Eat a little, then I'll have some."

The soup was only lukewarm, but Florie savored every swallow. It wasn't the filling fare served in Mehadia's wheat field, but it was food. "What happens next?" she asked as she licked her lips clean of broth.

"A slave auction," Zora said. "Did you notice when we came in that most of the cells are full? It'll happen soon."

"That may be, but I plan to eat and sleep when I need to, and I'll find a way out later," Florie replied flatly. "I'm a slave to no one."

"You'll sing differently once your new master takes hold of you," Zora warned. "Just wait until our turn."

Florie winced. "What do you mean *our turn*?"

"I've heard the Turks usually auction the children first. You don't even want to think about them. Then it's the older and plainer women as field hands and scullions. Next come the pleasure slaves for the harems. That's us." To emphasize her point, Zora pushed up her breasts provocatively. "You've hair the color of gold coin, very unusual. You'll see what I mean."

With Zora's words cascading through her thoughts, Florie gathered some of the straw layering the stone floor into a crude bed of sorts. She draped her forearm over her face and closed her eyes. An image of her parents drifted in her daydream. She wished they were there to give her comfort, to take her away from this nightmare. But ten years had passed since Papa had gone to fight during the Hungarian uprising against the Austrian emperor. He never came home. And Mama … it was just too painful to recall those final, terrifying moments. Then, parentless, the horror of being swept into the tide of refugees fleeing to Wallachia to escape the rampaging Austrian troops. Now Mehadia was gone, and Tamas, too. Her world seemed filled with loss. To the restless whispers and occasional sobs of her cellmates, she drifted into an uneasy sleep.

**

Iron doors slammed. Guards shouted. Women shrieked.

Florie woke with a start, her heart hammering like a maul on raw iron. The other girls in the cell huddled together, quivering with fear.

"This is it," Zora said, her jaws clenching. "The auction is starting."

The clanging of doors mixed with the screaming drew closer. Florie gulped as she remembered the Serbian's warning: the children first, then the older women. Their turn would come last.

An hour crept by, then two. The shrieks diminished. In the ensuing stillness, Florie gritted her teeth and clamped her hands into fists against her nervous trembling.

"It's soon now," Zora whispered.

As if on cue, a key turned in the lock and the door creaked open. Two turbaned guards, one bearing a whip, strode boldly into the cell. They positioned themselves on either side of the door. A third, more exotic figure waddled in.

Florie sucked her breath in surprise. She had never seen a black African before. This one's meaty arms and bared, plump legs quivered as she entered the cell. Her ebony skin glowed with oils; her lips were smeared red, while silver paint outlined her eyes. A gauzy linen robe draped over one shoulder stretched across her ample hips and bosom. She cradled an enameled tray filled with hairbrushes, small wooden boxes, and elaborately decorated round tins. Behind her traipsed three more women hefting buckets of steaming water, stacks of thick towels, and folded robes.

The African set her tray down and gestured broadly with a wave of her hand toward the ten women. "All of you, take your clothes off," she ordered, her words oddly accented. "Here is soap and water. Wash your faces and your bottoms so you don't stink. Then put these on."

The garments handed out by the African's assistants were simple caftans with hoods and drawstrings at the neck and shoulders. The captives, including Zora, meekly stripped off their soiled, tattered clothing. After a quick scrubbing, they slid the caftans over their heads. The African opened several tins on the tray and dabbed a thick finger into one of them. She spread dark kohl around the eyes of each of the women. From another tin, she rubbed a light pink paste into their cheeks. A darker ruby coloring highlighted their lips.

The African stepped back and surveyed the slaves with a critical eye. She turned to Florie. "What are you waiting for?" she asked impatiently, her tongue flicking over her lips. "Drop your dress, wash up, and put this on. The governor is here today and wants to see only the prettiest. You're a blondie, sweet one. You'll be the last to go. What shall we call you? How about Zelda? Maybe Astiza. Every slave needs a name."

"My name is Florence, and I'm not a slave."

The African's eyes widened. "You're an impudent bitch, and you'll be a slave soon enough. Then Florence it shall be. Your new master can change your name if he chooses."

Florie fought against the icy touch of panic as she sponged water over her bare body. She wouldn't give in to such weakness, she vowed silently as she bit her lip. No one would ever own her.

The African grinned, her teeth gleaming brightly, and applied kohl around Florie's eyes before painting the young woman's cheeks and lips. One of the attendants brushed her golden hair until it shimmered like freshly cut wheat. Florie shuddered as she shrugged on a blue and white striped caftan.

"You may well break Emile Zeb's auction record," the African murmured as she paused to admire her handiwork. After packing her cosmetics, she waited near the door until another guard appeared.

"It's time," the African said. She wiggled a finger at the captives to follow the guards.

The dank air in the corridor caused Florie to shiver. Under the light of a flickering torch, the ten young women were led to a narrow staircase that spiraled to an upper level. The roar of many voices drifted to them.

"Now we're in for it," Zora said casually, reveling in the discomfort and fear of her fellow prisoners. "Now *we'll* be sold. It won't be such a big thing."

Florie heard men laughing. She tried to swallow but her throat felt dry as milled flour. Her pulse pounded faster than she could count. Taking a deep breath, she climbed the stairs.

The cacophony of voices increased in tempo and intensity as she and the others ascended to the next level and marched through an arched door leading to a vast, domed room. Light filtered through tiny windows plastered into the curvature of the ceiling. Smoke from cigarettes and hookahs roiled at the entrance to the bidding floor. Then they were through the tobacco haze, through the fringe of jabbering, gesticulating men gathered near the auction block at the center of the dome. Perhaps a hundred bidders, some reclining on brilliantly hued cushions, were spread in a semicircle.

Florie swallowed hard and wiped her sweaty palms on her striped caftan. Her gaze drifted over the men, barely noticing their turbans, multicolored robes, and lusting, olive-skinned faces. To her they all looked the same, like wolves hungry for her flesh. She saw no mercy, no pity in their eyes as they cursed and jostled one another to be closer to the bidding block. The banging of a brass gavel on a metal plate startled her.

A hook-nosed Bulgarian factotum, swathed in dark robes and seated at a low desk near the auction block, pounded his gavel for silence. A leather-bound book, inkhorns, pens, and an abacus inlaid with rare woods were arrayed across the desktop.

Florie's eyes narrowed. The slave catcher who had violated her in the wheat field stood just behind the man with the gavel, his muscular arms crossed over his chain mail shirt. Scabbed scratch marks puckered his cheek. For a moment, the deep wound of her rape flared brightly in her mind. She wanted to scream her hatred, to fling herself at the slave catcher, to pound his head against the ground until the gray slush of his brains spilled out. Then the moment passed. Anger will get you nowhere, she thought bitterly.

The slave catcher smirked when he saw her.

The Bulgarian hammered on the metal plate again and called for attention in his mother tongue. "Be aware, all who are gathered, of the auctioning of a stock of fine slaves fit for the most discerning of harems, or for those of you who need only a single one to keep you warm." Laughter rippled among the men. "Today, in this final phase of our sale, we auction ten of the finest women we have procured. It is also our pleasure to have in attendance His Excellency, Zast Ohmed Pasha, Governor of Vidin."

A thin, mustachioed man, his eyes glittering coldly from skull-like orbits set in a narrow, ascetic face, flicked his hand in acknowledgement. Florie, just able to understand the factotum's words, saw the governor's dark, curious gaze turn upon her, methodically appraising her from feet to face. She shivered.

"The Honorable Emile Zeb welcomes you to this auction," the factotum cried, his voice rising with excitement. "The rights of exchange are gold or silver, Turkish lira, piasters, or any modern currency drawn from a reputable bank and delivered at the correct rate of exchange."

The gavel pounded again, and Emile Zeb emerged from behind a fringed curtain. Stoop-shouldered and walking with a slight limp, Zeb appeared to be middle-aged with a wispy beard and watery brown eyes. He gazed about the room, gauging the wealth gathered there. He dipped his head with appreciation toward the governor, usually the most successful bidder.

"Magram Bur, bring forth Elira, the first on our program," Zeb ordered in a sonorous tone that belied his slender frame.

Bur, the slave catcher in the mail shirt, led a young woman to the auction block. Unruly black hair framed a face with high cheekbones and frightened eyes. At Zeb's order, Elira turned in a slow circle. He loosened the shoulder lacings of her dark blue caftan. The upper portion of her garment dropped, revealing pert breasts and tanned, sinewy arms. Tears trickled down her cheeks. Florie thought she might be fourteen or fifteen years old.

Several men approached the bidding block. They squeezed Elira's calves and pinched her thighs and arms. One inspected her teeth.

"As you can see," Zeb began, his gaze once more sweeping across the crowd, "Elira is strong and desirable. Her teeth are sound, and her backbone straight as a mountain ash. She will perform whatever duties you might ask of her. We will start the bidding at two thousand piasters—two hundred liras."

The bidding started slowly, but quickly increased in tempo. When the factotum's gavel finally sounded, Elira had been sold for three hundred and fifty liras to a rich cloth merchant from Temesvar. She stoically retied the laces of her caftan to hide her nudity before Magram Bur escorted her from the platform. The factotum duly registered the sale in his leather-bound book, collected the money, and handed the buyer a receipt.

The girl's future had been decided in less than ten minutes.

Over the next three hours, eight more women were led to the auction block. Zora, her bravado gone, sobbed loudly in humiliation as a guard peeled her robe to her waist. Men gathered, pinching and squeezing. She tried to cover her breasts with her hands. Panting with passion, an elderly Bulgarian in a mauve turban, his eyes never leaving her bosom, drove the bid to five thousand piasters before the gavel sounded.

"Our last beauty today is of great rarity," Emile Zeb cried as he ostentatiously rubbed his hands together. "Usually one of her type would be found in Prussia, or in the kingdom of the Swedes. Her eyes and hair and skin set her apart from all others we have offered. But enough of my prattle! Behold! Florence!"

Florie shrugged away from Magram Bur as she stepped onto the block. His touch made her skin crawl. Her breath came in short, quick gasps as Zeb pushed the hood back from her head. She heard the buzz of many voices as the bidders pressed more closely toward her. The governor, his reptilian gaze gleaming coldly, leaned forward, felt the firmness of her calf, his hand gliding halfway up her thigh before he settled back on his cushion. Her knees almost buckled. Other men squeezed her arms, or examined her hands. Many touched her hair.

She shuddered as she remembered Zora's words. *Please, God,* she prayed silently, *let my master be a kind one!*

The gavel sounded. Bidding was about to start.

Chapter Two

Atholl, Highland Perthshire, Scotland
Autumn 1858

A shiver prickled Sam Baker's spine as he washed his bloodstained hands in the tumbling, icy waters of the River Tilt. He plunged his broad-bladed hunting knife into the flow, wiped it clean on his coarsely woven shirt, then inspected its keen edge in the lowering sunlight before sliding it into its sheath.

"I've never seen hounds work a stag like that before," said his companion, the Maharaja Duleep Singh, shaking his head in wonder. "And I doubt if I'll ever see such knife play again." He stood in his stirrups to better survey the carcass of a huge red stag lying just beyond where Sam washed. The stag's antlers swept upward like the branches of a great oak.

"But this is the only game they know." Sam grinned, waving his thumb at the pair of dogs panting next to the stag. Water from the Tilt beaded his thick, reddish-brown beard. "In Ceylon, we hunted deer with the hound and knife. We saved rifles for bigger game like elephant and water buffalo."

Singh chuckled and shook his head. The hereditary ruler of the Punjab, he sported a turban of burgundy silk, while his dark blue jacket almost writhed with gaudy gold piping. A leopard skin pad spread over his saddle imparted a romantic and barbaric appeal. His dusky complexion and oiled, jet curls and mustache had earned him the soubriquet of Black Prince of Elveden, yet his delicate, almost effeminate, facial cast and full lips clashed with Sam's brawny ruggedness.

"You know that you'll be the talk of everyone back at Blair House," he said. "The Duke of Atholl only invites select company to stalk his deer."

"I wish all of Atholl's guests would just leave me alone," Sam grumbled, flexing his powerful arms.

"You're a novelty, Sam. You've written books, and you hunt stags with a knife. You plan to head to Africa to search for the sources of the Nile. You want to be famous, but you don't want to be stared at. You don't want your name to be forgotten, yet you want these people to forget about you. You are, indeed, an enigma."

Sam glared at his diminutive comrade. *Enigma.* The word reminded him of something his father had drilled into him years ago. They had had their disagreements, perhaps stemming from when the senior Baker had sent young Sam to school in Germany as punishment for his indifference toward his lessons. What had Father said? *You are made from curious parts, Sam. How will you succeed when your nose follows every new scent? Don't try to be something you're not.*

"Well, let's head back to the duke's house," Sam growled. Nobody in the world could tell him what he could or couldn't be. "If I'm lucky, that crowd will admire the deer and forget about me."

"I wouldn't count on it," Singh muttered just under his breath.

***

"Look, there goes father now. See how grandly he rides," eleven-year-old Edith Baker cried as she watched Sam canter by. She bounced on her toes in anticipation and pushed back the lock of red hair that had slipped loose from her gaily-colored ribbon.

Agnes and Constance, her younger sisters, watched wide-eyed as their father passed the broad lawn in front of the Duke of Atholl's Blair House. Baby Ethel, not yet three, lay sleeping on a bench, missing the spectacle of riders, dogs, and trophy stag. "Did Papa shoot that huge deer?" Constance asked, her gaze shifting to Edith.

The elder girl laughed. "No, silly. You know Papa. He never does anything the simple way. He hunted it with his big knife."

"A knife?" Constance's eyes grew even larger.

"Is he really going to Aferca?" Agnes pulled on her older sibling's hand. She wasn't sure of the proper pronunciation. "Since Mummy has gone, I don't want him to go, too."

Edith's laughter died. She squeezed the smaller girls against her hips. "If he goes, sweetheart, it will only be for a little while."

"There now, young ladies, we'll be able to see your father from over here," said the girls' Aunt Min as she lifted Ethel and cradled her in her arms.

Minerva, Sam's younger sister, had been devoted to the children's welfare since the sudden death of Henrietta, their mother. As yet unmarried, and with no immediate prospects in sight, she had virtually adopted them as her own. She understood and forgave her eldest brother's passion for sport, his leapfrogging from country estate to manor house accepting invitations to shoot or fish. It's his way of coping with his loss, she told herself. And now this silly talk of him going to Africa. It would be up to her, she decided, to make sure her nieces received a proper education and Christian upbringing.

Sam dismounted and jogged toward them as his daughters pointed at him and jumped up and down with glee. The lacing holding his hair back in a tail had come undone and long strands floated about his shoulders.

His short bark of mirth mixed with their childish screams of delight as he lifted each of the girls high above his head, holding them aloft for a second, and then pretending to drop them before enfolding them in his arms.

"Sam, please. How will I ever get these children settled down?" Min scolded. "Go take care of your deer."

With a broad grin, Sam planted sloppy kisses on his daughters' foreheads. When he feigned the same kiss on Min, she stiff-armed him away.

"Don't you dare! Not in front of them," she said severely. "This is a Christian household."

Sam laughed, waved to the girls, then strode quickly back to his horse.

Min wasn't smiling. This sporting holiday at Atholl's estate was not to her liking. Indeed, it was time to head back to the more properly austere halls of Lochgarry House where there were books and music, but no guns or knives.

***

Sam ducked into Blair House before the Duke of Atholl's admiring guests could surround him. He kicked off his muddy boots and padded in stocking feet down the carpeted halls.

"Ah, Sam, there you are," the duke called from his library. "That was an amazing demonstration you put on today. You and those dogs brought the stag to bay right on the banks of the Tilt for all to see. Simply Homeric."

"Thank you, Your Lordship," Sam said, nodding to his pot-bellied host seated in an overstuffed chair, sipping brandy and smoking a black cigar. He liked Atholl, liked his comforting presence and the sport his highland estate offered, liked his brandy. He didn't notice another guest slumped in a Queen Anne upholstered in expensive maroon leather.

"You're in here early," Atholl said, the thick burr of the Scots woven into his speech. He blinked watery blue eyes. "I would have thought that you'd still be enjoying the accolades of my guests. Eh, Sam, now what?"

A thin smile curved Sam's mouth. "Africa. I still want to go to Africa. It's the damned Nile that calls. No one knows where the river begins. You know the stories. It springs from the earth in a great waterfall and descends over cliffs of solid gold. I think we both know that's a lot of rubbish. Solid gold, indeed! But there's little doubt that if the Nile truly flows from the Mountains of the Moon as Ptolemy suggested, whichever country controls its headwaters controls central Africa. That means trade in grain, salt, ivory, and metal ores. I want to claim those headwaters for

England, and set my name in history."

"But the only way you might get permission for such an expedition would be through the Royal Geographical Society, which would forward it to the Foreign Office," said the tallish man unfolding himself from the Queen Anne. A thick growth of hair above his ears fringed his majestic forehead and baldpate.

"Let me introduce Sir Roderick Murchison, President of the Royal Geographical Society," Atholl said with a flourish of his glass.

Sam reached out and shook Murchison's hand. A firm grip, not what he expected from an academic.

"While I appreciate the thought of you wanting to explore the Nile, we, at the Society, have a few problems with that idea," Murchison said after a sip of brandy.

Sam swallowed. Taking criticism was not his forte.

"First, the Society has already pledged funds to Captains Burton and Speke to explore the sources of the White Nile," Murchison continued. "They plan on heading west from Zanzibar, following the old caravan routes directly toward the Mountains of the Moon. Your version takes you down the length of the Nile from Egypt into the unknown south. That's perfectly impossible. The distance you propose to follow is four times greater than what Burton and Speke will face.

"Secondly, there's little doubt that the presence of another white man in the region would simply stir up trouble with the natives, something we don't want the captains to endure."

Sam felt the muscles bunching in his shoulders, and was surprised how tightly he clenched his fists.

"And thirdly," Murchison concluded, ticking the points on his fingers, "your reputation is that of a big game hunter, a regular nimrod if you will. I've read your books on hunting in Ceylon. It's ripping stuff, but I don't know that you have the inquisitive metal of a Dick Burton. Good Lord, man, it's 1858. We're in an age of scientific and geographical discovery conducted by experts in their fields. Burton alone speaks more than a dozen languages. Britain needs heroes like Burton and Speke. I suggest that if you want to visit Africa, put together a shooting trip, enjoy the sport, and avoid the limelight."

Sam forced himself to take a deep breath to keep his anger under control. "And if I don't?" he asked coldly.

"Then you'll have to go it alone. You can expect no financial help from either the RGS or the government. If you still persist on traveling to Africa, the Society will make arrangements for you to explore the Blue Nile. You can also expect a delay for as much as a year."

"The Blue Nile? A year?"

"Aye. The glory of the White Nile is reserved for Burton and Speke. It will take them as least a year to complete their investigation."

"But the Blue Nile holds none of the mystery as the White," Sam blurted desperately. "Most of it has already been mapped. Just a few tributaries remain."

"Take what we offer, or stay here and hunt deer or fox or snipe, or whatever it bloody well is that you hunt."

"My only choice?" Sam knew the answer even as he studied Murchison's face.

"Your only choice."

"A year? And what am I supposed to do until then?"

Murchison hooked his thumbs in his vest pockets. "That, my good man, is your problem, not ours. If you go, and if your work is professional enough, we'll publish your findings and invite you to lecture the Geographical Society. You'll have your footnote in history.

"Now, if you'll excuse me, Your Lordship," he nudged his chin in Atholl's direction, "I will leave your company and join the other guests. There is a certain young lady who has asked me about the botany of Peru."

Atholl waited until Murchison left the library, then jabbed at Sam with the stub of his cigar. "If I know Roddy Murchison, that young lady will probably have to pay him for information. He's a penny-pinching twit so tight he farts dust. Eh, Sam, he's as good as said no to your African excursion."

Sam grunted his displeasure as he shook his head. "No is not an option for me, my friend. I'm thirty-seven years old. My father hopes I'll take over his sugar business some day. But the thought of being a clerk the rest of my life chills my brain. Commodore Ross has searched for the North-West Passage, and David Livingstone is exploring along the Zambezi. I've done nothing. The entire world will be plumbed and examined, and I'll grow old selling sacks of Mauritius sugar. No one will ever remember Samuel White Baker."

"But what of your daughters? Surely you can't leave them."

"Aye, and that's the rub," Sam said, scratching his head. A pang of guilt skittered through his thoughts. "Since Henrietta died, well, I've done the girls little good. They need to be educated in the proper fashion, not in the haphazard way I'm used to doing. They need a strong woman to guide them, to raise them properly."

"Have your sister keep them. I dare say that she's a better mother than you'll ever be," laughed a third man just entering the room. Amusement danced on Duleep Singh's face. The twenty-year-old maharaja idolized Baker's masculinity, his easy way around horses, and his familiarity with rod, rifle, and gun.

"True. I'm sure Minerva would relish the idea," Sam returned. "But what will I do for the next year?"

Duleep Singh idly spun a barrel-sized globe mounted in a walnut and brass tripod. His slender, manicured finger drifted over the European continent. "Sam, let's go on a shooting trip away from England," he exclaimed, his dark eyes gleaming brightly. "It's quite the rage to hunt wild boar and roe deer in the Balkans. We'll cross the Channel, and take trains from Paris to Budapest. No servants. Just us two and our guns."

"And we can ride a river steamer down the Danube, and stop and shoot ducks and geese and snipe wherever and whenever we want," Sam agreed excitedly. "I hear game is plentiful in Bulgaria. With my daughters staying with Min, we can do as we please."

"Then Bulgaria it is," Singh said with a grin. "We'll easily be back before a year is up, and then you can go to Africa and become famous."

***

A haze of brown gun smoke drifted lazily over the rim of the frozen marsh bordering the Danube River. "I'm afraid hunting has come to an end, my friend," Sam said as he retrieved the gray partridge he'd shot. "I've never seen cold weather blow in so quickly."

Duleep Singh blew on his hands to warm them. It had been six weeks since Sam and he had left England on their shooting trip. The glorious weather they enjoyed during their journey through France and Central Europe had deteriorated into heavy frost and stinging sleet squalls.

"I should think so," Singh carped, his teeth chattering. "When we sailed from Budapest a week ago, it still felt like summer. Now winter threatens to strand us here. We should have stayed in Buda. At least it had a nightlife."

Sam admired the little game bird's colors before he stuffed it into his belt pouch. He retrieved his shooting diary from his coat pocket, then recorded his bag, the weather conditions, and the number of shots he had expended: six partridges, eight shots. "Come now, Your Highness, the sport has been quite good today, don't you think?" he said.

"If you like freezing your arse off," the maharaja said. "We've only been here a day and I already hate this place! What is it called anyway? Vidin?"

Sam nodded as he replaced the diary in his pocket. With the Danube frozen over, their hunting expedition was at an end, and they were stuck in this Bulgarian backwater. Vidin had once been a thriving outpost of the Roman Empire. Now the shabby town served a different purpose as a center that traded in flesh to the farthest reaches of the Ottoman Empire.

By the time the two friends returned to the city to deposit their guns and horses, the sleet had stopped and a watery glimmer of sun peeked through dreary clouds. The muezzin's call to prayer had just ended. Beyond the mosque with its elegant minaret squatted the ancient citadel of Baba Vida, its tile-roofed twin towers maintaining a commanding, watchful presence over the river.

"This place is a real dunghill," Singh griped petulantly as he shivered. "I'm for a coach to Bucharest, and from there, to Rome. I lust for a Latin lady, not for some Bulgarian beastie. Our ideas of penetrating foreign lands are quite different."

Sam rolled his eyes. "All right, we'll hire a coach."

"But at this moment, I'm incredibly bored." Singh sighed. "Why don't we see what Vidin offers for amusement?"

"I don't know if that's a good idea," Sam objected. "This land belongs to the Turks, not to the Queen. Perhaps a brief visit to the bazaar."

After paying for coach fare, Sam and his friend entered Vidin's sprawling bazaar. The noon prayer was over and prayer rugs rolled away. Craftsmen and merchants plied their wares, calling out the virtues of their handiwork in a dozen dialects. The tap-tap of tinsmiths' hammers on bronze and copper mingled with the chop-chop sound of woodcutters' axes splitting logs for home and hearth. In the food market, the pungent aroma of *carnatzlachi*, spicy sausages sizzling over charcoal grills competed with the semi-sour odor of *ciorba*, a soup filled with cucumbers and dill.

The locals paid scant attention to the two travelers as they entered a low, rambling structure that swelled to a whitewashed dome at the far end of the bazaar. Bronze lamps with flaming wicks drifting in pools of buttery oil spread flickering light across a corridor jammed with men.

Sam nudged an elderly Bulgarian wearing a mauve turban and shoes with upturned toes. The old man clutched a portable writing desk under his arm. "What gives?" Sam asked in Turkic.

"Eh?" The old fellow craned his neck to catch a glimpse of the arched chamber ahead. "It's an auction," he replied. "A slave auction. Fine women."

"We shouldn't be here." Sam gulped.

"But think of the spectacle," Duleep Singh replied excitedly, perching on tiptoes to see above the throng. "Do you know of any other Englishmen who have ever seen a slave actually auctioned?"

Sam grumbled his disapproval. Strong misgivings were already building in his mind as they entered the chamber. Tobacco smoke hung heavy at its center. A collision of tongues assaulted his ears. Human beings were going to be sold.

He tried to push past the aged Bulgarian in the mauve turban.

"Good slaves today. Lovely women, I've heard," the old man crooned, refusing to budge. "Some are likely Wallachians. I've heard tell there's even a yellow-hair, but the governor will get her. One must be careful in bidding against him. He doesn't like to lose. If we're truly lucky, maybe there will be some Serbian farm wenches." He rolled his eyes in anticipation. "Those Serbs, tits like melons just quivering for a man."

Sam glared at the ancient fellow. Slavery had long been a staple of trade in northern Africa, the Guinea Coast, and the hinterlands of the Sudan. He had met slaves in Turkey and Persia while on a hunting trip with his brother years earlier, but there it had seemed a simple economic and cultural expedient. He had never visited a slave auction before, and the thought of white, Christian women being sold into bondage was particularly revolting.

As he turned to leave, Duleep Singh hooked his arm. "I'll probably never have a chance to see such a proceeding again," he said, his voice vibrant. "Let's watch for a bit. There's nothing else to do until the coach arrives. Do you understand their infernal language?"

"A little," Sam said as he shook his head in frustration and shrugged loose from his friend's grasp. He stepped back and leaned against the wall. He wasn't about to abandon Singh, but he wasn't going to enjoy this disgusting display either. Better to get this over with, and then we'll catch the coach, he thought irritably.

He glumly surveyed the crowd. Close to the bidding platform sat a thin man in a military uniform. His black hair was slicked back, giving him a distinctive skull-like appearance. Other be-medaled officers were gathered around him. That would be the governor the Bulgarian had mentioned.

The line of women about to be auctioned snared Sam's attention. Most of the pathetic creatures had their heads down in a posture of dejection. There was a rhythm to their sale, the auctioneer calling out their charms while acknowledging bids from the audience. Excitement swelled among the bidders, their shouts and challenges ringing. One by one, the women were sold, with sobs and tears aplenty. Only one woman, clothed in a blue and white caftan, remained. Her face was partly hidden by the folds of her hood. Sam caught a glimpse of her profile, and of golden hair peeking from under cloth's edge. He wanted to see more. A seated man banged a gavel, and he glanced away. When he looked back, the woman in the striped caftan had moved a pace into the shadows. He snapped open his pocket watch. It was nearly time to catch the coach. He reached toward Duleep Singh's arm.

"Our last beauty today is of great rarity," the auctioneer intoned. "Behold … Florence!"

With a wave of his hand, Emile Zeb directed the slender girl cloaked in the blue and white striped caftan to step to the bidding platform. He drew the hood back from her head.

Sam swallowed hard, sure that his heart had skipped a beat. Wheat-colored hair brushed into a foaming mass framed a youthful face of delicate features with just a hint of rose on her cheeks; her lips had been painted a darker rose by the slave traders. Her piercing blue eyes, made more startling by the dark shadowing of kohl, strove to maintain poise and strength as potential bidders squeezed and stroked her arms and legs. She was helpless and knew it, but refused to give up her dignity. Her beauty and unspoken courage captivated him.

"Bidding starts at three hundred liras," Zeb called.

Fingers began gesturing numbers as the crowd hungrily upped the bid.

"Five hundred!"

"Five-fifty!"

"Seven hundred!"

The factotum scratched numbers on parchment and slid multicolored balls on his inlaid abacus.

Zeb sought more bids. "Observe her delights," he said enticingly as he loosened the lacing at the shoulders of her caftan. The garment slid to Florence's waist. Full breasts quivered with her fear, but she stared straight ahead, her fists clenched. The cords in her neck tightened.

Zeb gently rolled a nipple between thumb and forefinger. "See how ripe she is."

Sam ground his teeth as the frenzied men gathered in the dome shouted their bids and thrust more fingers into the air.

"One thousand liras," cried Ohmed Pasha, the governor. The sight of the slave's white flesh had stirred his passion. This was by far more than he had ever bid on a slave woman before. His grin was a cruel, compressed slash.

The factotum scribbled madly.

The slave girl's jaw trembled as she struggled to remain strong. For a moment, Sam thought he saw his own daughter standing on the block. He imagined Ohmed's hands on her, and it made him furious. A red mist of anger clouded his vision as he elbowed his way through the throng until he reached the base of the auction block. Her eyes were wide, staring at him in wonder and fear. He saw the gavel rise to end the bidding.

"One hundred English pounds," he bellowed in a voice that echoed from the high curve of the dome.

In the volatility of summer storms, silence often follows the drumbeat of a thunderclap. In the slave auction dome of Vidin, such silence followed Sam's words. Near a hundred pairs of eyes turned toward him. Emile Zeb gulped. Had Sam bothered to glance about, he would have seen Duleep Singh's jaws working spasmodically and the governor's hand drop to the dagger in his sash. But his eyes never wavered from the slave girl. Her surprised gaze had locked on his at the moment of his outburst. It bored to his very soul.

The silence of the dome slowly gave way to murmurs. Beads on the factotum's abacus clacked together as he converted the sum. He said something to Emile Zeb.

"The bid is one hundred English pounds," Zeb cried. "Five thousand Turkish lira, or 15,000 piasters."

Many bidders shook their heads in disbelief. The foreigner's bid, they agreed, was outlandish, despite the woman's beauty. The governor's bid had been one thousand liras. Wealthy as he was, Ohmed Pasha could not meet the Englishman's price.

Emile Zeb implored the crowd to bid higher, although inwardly he was beyond ecstasy. He had already figured the percentage of the money he would receive. A moment later, the gavel fell. The factotum entered £100 into his book.

Singh clutched Sam's arm desperately. "What have you done?"

Sam ignored him. He was still focused on Florence, her robe and hood restored, as she was led away by a guard. She turned. Her eyes met his again. He still read fear in them, but more surprise.

"You fool! You've bought a slave girl," Singh rasped.

Startled, Sam blinked in confusion as he signed a bank draft and accepted a receipt of purchase from Zeb's factotum. He folded the paper without reading it and tucked it into the back of his shooting diary. Singh's words echoed in his brain. The magnitude of his outburst slowly sank in. Good God! An English gentleman with a female slave? If his family or friends in England heard of this fiasco, what rumors would spread? Could he ever return to his home? How would his daughters react? What had he done?

"I ... I just couldn't see that poor child sold into bondage in this God forsaken land," he mumbled.

"Now what will you do with her?" Singh demanded, sensing his own life might become more complicated if he continued to accompany Baker.

"We ... I should give Florence her freedom," Sam stammered as he nervously plucked at his beard.

"And how long before the likes of the governor will have her under chain again, or before he and his friends cut our throats? I'm sure Ohmed Pasha could easily fabricate some kind of formal report to London on how we were murdered by thieves."

Sam glanced at the governor and his minions. The pasha stared at him through narrowed eyes, fists on hips, his stance projecting anger and danger.

"Then we'll take her away from Vidin and the pasha," Sam said as he struggled to think clearly. Henrietta had always warned him not to be impetuous, to measure the full circle of a decision before making it. Henrietta! He tried to recall his wife's features, but his memory of her unexpectedly blurred. The only image he conjured was one with yellow hair and fearless blue eyes framed by a caftan's hood.

What *had* he done?

Chapter Three

Snow squalls swirled across the Wallachian plain as a coach containing three passengers rumbled over rutted roads toward Bucharest. Florie sat stiffly next to the bearded man who had purchased her, but shivered as an icy wind buffeted the coach's closed windows and found gaps in its frame. Everything seemed to dance in a muddled blur through her mind. She didn't even recall being helped into the coach, but she *did* remember the last terrifying moments on the auction block. Her jaws had clenched when her caftan was pulled down. She remembered glimpsing the pasha as he bid, reading the lust flickering in his skeletal eye sockets and how that had chilled her to the bone. Then the bearded man wearing a Western coat had pushed his way through the crowd, shouting and waving his fist. She didn't know what he had yelled, but the boisterous gabble in Emile Zeb's auction dome had suddenly gone silent as a cemetery. And now she rode in this coach with him and another stranger.

The bearded man tapped her shoulder. She recoiled. His eyes widened with surprise. Then he asked her something in an unfamiliar tongue. His tone was not threatening; he seemed concerned. She shook her head. The brown-skinned man seated across from her spoke angrily. Again, she shook her head.

"You must try to get her to speak," Duleep Singh said.

Sam grimaced sourly. He had tried English, Turkic, then French, but obviously the slave girl did not understand. He mouthed a few words in the Bulgarian tongue. Her attention perked. Then he spoke in German.

Florie's eyes widened. "*Meine name ist Florence Barbara Maria von Sass,*" she said quietly. "*Ich bin Katholisch.*"

Sam smiled. "*Guten tag, Fraulein von Sass. Ich bin Samuel Baker, von Britanien. Ich bin Sam.*"

"Congratulations, Sam." Duleep Singh laughed bitterly. "You've not only bought a slave girl twenty years younger than you, but a Catholic one at that. And she doesn't even speak English. That should go over well at home."

Florie sensed the agitation growing between the two men. She also sensed she was the object of their aggravation. *Why did this Samuel Baker buy me?* She was certain the English did not keep harems. *When he bid, there was no evil in his face. If he bought me only to free me, then my most incredible prayers have been answered. But why didn't he leave me in Vidin? What is his purpose?* A second cold draft whisked through a gap in the window frame and she shivered again.

"*Bis du kalt?*" Sam asked.

At first she wanted to say no, to let Samuel Baker know that he did not have to take care of her. But when she shuddered for a third time, she allowed herself a small nod.

Sam shrugged off his coat and draped it around Florie. Her fists tightened as his hands touched her shoulders. He looked at her with concern. "The Turks did not treat you well, did they?"

The tiny tremble of her lip betrayed her pain. *No weakness,* her inner self seethed. *He will only pity you!*

"Be assured, Florence, that I mean you no harm."

Her eyes searched his. She was sure she read honesty and strength. "What … what will you do with me?" There, she had asked the question. She hoped her voice sounded strong.

Sam did not answer immediately. He flicked a look at Singh, but the maharaja's eyes were closed. "I truly don't know," he finally replied. "We will decide when we reach Bucharest."

We? Had she heard him correctly? We. He said *we* will decide! He had spoken to her as an equal, not some chattel to work in the fields, or pleasure a man in his bed.

Florie felt some of her fear drift away. Her body relaxed. The memory of the slave floor, the bidding, her rescue by Samuel Baker, swirled into a jumbled panorama of images and emotions as she struggled to stay awake. Her eyes closed and her head nodded.

Sam glanced at the young woman sleeping on his shoulder and gulped.

***

Florie, wide-eyed, pressed her face against the coach window. Her breath fogged the glass near her mouth. It was almost too much to take in. Bucharest seemed to stretch forever. Brick shops and wooden houses flanked long avenues. Farmers with bundles of firewood strapped to their shoulders trudged next to rickety carts piled high with sacks of turnips and beets. Ox-drawn wagons loaded with charcoal or straw clogged the thoroughfares. The recent snow had been trampled to a gray mush. A thin, brownish haze spewed from the innumerable coal and wood fires heating homes and businesses hung over the cityscape. Even the clanging of bells from a nearby church seemed muted in the gloom. It was dirty and noisy and rife with stagnant, unfamiliar smells. It was absolutely wonderful!

The coach clattered down a boulevard lined with bare-branched linden trees. Shoppers clutching packages bustled from one shop to the next.

"Herr Baker, where are we going?" Florie asked hesitantly.

"Please call me Sam," he said. "You can't traipse around Bucharest dressed only in that silly robe. It's winter, for pity's sake."

Duleep Singh chuckled as Florie's cheeks reddened.

The coach stopped at a storefront with elegant, blue-painted letters decorating the sign above its door. Florie shook her head. Although she could read after a fashion, the words on the sign were a mystery. She glanced at Sam questioningly.

"It's the dress shop of Madame Kopecky," he said, catching her eye. "We have business here."

Florie shivered as Sam helped her from the coach. A passing shopper stared at her curiously. She blushed again.

"Don't worry, I'll find a room for us at a good hotel," Singh said, leaning from the coach seat as Sam closed its door.

"Find *three* rooms," Sam advised. "And have a bath ready for her. Meet us back here in three hours."

A little brass bell above the door tinkled merrily as Florie and Sam entered the dressmaker's shop. Madame Kopecky, a smallish woman with round-lensed spectacles pushed over her forehead and into her graying hair, surveyed the pair wonderingly.

"Madame, a dress for the lady, please," Sam said in German. "One that you have in supply that can be quickly altered to fit. Payment in silver coin, of course."

Florie's mouth felt dry as wheat dust. She did not like the way the little woman was studying her. She stepped back behind Sam and whispered, "I have no money. You can't buy this for me. You've already done so much."

Sam turned and guided her toward Madame Kopecky. She wanted to jerk away, but the gentleness and warmth of his touch left her confused.

Kopecky's thin lips curved in an austere smile as she dropped her spectacles to the bridge of her nose. She measured Florie with a critical and practiced eye before lifting a dress from a display form. "This should do nicely, *mein Herr*," she said to Sam. "Only a few minor alterations will be needed."

Sam nodded. "Go with her, Florence," he said softly. "She'll take your measurements."

With a curt nod of her head, Madame Kopecky directed Florie into a curtained room. She slid a cloth tape measure under the young woman's arms and around her breasts. The bulge of flesh under the caftan was soft, unconfined. Kopecky's brow furrowed. She slid her hands over the material covering Florie's hips. The contour was smooth. Thrusting the curtains apart, the dressmaker stalked toward Sam.

"*Mein Herr,* the young lady has no undergarments," Kopecky sputtered apprehensively. "I do not know what to say."

Sam, flustered, reached into his pocket and produced several coins. "You won't have to say anything, Madame. Just make sure she has all of the necessaries a young lady requires. You have such items?"

Kopecky peeked at the coins Sam handed her and nodded. Yes, the combination of bribe and payment for underclothes was certainly enough to get rid of her apprehension. With a polite gesture, she directed him to an overstuffed chair occupying one corner of the shop. He plopped into the chair and clasped his hands behind his head. In a few minutes, he was snoring.

Florie let out her breath in a long, nervous sigh. Kopecky's fingers were cold against her skin as the dressmaker helped her slide the caftan off. Goose pimples crept across her body. Kopecky unwrapped a brown paper bundle, revealing a white linen chemise, drawers, and petticoat.

"I've never had such fine things," Florie whispered as she ran her hand across the soft material.

"It's a wonder you don't have anything on at all," Kopecky said, pursing her mouth.

"It is a long story."

"One I don't need to hear."

An hour sped by as Madame Kopecky measured, snipped, and stitched. At last she put down her tape and scissors, smoothing out tiny wrinkles with her hands. "You are ready."

Madame Kopecky dramatically drew aside the curtains leading to the fitting room. Biting her lip, Florie strode gracefully into the larger chamber. She pressed her hands against her hips, feeling the texture of the serge cloth. In a full-length mirror, she admired the fit and style of the dark blue dress trimmed with lace around the collar and its double row of black buttons down the front. Her heart thumped madly as Kopecky shook Sam awake.

Smothering a cough, Sam rose from his chair, goggle-eyed with wonder. A swallow stuck in his throat as his gaze swept over the beautiful young woman. He clumsily played with the brim of the hat he clutched at mid-waist. This was not his little daughter, his Edith, he had envisioned in his recent daydream. And this was certainly not his wife Henrietta.

"A warm shawl for the lady, please," he mumbled, his eyes never leaving Florie with her hair freshly combed, her new blue dress accenting her beauty.

Florie smiled shyly as Kopecky arranged a thick, gray shawl with crimson tassels around her shoulders. Then her face burned hot with embarrassment when Sam whispered, "Lovely."

"Thank you," she said softly.

"We're not done yet. We still have a few more stops to make."

They next visited a shoemaker who promised sturdy, yet elegant, footwear by morning. Then a shop featuring women's necessities where Sam purchased a set of green tortoiseshell combs, toiletries, and a canvas travel bag trimmed in leather and sporting a shoulder belt.

Florie marveled. He seemed to know everything a woman needed. She wondered how she could pay him back.

By the time they returned to Madame Kopecky's storefront, Duleep Singh and a coach were waiting.

"We have rooms at the Hotel Amsterdam," Singh reported. His eyebrows arched with surprise as Sam helped Florie to her seat. "A most charming transformation," he said appreciatively.

Florie smiled at him, not understanding his words.

The coach eased to a stop in front of a broad stretch of stone stairs leading to the carved doors of the Hotel Amsterdam. Rearing marble lions flanked the entrance, their ferocity only slightly dulled by the soot-darkened snow mantling their manes. Inside, birch logs flamed in the hearth of the great room, and a carpeted stairway curved to the hotel's second floor. They followed a chambermaid carrying thick towels upstairs.

"This is your room," Sam said to Florie.

Disbelieving, she entered hesitantly. A canopied bed filled one corner. Beside it were a dressing table and a chair upholstered in dark blue and gold brocade. The chambermaid backed away after depositing the towels on an oval table next to a porcelain and copper bathtub filled with steaming water. Florie couldn't remember her last hot bath. With a chirp of glee, she began disrobing almost before an embarrassed Sam could beat a hasty retreat to his own apartment.

***

While Florie luxuriated in her bath, Duleep Singh joined Sam in his room. He poured a brandy before slouching into a leather-covered chair. "Well, my friend, have you decided what you will do next?"

"I think I'll give her some money and she can be on her way," Sam replied with a shrug.

Singh clucked his tongue in a scolding fashion as he stared into the amber contents of his glass. "You've bought this girl, rescuing her from a deplorable fate. Do you think you can just walk away from her? This Florence von Sass has nothing in her world but you. And, by the laws of this land, she *is* your property."

"I've buried my wife and I have four daughters." Sam groaned as he combed his fingers through his hair. "I can't take care of this woman, too. Not now. My future lies in Africa, not anywhere else."

"All reasons why you shouldn't have bid at the auction."

"She was helpless," Sam said, his voice rumbling with agitation. "Those Turks were ogling her, waiting to put their hands on her, especially the governor, Ohmed Pasha, or whatever his name was. I just couldn't let that happen."

Singh waggled his finger as if he were admonishing an unruly child. "And what if Florence doesn't leave you? How will she fit into London society? Better yet, return with her to England and how will *you* fit into society? Your countrymen have most peculiar and ambiguous standards, my friend. Extra-marital affairs are tolerated among the upper class, but it's all swept under a carpet of decency. That moral code means you and your family might be the center of scandal in your own land. I doubt the Foreign Office and the Royal Geographical Society would further entertain the idea of you going to Africa."

Sam heard Florie singing softly from her bath in the next room. He glanced helplessly at his friend. "What do you recommend?"

Singh smiled and drained his liquor. "That, my dear Samuel, is a problem you will have to figure out alone. I'm leaving for Rome in the morning. The sport in this land has dried up, and the cold is set into my bones. I need warmth, women, and food not smothered in peppers and onions."

A knock sounded softly at the passage door connecting their room to Florie's apartment. Sam swung it open. She stood framed by the doorway, a towel wrapped about her head, her body covered by her caftan. Damp, golden curls clung to the soft curve of her neck, bared by the open lacing of the caftan. Her cheeks were ruddy. She tipped her chin slightly at Duleep Singh, but smiled warmly at Sam. "*Guten nacht,*" she murmured demurely.

"Good luck, Sam," the maharaja said as the door closed behind her.

***

Zast Ohmed Pasha, Governor of Vidin, walked in a small, tight circle in his office in the Baba Vida, his hands clasped behind his back. Muscles quivered along the lines of his jaw. He was a man used to getting what he wanted, no matter the cost. Governorship did not come from being meek or squeamish. He shot a hard glance at Emile Zeb, the slave seller.

"You look troubled, Your Excellency," Zeb said as he rotated his bony hips more deeply into a plush cushion near Ohmed Pasha's desk. "Are your concubines keeping you up at night?"

The governor scowled fiercely. "It's that damnable yellow-haired wench you sold, the one the Englishman bought, may he be cursed as an infidel dog. No! Stole from me! I can't get her out of my mind. She haunts my thoughts."

"It is not often that such fine flesh comes to my block. I doubt I will see the like of her again for some time," Emile Zeb said, nodding solemnly.

Ohmed's dark eyes blazed hopefully. "I've received a report that this Samuel Baker has taken her to Bucharest. Surely, Zeb, a man of your experience and connections can find a way to bring her back."

"You mean get rid of the Englishman and steal the girl. My contacts are spread from Bucharest to Cairo, and beyond to Khartoum deep in the Sudan. I can get her back, but it will be costly."

"And Baker?"

"That's more troublesome. Putting a knife in the back of a foreigner, especially an Anglo, only brings more angry Anglos to the scene. That kind of thing must be done delicately."

"Do it," Ohmed Pasha said angrily. "I don't care about the cost. Bring me the wench and kill the Englishman. See to it personally."

"Thy will is my will," Emile Zeb said, bowing low. "I will be in Bucharest in three days."

As he left the room, he allowed himself a sly smile. *And I will be that much richer*

Chapter Four

Goose down and soft cloth matting plumped the mattress Florie lay on. The sheets were white and crisp. A heavy, down-filled comforter trimmed in dark blue thread swallowed her body like a cocoon on the underside of a midsummer's milkweed leaf. The pillow was so soft it felt as if her head would drift completely through it. She glanced about the room. The dress Sam had bought for her hung nearby. The muted drone of his voice came from next door.

She pinched herself to see if she was dreaming. The pinch hurt. This was real.

With a contented sigh, she tried to will herself to stay awake, to relive all of the events since she'd been swept away from the dark, hopeless pit that was Vidin, but, swathed in the warmth and softness of the bed, her tension melted away and her eyes grew heavy. In the gauzy netherworld of dream-sleep, her body twitched. A familiar voice called her, a voice she hadn't heard since she was seven years old: Mama's voice, but filled with terror. Oily columns of black smoke roiled skyward, and men screamed in agony as impossibly large musket balls sliced through them, shearing away limbs and faces. Papa tottered toward her, a ragged hole where his belly had been. His face was melting in gobbets of ruined flesh. Mama dragged her away, thrusting her into the flabby, comforting arms of her nurse, Alma.

"I won't cry, Mama," Florie moaned, thrashing in her sleep as her nightmare built to a crescendo of horror. Alma was carrying her to safety, away from her burning village, forcing her face against her shoulder so she wouldn't see the Austrian bayonets pierce Mama, or hear the maniacal laughter of the soldiers as they stomped the life from her convulsing body.

Florie screamed and jolted upright in her bed, her eyes wide with fright.

"Florence, wake up! What is it?"

Strong hands on her shoulders were shaking her before she blinked away the macabre dregs of her nightmare. Her arms circled Sam's neck and she buried her face against his chest.

Unsure how he should calm the trembling woman, he hesitated. Then he gently stroked her hair until her shivers ebbed. "It was only a bad dream," he said soothingly, remembering how he had calmed his daughters when they woke in the throes of a nightmare. "You're safe." He rose from the edge of her bed to leave. Her fingers wrapped about his arm with surprising strength.

"Please don't leave me," she said, choking back her fear.

"Leave you? Whatever do you mean?"

"Please."

Sam gestured with his thumb toward a corner of the room containing the brocade-covered salon chair. "If you wish, I'll just settle into that chair for a little while."

Blue eyes flashed her thanks as he slumped onto its seat. His hands folded over his powerful chest. She remembered those hands stroking her hair. As she drifted back to sleep, she wondered for a fleeting moment how his touch would feel on her naked skin.

***

Duleep Singh departed by coach for Rome in the early morning while Florie slept. "Find a way to leave her," was his final advice as Sam saw him off. With that warning ringing in his head, Sam trudged wearily back toward the hotel, wondering how he had gotten into such a mess.

As he passed the British consulate, an elegant black brougham pulled to the curb and a mustachioed man in a dark suit and carrying a leather valise stepped down without looking. The two men nearly collided. The gentleman offered his apologies and then stopped. "Sam Baker? Is that you?"

Sam blinked in surprise. "William Price? What are you doing in Bucharest?"

"Why, I could easily ask the same of you, old man," Price said, doffing his hat and offering his hand. "Weren't we in Perthshire shooting grouse last year?"

"We were." Sam smiled, remembering how he and Price had each taken a dozen brace of game birds on a windy afternoon.

"Surely you didn't come all this way just to hunt in Romania? I do remember that you were always quite the sportsman."

"I did, William. But I've run into some complications, and now I'm ready to leave."

"Pity," Price replied, his brows curved with thought. "If you could have stayed a bit longer, I would have offered you a business proposition. I need someone I can trust. I represent a number of investors who are building a railroad from Bucharest to the Black Sea town of Kostendje. We are sure it will make quite a lot of money transporting grain and other food stuffs for the Russian market, but we need a managing director."

Sam paused. He remembered Duleep Singh's warning about owning a slave girl. Perhaps William Price, Member of Parliament and entrepreneur extraordinaire, could offer him a way out of his predicament.

"I think, William, that we should talk over tea."

***

Florie was still sleeping when Sam returned to the hotel. He sank into the chair in her room, his chin on his chest, his eyes narrowing as he watched her rhythmic breathing. In his mind's eye, he saw her stepping from the fitting room of Madame Kopecky's shop. She was beautiful, young, and vibrant, with a strength that had endured the outrage of slavery. He remembered how her blue eyes had locked onto his, had seemed to sear his very soul.

But this was not how he'd expected things to go. Singh had been right. How could he ever explain his purchase of a slave girl to his friends and family? Society would never accept it. His thoughts wandered to Henrietta. She had succumbed to typhus while they were traveling through the Pyrenees, leaving him with four daughters to care for. He closed his eyes as he recalled her on her deathbed, skin waxen, barely breathing. Then, with her remaining strength, she had pulled him close so he could hear the husk of her voice. *Please, Sam, promise to love the girls and watch them grow.* Those were the last moments he had with her. He remembered candlelight shadows on his daughters' faces, painting their tears in with a soft glow after he told them their mother had passed. It would be hard enough leaving them behind when he traveled to Africa; staying with Florie meant taking on a responsibility he didn't want and didn't need. It was better to get it over with now. He would tell her he had accepted William Price's job offer as managing director and would be leaving for Kostendje on this morning's coach.

Mustering his courage, he cleared his throat. "Florence?"

Florie didn't stir. Her lips were slightly parted. He followed the curve of her bared arm to her neck, to the soft lobe of her ear. Golden hair cascaded loosely over a plumped pillow, framing her face in a way that made her vulnerable and desirable all at once. He remembered her nakedness on the auction block. For a moment, he longed to take her in his arms and explore her body.

No, his inner self warned. *If I stay with her, Africa will be lost to me forever.*

Slowly, deliberately, he backed away. She didn't awaken when he left the room and closed the door behind him.

***

A church bell pealed from down the street. Florie yawned and stretched her arms, then snuggled more deeply into her pillow, soaking up the warmth provided by the goose down comforter. The residue of her nightmare had drifted away. She slowly opened her eyes and peeked about the room to ensure that all she remembered was real. Yes, there was the blue dress still hanging from a wire in the armoire, and next to it was the canvas travel bag with its long, leather shoulder strap. A set of four tortoiseshell combs was spread across a small dressing table. Sam had bought them for her after they had left Madame Kopecky's shop. These all had to be gifts from his heart.

The bell tolled twelve times. Twelve chimes? Through the curtains she saw the wan winter sun had risen high. Why hadn't Sam awakened her? Sliding from her bed, she knocked on the door to the adjoining apartment. No answer. Perhaps he and Duleep Singh were out. Maybe he was just arranging passage out of the city, or settling the bill at the hotel desk. Men, after all, had their own ways of doing things. She fought back the tinge of panic that she was alone again. She just needed to be patient.

Long minutes ticked by on the clock atop a nearby bureau. The enigmatic, smiling sun-face painted on the lower portion of the clock's cabinet seemed to mock her. An hour dragged by. She fidgeted. The rhythmic toll of the church bell announced it was mid-afternoon.

Disquieted, Florie rose from the chair and plodded to the tiny dressing room. After performing a brief toilet, she deftly wove her blond tresses into a thick braid and slipped on her blue serge dress. She stared at her reflection in the mirror as she fumbled with the last button. She opened a box on the floor next to the door. Inside were her new shoes. Had Sam set them there? Where was he? The dark ghost of apprehension grew.

The desk clerk, a mousy man with a thin mustache, noticed Florie descending the stairs and hurriedly busied himself with slipping envelopes and messages into numbered pigeonholes behind the counter. He wasn't sure of the status of the woman, but he doubted she was Mssr. Sam'l Baker's wife. There had been no Mrs. Baker registered in his book. The matters of the hearts of travelers who came to his door were none of his concern, but the whole affair seemed quite strange: an Englishman, a dark-skinned foreigner with effeminate features, and a lovely doxy all in adjoined rooms! He was glad that both the Hindu and Baker had checked out. Best to get rid of this woman as well. He couldn't have dubious characters settle into his hotel and ruin its reputation.

Florie waited impatiently for the clerk to acknowledge her. She cleared her throat.

The clerk turned, feigned a look of mild surprise, and bowed slightly. "Yes, *fraulein*, how might I serve you?"

"I was to meet Herr Baker," she replied.

"Ah, Herr Baker. I'm afraid he checked out very early this morning."

Florie caught her breath. "Checked out? Where … where did he go?"

The clerk shrugged and retrieved a thick envelope from a pigeonhole. He was sure this woman was some unsophisticated peasant wench fresh from the farm, and now dealing with a broken heart. Yes, better to speed her on her way.

"I'm afraid Herr Baker did not leave a forwarding address. He did, however, leave this for you," he said, handing her the packet.

Florie stared at the envelope, pinching it between thumb and forefinger as if it were a damning writ delivered to her by a constable of the court. A lump formed in her throat as she clumped up the stairs to her room. She dropped onto the brocade-covered chair and closed her eyes, struggling to sift through the collision of thoughts and emotions. Sam had left her! Had she said or done something to offend him? Why hadn't he at least spoken to her? A bolt of bitterness lanced through her gut. Her own emotions had betrayed her, had lulled her into a sense of security she felt when she was with him. She had been alone for so long that his friendship and care for her had crumbled barriers she had painstakingly built. But now he was like others in her life: her parents, old nurse Alma, even poor Tamas Comanasti, all gone, dead to her, abandoning her on the edge of a chasm of emptiness.

No time for tears. I promised Mama I wouldn't cry!

Squaring her shoulders, Florie opened the packet Sam had left at the desk. A wad of British currency and Turkish liras spilled onto the bed, more money than she had ever seen in her life. But, more importantly, there was a letter crisply folded into quarters. The letter, written in German, was in Sam's hand. She stumbled over unfamiliar words:

Dearest Florence,

You are a free woman to make choices of your own and not be burdened by any problems or difficulties I might bring. The truth be known, I have daughters of whom the eldest approaches your age. Their mother is dead, and for her I yet grieve. God has blessed me with the time I have come to know you. He will continue to watch over you, just as He directed me to save you from bondage.

My dream of Africa awaits me. For the moment, however, I have found employment, and on this day travel to Kostendje on the Black Sea. The money I have left for you will help you to start the new life you deserve. Forgive me for leaving you in silence, but it is for the best. Your path is one you, alone, should choose.

God grant you wisdom and safekeeping.
Affectionately,
Sam'l Baker

Florie carefully refolded the letter. *God has blessed me with the time I have come to know you.* Sam's words rippled through her mind, leaving her feeling barren. *Your path is one you, alone, should choose.*

"Where would you have me go, Sam?" she asked quietly. "You're the only good thing that has happened in my life."

Drawing in a deep breath, she began packing her few belongings into her travel bag. Where would she go? Back to Mehadia? That life, like Tamas Comanasti, was snuffed out. She couldn't stay in Bucharest indefinitely. What other place was there? The jumble of thoughts only made her head ache.

When she had finished packing, she sank onto the edge of the bed and glanced about. There was the chair Sam had slept in after her nightmare. His room, now vacant, was a few steps away. Her travel bag contained his gifts. She wore the dress he had bought for her. The hotel room suddenly seemed to close in on her. The sun-faced clock tolled the late hour. Fresh air. She needed fresh air to sort out her feelings.

The hotel lobby was empty. From behind his desk, the clerk glanced at Florie curiously as she walked by with her bag slung over her shoulder. Outside, a thin frosting of snowflakes drifted earthward from metallic, melancholy clouds. A snowy slush coated her new shoes as she trudged aimlessly toward the city center, past Madame Kopecky's, then the café where Sam had treated her to a plate of sugary sweets and cocoa. A tear threatened the corner of her eye.

An image of Sam materialized in her mind. He had given her a new start, had offered a path of *her* choosing. The possibilities of independence were frightening and thrilling at the same time. *My life— my choice,* she decided as she smoothed her hands over her dress, *and it begins now.* Yes, the first thing to do was to contact the coach line that operated between Bucharest and the Black Sea. Sam had left plenty of money to book passage. Then she would find him in Kostendje, and find a way to pay him back for her clothing, shoes, and combs—and for her freedom.

With her decision made, Florie strode purposefully back toward the Hotel Amsterdam. The desk clerk would know where the coach station was located. As she neared the hotel, the wavering glow from a solitary file of gas-fed streetlights along Bucharest's main avenue imparted a surrealistic landscape of flickering gray shadows and plunging pools of darkness. A flutter of movement at the base of one luminescent halo caught her attention. Two men hugged the night beyond the last lamp, but one of them had strayed into its puddle of light.

Magram Bur! Florie caught her breath in fright and ducked behind a linden tree. Even at this distance, she recognized the man who had pinned her to the ground at Mehadia, his stink still vivid in her nostrils. Bur's companion limped into the light to whisper something to him. There was no mistaking Emile Zeb, the creature who had sold her in Vidin. Their focus was on the hotel. There could only be one reason they would be lurking outside its door! Rage seethed deep within her, welling past her fear of being kidnapped in a thick wave. Not ever would she return to the slave pens and the likes of the Ottoman governor!

The linden tree was large enough to hide her, but she couldn't stay behind it forever. Throwing caution to the night wind, she eased back, trying to keep the tree between her and the slavers. They continued to watch the hotel. Another dozen feet and she would be around the corner and away from the gaslights. Darkness would then be her friend. She stepped backward three more paces. Her foot suddenly slipped on a patch of ice and she gasped loudly as she regained her balance.

Magram Bur turned toward her. "Zeb Effendi, it's the yellow-hair!"

Florie skidded over the icy area. The pounding of feet caused her to look up.

Magram Bur sprinted through the pools of gaslight toward her, his arms pumping furiously. Behind him, Emile Zeb shook his fists.

For a fraction of a second, Florie thought about darting away. But what chance had she to outdistance the burly slave catcher? Her only hope was his speed.

"Don't let her get away," Zeb shrilled as he limped after Bur.

Florie balanced on the edge of the icy walkway. The snow piled behind her would give her better footing once she ran.

Only a dozen feet from her, Bur bared his teeth in a ferocious grin and his hands opened, claw-like. A moment too late he saw the glare of gaslight on the ice. Then his lead foot slid, his legs splitting from under him. His arms swung like desperate windmills, both feet flying into the air. He landed heavily to his back, his head smashing against the ice with a resounding *thunk*.

Florie stumbled into the snow, her heart pounding and limbs trembling. With her bag clutched tightly, she turned and ran, not daring to look back at the slave catchers. Her feet felt like frozen clods as she lurched toward a lane unlit by lamps, then down an alley, another street, and another alley. She lost her sense of direction. Finally, lungs aching and teeth chattering, she leaned against a rail fence. How far had she come? She listened for pursuit above the thudding of her heart. No one had followed her.

A horse neighed softly, making her jump. The wind carried the familiar tang of animal dung, straw, and leather, smells such as those found in Mehadia or any farming village. They meant there was a stable near by.

The rail fence she leaned against formed a corral of sorts. By following the rails, she contacted the corner of the stable, then barely squeezed through the gap between the sliding gate and its frame. Fresh smells of animals filled her nostrils. A horse caught her scent and nickered from one of the stalls. With hands outstretched, she felt her way through the darkness until she bumped into an object that shifted slightly. Her fingers curled around the rungs of a ladder and she climbed into the soft, earthy comfort of a hayloft. Nestling into its stack of hay, she fought to stay awake to sort out what had just happened. Outside the stable, all was calm. There were no pounding feet, no Emile Zeb or Magram Bur. Inhaling a deep breath, she slowly relaxed. Her eyelids grew too, too heavy.

***

A shaft of sunlight lancing through the stable's grime-crusted windows woke Florie from her deep sleep. Motes of grain dust drifted lazily through the sunbeam. While the barn reminded her of Mehadia, this wasn't Mehadia.

After brushing wisps of hay from her dress, she pulled her legs close and hugged her knees. Her thoughts spun dizzily as she tried to patch together sketchy images from the night. She pictured Emile Zeb waiting for her in the street, the hulking Turk that had raped her standing next to him. If the Turk hadn't slipped … her stomach revolted and she retched. She choked back a sob as she clambered down the ladder, plunged her hands into a water trough, and scrubbed her face vigorously.

Panic gripped her as suddenly as it had in the darkened street. Zeb and his cutthroats had found her to take her back into bondage, and if the slaver catchers had found her once in Bucharest, they would find her again. Had Sam been with her, he, too, would have been in danger.

As Florie's gaze swept around the stable in misery, she spied a soiled shirt hanging from a peg near an empty stall. Held against her chest, its shapeless weave hung halfway to her knees and was bulky enough to partially hide her curves. A desperate plan began to percolate, one that kept her close to Sam, but where she didn't have to face him, at least not yet. Yes! Here was a battered hat and tattered trousers with grimy suspenders belonging, no doubt, to a stable hand to slip on when he did chores. The trousers were baggy, but they would suit. When there was time, she'd buy a length of soft cotton to bind her breasts and flatten her chest. These were clothes that would help hide her sex. That left only one thing she could still do while in the stable.

Florie picked through a chest of farrier's tools until she found a curved knife used to trim horse hooves. Although the blade was pitted and worn, its edge was sharp. She undid her thick braid and shook her hair loose. There was no mirror in the stable, but there was water in the trough. Her reflection wavered as she bumped its side. "Coward," she said. She stretched out a thick lock of hair and sawed through it with the knife. A few of the severed strands floated on the water. More cuts, more hair, until only a ragged bristle remained.

The image in the trough was hers, she knew, but now it resembled more the face of a boy, especially after she rubbed a fingertip's worth of saddle polish over her cheeks and jaw line. There, she thought, neither Sam nor Emile Zeb and his thugs would recognize her. Today she would find the stagecoach station, purchase a ticket, and travel to the Black Sea to look for work and to be near Sam. It might take weeks or months, even years, but she would repay him. Only then, she believed, in a bittersweet way, could she truly be free.

Chapter Five

27 March 1859
Kostendje, Bulgaria
My Dearest Edith,

I beg your forgiveness in not writing the past month. I hope you and your sisters are minding your Aunt Min and keeping well with your studies. Please ensure that Agnes continues with her geography, and Constance with her letters. Help especially with little Ethel.

I will not be able to return for some time yet. A position has opened to me with a railway that is extending from the Danube to Kostendje on the Black Sea. It is a huge effort, but an important one that benefits the commerce of this region. Perhaps you recall Mr. Price from our trips to Perthshire? He is one of the directors of the railroad, and has engaged me to be the Managing Director. I have quite some number of workers under me.

Kostendje was once an ancient Roman port. In those days, it was called Tomis, the place where the poet Ovid was exiled. We have had to break apart the marble baths and walls constructed by the emperor Trajan. Once the rail line is completed, the farmers of Romania will be able to send their produce to Russia. This is indeed a monumental undertaking since ours will be the first rail line to be completed in the lands of the Ottomans.

My sweet Edith, you are the eldest and must watch and care for your sisters until my return. Please give all a hug and kiss for me.

Love,
Papa

Sam folded his letter to Edith and gazed out the cracked window of his cramped office near Kostendje's harbor. He imagined Min's home in Richmond and his daughters playing together, maybe outdoors if it wasn't too cold or snowy. That image seemed more than a world away.

The large map spread across his desk traced the proposed route of the Danube & Black Sea Railway. Although work had begun on the line the previous year, it had stalled. Removal of debris and rocks had been spasmodic. Too often, work crews sat idle due to poor decision-making by their foremen and a lack of orderly supply. English investors in the rail company had grown uneasy and had sent William Price to investigate. Price had immediately fired the previous managing director, a whiskey-swilling Welshman who had succeeded in setting the Christian and Muslim workers at odds with each other. He had been most fortunate, Price admitted to his new manager, to have found Samuel Baker, Esquire, open and ready to assume that managing position.

Sam sipped his coffee and smiled at his success. Since he had arrived months earlier, rails now extended well beyond the western hills. More ties and rails were stockpiled. He had even helped unload supply wagons to make sure all goods were accounted for. There had been no pilfering from company stores under his watch, a fact he reflected on with pride. And it felt good to plunge into hard work that tested his mind, yet kept him physically active. It had been a wise decision to leave Bucharest at Price's invitation when he did. In a few more months, he would return to England to prepare for Africa.

A distant peal of thunder boomed. He glanced out the office window. A March storm blossomed over the Black Sea. Although still hours away, its banks of dark, beetling clouds promised strong winds and driving rain. The transition from winter to spring could sometimes be violent.

An unfolded stack of newspapers, most two weeks to a month old, sent to him by the British consulate in Bucharest beckoned his attention. Dog-eared and soiled, they gave him a measure of information regarding the outside world. Emperor Louis Napoleon of France, noted a headline in *The Times*, was considering war in Piedmont. Queen Victoria and Prince Albert were at Balmoral. The American president, Buchanan, had entertained guests from Japan. One headline immediately caught his eye: Speke and Burton Discover the Source of the Nile.

Sam devoured the article. John Hanning Speke and Richard Francis Burton had arrived in Zanzibar after a perilous journey of many months into the interior of Africa. With Burton recuperating from illness in Aden, Speke had returned to London and addressed the Royal Geographical Society, proposing that a lake he had discovered among the mysterious Mountains of the Moon was indeed the fabled source of the Nile. Speke had dubbed the lake Victoria, after the queen.

Rubbing his jaw ruefully, Sam meditated on the news. So, the source of the Nile had been found—according to this. Strange that Speke had not waited for Burton to join him before making such a pronouncement. Sam had met Speke before and liked him, but also realized the officer was not of scientific or literary bent. Speke was a big game hunter, not unlike Sam himself. Burton, on the other hand, was a renowned linguist, adventurer, and explorer. His fabled journey to Mecca had garnered attention throughout the civilized world. Burton would ensure that the discovery of such a lake was backed by scientific evidence. The newspaper article mentioned nothing of evidence. Besides, how could the mighty Nile be fed by only one lake? Like many other geographers, Sam had always been convinced that there were numerous highland lakes and rivers feeding the great river. What Speke and Burton had discovered was surely just one of those water bodies. And now that the two explorers had returned to civilization, Sam could begin assembling his own expedition.

He carefully folded the newspaper. Burton and Speke had made some kind of monumental discovery, but other mysteries of the Nile still waited. It was his destiny to unravel them. Finish this railroad and the depths of the Dark Continent could still be his—no, *had* to be his, or he would end up a nobody, not even the footnote in history that Roderick Murchison had all but promised.

Deciding to keep the newspaper, he tried to open a desk drawer but it wouldn't budge. Something inside was wedged tight. He pulled harder and the drawer flew open. His little shooting diary tumbled to the floor, one cover creased.

Sam clicked his tongue sadly as he retrieved the diary and opened it. The last entry recorded his hunt on the Danube with Duleep Singh: Mixed marsh and pasture near Vidin, Bulgaria. Cold north wind. Six partridge bagged. Eight shots.

"Too long between hunts," he said to himself. "Too damned long." As he closed the book, a bit of folded paper slipped out from inside the rear cover. He straightened the paper and glanced at it. It was the bill of sale for the purchase of a female slave named Florence.

Sam stared at the paper as he sank back in his chair. William Price's offer to work on the railway to Kostendje had been so sudden, and the decision made so quickly, that it had been easy to abandon Florie in Bucharest. It hadn't even required a goodbye, just a note with some money. No scandal, no emotional baggage. It had been a surgically clean severing, until now.

In his mind, he was once more draping his coat about her shoulders in the coach to Bucharest. Her face was tilted to his, her cheeks reddening as their arms touched, her blue eyes flashing a warning. She was strong, yes, but he remembered how her hands folded together with little girl glee when he had bought her the tortoiseshell combs. He recalled her every feature, recalled everything from the moment her blue eyes locked with his in the auction dome of Vidin to his last glimpse of her sleeping peacefully in her room, her golden hair piled loosely over her pillow, her vulnerability all too evident.

With a shake of his head, he tried to fight the building sense of guilt:

guilt over Henrietta's death, guilt over leaving his daughters, guilt over deserting Florie. He should have awakened her, been honest with her.

In the few days he had spent with Florie, he had nearly forgotten the dull ache he still felt when he thought of Henrietta. He couldn't put his finger on it. Was it Florie's dignity and bearing that made her so attractive, or the uncommon fearlessness she seemed to possess? True, she was beautiful, but it had to be more than that. Maybe they'd simply connected when their eyes had first met. It didn't matter what it was. It was ridiculously complicated. If only he had kept his big mouth shut back in Vidin.

Sam stashed the diary back in the drawer. Soon he'd be exploring the Nile. His guilt would burn away under the tropical sun. Africa was, after all, no place for a woman. Maybe it was a good thing he'd left her in Bucharest, had come to work for the railroad. But of a sudden all the work in the world couldn't erase his vision of her haunting blue eyes, couldn't erase his abandonment of her

You've done everything to mess things up. If you weren't such a coward, you wouldn't be worrying about her now. Piss on the scandal! It was your duty to protect her and you left her behind! For all you know, she's dead.

A deafening drumbeat of thunder suddenly rattled his window. He stared at the boiling thunderheads, looming closer now, and more threatening. Lightning played over the dark waves. The gentle breeze that had been blowing from the south died abruptly, and the moisture-heavy air grew oppressive. The approaching storm jolted him back to his job. The steamship *Adrianople*, carrying a heavy cargo of rails, was due to arrive that very afternoon. He doubted its captain would make it to port before the storm erupted.

The gale broke with a fury that startled him. A blast of sultry wind burst his door open. He bounced out of his chair, his thoughts of Africa and Florie shattered by lances of lightning crackling through the darkness. Rain shafted down in a slanting torrent. Above the demon's song of storm wind, he thought he heard the clanging of a bell. He held his breath as rain matted his hair and stung his eyes. There it was again, the frenzied pealing of the harbor bell. A ship was in danger out in that surging, crashing sea.

Sam flung himself through the open door and dashed toward the waterfront. To the west, towering columns of storm clouds nearly hid the setting sun. To the east, lightning splintered the blackness above the sea. Thunder reverberated from the cliffs above Kostendje. Dozens of townspeople and railway workers had gathered on the beach to light enormous bonfires, their shadows dancing against the whitewashed buildings. As he approached, he heard the hiss of rain striking the flames. Henry Barkley, one of his railway employees, crouched at the lip of the beach, a telescope pressed to his eye.

"Barkley, what is it?" Sam roared over the wind.

Barkley jumped in surprise and then handed over the telescope. "It's the *Adrianople*," he cried. "She was sighted just before the storm broke. I've lost her for the moment, but I think she's up on the rocks to the southeast. Her boilers seem to be out, and I don't think she'll make it into the harbor."

"Then we'll go out after them if we need to," Sam said.

"But it's too damned dangerous to take boats into that storm surge," Barkley objected. "We're getting a rocket ready now for a better look."

With a hissing, cracking sound, a rocket arced from the beach and over the breakwater, exploding in the black sky beyond. Sam peered through the telescope to the southeast and cursed in awe as he glimpsed the churning waves swelling and crashing in a maelstrom of rain and motion. "Fire another," he shouted above the storm's din. For a moment, he thought he had seen the *Adrianople*. Within seconds, another missile flared into the dark sky. Its eerie, explosive flash illuminated the ailing vessel canting to starboard, much closer to the harbor than he had expected. At least the captain seemed to know what he was doing in attempting to preserve his ship. Twin cables, one on each side, had been played out at severe angles. But the powerful wind continued to drag the ship and its anchors closer to the rocks. In moments, those jagged projections would cave in its hull. With its heavy load of rails, the ship would sink almost instantly.

Sam reacted quickly. "Bring ropes and torches," he yelled.

Villagers scrambled to the boat sheds and retrieved coils of thick, sturdy rope. Others lit torches from the beachfront fires, the flames sputtering in the rain. A few young men grabbed barrel-sized cork floats used to mark fishing nets and joined their fellows clawing across the slick rocks of the breakwater.

Above, a bright streak arced high and exploded, the rocket's actinic glare revealing the *Adrianople's* death throes. One of the anchor cables tying the ship away from the rocks snapped. Lifted by an enormous wave, the vessel rolled heavily, smashing into the rock fangs. Sam heard the timbers of the hull fracture. The foremast splintered and reeled into the darkness. Huge volumes of water poured into the broken ship, causing it to heel in a short arc, its bow pointing toward the rescuers three hundred yards away. As the remnants of rocket light flickered out, he glimpsed the ship's crew struggling to launch a boat. The rowboat shoved free and rode on the crest of a boiling wave as the sailors paddled furiously toward the harbor.

"There! Over there," cried one of the young villagers, waving his torch from his pinnacle of rock. "There's a spar in the water and a man by the bow!"

Sam shaded his eyes against the sting of seawater and spotted the pale oval of the sailor's face bobbing up and down among the pounding waves. His arms appeared to be wrapped around the broken spar.

Sam sprinted down the beach to an overturned scull. With a straining of muscles, he heaved the little boat unto its keel and dragged it into the surf. Waves lifted it, threatening to tear it from his grip. Then he was inside, freeing its oars and dipping their broad blades into the foaming water. The sea surge pushed him sideways and he feared the scull would capsize. Paddling urgently, he straightened his course and drew past the breakwater. To his right, waves battered the *Adrianople*, flowing into the hole in its side, then spewing out as the hull shifted.

Fighting the sea's fury, Sam slowly closed the distance to the man hugging the spar. Blood flowed from a wide gash on the sailor's forehead, washing away with each wave, then bubbling back. The man's eyes were wide with fear. The scull bumped against the spar.

Sam clutched the sailor's arm. "On three, kick as hard as you can and I'll haul you aboard. One! Two! Three!"

With a grunt, he leaned backwards, drawing the drowning man into the scull. The sailor choked and spat water.

"We have to fight as close to the rocks as possible," Sam cried above the roar. "They'll have ropes ready for us."

With agonizing slowness, he brought the little boat about. A wave crashed over them, then ebbed, leaving a foot of water in the scull's bottom. Another wave like that, Sam reckoned, and they'd sink. Bending his back, he rowed toward the breakwater. Torches flared, ghostlike, through the driving rain. Fifty yards remained. Forty. Thirty. Screams of encouragement rose from the villagers.

A monster wave crushed down on the scull. Sam gulped air the instant before the wave sucked him deep. He stroked upward and broke the surface in time to see the injured sailor splashing helplessly. His fingers closed on the man's collar before he could sink below the waves. Too weak to continue, the sailor clung to Sam's arm. The shattered hulk of the overturned scull drifted beyond their reach. In the bitter struggle to swim against the storm's surge with the dead weight of the sailor, Sam felt his body turning to lead.

Someone on the breakwater shouted. A brave villager grabbed a cork float and dove into the sea. Pushing the float in front of him, the villager kicked toward Sam and the injured seaman, an umbilical cord of rope trailing back to the rocks. Sam grabbed the float and wedged it under the seaman's arms. The line tightened. With his head lolling, the sailor was dragged through the waves, hauled to a boulder, and lifted to safety by Barkley and two townsfolk. An instant later a massive swell smashed down. When it receded, the villager who had had come to the rescue had disappeared.

"God save me," Sam gasped as he sucked in a breath and plunged underwater in a surface dive. With desperate strokes, he searched, found nothing, then kicked back to the stormy night sky empty-handed. The people on the rocks called to him, begging him to save himself. He drew another deep breath, curled and dove again, sweeping downward until he finally hooked the villager's limp arm with one strong fist. They broke the surface together, choking and spitting. Willing hands plucked them from the sea.

Doubled over with exhaustion, the villager retched seawater. A rocket burst overhead in a whiz-bang of sound. Sam dropped a thankful hand on the man's shoulder. In the pulsing, reddish glow, a youthful face with close-cropped hair turned toward him.

"My God! Florie!"

Chapter Six

Fear flashed across Florie's face as she pulled free of Sam's grip and faced him. Townspeople gathered around, patting them on the back. Someone threw blankets over their shoulders. Others carried the injured sailor to shore.

Florie and Sam stood alone on the slick rocks. His hand slipped over her wrist, preventing her from leaving. "What are you doing here?" he yelled above the roar of wind and waves. Lightning crackled overhead.

"I saw you go into the water," she cried as she struggled loose. "I just couldn't stand by. Please don't send me away."

"What are you doing here?" he shouted again. His fists were clenched. A vein bulged in his forehead. "Send you away?"

Startled, Florie stepped back a few paces. His anger confused her. "I have no other place," she said. "You're here and I'm here. There is nothing else."

"You could have been killed!"

Her voice broke with emotion as she tried to shout back at him. The blanket fell from her shoulders.

Sam drew in a deep breath. The driving rain slowly weakened, although thunder still rumbled through the clouds. A cold wind knifed in from the sea. He saw her shivering.

"Take my hand," he ordered, his words hard-edged with agitation.

Florie retreated as she measured the distance to the next rock. Her teeth chattered. How could this angry man be the Sam who had saved her from slavery?

"Please take my hand." His voice softened. "I have a private house on the cliffs above the sea. It's not much, but it's better than the railway office."

After a moment's hesitation, she finally extended her hand. His grip was firm and warm, his flesh wet from the storm. As she drew near him, her legs folded from exhaustion. He swept her up in his arms, holding her tightly to keep his balance on the wet rocks. Then they were on the shore, past the torches flickering weakly on the beach, past the ropes, cork floats, and surprised villagers.

The path to his house was a long one. Cradled against his chest, Florie heard Sam's heart hammering. His arms, strongly muscled, held her as easily as if she were a child. By the time he kicked the door to his house open, she was shivering uncontrollably. He laid her on his bed and tipped a bottle against her lips. Brandy burned down her throat. His fingers fumbled with her wet clothing. She wanted to fight back through the thick blankets swaddling her, but she was too weak. He ran his fingers through her unfamiliar, close-cropped hair and she groaned. Then slowly, as she warmed, Florie drifted into a deep sleep.

***

Sunlight shafted through the only window in Sam's house. The embers glowing in the hearth gave off a delicious heat. The coarse woolen blankets scratched against her skin.

Shocked that she was naked, Florie sat up. The terrible storm, the ship sinking, Sam struggling in the water with the injured sailor, their confrontation on the rocks—it all flooded back in a whirlpool of anxiety. She scanned the outer room, but it was empty. Her clothing was draped over a chair in front of the fireplace. With the scratchy blanket wrapped around her, she tiptoed to the chair and donned her heavy shirt and trousers. Her shoes, near the hearth, still looked wet.

Sam knocked twice on the door. He entered as she buttoned the last button on her shirt. He stood there, framed by the doorway, his hands on his hips.

"Last night, I thought you were a boy," he finally said, pointing to her hair.

I've been living that life for a long time, ever since ... since you left me in Bucharest," she replied softly. She saw his eyes flare in surprise, and she backed away from him until her shoulders contacted the wall. *Why do I suddenly fear him?* Her mouth felt dry. "I didn't know if you would ever want to see me again. After that, I cut my hair, and wore these clothes. Nobody notices me in them. They think I'm a farm boy come to work in Kostendje. I've been watching you for weeks. I should have told you I was here. I'm sorry I'm such a coward."

Sam studied her. The bristle of her hair was unevenly cut, more a short thatch in some spots. He tried to imagine her in front of a mirror, sawing through her hair with a knife. The bulky, shapeless shirt hid her breasts and hips. Her trousers were ragged and soiled. But her blue eyes, those startling blue eyes, cut to his soul.

"This is no place for a woman," he said tersely. "Why did you come here?"

Florie's hands balled into fists as if she needed them to defend herself against his interrogation. "Because I don't know anyone else, because I was afraid. I have no family, no village, no country, no place else to go."

Sam ran his tongue over his teeth. This was not how he had expected to find her, to talk to her. "Listen, please," he said, biting back his irritation. "I left you in Bucharest because I couldn't take you with me.

Soon I'll be returning to England. My children and family—well, I can't very well tell them I purchased a woman at a slave auction."

"But you gave me my freedom." She struggled to keep her tears in check. "You bought me clothing. You—"

"What I've done is done," he interrupted. "From England, I head to Cairo, and after that, into the depths of Africa." He tried to make his voice sound convincing. "Too many dangers. I wouldn't do that to you."

"If I were a man, would you take me? I have some money to pay you back. Just don't leave me alone again."

"It's unthinkable," he said, shaking his head. "Money? You owe me no debt. I'll arrange safe passage for you back to Bucharest. If you need more money—"

"But I can ride and cook and mend. I'm not afraid to go to Africa."

"You're not listening to me," he retorted as he turned away in frustration.

Florie sank numbly to the edge of the bed and stared at him. What had she expected him to say? Had she really thought he would welcome her with open arms? *You're a foolish child. A stupid, foolish child!* Sam might be angry with her, she acknowledged as she slipped on her damp shoes, but he couldn't make her leave Kostendje until she chose to go. The haunting look they had exchanged on the auction floor in Vidin burned in her mind.

"Where do you think you're going?" Sam asked gruffly as she pushed past him and out the door. "And what am I supposed to do with you?"

Florie spun angrily toward him. "Nothing! I … I've been working in the stable in Kostendje. The owner found out I was good with animals, so I earn a few coins helping him and he lets me sleep in the stable loft. He, too, thinks I'm a boy." She paused, waiting for his response. "I'm going back to work now."

"Stable?" Sam chewed on the word. "But it's too damned dangerous for a lone woman in Kostendje." He wanted to shout that at her, but he forced himself to remain calm. Her stubbornness aggravated him, but he sensed there was something more that she hadn't told him. "What happened in Bucharest?"

Florie's mouth formed a thin-lipped frown. She squeezed her fists more tightly. The terror she'd felt when Zeb and his henchman had tried to kidnap her had been shoved into a closet in her mind. Now that memory flared vividly. "Emile Zeb and his slave catcher found me," she replied after a long pause. "They came to the hotel to take me back to Vidin. I managed to run away. That's why I changed my identity, so Zeb couldn't find me."

"Zeb?" Sam's brows drew down in disbelief. "Slave catchers found you?" He blinked rapidly as he digested her story. Despite his misgivings, it was impossible to turn her out with slave catchers on her trail. "You can live in this house," he said slowly, waving off her objection. "There's only one path leading up here, and only one door into it. It's much safer than in town. There is no argument about this."

"But what about you?"

"I'll sleep in my railway office," Sam replied, puffing his cheeks and slowly exhaling. "Tomorrow, I leave for Medzidia to check on the progress of track laying through that town. Now, let me help you gather your things from the stable and move them up here." He looked fierce and angry, but his voice was surprisingly calm. "Oh, and I'd better leave this with you." He dug in his pocket, produced a tiny key to unlock a drawer on a small cabinet, and removed a walnut box. He laid the box on a table and opened it. A short-barreled revolver filled one compartment. A brass powder flask, a bullet mold, and a round tin of percussion caps filled smaller compartments. He removed the pistol and checked its cylinder. The gun was empty. "I carry it when I have to deposit railroad funds. Do you know how to use one of these?"

Florie gasped in bewilderment as he pressed the pistol into her hand. His skin felt cool against her moist, hot palms.

"You cock the hammer back, point, and squeeze the trigger," he continued. "Try it."

With her heart beating more quickly, she raised the pistol and squeezed the trigger. The hammer snapped down loudly.

"Excellent," Sam said with a smile. "You remind me of my daughter Edith. I taught her to shoot, too. Now learn to aim."

Florie blushed as he stood behind her, helping her straighten her arms to sight along the pistol's frame and barrel blade. With his body touching hers, she thought of being alone with him in a way that would never remind him of his daughter.

***

Florie pushed back a wayward lock of hair with a flour-dusted hand. She had been baking bread, and fragments of dough clung to her apron. A kettle of soup simmered on the small wood stove in Sam's house above the sea. She almost dropped her rolling pin in surprise when someone rapped on the door.

"I didn't mean to disturb you," Sam mumbled apologetically when she opened the door.

"This is your home, not mine," she said as he entered. It was the first time she had seen him since they'd hiked along the coast a few weeks earlier, collecting oddments of antiquities from the shattered, overgrown ruins of Roman villas. She remembered sitting quietly on the edge of a chipped, marble step, her hands folded together, drinking in every word as he explained the history of the region. Then they strolled along the cliff, watching the movement of the sea. Now, her mouth felt strangely dry. She hadn't realized how much she missed him.

"You … you must be very busy working on your train," she said.

"Yes, very busy," he replied absently as he sniffed the aroma rising from the stove. "Rabbit stew?"

"Yes, would you like some?"

"Perhaps later," he said, licking his lips hungrily. "I've come for my shotgun and shooting jacket. A fellow from Kostendje said he saw woodcock in the thickets to the west. I'm joining him and his brother for a little hunt."

Florie watched him with wide-eyed wonder as he opened the trunk case, lifted out the Damascus barrels of the Thomas Bland twelve-bore, and assembled them to its frame.

"I'd like to go with you, if I could," she said hopefully. "Maybe you'd even show me how to shoot a bird gun."

Sam's face creased with a frown. Perhaps it was her little girl look, with arched brows and teeth biting lightly on her lower lip in anticipation, that changed his mind. He grinned. "Then you must hurry," he declared as he grabbed his gun and headed for the door. "There are boots in the corner. They'll be a bit big for you, but you'll need 'em. And wear a hat. It looks like rain later today."

Moments later, Florie joined him. Her heavy shirt, floppy-brimmed hat, and over-sized knee-high boots made her look like a peasant lout fresh from the barnyard. But there was no mistaking the soft bulge of her breasts against the fabric. Sam turned away, embarrassed that she might have seen him staring.

A half hour of steady walking, she in more of a trot to keep up with his long strides, brought them to a dense network of alders and willow thickets. The two hunters from Kostendje were waiting for them, contentedly smoking their pipes. At their feet, a hunting dog, running in small ovals, sniffed anxiously at the edge of the marshland. They greeted Sam, eyed his companion curiously, and pointed toward a tangle of alders a hundred yards away. With the dog working back and forth through the tall grass, the party marched forward.

Sam crouched slightly before slowly rising to his tiptoes to peer into the dense brush. He knew the little pointer had entered the thicket somewhere ahead of him, but it was nowhere in sight. The tinkling of the tiny brass bell at its collar hinted that the dog had slowed its pace, a sign that game might have been scented. The tangle of brambles and alders was a place meant for beasts and birds, not men.

The clinking of the bell stopped. "The dog is on point. Be ready," he said.

A woodcock burst from the thicket, corkscrewing skyward with rapid surges of its powerful, stubby wings. Its peculiar *peent*ing cry sounded as it leveled off before speeding in escape toward a neighboring thicket across the bog. A second bird erupted from under the dog's nose.

Sam squeezed the front trigger of his twelve-bore. The gun bucked against his shoulder, sending its charge too far behind the lead bird. He heard the other men firing as he focused on the second woodcock with his left-hand barrel. Again the shotgun roared. The buff-colored bird with the long beak dropped in a flurry of feathers.

"I'll go in after it," Florie called over her shoulder.

Sam paid little attention to her as he reloaded his smoothbore. He was still fitting caps over the ignition nipples when he finally looked up.

"No, don't go in the bog!"

Too late. Florie had already entered an area of thick grass and mud. From a distance it had looked deceptively firm. Now the muck was sucking midway up her calves. She was stuck.

Sam doubled over in laughter. Florie forlornly watched the mud ooze over the tops of her boots. She looked up at him as he laughed, a quivering pout forming on her lips. "Help me … *bitte*."

Still chuckling, Sam picked his way to the edge of the bog. He edged in slowly, feeling the muck cling to his legs. "Wait still a minute and I'll be right back," he called. "I have an idea."

"I don't want to be eaten by a swamp." There was no panic in her voice.

Sam laid his gun on firm ground, drew his knife, and entered a dense growth of birch saplings. He hacked an armload of the whitish-gray boughs before returning to the bog. By tossing the branches onto the ooze, he created a thin carpet to where Florie stood stranded. Stepping cautiously on the rough mesh, he sighed with relief when it didn't break under him. A moment later, he eased next to her.

"I'll grab you under the arms," he said, trying not to laugh. "You lift your feet out."

Grasping her firmly, he heaved upward. Florie kicked free, but her boots remained encased in the mud. Barefoot and in Sam's arms, she smiled prettily at him. "*Danke*."

The branchy carpet promptly snapped. Sam fell backward, landing seat-first in the muck. Florie fell on top of him, pushing him even deeper. The rank odor of bog enveloped them.

"Some rescue," she said sarcastically, gathering a dollop of mud in her fist and plopping it firmly on the top of his head.

With slime dripping down his face, he grabbed her ankles, tilting her legs until she fell off his lap and into the ooze. She came up with more handfuls of mud. Before she could deliver her soggy payload, he kissed her firmly on the lips. Startled, the mud balls dropped from her hands as she drew back from him.

But Sam didn't seem to notice. Just beyond another thicket, the bell had stopped jingling. A woodcock had been pointed. The hunters called his name.

"Come on," he cried gleefully. He grabbed her by the wrist and hoisted her to her feet. "Get your boots. More birds!"

Florie didn't move. Her breath came in short, ragged gasps. The thought of a man touching her in a pleasurable way suddenly frightened her.

***

Rain fell through the waning daylight, dousing the hunters as they left the thickets and parted company, their game bags full. As he and Florie hiked toward his house, Sam laughingly recounted the shots he had made, sometimes hefting his twelve-bore and swinging it at an imaginary woodcock. Florie remained silent. She walked several paces behind him, her eyes roving over the sweep of his shoulders, his fluid motion as he brought gun to shoulder. She remembered his kiss in the bog, felt it burning on her lips.

By the time they reached the house, the rain was pelting more fiercely. Mud from the swamp sloughed off their trousers. They kicked off their sodden boots.

Florie bent over a stack of wood. "I'll start a fire so you can clean up." Those were her first words since he had kissed her. "The stew will be hot in a few minutes. Please, you'll stay for some?"

Sam nodded his head appreciatively.

"Give me a moment so I can change into dry clothes," she said.

As she pattered toward the tiny bedroom, he mused over her bare, wet footprints on the floor, small and slender compared to his. Uneven curls clung wetly to the soft curves of her neck. He found himself wanting to explore the secret pleasures of that neck. He quickly turned away.

Florie retreated to the bedroom and closed the door, her palms suddenly moist. She had caught Sam staring at her, but why? She caught her breath as she glimpsed her image in the tarnished mirror on the wall. Her hair, slowly growing out, needed brushing. Her bulky shirt was stained. Mud streaked her face. What a frightful mess for any man to see, she thought, and Sam wasn't just any man.

After peeling off her wet shirt and trousers, she delved into the narrow wardrobe in the corner of the room. There was the blue serge dress he had bought her. She wondered if he would remember it.

When she emerged from the bedroom five minutes later, she caught Sam sipping stew from the kettle simmering on the stove. He looked up, paused in mid-sip, and then set his spoon down. Florie, in the dress he had found for her in Bucharest; Florie, with her hair growing back unevenly and her face washed clean, stood radiantly in the doorway. He gulped and pulled back a chair for her.

Neither of them spoke for the rest of the meal. After he had devoured the last morsel of stew and sopped its gravy with freshly baked black bread, he finally rose from the table. "It's getting late," he said. "The rain has let up some. I thank you for the fine meal." He gently lifted her face to his and kissed her on the forehead.

Florie's heart pounded so loudly she was afraid Sam would hear it. She desperately wanted him to stay in the house with her. But if he did, what would he do? All she could think of was the slave catcher who had savaged her, who had ripped from her what she had wanted to give of her free will at a time of her choosing.

Biting her lip, she eased the door shut after he left and blew out the candle.

***

A month later, Sam knocked in his familiar way. Florie flew to the door, her pulse racing with the idea of seeing him again. He had been in her thoughts constantly since the woodcock hunt. But her welcoming smile quickly faded as he entered, somber-faced. Then she noticed the letter he pinched between thumb and forefinger.

"What is it? What's the matter?" she asked, sensing bad news.

"This came from England today," he replied dismally. "It's from my sister Min. My father has died and I have to return home to settle family matters. I'm the eldest son, so it is my duty."

"I'm so sorry for your loss," Florie said in a small voice. "I understand."

Sam was quiet for a long uncomfortable moment. "No, it's more than that," he said finally. "My sister also wrote that I have received approval to travel to Africa."

Old fears peeked from their dark closets in Florie's mind. "I ... I will wait for you here," she whispered.

"You don't understand," he retorted sharply, more sharply than he intended. "When I return to England, it won't only be to take care of family matters, it will also be to prepare for my trip to Africa. I won't be coming back here."

"I'll be waiting for you," she said, shaking her head as if she couldn't grasp what he was saying.

He gripped her shoulders. "Florie, are you listening?"

Her lips quivered as she fought to hold back her tears. "I just want to be—"

"Want to be what? Be with *me?* You can't come with me. I have four daughters and I'm twice your age. I bought you as a slave girl. There would be no place in England for us."

"But I love you."

Sam pursed his lips tightly and released his grip on her shoulders. Images of Florie on the slave block, sleeping in the hotel room, hunting woodcock with him, tumbled through his mind. Then he slammed the door on those memories. Africa was calling.

"You don't know what you're saying," he said in exasperation. "You're too young to know what love is. Please, don't make this harder on yourself." He paused in the doorway. "I'll leave money for you and arrange for you to live in this house if you'd like. The train leaves for Bucharest in the morning. I have to go to England. Please forgive me. I don't mean to hurt you."

As he tried to kiss her on the forehead, she turned away, her eyes closed, her back pressed against the wall for support.

"Goodbye, Florie."

Emptiness crushed down on her as he turned and went out the door. He had left her again. It was too painful to even cry. She pounded her fists against the wall, his abandonment ripping through her. No, she wouldn't give him up this easily. She stumbled after him, into the darkness, but he was already out of sight. The crash of breakers far below warned her that the cliff's edge was near. If she strayed too close ….

A single birch tree loomed ghostlike in the darkness. Its pale skin felt cool on her forehead as she leaned against it. She stared into the night, hoping he would reappear.

"I love you, Sam," she called loudly. There was no answer, not even an echo. She clutched the tree desperately. It served as an anchor of sorts. "I've loved you since I first saw you," she said quietly, knowing that by now he was far down the path. "I'll be waiting for you right here. Please don't forget me."

***

With the sun lifting above Kostendje, the squat locomotive of the Danube & Black Sea Railway hissed as steam began to build in its belly. Its coupling rods surged against iron wheels. A whistle blew as the train bucked in fits and starts, creeping forward until it reached continuous motion.

Sam glanced out the soot-speckled window of the passenger car. As the train chugged out of town, he saw his little house perched on the cliffs above the restless sea. In ten days he'd be in England. He had tried to catch a few moments of sleep in his office, but he kept seeing Florie, desolation etched on her face. It was baffling. How could she love him? She was only a child. No. It was more than baffling, it was distressing.

As the house disappeared from view, he wondered if he would ever see her again.

***

Six men formed a rough circle inside the stable in Kostendje.

"Are you sure this is where the girl has slept?" Magram Bur growled as he kicked at the dirt floor in agitation. After he had cracked his head on the ice in Bucharest, the yellow-hair had simply disappeared. It had taken weeks to root out that the Englishman, Baker, had gone to Kostendje. It made sense that she might follow him. But a search of the town had revealed nothing, until a bribe offered a clue.

"This is the place, Effendi," said Vulkho Zhivkov, a rat-faced Bulgarian with a stiff bristle of beard. "The stable owner said a boy stayed here for a time, a boy with short, yellow hair. It's her, I tell you, but with her hair cut. She's the one Emile Zeb wants, the one who escaped from you. We've been searching for a girl while she's been disguised as a *boy* and operating right under our noses."

Magram Bur scowled fiercely and traced the puckered scars on his cheek with his forefinger. The yellow-hair would not elude him again. When he caught her, he'd teach her another lesson like he had in Mehadia. "And where is she now?" he demanded.

"No one knows," Zhivkov replied. "The English dog, Baker, left by train this morning. He had many bags with him. I have word he is traveling back to his homeland."

"And was she with him?"

"No, Effendi. Baker lived in his railroad office, or worked on the line. I have never seen her near him. She is nowhere to be found."

"Fool!" Magram Bur grunted. "The yellow-hair must be here, and Baker would have known where. Spread out. Check every warehouse, every barn and worker's tent in this rat's nest. Watch every road. Keep an eye on Baker's office. She's hiding here somewhere and we'll find her, or Ohmed Pasha will have our heads. A gold dinar to whoever brings her to me."

Vulkho Zhivkov grinned greedily. He knew Kostendje's back streets and alleys better than anyone. The yellow-hair was not in the town. She was hiding somewhere in its outskirts, of that he was certain. Ferret her out and the reward would be his.

Chapter Seven

Lochgarry House hadn't changed a whit, Sam decided once he finally arrived at his sister's home after the long journey across Europe and the English Channel to London and its suburbs. Primrose bushes still flanked Lochgarry's walkway. Ivy crept along its walls on the north side, sending long, green tendrils up the brick chimney. The oak door bore the familiar brass knocker in the shape of a sailing ship.

The house remained the same; it was his daughters who had changed. Edith, now thirteen, had the high cheekbones and dark hair of her mother. Agnes had grown two inches taller, but was still the quietest of the foursome. Constance, with bright freckles across her cheeks and nose, ran everywhere rather than walked. And Ethel was no longer the babe in arms he had left.

"Please, Papa, tell me more about Africa," Edith pleaded after they had shared their first meal together in months. She squeezed his hand with a desperate fury. "Schoolmaster Naseby says it's a savage place. I'm so afraid you will come back changed, that we'll all be changed!"

"We'll be fine," Sam reassured her as Min's maid cleared away dishes. "The business of exploring is to give names to places that have none. See? Look at this map."

With a crinkling of paper, he unfolded a large map published by Brightly and Kinnersly of Suffolk. Gay colors outlined the African continent. "Because we have no knowledge of the central part of Africa it has simply been called *Negroland*. Further to the south we have the *Land of Hottentots*." He pointed to the hand-colored image of an African native with a thighbone twisted in his hair and a mouth filled with dagger-like teeth. "This smacks more of overblown imagination than true geography. What I will do is visit these places, map them, and give them proper names."

Agnes and Constance dashed to the table to see what their father was showing their older sister. Agnes understood the concept of maps, but Constance preferred to dance about, grimacing like the African native with the thighbone in his hair. Ethel, barely four years old, clung to her aunt's hand. The illustrations on the map frightened her.

"I promise I will bring back a wondrous gift from Africa just for you," he told his children as he hugged each in turn. "Now, with your aunt's permission, into the library. It's time for some stories."

With his daughters clinging to him, he retreated to an overstuffed chair. By the time he had finished his tales of sailing on a corn barge through the rapids of the Danube and saving the sailor from the *Adrianople*, Ethel was sound asleep.

"One more story, please, Papa," Edith begged. "What happened after you rescued the sailor?"

"No more tonight," he said gently. Edith's question resurrected the image of the young woman he had left on the cliffs above Kostendje.

"Come, my dears," Min said as she lifted Ethel from Sam's lap. "You can see your papa in the morning."

After kissing his daughters goodnight, Sam settled back in the chair. They seemed to be flourishing under Min's tutelage, although she constantly referred to them as "my girls", a possessive he'd noticed immediately. In a way, she reminded him of Henrietta: round-faced, hair drawn back in a bun, religious, loving, but unforgiving in her moral outlook. But she was his sister, and his girls loved her.

Min returned to the library. She looked over his shoulder at the map half-folded on her table. She touched her hand to her cheek. "I declare, Brother, I saved a copy of the paper for you. It mentioned something of Africa and something about explorers, I believe. Wait, I'll get it." She returned with a folded copy of *The Times* dated 27 April 1860, already a month old. In large, bold type its headline announced: "Speke & Grant Leave for Africa."

Sam pored over the article. John Hanning Speke, who had claimed Lake Victoria as the birthing place of the Nile, was returning to Africa to ensure the scientific accuracy of his discovery. Apparently, he and Richard Burton had a falling out—probably because Speke had presented their findings to the Royal Geographical Society without Burton being present, Sam guessed—and would be joined by Captain James Augustus Grant on this second expedition. Backed by £1,000 supplied by the RGS, the pair had left Portsmouth aboard the *Forte* bound for Zanzibar. As before, Speke planned on trekking westward to scientifically prove the lake was indeed the fabled source of the Nile. Then he and Grant would follow the course of the river to the north and on to Khartoum, the city in the depths of the Sudan where the White and Blue Niles converged to form the Nile.

Sam paused to digest the news. Speke was now not only world famous, he was backed financially by the Royal Geographical Society. Sam realized, with a pang of anxiety, that if he didn't hurry, there would be nothing of Africa left for him to discover.

"But if Speke and Grant only search for the Nile's origins at this so-called Lake Victoria, then they are traveling from east to west," he reasoned aloud. "The only real way to determine the sources is to follow the White Nile southward from Khartoum. Speke should realize there must be more than one lake that feeds such a great flow."

His face suddenly brightened. "Min, I'm leaving for Atholl's Blair House after Father's memorial service. The Duke has invited some influential people to his highland games that may be able to help me purchase supplies, collect guns, and arrange for passage. Once I'm done with that trip, it's off to Egypt to explore the Nile. And it's not just the Blue Nile as the RGS wants me to follow, but the White where the true mystery lies."

"It's a fool's errand you'll be on, Brother," Min said. She wanted to ask him if he had even taken time to grieve for Father, but she bit that back. She knew the two men hadn't been close. "You've just returned home and now you plan to up and leave. Have you decided on a partner? Perhaps that sportsman, Oswell, might accompany you. You really should have another white man with you, somebody you would trust your life with."

"You know I'd rather go alone," Sam replied. "I don't trust people readily, and rely on them even less. I'll end up doing all the work and have to share the glory. But to be safe, perhaps I'll find a dependable sporting chap at Atholl's who might like a jaunt to Africa."

Min smiled knowingly. Secretly, she was happy he was planning to depart for Africa. That meant a year, maybe two, of his absence during which she could teach and love his daughters—her girls—even more.

"Whatever you decide, we'll be waiting for you when you return."

Sam winced. He had heard those words before.

***

Gentlemen in tall hats and fashionable coats strained to catch a glimpse of the athletes competing in the highland games on the Duke of Atholl's estate. Ladies, their open parasols resembling a field of pastel blossoms in the late afternoon sun, stood on tiptoes and craned their necks. The hum of their voices blended with the soft soughing of a breeze through the crowns of ancient oaks and carefully pruned junipers.

But it wasn't the sight of the brawny men tossing the caber that aroused the curiosity of the duke's guests. Rather, their attention was drawn to the wide-shouldered hammer thrower wearing Atholl's plaid. His last heave had dropped the twenty-two-pound ball and shaft better than a foot further than his nearest competitor.

Suzanne MacKinnon, the Duchess of Pembroke, absently twirled her parasol as she smiled coquettishly at the young women clustered about her. The pale yellow ballooning of her hoop skirt matched the color of the umbrella. Her reddish hair was pinned in a stylish manner under her elegant, modestly brimmed hat. Although in her forties, she was trim, attractive, and very aware of the spell she cast on men.

"That, ladies, is Samuel White Baker," she said, nodding her head in the direction of the bearded thrower.

Lucie Parsons, the third daughter of the Earl of Dumfrieshire, lifted on tiptoes to gain a better glimpse. She was half the age of the duchess, with a ripe swelling at her hips and bosom. "They say he's lived in Ceylon; a tea planter, I believe," she trilled, her questing eyes never leaving the man with the auburn hair as he pivoted his torso for another throw. "Buried his son there, I hear."

"No, it was coffee, and he lost his wife several years ago while tramping in the Pyrenees," Lady Pembroke corrected as she idly spun her parasol. "He should be over his grieving by now. That makes him rather eligible, don't you know."

Lucie turned toward the older woman, her brow furrowed with confusion. "But he has four daughters," she exclaimed peevishly.

"To be quietly packed off to boarding school," Pembroke said, smiling slyly. "He has money, land, a sound lineage, and he's literate; he's even written two racy books about his adventures in Ceylon. And now he manages a railroad somewhere in Eastern Europe. All he really needs is a strong woman to care for him."

Lucie abruptly felt herself flushing from more than the heat of the afternoon sun. Tiny beads of perspiration dotted her upper lip. She discreetly patted her face with a lace hanky plucked from her sleeve. "But he looks half the savage," she said, her eyes burning brightly under the canopy of her hat. "That shirt he's wearing is the kind the rustics wear. Gentlemen don't dress like that. Why, it's 1860, and we're a civilized people. Look how he handles that hammer as if it's a toy."

"Aye, the hammer," Lady Pembroke said. Her gaze swept over the broad expanse of his chest and the long-shafted hammer gripped in his fists, metaphors of his virility. "If only my husband looked half the man that one does." A hot flush of desire crept from her belly through her thighs. "Come ladies, let's meet Mr. Samuel White Baker."

***

Sam wiped sweat from his brow. His last throw of the heavy hammer had sailed even further than those before. Warm hands suddenly curled around his bicep.

"Mr. Baker, I must introduce you to Lucie Parsons." Lady Pembroke's cheeks were flushed. Her fingers squeezed more tightly.

Sam smiled politely and allowed himself to be swept along by several of Atholl's other guests. Pembroke quickly released her grip on his arm as someone produced a bagpipe and began skirling a raucous tune. She had been discreet, appearing to have only been caught up in the excitement of the moment, but he read more than momentary admiration in her eyes.

In Ceylon, he had seen female panthers stalk their prey, and this was too eerily similar. Fortunately, Atholl hooked his arm and led him toward a group of men walking toward the house.

"That last toss was most marvelous," Atholl said, his leathery face crinkling with a grin. "There are a number of people who are interested in meeting you."

"As long as a certain lady isn't among them," Sam said with a quick glance over his shoulder.

"Ah, Lady Pembroke, I'm sure. She's a nymph in bed, you know. I was quite taken with her for a while. But don't tell my wife."

The group of men waited for Sam and Atholl to catch up.

"You know Rear Admiral Murray, Lord Wharcliffe, and William Cotton Oswell?" Atholl asked.

"Of course," Sam replied, shaking their hands.

"I understand that you're leaving for Africa soon," Admiral Murray said, brushing at his white whiskers. "It seems like only yesterday that you hunted stags on the Tilt with that bloody big knife of yours."

Sam laughed. "Aye, but I think I'll need something bigger than a knife for where I'm going."

"Damn it all, Sam," Oswell exclaimed, his ruddy complexion even rosier from excitement and whiskey. "I've traveled to the Upper Zambezi with David Livingstone and hunted buffalo and big elephants there. I want you to take my ten-bore. It's built by Tatham, and a better elephant rifle doesn't exist."

"Hear, hear," Murray shouted above the applause. The old sailor patted his paunch and then clapped Sam on the shoulder. "And I want you to take my ship's telescope. It's a fine glass, and was with me on the *Dryad* during the Borneo affair."

"And I'll see to it that you have thermometers, barometers, and additional scientific instruments to measure the elevation and climates of the African watersheds," Wharcliffe added.

A beefy hand wrapped around Sam's in a powerful grip. Dark eyes peered from above puffy cheeks and a thick beard.

"I'm John Petherick, Sam," the newcomer introduced himself. "I've just been appointed Her Majesty's consul to Khartoum in the Sudan. I can't afford to give you any such grand gifts as the others have, but I promise that should you reach Khartoum, I'll make sure that you have proper lodging and what food you need."

"Thank you all for your support," Sam said, pumping Petherick's hand. "I'm truly indebted. However, I'm still looking for someone to go with me and perhaps share the expense."

The smiles disappeared. Sam glanced at the men. There were no takers.

They all think I'm going on some idiotic quest. The Blue Nile holds no riddle; it will give fame to no one. I'm on my own.

"Three cheers for Samuel White Baker," Atholl shouted to break the strained silence. "He'll be the one that comes back famous. We'll all wish we'd gone with him then."

***

Lochgarry House was quiet as Sam strode into its library. The long ride by coach from Atholl's Blair House had left him pensive. After the games, Lady Pembroke had invited him to lunch, but he quickly declined. There was too much to get ready, he assured her. Perhaps the next time he was in London. He remembered how her tongue had flicked wetly over her lips.

He had met with his younger brother James to determine the direction of the Baker family's business now that their father had passed. With middle brothers John and Valentine out of the country, James managed the reins of enterprise. Sam guaranteed James that he had no intention of interfering.

With his business done, Sam visited his daughters for the last time before leaving. Min had them seated properly until he walked into the library. Then they dashed to him with tearful embraces. After Min had ushered away the younger girls, Edith, alone, remained. She cried on his shoulder when he told her he would be leaving again.

"Please, Papa, take me with," she begged. "You've taught me so much. I can help you keep your notebooks. You know I can ride and shoot. I'm not afraid to go to Africa. I'm not afraid of anything. If you go alone, there will be no one to take care of you, to watch over you, to mend your clothes, to … to love you."

Sam gulped as he gently pressed the tears from Edith's cheeks and escorted her to her bedroom. Her words reverberated in his mind. He hadn't seen a woman's tears since Kostendje. The barriers he had carefully built the past few weeks were crumbling.

That night, he slept fitfully. A hazy image of Lady Pembroke, part woman and part snake, luring him to bed threaded through his dreams. He woke, groaning and sweating. As he rubbed his brow, he thought of Florie, sparkling blue eyes under an uneven crop of golden hair. A terrible sense of loneliness and loss pervaded.

When he rose in the morning, he knew he had to return to the Black Sea.

***

Florie smoothed her hands lovingly over the back of Sam's chair. Moonlight flooded through the little window. It was a quiet, breezeless night. From below, she heard the soft slapping of the Black Sea against the rocks.

Memories stirred. His kiss while hunting in the marshland still haunted her. If only he were here to sweep her into his arms, to share the little house with her. But Sam had been gone nearly a month, and every day seemed to stretch for an eternity. She said she would wait for him in his house, even if he denied he was returning. This was his home, his chair, and his bed. She would hold on to them as long as possible.

Stooping, she blew out the little candle on the table before slipping on her nightclothes. Moonlight lit her way to the bed. She drew back the covers and felt under her pillow. Yes, protection was there.

As she struggled to stay awake, her thoughts drifted to her childhood in Hungary, then to Wallachia. Too much loneliness there, she decided. But the moonlight shining through the window reminded her of one night in Mehadia when ragged clouds, like frayed strands of lace, glided over the orange-yellow face of the full moon. In those moments when the moon was shrouded by clouds, the shadows creeping across the meadows were colored dark charcoal; then, when the soft wind caressed the veil away, a ghostly landscape was revealed, one checkered with fields of barley and wheat, roads running like corrugated veins from fields' end to the village nestled in its mid-October slumber. Though she was tired from the day's fieldwork, she was mesmerized by the shadows shifting and gliding across the swales and pastures. She softly hummed a quaint tune, lowering her voice whenever the clouds puffed across the moon's glowing face. The melody formed into words from an old poem Mama had taught her:

Hail Mother Moon o'er autumn night,
Thy pale caress of heavenly light
Wakes lovers' hearts under dusky sky,
With a solemn promise that winter is nigh.

Could it be, she wondered, that lovers do meet under a harvest moon? She was sure Sam was the one whose heart beat as one with hers.

Florie sighed and pulled her blanket more tightly. Fidgeting under the covers, she turned restlessly from one side to the other. More thoughts. Finally drowsiness.

From outside the house came the sound of stone bouncing from stone. She was awake in an instant, her heart thudding. Something scraped. A hushed voice—or was that a puff of wind? The doorknob twisted, slowly, but the lock held. She reached under her pillow for the revolver Sam had given her. Her thumb eased back its hammer.

"Sam, is that you?" she called, her voice little more than a whisper.

The door suddenly exploded inwards, screws from its hinges ricocheting from the walls. A dark shadow, silhouetted by the moonlight, burst into the room. Florie twisted away as Vulkho Zhivkov groped for her arms, pinning one down. He cursed as her fingernails raked his face. She jerked free, lifted her pistol, and fired.

***

With slow jolts, a locomotive of the Danube & Black Sea Railway eased to a stop. The tinny keening of its whistle roused Sam from his reverie. He had been daydreaming about the last night he had seen Florie when she blurted her love. In his mind, he first replayed that conversation, then the one he had with her when they had ridden in the coach from Vidin to Bucharest. It was something about how the Turkish slave catchers had mistreated her. She had looked to him for protection and he had turned her away. Now he had to find her, had to make things right.

When his car drew even with the platform at Kostendje, he stepped onto the wooden landing. With his battered valise clutched in one fist, he began the long walk up the dusty path to the cliffs above the city. As he neared his house, he noticed the little garden Florie had tended was weed-choked and desiccated. The strings of peppers and clusters of dill she usually hung to dry were missing. Then he stepped back in surprise. The door was broken from its hinges and propped into place; it crashed inward when he touched its knob. Inside, he found the table tipped over. Shards of glass littered the floor. The blankets on the bed twisted in a heap. A candleholder upside down, the candle broken. Forbidding, dark stains on the floorboards.

Sam dropped his valise, his heart in his throat. Both rooms were empty. She had been here, but now gone. The jumbled vacancy spoke of terrible violence.

"Florie," he shouted, his voice loud in the little building. Uncertainty gripped him. "Florie?"

Turning in a half-circle, he searched the emptiness of the Black Sea. Where could she be? Someone in town had to know something. Smothering an oath, he bounded down the path toward Kostendje, his jaws grinding. Whose blood stained the floor? Had the slaver catchers found her? What if she were dead? Mocking voices beat at his brain as he dodged past a cargo wagon that was easing to a stop near the stable. He almost cursed the wagon for partly blocking his path. Then he caught a glimpse of the driver working the long-handled break lever. The driver's face, partly obscured by a floppy hat, seemed familiar. Sam skidded to a halt by the front wheel, his hands on his hips, as the fellow rose from his seat.

"Hello, Sam," the driver called, an ox-hide whip clutched in one fist.

His eyes widened with surprise. "Hello, Florie," he said wonderingly. He glanced at the whip. "Planning to use that on me?"

A faint smile curved her lips as she placed the long lash in its holder next to the seat. She pushed her hat back, revealing close-cropped hair.

"I see you've done your hair again," Sam said, gesturing with his chin.

"You were gone a long time. After a while, I didn't think you'd return," she retorted coolly, combing her fingers across her scalp. "Vidar Dubrin hired me to drive wagons. I even sleep in a wagon in his camp. That's easier to do when you're a boy."

Sam offered his hand to help her from her seat, but she ignored his courtesy and jumped lightly to the ground. "Why are you here?" he asked, waving toward his house. "The door, it's been broken in."

Florie glanced up the hill. "I stayed in your house after you left," she said quietly. "I had no place else to go."

"What happened?" he demanded, gripping her by the shoulders.

"Why are *you* here?" she countered, shrugging away. Those unsettling blue eyes flashed her warning.

"I ... I'm going to Africa," he exclaimed, surprised by her hostility. "Most of my supplies are probably in Alexandria by now."

"Then you came to say goodbye?"

"Yes. No." He felt flustered. "What the devil happened up there?"

Sam studied her face, the challenging tilt of her chin, the slight quivering of her lips. Her bare arms folded on her breast were brown and sinewy. She had changed since he'd last seen her. This wasn't the teary-eyed woman-child gushing her love for him. A hard-edged confidence radiated from this Florie.

"I killed a man," she said bluntly.

Sam's brow creased. "What did you say?"

"I killed a man. He broke in as I slept. I shot and shot until my gun was empty."

"Are you hurt?"

"No."

"Was he Zeb's man? How did he find you? What the hell is going on here?"

"You didn't answer me, Sam," she said, ignoring his questions. "Why are you here?"

Sam grimaced and stared at the restless sea. He kicked at a stone on the roadway. "I ... I'm leaving for Africa. I need a partner that I can trust. Will you join me?"

Florie's eyes narrowed. "I have a job now. I'll be able to start paying back my debt to you."

Perturbed, Sam kicked more stones. "There is no debt you owe me. And what if Zeb's men come back? What then?"

Florie pursed her lips in thought as she scrutinized Sam. Was he the man she loved, or was he the man she only thought she loved? He had given her freedom, but had abandoned her twice. Perhaps she wouldn't truly know if she loved him unless she joined him. Besides, Emile Zeb's thugs would never find her in Africa, and they'd never be able to hurt Sam. There was little doubt they were still searching for her. She remembered the face of the man she had shot, remembered his puffy cheeks and bristly beard, his blood splattering across her bedcovers. She had buried him by herself, scratching a hole in the hard ground with a pickax and covering the corpse with soil and stones. That experience alone had shaken her to the core, but had made her stronger, too.

"I'll go with you, Sam, until I feel I've repaid my debt. Not another word about that. It's the only way I'll go."

Chapter Eight

The Nubian Desert
Summer 1861

The brass ball of sun glared mercilessly from a cloudless, cobalt sky. Florie adjusted her broad-brimmed straw hat and wiped a dribble of sweat from her brow. Nothing in the world she knew rivaled the hellish landscape stretching before her. She squinted against the tortured bands of heat that danced and shimmered across a nearly barren plain. Only distant, low hills of black basalt, glowing with a furnace-like intensity, broke the vast expanse of yellow sand.

Sam yelled as the column of camels and Bishareen drivers slowed their pace. Some of the tribesmen groaned and beseeched Allah for mercy. Many of them, experienced though they were, had already consumed their shares of the water he had tenaciously guarded for the march across the Nubian Desert. To go too slowly was to court death.

Florie marveled as Sam grabbed the reins of a balky young camel and yanked hard, forcing the animal to move. Where did he get his vitality? He'd been a whirlwind of activity since leaving Kostendje months earlier: transporting supplies, hiring camels and porters, weighing their stores, and calculating the weight a camel could carry through the desert. He'd hired a young Egyptian scholar to instruct them in Arabic, and a gruff, vulgar camel skinner to teach them to ride. Sam had also found tents, one for him and one for her, which could be erected quickly. He had even purchased a little enameled bathtub just for her. The tub reminded her of the dress and combs he'd bought her back in Bucharest in what seemed a lifetime ago. He might not say it, but she knew he cared.

Had five days passed since the caravan had left the course of the Nile at the Egyptian village of Korosko? Sam's goal was to plunge southward into the heat-baked expanse of the desert to avoid the extra days of travel required to follow the river's pregnant curve to the west. It meant a forced march across burning sands to reach the town of Hammed before men and camels perished. From Hammed to Berber was a short distance; beyond that lay the mysterious highlands of Abyssinia.

"Old Beelzebub's done his business here," Sam said with a grimace as he jerked a thumb toward glazed shards of volcanic slag littering the sands. Rib bones and skulls of long-dead camels bore mute testimony to the unforgiving clutch of the desert. "Looks like it's been puked out of Hell itself."

Florie again adjusted her hat over her golden hair, now growing out. The molten air seemed to sear her lungs, the moisture wrung out of her body by the savage grip of sun and sand. Her back and hips ached from the *makloufa,* the hard, unyielding saddle, padded though it was with a bright cushion. The bobbing gait of her camel had left her nauseous when they had started their journey, but now it was only a minor discomfort.

"It feels like it, too," she gasped as she swayed in her saddle and squinted against the glare. The thermometer hanging from the pommel of her *makloufa* read nearly 120 degrees Fahrenheit. Even the tough Bishareen cameleers were showing distress. With the sun nearing its zenith, she hoped Sam would soon find shade.

Sam saw Florie weave in the saddle. "Let's move in over here," he called, directing the caravan with a sweep of his arm.

An overhanging outcropping of gray granite provided a measure of relief for the thirsty men and camels. Water bags made from gazelle skins were lifted to parched lips, only to deliver a few drops of precious moisture. The heat had literally evaporated the remaining fluid out of the stoppered skins.

Amidst the Bishareens' cries of supplication to Allah, Sam lifted the edge of a carpet laid over the back of one of the pack camels. From a harness hidden by the carpet, he eased a ten-gallon oaken cask, its lid padlocked firmly in place. He produced a key from a thong about his neck and opened the barrel. Water sloshed lightly over its rim.

"I've been saving this ration for just such a time," he said as he passed a brimming cup to Florie. "It's still two days to the well at Hammed, but we should have enough water to last. After that, it's a week's jaunt to Berber."

With wondering eyes, she accepted the cup, and though she longed to gulp it down, she paused. She glanced at the Bishareens, their eyes bulging and faces caked with sand. Smiling, she passed the cup to Hadji Achmet, the leader of the cameleers.

"Florie, that was for you," Sam admonished.

"These men are our employees. I wouldn't have them think that we don't care for their well being," she said with a tiny frown.

Hadji Achmet, a Bishareen with a dead-white smear of scar across his forehead, accepted the cup from Florie. He lifted his fingers to his lips.

"God is merciful, *Sitt,*" he said. The other cameleers intoned the name of Allah, then *sitt.*

"What is *sitt?*" she asked as she passed another cup of water about.

"That, my dear, is the Bishareens' recognition of you as a great lady. You carry much honor in their eyes by offering them drink first." Sam's eyes twinkled. "Now, *Sitt,* take that small bucket and help the men water the camels."

***

Florie rubbed her eyes, not sure if the dust in the air was deceiving her. The towns of the Arabs, her father had once told her, had towers of white stone that rose into the air like ivory spears, and great buildings with domes of gold. Gardens hung from walls painted the colors of the rainbow. Fountains gushed in every yard. But Berber wasn't at all like that. The town they finally reached consisted of little more than mud and thatched huts pitched haphazardly around a crude system of dusty, crisscrossing roads. Beyond the central town with its ubiquitous bazaar, the ominous bulge of a fortress dominated a low ridge. The color of Berber was dirt brown, broken only by the shimmering blue of the Nile.

A short, round-faced man clothed in a dark blue robe and bright red fez padded toward them. A dozen soldiers armed with antique muskets decorated with brass nails followed him in a ragged formation. The man bowed. "His Esteemed Excellency Halleem Effendi, Governor of Mudir, sends his greetings and welcomes you as distinguished visitors to Berber," he said. "My name is Hasan, and I will guide you to the governor's personal garden where you may rest."

"Thank you, and we most graciously accept the governor's hospitality," Sam said.

Hasan led the tiny caravan to the outskirts of the city where the house of the governor lay bordered by the great river. Florie gasped with joy as she and Sam entered a grove thick with date palms and carefully cultivated lemon and citron trees. The cool waters of the Nile lapped gently at the fringes of the verdure. Colorful Nilotic birds chirped and sang from perches in the tall palms. A soft breeze off the river, carrying the fragrance of lemons and hibiscus, stirred her hair. *This* was the garden her father had described.

Halleem Effendi, a slightly built man of later years with a closely-cropped white beard, arrived shortly after the muezzins had finished the *Maghrib*, the evening prayer. A blend of deep lavenders and streaks of burnished brass lit the evening sky, transforming the Nile into an enormous, exotically scaled serpent constantly gliding to the north. Against this fluid backdrop, the governor and his party sat on carpets across from their visitors. Sam presented his *firman*, an order from the Viceroy of Egypt calling on all Egyptian subjects to provide assistance to its bearer. Halleem Effendi studied the parchment written in both English and Arabic. After a brief discussion about the health of the viceroy, coffee was served and pipes smoked.

"So what brings you to Berber, Mr. Baker?" the governor asked. "You have many guns. Is this, then, to be a hunting expedition?"

"Your Excellency, while I thoroughly enjoy sport, I'm here to investigate the great Nile," Sam began after sipping his coffee. "As you well know, other Europeans have tried to map its length and solve its mysteries. Perhaps you have heard of my countryman, James Bruce of Kinnaird, who traveled the Blue Nile decades ago?"

Halleem Effendi shook his head. "The comings and goings of the great European race are beyond the knowledge of this poor son of the desert. But if you are saying that you would further your peoples' desire concerning the Blue Nile, I can arrange contact between you and the King of Gondar in whose lands the great river begins."

Sam politely allowed the governor to suck at his water pipe. A thin cloud of smoke wreathed the official's head.

"Thank you for your offer, Your Excellency," Sam said as he unrolled a length of heavy paper. Using stones to anchor its corners, he revealed a map of Africa. He stabbed at the map with both forefingers. "You see, from here to here is what is known of the length of the Nile, but nothing of its sources. Does it flow from a great inland lake, or a series of watersheds? Or does its life begin among the fabled Mountains of the Moon? While much of Africa's coastline has now been explored and mapped, the interior is virtually unknown. The maps drawn today are little better than those created a hundred years ago."

The governor stroked his beard thoughtfully before responding. "So, Mr. Baker, you have come to Berber for exactly what purpose?"

Sam jabbed his forefinger at the emptiness of central Africa on his map. "It is not the Blue Nile that calls me, Your Excellency. I'd like to follow the White Nile, too, and discover its headwaters."

"Surely you are not serious, sir," Halleem Effendi said, his brows knitting.

"Quite serious."

"Then you must know of some route that no other person knows of to take you to the crown of the Nile?"

Sam shook his head firmly. "I don't, but that won't stop me."

The governor sucked deeply on his pipe, then released a cloud of smoke with a noisy whoosh. "But you know that the pharaohs of the Ancients, as well as the Romans, all tried to find the fountainhead of the great river, and failed. The sources of the Nile, indeed! You, of course, will not return. The savages who live to the south will see to that."

"I'll still try," Sam said, shrugging.

Halleem Effendi tilted his head slightly, catching the gaze of the woman who sat, in deference to the men, behind Sam. "Surely, Mr. Baker, you have consulted the *sitt* over this matter, and she has accepted your decision as a good wife should. If you are determined to follow the Nile, I will personally arrange passage for her back to Cairo."

Florie caught her breath. "I'm going with him, Your Excellency," she said. Both Sam and the governor glanced at her, surprised that she understood more of the Arabic than they had credited her.

"Why that's preposterous," the governor exclaimed, tugging his beard in agitation as he addressed Sam. "You would take a white woman into the unknown heart of barbarism to find the beginnings of a river? And what unspeakable things could happen to her if you should perish? The viceroy's *firman* would not protect her."

There was a strained silence. Several members of the governor's staff stirred uneasily.

"I thank Your Excellency for your concern," Florie said as she glanced from Halleem Effendi back to Sam. "I'm a good shot and quite strong. I wouldn't consider being left behind. If Mr. Baker should go without me, I would still follow."

Noting his arguments were falling on deaf ears, Halleem Effendi rolled his eyes and released a final puff of smoke. "May Allah protect us from mad Englishmen, and their even madder wives," he said. "You do not know what you are getting yourselves into."

***

Sam gazed into the distance, bronzed arms akimbo, a stern look chiseled on his face. From the back of his dromedary, he studied a brown and barren landscape. Behind him, Florie tapped her camel lightly on the neck with a short stick. The rest of the caravan, tended by the Bishareens, trailed.

Barely an hour of daylight remained. Sam suddenly raised himself in his saddle and peered through Admiral Murray's telescope. He had done so several times since leaving Berber, expecting a shadow on the horizon as the banks of a river. So far, the shadows had only been shadows—until now.

"There," he exclaimed excitedly. "I see another line of vegetation. It has to be the Atbara River where it joins the Nile." He glanced at Florie as he kicked his camel into a trot. "It's closer than I thought it would be. Hurry! I've got to see it."

This is what the Royal Geographical Society has sanctioned me to do. His thoughts were gleeful as their riding camels galloped over the low dunes. *Explore the tributaries of the Nile. This is my destiny!*

Twenty minutes later, Sam dismounted and pushed through the fringe of brush edging the riverbank. He skidded to a halt and took two steps back in astonishment. Four hundred yards of heat-baked river sand greeted him, its whiteness painful to gaze upon under the setting tropical sun. There was no water, no river. Steep banks ten to twenty feet high hemmed in the bone-dry course. Thickets of browned and withered mimosa thorns crowned the banks. Dome palms thrust through the shrubbery, their fan-shaped leaves colored like worn leather.

"Is this the river?" Florie asked in a hushed voice. Compared to what Sam had described during their journey, it was greatly disappointing.

"Yes," he replied somberly. He shaded his eyes with his hand as he peered upstream. "I think we may find water as we follow it. It is June, after all, the dry season, though that should be ending soon."

Florie nodded her head hopefully. She trusted Sam implicitly.

By sunset, the Bishareens had arrived and a camp was constructed on the riverbed. Tents were lifted on wooden frames and guide ropes strung tautly to stakes hammered into the ground. Dhurra, a type of sorghum, was fed raw to the donkeys, while the camels received pouches of dried corn. The cameleers doled out flat loaves of dhurra bread and dates amongst themselves.

Around a campfire made from dried, brittle palm fronds and underbrush, Florie and Sam shared some dried meat, dhurra bread smeared with honey from a small jar, and a cup of camel's milk. From the riverbanks, insects chirped.

"Tomorrow, I'll started exploring," he said with a satisfied smile. He leaned toward her and clinked her cup in a toast.

"You mean that tomorrow *we'll* explore," she replied before sipping the milk.

Sam caught the glint in her eye and decided to keep silent.

Chapter Nine

Birds screeched raucously, welcoming the new day. A pale rosy haze in the east signaled that dawn was perhaps a half hour away. Florie shivered slightly in the surprisingly chill air, her bare toes digging into the sand. The grit on the surface was cool, but an inch or two below it felt warm. She heard Sam sleeping inside his tent. Creeping softly to the tent flap, she peeked in. He was muttering something, but she couldn't make out what it was. Leather gun cases were stacked next to his bed. His clothing was folded neatly, his Piccadilly knife and boots close at hand. She had promised to wake him if she stirred before he did. For the moment, however, she felt content just to watch him sleep.

Sam fidgeted, then rubbed his eyes and sat up. "Were you going to let me sleep all day?" he asked when he saw her peering in. He combed his fingers through his hair, trying to straighten the disheveled mess. "Half the day is gone, and I've got a river to explore."

"I'll get coffee started, then I'll dress to go with you," she said cheerfully.

"I think it would be wise if I go alone," he grumbled. "Who knows what dangers are out there."

"All the more reason to have a second gun to back you up," she replied, her buoyancy undiminished. "You're the one who said you needed someone reliable to come with you." She stooped next to the campfire and added twigs and other tinder to the few embers still glowing from the night before. A thin, brown column of smoke coiled into the air. Flames sparkled and snapped. Small branches and larger pieces of wood were added. Within ten minutes, a kettle of water was boiling. She carefully doled out two teaspoons of coffee grounds into the water. The rich aroma filled the air.

"That's mean coffee you make," he announced pleasantly after sampling from the cup she offered. "But I still don't think you should come with me. Or do you think I'm running out on you again?"

"Where would you go?" she asked soberly. "The next sand dune? Please don't make light of leaving me."

Sam sipped his coffee thoughtfully. The smile he had seen when she stood at the door to his tent now evaporated. "I won't," he finally said. "But if you're going with me, then be ready in five minutes."

With a whoop of delight, Florie disappeared into her tent.

As she dressed, Sam retrieved his notebook from its waterproof bag, sharpened a pencil with his knife, and wrote a new entry:

20 June 1861

We have found the Atbara, a tributary of the Blue Nile. What disappointment! It is mostly sand and rocks. I'm hoping the rains come soon to fill its course. Only then can I discover how the Nile is fed. I feel the Geographical Society has sent me on an academic errand. I should be searching for the true source of the White Nile in Africa's heartland. How I envy Speke and Grant.

After a spartan breakfast of bread and coffee, he returned to his tent and unpacked his favorite rifle. Nestled in its case lined with green billiard felt was his 24-bore rifle built by Thomas Fletcher of Gloucester. It had a fixed rear sight and two folding leaves for longer range shooting. The little double-barreled gun was not the most powerful in his arsenal by far, but for most game it was plenty potent. Besides, he loved the balance of the weapon, the way it seemed to spring to his shoulder and line with his eye as if it were an extension of his arms.

"This is for you," he said to Florie as he handed her the Fletcher. "It doesn't kick as much as my big rifles. But for God's sake, don't shoot at anything unless I tell you."

Her eyes glowed with appreciation. "And what are you going to use?"

With a grin, he hefted his massive four-bore, single-barrel rifle. The twenty-pound gun made by Holland of London fired a half-pound bullet backed by twelve drams of powder. He had shot the big rifle only a few times before; its recoil was ferocious.

"But you'll only have a single shot," she objected.

"It's all I'll need."

Sam saddled two of the donkeys, hooking a water bottle over each saddle horn. Then he woke Hadji Achmet. "The *sitt* and I will travel up the river for a few miles. Rouse the men in a few minutes and follow us in case we shoot any game."

Florie had already mounted her donkey, her rifle balanced carefully across the saddle. She had tucked her golden hair under her broad-brimmed hat, pulling it firmly down over her forehead. The soft white sand muffled the sounds of the donkeys' hooves as they left the camp.

The riverbed ran straight for over a mile before bending to the south. As they approached the bend, Sam leaned from the saddle to study the footprints of numerous animals. Another half mile brought them to a large, brackish pool that stretched from a depression at the foot of one bank about sixty yards toward the riverbed's center. Sand grouse that had gathered at the fringe of the moisture to drink erupted in flight. A crocodile lunged into the water from its resting place in the mud. Before he could throw his rifle to his shoulder, the reptile disappeared, its passing marked only by an oily, V-shaped ripple. The water was deeper than it looked.

"Look how this bends and twists," Sam said.

Florie's gaze followed the high, undulating banks that marked curves in the riverbed. A fringe of large boulders had collected at the bottom of every bend. In the stone-scoured curves and depressions were pools and lakes, all that remained of the once mighty flow of the river. She sensed eyes staring at her. Somewhere in the jumble of rocks just ahead, a gray shadow leaped between boulders. Seconds later, it emerged on the top of the rock heap and bared its fangs. Yellow-rimmed eyes set close above a naked, doglike snout seemed to focus on her.

"My God," she gasped in awe. "It watches us as if it were human."

"Baboon," Sam said. "Oswell, a friend of mine from England, told me they hunt in packs, surround their enemies, and attack from all sides."

Just like humans, Florie thought as she turned in her saddle while the donkeys ambled past the rock pile. The first baboon was still perched there, but others, including thin-limbed babies, soon joined it. A few males bared their wicked-looking teeth in warning, but the troop was content to let the riders pass peacefully.

Then something whitish in color appeared at the edge of larger lake. "Are those people or just a mirage?" Florie asked, squinting against the glare of the newly risen sun.

Sam rose in his stirrups and shaded his eyes with his hand. There was movement. Through the telescope he detected several people robed in white caftans herding goats toward the edge of a mile-long pool that glimmered a few hundred yards away. The pool had been hidden from view until he and Florie had cleared a long, curving bank. A number of tents, partially hidden by mimosas and dome palms, were clustered at the top of the bank. Thin tendrils of smoke from cook fires drifted skyward.

The goat herders on the Atbara's bed had driven their flock to within a dozen yards of the pool's edge. A few of them were digging in the sand, allowing water to fill the holes so their goats could drink. As Sam surveyed the edge of the lake, he understood why the herders had not allowed their animals to wander to the water's edge. Several large crocodiles lay basking in the early morning sun. He sighted one, looking more like an old log than a dangerous reptile, swimming near the shore.

A young goat, its tan hide dappled black, left the pack crowded around the lip of one of the water-filled holes and nonchalantly trotted toward the pool's edge for an easier drink. A herder, probably a young boy or girl — he couldn't be sure from this distance — waved a stick and ran after the goat. The crocodile drifting offshore suddenly submerged.

Sam, sensing danger, dug his heels into the donkey's ribs. The animal bawled in surprise and leapt forward.

"Wait here," he called over his shoulder to Florie.

The goat drinking at the pool's edge bleated in terror as the water churned. A dark, savage bulk heaved through the froth. Then the goat was gone.

Florie gulped. "Sweet Jesus!" She gave rein to her donkey and bolted after Sam as the horrific scene unfolded with lightning speed.

The child bravely, but foolishly, ran knee deep into the bloodied water, thrashing the surface with the stick. Another crocodile submerged. Perhaps sensing his impending doom, the child froze, letting the stick droop. The water swirled menacingly in front of him and a reptilian snout poked above the surface.

Sam flung himself from the saddle and cocked the hammer of his four-bore. There was no time to run closer or yell a warning. In an instant, the big rifle was at his shoulder, its sights lining on the crocodile's skull, his finger tightening on the trigger. The explosion and recoil blew him backwards, seat first, into the sand. His ears rang painfully. Blood dribbled between his eyes as he struggled to clear the cobwebs.

Florie knew Sam's single-shot was empty. She leapt from her saddle and ran through the brown haze of gun smoke to clear her view. Her thumb rotated her rifle's hammers to full cock. She gasped at what she saw.

In the pool, the water boiled madly. A huge tail whipped through the air as the crocodile twisted in its death agony, its creamy belly stark against the muddy liquid. The bullet had struck the instant the monster's head had emerged. The great reptiles that had been sunning themselves glided into the lake with amazing speed. Within moments the dying crocodile was being torn apart by its brethren, huge bodies convulsing and rolling in a feeding frenzy. Jaws chomped, herders screamed, and panicked goats bleated. The child, motionless as it was sprayed with blood and mud, suddenly wailed in terror and sloshed from the pool.

Through the cacophony, Florie heard cries from the tents at the top of the bank. Arab tribesmen poured down the slope from their camp, curved swords and spearheads glinting in the sunlight. They surged toward Sam who busily loaded his massive rifle. Taking no chances with a *feringhi* interloper, the tribesmen surrounded him with a menacing wall of steel. If they attacked, it would be over in an instant. The Arabs edged closer.

Thunder barked loudly across the dry belly of the Atbara River. Many of the Arabs jumped with surprise. They turned toward the new intruder. No one had even noticed the woman standing next to the donkeys.

Florie strode briskly toward the ring of shocked men, the hammer on her remaining barrel cocked, the muzzles weaving from one tribesman to the next. She choked back her fear. Her second shot would not be in the air.

"Are you all right, Sam?" she asked urgently as the circle of tribesmen opened to let her pass. Her eyes remained glued on them.

"Why didn't you run?" he growled in reply, fearful of the danger she had put herself into.

"And go where?" she snapped as she stood next to him.

"Anywhere but here."

Camels suddenly bawled and donkeys brayed. Hooves pounded on the sand of the riverbed. A group of riders jolted to a halt amidst a swirl of dust. Hadji Achmet, mounted on the foremost *hygeen,* had one of Sam's ten-bore rifles balanced across his lap. Behind him were the rest of the cameleers, all armed. He quickly slipped from his saddle, and then bowed to one of the Arabs, touching his fingers to his lips.

A tall man stepped from the throng and returned the greeting. Standing over six feet in height, he had broad shoulders, a magnificently arched nose, and a thick white beard that descended to the middle of his chest. A white turban covered his head, while a cream-colored cashmere *abbai* clothed him from his throat to his ankles. He surveyed Sam with hard, dark eyes as Hadji Achmet spoke rapidly.

"I am Achmet Abou Sinn, sheik of the Bishareen," the tall man said. "Your coming is like the blessing of a new moon. Our young goat boy, Basheet, would have been but a morsel for the great beasts of the water, but your timely presence has spared his unworthy life."

"And I am Samuel Baker of the English," Sam replied, his eyes never leaving those of the sheik. "It is purely God's will that I arrived when I did."

"Yes, I am familiar with the English," Abou Sinn said. He shifted his gaze to Hadji Achmet. "And I see my son is still working in the land of the Egyptians. What is it you do with this Englishman?"

"Yes, Father," the burly camel driver replied meekly. "This is Baker Pasha and his *sitt.* They are—"

"What? A white *sitt,* here?" Abou Sinn cried in disbelief. "I have seen but one such creature in my lifetime. That is she? Surely that is a stripling boy at his side, not the wife of the Englishman. Let her be under the cover of a tent so the sun shall not strike her."

Abou Sinn, eyes rolling in wonder, gracefully offered his hand to Florie. She giggled as she accepted and allowed him to lead her up a narrow path to the top of the banks, then into an open tent. Stretcher-like cots called *angareps* were arranged on one side of the tent. Elaborately woven carpets and cushions covered the *angareps.* As she sat, she caught

Sam's appreciative glance. Her confidence soared. She listened carefully as the sheik questioned Sam.

"You would seek the birthplace of the great river?" Abou Sinn clucked his tongue ruefully. "Not good, not good. You cannot go to the south. The rains will be falling there soon and all will be a sea of mud. The seroot fly bites everything that moves. Camels and donkeys will die; only goats can survive. There are barbarous men to the south as well, ones who would kill you and enslave the *sitt.*"

"I know there are dangers, but it is what I have come to find," Sam said firmly.

"Then if you continue, you will travel for a full moon before you enter the land of the Hamrans," Abou Sinn said, spreading his arms helplessly. "They are famed as elephant hunters, and I think you would enjoy their hospitality." The sheik hesitated, nodding his head toward his son. "To ensure such, I will order Hadji Achmet to remain in your service. He has followed the Hamrans on the hunt and knows their ways. Once you enter their territory, they will test your bravery and invite you to kill elephants. If you show courage, they will allow you to pass through. If you are killed, well then ...."

"Don't worry," Sam said. "I won't disappoint them."

"I do not know if your *Jenna el Mootfah* can stop a bull elephant," Abou Sinn chuckled, pointing at the Holland four-bore.

Florie tugged at Sam's elbow. "What did the sheik say?"

"Eh? *Mootfah*? He calls it Child of the Cannon. "

Florie laughed and pointed at the purplish knob on his forehead caused by the recoil of the big gun. "Yes, child, a baby cannon! It's a good name. That's some baby you have, Sam. She kissed you well."

"Basheet, the boy you saved from the devil in the pool, will follow you as your servant," Abou Sinn continued, nodding approvingly. "He has some of the European language he learned as an orphan raised among white missionaries. When they all died of the fever, we found him, barely alive, and he has been among us since.

"Past the Hamrans lies the junction of the Atbara and the Setit. Go beyond that, Allah forbid, and you will be in the highlands of the Abyssinians and the domain of the warlord Mek Nimmur, the Leopard King."

"Leopard King?" Florie asked.

"Yes, *Sitt,*" Abou Sinn replied, nodding gravely. "As a young man, Mek Nimmur killed a leopard with only a knife. There is no more deadly beast than an angry leopard. Today, he is at war with the Egyptians and any others who enter his territory. His way is of the slave trade. I, myself, have lost a daughter to him, may Allah have mercy on her and burn the eyes from his head."

Florie fought the cold grip of fear at the thought of marching into a slave trader's lands. A vision of the auction floor at Vidin swam muddily through her mind. What was Sam's phrase? Something about a frying pan and fire?

Sam unfolded his map and pointed at the thin blue lines denoting the possible path of the Nile. "And is there a great lake that feeds the Atbara and Setit, and delivers its waters to the mighty Nile?"

"I have heard that there are lakes far to the south of the *Bahr el Abiad*, the White Nile, but those may merely be fables," the sheik said, wagging his head slowly. "Of the Atbara or Setit or even further to the River Dinder, I have not heard of such a lake feeding the Blue Nile."

"Then I'll have to go and see with my own eyes what lies in that direction," Sam said as he re-folded his map.

Abou Sinn bowed his head knowingly. "It will be as Allah wills."

"As Allah wills," Florie whispered to herself as she and Sam left the tent, walked down the riverbank, and approached the camp erected by the Bishareens.

In the west, the molten ball of sun sank in an indigo African sky, melting into an evening palette of pale rose, soft peach, deep violet and other colors she couldn't name. Animal sounds—hunters growling, prey screaming in their death throes, birds screeching under the rising moon—echoed in a bestial symphony that carried on through the night. And the stars in the heavens glimmered in patterns she had never seen before. Sam suddenly extended his telescope.

"What is it?" Florie asked when he smiled broadly. "What do you see?"

"It's a little dark to tell for sure, but I think I see clouds building in the east," he replied. "That means rain, and if it's raining there, the rivers should soon be flowing."

Basheet, the young goat herder from the Bishareen camp, watched them study the clouds. He was perhaps twelve years old, with intelligent, glittering eyes and a ready smile.

"When the rains come, the river will cover all of the land as far as you can see," he said, turning about in a circle and pointing in all directions. "It will be soon, I think. See how the clouds are changing colors? The rains will soon be here."

Florie laughed as she remembered the stories her mother had told her. "Like Noah's flood, when God sent a rain that covered the entire Earth."

"Yes," exclaimed Basheet excitedly. He wasn't quite sure what she meant by the entire Earth. "The river covers everything. When it comes, I will warn you."

***

After the full moon had risen, Sam lingered over a brandy outside his tent on the riverbed. The trilling of birds had been replaced by the rhythmic chirruping of bullfrogs at the pool's edge. The breeze, still warm so late in the evening, caressed him with the scent of lemons from a nearby grove on the bank. He discerned Florie's silhouette against her tent wall, her shadow cast by the meager glow of a single candle. The thin sound of water dribbling in the small, enameled tub meant she was performing her bath, a luxury she had been forced to forego during the trip through the desert. The faint fragrance of lavender drifted through her partially opened tent flap. Her back was to him as she sponged her face and belly. The light bronzing on her arms and neck from exposure to the Egyptian sun contrasted with the whiteness of her shoulders and buttocks. He tried to look away, but couldn't. The curves of her hips, a half-glimpsed breast, the water dripping down her legs. His pulse quickened.

Florie glanced over her shoulder and caught her breath. She saw him watching her, and she stepped from the tub and away from the flap. A few moments later she emerged into the night air, her striped caftan covering her. Sam, his face flushed crimson, tried to walk past.

"Sam," she called softly, "wait." Her eyes searched his. "I heard Halleem Effendi call me your wife, and now Abou Sinn thinks the same. I won't have you embarrassed by that again. I'm used to shaving my head and pretending I'm a boy. I'll do so again."

Sam noticed her trembling although the night air was warm. "Tomorrow, we'll travel upriver to find out if it's really a source of the Nile," he said, looking first at his feet, then meeting her gaze. "Where we go, none will know us. Besides, I rather like your hair now."

With his laugh, the tension she felt a moment before fled.

"I'm sorry I was watching you," he added, looking away. Before she could respond, he walked to his own tent and ducked in.

"I'm not," she said, breathless.

Chapter Ten

The camp slumbered quietly when Florie suddenly jolted awake. She wasn't sure how long she had slept, but it couldn't have been for more than an hour or two. The air was muggy, heavy with the threat of storms. But it wasn't the sultry night air that had awakened her; it was something else.

With her revolver in her fist, she swung her legs from the cot. There, she heard it again. It was a low rumbling growl, reminiscent of distant thunder. There had been only a dark line of storm clouds far to the east earlier in the evening; those certainly couldn't have traveled that quickly. She pushed the tent flap open. Above her was a clear sky, milky moonshine lighting the Atbara's floor, stars glimmering like chipped diamonds in the dark void. Normally, thunder rolled and ebbed, slowly growing stronger as the storm neared. This sound, this tumbling roar, was constant and it was definitely getting louder very quickly.

Torches flared along the ridges of the river. She heard shouts from the Bishareen camp. One of the tribesmen skidded down the bank and sprinted toward the travelers' tents. "El Bahr! El Bahr!" the Bishareen cried, gesticulating wildly up river.

Basheet wriggled from under his blankets near the fire, his eyes wide with fright. "He says it is the river. It comes!"

Florie stared, mesmerized by the sullen roar. The black banks of clouds she had seen to the east meant it had been raining in that direction. And now the product of that deluge was surging toward them.

Sam's head poked through the tent flaps, his ear cocked toward the rumbling sound. "Florie! For Christ's sake, move," he yelled at the top of his lungs. "The river is flooding! Take the guns up the bank! I'll jack the tents! Hurry!"

Sam grunted as he yanked the deeply driven tent stakes out of the ground. With the support ropes free, he gathered the smothering folds of canvas into his arms, pivoted, and pitched the collapsed tent across the bare back of one of the donkeys. The beast, sensing the danger, brayed and bucked.

To Florie, it appeared as if everything was moving in slow motion. Mucous blew from the donkey's nostrils. Basheet dropped a box containing the flatware and was carefully placing each spoon, knife, and fork back it its appropriate slot. She saw Sam's muscles bunching across his bare chest and arms as he strained against a stubborn stake from her tent. The stake suddenly jerked free in a spray of earth, its jagged, battered cap scraping across his ribs, ripping through his thin shirt and into his flesh.

Sam grabbed her by the shoulders, his eyes wide with concern. "Damn it, woman, I need you to help! If you can't, then skedaddle up the ridge. I'll join you in a few seconds."

With confusion wrinkling her brow, she blinked first at Sam, then at the ominous black shadow filling the gorge upriver. It was as if a deadly torpor had crept into her limbs. Clamping her jaws, she willed herself to move and began shoveling gun cases to Hadji Achmet and a few of the Bishareens who were not engaged in driving the camels up the banks. "Shit," she cried as one of the leather straps broke. The gun case flew open and its rifle thrown into the sand. She plucked up the gun, but stubbed her toe on the broken case. With her teeth gritted against the pain, she wrapped her other fist around the handle of her beloved bath basin. Behind her, Sam hefted a heavy trunk to his shoulder.

There were a few more moments of hellish activity, and then the men were moving up the bank with camels, donkeys, and supplies. Left behind were a few scraps from supper, the dying embers of the campfire, and the broken gun case. The rain-swollen flood surged across the distant lip of the pool.

"Hurry," Florie cried over her shoulder to Sam as she raced up the path leading to the riverbank. When she reached the lip of the bank, she spun toward him. "Hurry!"

A glimmer of the river's oily darkness in the glow cast by the Bishareen torches caught her eye. Its flow was irresistible, its roar reminding her of the locomotives in Kostendje, but without the shrill whistles and thick worms of stinking smoke. With eyes wide, she watched Sam sprint after the disappearing cameleers, hooking his free hand around the broken gun case as he ran. Soaked by the flood's spray, he clambered up the bank, kissed her as he gained its top, hugged Basheet, and kissed her again. Had he been a step or two slower, he would have been swept away by the muddy deluge.

"It's been raining in the Abyssinian highlands," he roared, a vast smile lighting his face. "It's been pouring there. The Atbara is filling. Here is the source of the Nile! This is what geography is all about!"

Lips aflame with his kisses, Florie looked at Sam as he laughed loudly, his hands slapping his thighs. She placed her hand over her breast to calm her pounding heart. *What kind of man treats me as his equal, his companion, and then leaves me weak and trembling with a simple kiss?* She stared at the dark waters of the flood to hide her confusion.

The river continued to swell, splashing the sand at their feet until it turned to mud. This certainly could not be from where the mighty Nile sprang, she thought. This was a torrent, but the Nile was an all-consuming serpent that wound its way through the deserts until its vast tongue lapped the salt of the Mediterranean. She was no geographer, but she was sure it would take many such streams to fill the Nile. She hoped Sam would look for all of them.

A thin wind riffled the leaves of the mimosa palms. Sam placed his arm around Florie's shoulders to keep her warm as they watched the moon rise above the thundering flood of the Atbara. Behind them, the men were already hammering tent pegs into the ground.

"I'm sorry I froze down there," she said, nodding toward the river. "There was so much to do and so little time, I just couldn't move. I won't let it happen again."

"In Africa, hesitation is the difference between life and death," he said, trying to sound stern. "Do that again, and I'll have Basheet take you home."

"You foolish old man. No one is sending me home," Florie cried in mock anger and playfully pushed him away. With a wince of pain, he stepped back.

"You're hurt." She groaned in dismay as the flickers of torchlight revealed a bloody rent in his shirt. Raw flesh glimmered redly through the tear.

"I'm fine. It's just a scratch," he mumbled. "Must have scraped my ribs against one of the tent stakes. Damned things are sharper than they look. A bit of cleaning and I'll be good to go on."

"You'll do no such thing," Florie declared, shaking her finger menacingly. "One of our tents is already being set up. I want you to sit in there while Hadji boils some water. I've stitched up plenty of cuts from sickle blades when I worked on the farms. If this wound isn't cleaned properly, poison will set in."

With a candle to light the tent's interior, she directed Sam to sit on the edge of a cot. Blood continued to seep from the six-inch gash along his ribs. She sponged the wound with hot water. "Salt should clean it," she said, "or a little spirits."

"Why that's almost barbaric," Sam replied with a shake of his head. "I have something better. In the medicine chest is a bottle with purple liquid called tincture of iodine. Wet your sponge with hot water, sprinkle iodine on it, and pack it into this damned cut."

Florie found the bottle and shook its contents tentatively. "In Mehadia, we always doused a wound with brandy and lit a match to it. Are you sure this will work?"

Sam rolled his eyes. "Good Christ, no wonder your people were fodder for the Turks. Yes, it definitely works."

With a few orange drops of iodine blotted on the sponge, she swabbed it against the angry red slash.

"Sweet Mother of God!" He flinched as he jerked away.

"My, aren't we sensitive?" she chided him.

She gently packed a lint pad against the wound and held it in place with her palm. Her fingers lightly brushed the hair matting his chest. His arm rested on her shoulder for support as she leaned close to him, his warmth and nearness flowing through her. She tried to hide her trembling as she slowly wound the long bandages around his torso and under his arm.

Sam cursed under his breath as she knotted the loose ends of the dressings to hold them in place. He uncorked a bottle of brandy and took a long pull. "And you wanted to waste this?"

"You'll sleep now," Florie ordered. "And in the morning you'd better hope that you're free of pus."

Sam grimaced as he swung his legs onto his cot and laid back. A peculiar lethargy stole over him as the brandy took effect. His muscles relaxed. His chest burned. In a few moments, he was asleep.

Florie brushed a loose strand of hair from her eyes. Seated on a crate of supplies next to him, she listened to his deep, even breathing. He sleeps so peacefully, she thought as she lifted his arm to inspect the bandages. A ragged red stripe stained the wrapping, but thankfully had not spread. She held his hand against her cheek, then her breast as if his touch would slow her wildly beating heart. "I do love you," she said quietly. "I hope someday you'll love me."

Tears wetted her face when she finally left the tent.

**

Zast Ohmed Pasha thumped his fist on the table. "What do you mean they didn't bring her back?" he snarled at the cringing man who had just entered his office.

Emile Zeb clutched his hands together, his face a mask of fear. Although he was a wealthy man, he knew he could easily end up in the Danube with the governor's knife quivering in his ribs. "Magram Bur tracked Baker and the slave girl to Kostendje on the Black Sea," he replied, his voice quavering. "She was nearly in his grasp when she was warned somehow. Bur searched the entire town, but she disappeared. We think she's with the Englishman now."

"And where is that cursed Englishman?" Ohmed Pasha demanded.

"My sources say they have gone to Africa."

"Africa?"

"It's true, Your Excellency." Zeb saw the anger in the governor's eyes turn to wonder. "I sent Magram Bur to Cairo to investigate. His message arrived last night. He reported that Baker has headed up the Nile and is traveling somewhere in Abyssinia."

"What of the yellow-haired girl?" Ohmed Pasha leaned toward the slave trader, his arms rigid pillars anchored to his desk.

"Bur says that the Englishman was traveling with a young man at first, but he thinks it is her in disguise. He is on their trail at this moment."

Ohmed Pasha pivoted on his heel to consult a map tacked to the wall. His finger tapped the blue-green continent labeled Africa, and then traced the course of the Nile.

He shook his fist menacingly. "You told me once, Zeb, that you have contacts in Khartoum. See to it that you don't fail me again. And when the Englishman is killed, make sure that it cannot be traced back to me."

Emile Zeb bowed and backed out of the governor's office. Once outside, he braced himself against a wall as his legs threatened to fold under him. He felt his heart racing. The pasha never made idle threats. The fire burning in the man's eyes made his skin crawl. He would have to find the girl—or else!

Chapter Eleven

24 June 1861

The Atbara is now a memory, Sam wrote in his journal. Tomorrow, a new river should be in sight. Will it, too, be flooded with muddy waters purged from the mountains? Will I see bamboos and reeds, and even whole trees, speed along its rampaging current?

My ribs feel much better and no rot has set into my wound. Florence ...

Sam stared at what he had written. Since the night of the Atbara's flood, Florie had been pensive. True, they still ate together and rode side by side, but she said little, and rarely asked for his help. Maybe I was too hard on her the night of the flood, he thought as he leaned back in his camp chair. The source of the Nile is my concern, not hers.

With a deft motion he crossed out Florence so her name was unreadable. He substituted F in its place. Should something happen to him and his journal reach his family, it would be better if they did not know a woman traveled with him.

***

Florie wiped beads of sweat from her brow and surveyed the river with a practiced eye. It had been a month since they had left the swollen flow of the Atbara to follow the curves of the Setit. This tributary, she was sure, was just like the Atbara: heavy storms in the highlands caused the river to flood. When the rainy season ended, the flow diminished. These rivers were like veins feeding the great arm of the Nile.

As she turned toward the camp, movement along the riverbank caused her to pause. She shaded her eyes with her hand against the glare of the August sun. "We have company," she called loudly.

Sam placed his notebook on the ground and surveyed the approaching horsemen through his telescope. He hastily collapsed the glass.

"Load your rifle and stay behind me," he ordered. "It might be some of Emile Zeb's men."

Four riders galloped toward them, each bearing a round shield of hammered bronze. Braided plaits of oiled hair descended to their shoulders. Mahogany skin glistened with sweat. Light, cotton robes barely covered their muscular physiques and long sword blades glistened menacingly. Their approach was without fear.

"They are Hamrans," Basheet said, his voice quivering fearfully. "They are *aggageers*—sword hunters. May Allah protect us."

The riders halted, swords bared, horses snorting in agitation. Sam thumbed back the hammers on his ten-bore.

"Wait," Hadji Achmet called urgently. "I know these people." He stepped toward the horsemen, touching his fingers to his lips in greeting.

"May Allah guide your steps and keep your lands rich with game, Sheik Abou Do Roussol," the Bishareen intoned.

Abou Do was a strikingly handsome man with a broad chest and flashing dark eyes. "We recognize you, Hadji Achmet, son of Sheik Abou Sinn, and may Allah bless him and keep him well."

"And blessings to you, your kin, and to your uncle, the great Sheik Owat of the Hamran," Hadji Achmet continued. "This is Baker Pasha of the English, and his *sitt*. They have come to see the rivers that feed the great Nile. Would you give them permission to cross your lands?"

Abou Do studied the big Englishman. The double-barreled rifle cradled in Sam's arms looked efficient and menacing. So did the smaller version held by his woman. She was a slight thing with hair like the sunrise and no extra meat on her bones. He was sure both strangers knew how to use their weapons well.

"As you know, Hadji Achmet," the Hamran chief began, "my people do not take kindly to visitors. It is all we can do to keep the peace with our neighbor, the Leopard King. What can your friends offer in exchange for passage?"

Sam, understanding most of the conversation, stepped forward and handed his rifle to the cameleer. "I have trade goods that would grace your families and your city."

"I have seen the Europeans' trinkets and baubles in the past," Abou Do countered. "We have no use for them." He leaned forward in his saddle as his gaze searched over the gun cases strapped to several of the camels. "You have more guns?"

"Yes," Sam said with a smile, "but none are for trade. We need them to survive."

"What is that one?" Abou Do asked, pointing to the largest and bulkiest of the cases.

Sam motioned to Hadji Achmet to unpack the massive Holland four-bore. The smallest of the Hamrans, barely Florie's height, slid from his horse and bent at the waist to inspect the rifle. He pointed in wonder at the barrel of the big Holland, inserting two fingers into its muzzle.

"That is *Jenna el Mootfah*." Hadji Achmet chuckled.

"*Sahe, Jenna el Mootfah kabeer*," Jali, the diminutive Hamran, agreed, nodding his head in astonishment. "It is true. It is the child of a very big cannon."

"To cross our lands, we ask that you hunt elephant with us," Abou Do said flatly. "Our people are hungry and elephants have been too wary of our hunters. We have been unable to get close to enough to bring one down."

Sam surveyed the Hamran riders. He did not see any bows and arrows nor trade muskets. "Do you use guns or bows?" he asked.

"Guns? Bows?" Abou Do frowned. "We are *aggageers.* We hunt with the sword." Four feet of double-edged steel shimmered in the morning sun as he swung his blade in a half-circle. Then he motioned toward the two men remaining in their saddles. "This is Taher Sherrif and his brother, Roder Sherrif. They are our best *aggageers.* As you can see, Roder Sherrif has tasted the anger of the elephant."

Roder Sherrif lifted a withered arm, more a crooked spike of dried leather ending in a vulture-like claw than human flesh. "Tusk," he said, a measure of pride in his voice. "It has not kept me from hunting."

Abou Do rubbed his jaw thoughtfully. "If Baker of the English would pay us with elephant meat, then he and his people can cross our lands to find his river."

***

Florie frowned as Sam confronted her, his back arched tensely, hands on his hips, head wagging his disapproval.

"Go with us? You can't be serious," he snapped. "We're hunting elephants, not antelopes."

"I'm not staying behind," she replied evenly, ignoring his body language. "You trusted me to come with you to Africa, remember?"

He continued to shake his head. "But it's too damned dangerous."

"Sam, I can ride and sh—"

"Ride and shoot. Yes, I know all about what you can do," he grated in exasperation. "But these are *elephants*."

Florie's eyes burned with determination. "I swore I'd never be left behind again. I know how to ride and shoot because you helped teach me. I'll follow you on foot if I have to. I still have my pistol." She patted the little revolver jammed under her belt.

"It's hopeless," he shouted to no one in particular.

Hadji Achmet cupped his hand over his mouth to hide his smile. Wonders of the *djinn*! The *sitt* was more of a man than some of his own men. "I will gladly give up the horse Jali brought for me if the *sitt* should like to ride," he said, trying to keep a straight face.

Florie smiled prettily at him. Sam shot him a stormy glance. "And Basheet can ride one of the donkeys to keep you company," he added grumpily.

"Good. I'm glad that's settled," Florie said as she swung her leg over the saddle and settled her feet into the stirrups. She turned to the Hamrans. "So, do the elephants come to us, or must we find them?"

The tone of her voice stirred the sword hunters to action and they quickly vaulted into their saddles. Sam, still shaking his head in disbelief at how rapidly the table had been turned on him, clambered aboard his mount and galloped after them. Secretly he was glad she wanted to share this adventure with him, despite its danger.

Twenty minutes later the hunting party cantered toward a distant bend in the river. Baobab trees, their bottle-shaped trunks supporting vast, leafy canopies, created islands of shadow and coolness. Dome palms waved in the soft breeze. Rose-colored limestone cliffs framed the valley. A picturesque creek snaked its way across the valley floor. At the steam's edge, a small herd of gazelles with lyre-shaped horns raised their heads from drinking, their ears twitching. They studied the intruders for only seconds before bounding gracefully away.

"This is beautiful country," Florie said serenely as she watched the antelopes disappear. "I was imagining a cottage nestled on the banks of that little creek. I was baking bread in a brick oven. You had been fishing and were holding up your catch to show me. This would be a wonderful place for us to live."

With a little sigh, she looped her thick braid in front of her shoulder so its golden swell cushioned her cheek. She caught Sam's gaze and wet her lips with her tongue.

"Are you flirting with me," Sam asked warily.

"Do you think I am?" she replied with a hint of a smile.

Sam gulped and didn't answer.

Jali suddenly reined his horse to a halt and leapt from the saddle. A greasy-looking mound imbedded with fragments of seedpods had grabbed his attention. Squatting next to it, he pressed his forefinger into the soft pile. He said something excitedly, then motioned toward a grove of trees surrounded by kittar thorns and lush marshlands.

"Jali says the elephant dung is still fresh, probably from earlier this morning," Abou Do explained as he shielded his eyes against the sun's glare. He inspected the tracery of tracks. "The elephants have been here to drink and have gone into the forest. But there are buffalo in there, too. Very dangerous, very unpredictable."

"The wind is against us," Taher Sherrif said, turning his head this way and that to test the breeze. "We won't be able to take our swords into the thorns to drive them out. It will be too dense for us to swing."

"Then let them smell me," Sam offered as he rammed home the powder charge and inserted the iron-covered, three-groove bullet into the broad maw of the Holland four-bore. "I've killed a lot of elephants in

Ceylon, and I'm sure that my Baby will do the same here. What I don't shoot, I'll drive downwind to your swords. I still think it's unwise to face such monsters with only a blade." He finished by ramming the bullet and wad down the barrel, and placing a percussion cap on the ignition nipple.

"Yes," Abou Do returned, nodding his head sagely, "and if your rifle fails to fire when the elephant charges, what will you do? An elephant can move faster than you can reload."

Sam smiled as he hefted the Holland. The swordsman had a point.

"Jali will go into the brush with you," Abou Do ordered. "There will be many tracks in there, but he will be able to find the correct ones."

"Then he shall carry my spare rifle," Sam said as he handed the Ceylon ten-bore to the grinning *aggageer*. "Just make sure you hand it to me if I should need it."

Abou Do jerked his thumb toward Florie and Basheet waiting a few paces away. "And what of the *sitt* and the boy? Surely you cannot take them into the thorns. Their skin is too delicate."

"I'm not afraid of a few thorns," Florie said. It irked her that she wasn't able to follow all of the conversation.

Sam clenched his teeth. He imagined her facing enraged elephants with only the puny Fletcher to stop them. The great beasts, easily capable of ripping trees apart, would mangle her beyond recognition. His mouth suddenly felt dry as sand.

"That may be, but I think it's best if you stand under that baobab tree on the edge of that marsh, " he explained tactfully to Florie. "If anything breaks that way, we'll need you to turn it back toward us." He had measured his words in a way he hoped Abou Do would notice.

The sheik tested the air again. With the breeze wafting their scent toward the trees, no game would flee in her direction. Yes, she would be perfectly safe there. "I agree that would be a good place for the *sitt*," he said.

Florie's gaze turned to where Abou Do had pointed. To her inexperienced eye, the location seemed perfect, offering both shade from the sun's blast and an open field for shooting. She flashed a smile of satisfaction.

As Abou Do and the Sherrif brothers remounted and galloped to the north end of the forest, Sam loaded the ten-bore rifle that Jali would carry. Florie watched as he checked for extra percussion caps, and made sure his powder flask was full. A short pull on the canteen cut his thirst.

He does things so nonchalantly, as if the danger of the moment barely warrants a passing thought, she mused. She wished she had his courage. She wished she could be at his side as he stalked the elephants. Without warning, she threw her arms around his neck, her fingers curled into his hair, her cheek pressed tightly to his. Then she released him, turning away so he couldn't see the fear in her eyes.

"Florie …. "

But she mounted her horse without looking back, and with Basheet in tow, galloped toward the baobab.

Jali cleared his throat as the woman and the boy disappeared into the tall grass. He had seen English Baker and his *sitt* embrace, and it puzzled him. No Hamran woman would ever show such a sign of affection while another man watched. It was barbaric!

A high-pitched birdcall thrummed in the air, stopped, then started again. Jali cocked his ear toward the sound. "English Baker, Abou Do has rounded the far end of the forest. We should go."

Sam nodded his head, and, after a last glance in Florie's direction, turned and jogged warily to the edge of the trees. Long, hooked kittar thorns seemed knitted together like a forest of daggers. He realized if the elephants charged while he was hung up on the thorns, not even his Baby four-bore would save him.

Jali, the spare rifle cradled in his arms, dropped to a crouch, then carefully crept into the brush, weaving back and forth to avoid the lacerating spikes. Sam followed. Insects buzzed. Little clouds of dust lifted, the fine sand sifting into his shoes. The smells of dirt, animal dung, rotting vegetation, and his own sweat clogged his nostrils. A thorn scraped across his forearm leaving a bright track of blood. Moisture beaded on his brow, trickling into his eyes.

Minutes passed as he and Jali painfully crabbed their way through the thorns. The Hamran abruptly held up a cautioning hand. He leaned toward Sam until his lips pressed against the Englishman's ear. "Buffalo," he whispered. "He's hurt. Very dangerous! Do you see him?"

Sam followed Jali's line of vision. A dark, massive shadow with thick, curving horns limped through the thorns. He discerned the remnants of a native's wire snare dangling from an angry, festering slash in the bovine's hind leg. Biting flies swarmed around the wound, adding to the beast's agony.

"We wait until it passes," Jali said in warning.

Scant moments later, Sam heard the flap of an elephant's ear and its guttural groan, although the great animal remained hidden by the screen of kittar brush. The buffalo had moved a few yards further away, but was still visible. Jali grasped Sam's ankle and held a warning finger to his lips. The gray bulk of an old bull elephant pushed toward them through a thatch work of thorns. Sam just made out the gleam of its tusks. It halted, and then nervously shuffled in a small circle as it sensed danger. Its ears flapped against its leathery hide. Sam tried to swallow, but his throat was as dry as the dirt he knelt on. He leaned forward, trying to find an opening through the thorns that would give him a better shot. As he cocked his head, he caught a glimpse of the elephant's eye. Its ear flapped again. Its stomach rumbled; its tail swished. A withered branch dragged across Sam's shirt, caught momentarily in the cloth, then snapped.

Trumpeting, the great bull feinted toward the thorns, then drew back, its ears widespread with alarm. It heard the hunters, but couldn't pinpoint them. Its trunk curled, trying to catch a scent.

With a curse, Sam forced his way through the final fringe of thorns, blood beading his arms where the hooks bit flesh. As he nearly tumbled into the clearing, he glimpsed the rest of the herd as it rushed to the north. The big bull caught his scent. Its immense ears were cocked and its trunk lifted as it prepared to charge. Sam threw Baby to his shoulder. Instinctively, he aimed at the center of the huge head as he had done so many times in Ceylon. Out of the corner of his eye, he saw a massive black shape hurtling toward him. Too late to swing his gun! Jali thudded into him, driving him to one side. The dark shadow thundered past so close that sweat from its hide smeared his arm.

"It was the buffalo," Jali cried as he pointed in the direction the black-skinned nightmare had disappeared. "It almost got you! But we leave it go!"

Momentarily unnerved by the errant charge of the buffalo, the bull elephant turned its head and again lifted its trunk as it tried to relocate the human scent. Sam ducked and went to a knee. The sights of his four-bore aligned on the elephant's skull behind the ear. The big rifle roared and bucked, spinning him half way around. Smoke from its discharge obliterated his view, but he heard the thud of the elephant as it collapsed. A second bull promptly appeared near its fallen comrade. It shrieked its anger, tested the air for scent with its trunk, then wheeled about and crashed through the forest on the heels of the rest of the herd. Sam and Jali dashed down a corridor of splintered and smashed trees created by the fleeing pachyderms.

"My brother *aggageers* will hunt now," the little Hamran cried triumphantly.

On the sprawling plain north of the glade and river, two dozen elephants fled toward another sheltering grove in the distance. Babies and juveniles appeared and disappeared among the forest of adult female legs, emerging further on coated with dust. The elephant that had come up behind the one Sam had shot lagged behind the rest of the herd. The protective female leading the group would have never let a bull among the herd, but this one, old and with one tusk chipped two feet shorter than its mate, seemed to be simply serving as a rear guard of sorts while the rest made good their escape.

The *aggageers* harried the bull, riding hard on its flanks, then darting away as it swerved to meet them. Their long hair streamed in the wind;

their lithe, gleaming bodies naked save for their loincloths. Galloping effortlessly, their horses kept pace with the gigantic animal.

Roder Sherrif spurred his mount under the trunk of the enraged elephant. As the powerful trunk curled toward him, he deftly guided his horse away. With the reins wrapped around his crippled arm, he called to the elephant, beckoning it with his free hand, "Follow me, Great One!" The bull thundered after him and didn't notice the riders closing in on his flanks. "Follow me!"

Taher Sherrif galloped toward the bull's hindquarters. He saw the great tendons of its hind legs stretching, then bulging, its tail out-thrust. He fluidly leaped from his saddle as the elephant slowed to veer after Roder. At that moment, Taher slashed his long sword against a huge rear leg. The razor sharp edge sheared deeply, slicing through thick muscle to the bone. Bawling its pain and anger, the bull lurched about on three legs, futilely trying to drive off its wounded limb. It stumbled. Unable to run, the crippled elephant stretched its trunk toward Taher. Abou Do swept in from the opposite side, slid from his saddle and dashed toward the great beast. Swinging from his heels, he slashed his sword into the other massive leg just as the elephant put its full weight on it. The tendon snapped. The bull sank on its haunches, squealing its fury. Blood flowed from severed arteries, mixing with the sand until a slippery crimson slurry formed. The great heart pumped more slowly, the blood flow weakening. With chests heaving from exertion, the *aggageers* waited until the elephant collapsed to its side, its last breath escaping as a cavernous groan.

"Two great elephants today," Jali yelled elatedly after he recovered his breath after his run from the forest. "They were old, but still strong!"

"That is good," Abou Do said as he watered the horses from antelope-skin bags. "The cows and young ones will keep the herd bountiful for our future. This meat will supply our entire village with great feasts for days to come." He turned toward Sam and saluted him with his sword. "We thank you, English Baker, for your help on this great day. We will, indeed, guide you through our lands."

A rifle shot suddenly echoed from the east. Five heads swiveled in that direction. A second shot roared.

"Florie," Sam cried. "My God! An elephant must have cut toward her!"

"No elephant. It's the wounded buffalo that ran past us in the forest," Jali said sadly, shaking his head with regret. "Much worse. Poor *sitt*."

Chapter Twelve

Florie swung her leg over the back of the saddle and dismounted with a little hop. With her rifle cradled in the crook of her arm, she surveyed the surroundings on the east end of the forest. Beyond her assigned baobab, a thick grove of *nabbuk* lotus stretched for several hundred yards, the emerald luxuriance of its foliage brilliant against the stark banks of the Setit. Its cloying fragrance wafted over her. Animal trails led into the *nabbuk* and adjacent marshland.

"Yes, *Sitt*, Basheet will protect you from any elephants that come near," Basheet prattled as he leaned against the baobab's trunk. "If you would only place the wonderful gun in my hands, you will have nothing to fear."

A wan smile flitted across Florie's lips. The Bishareen goat herder had been talking virtually nonstop since they had dismounted under the spread of baobab branches. She'd grown very fond of him in the weeks since he had joined them, showing him how to sew with needle and thread, paint with the watercolors Sam had brought to enhance his sketches, and teaching him basic words in English and German. He, in turn, had shown her how to make soap from hippopotamus fat and to dye cloth brown with the juices of the mimosa fruit. Together they had captured butterflies with small nets, pinning the specimens in Sam's special scientific cases.

For a moment she wondered if Sam would ever marry her, if she would ever have children; raise them, teach them, love them. But even as her thoughts turned to having a family, a dark shadow clouded her mind. She was seventeen when Emile Zeb's slave catcher brutalized her. That seemed long ago, but the anguish and rage over her violation remained. Although she wanted to give herself to Sam, the thought of a man's hands on her left her trembling.

"*Sitt*, why are you crying?" Basheet asked with concern.

Embarrassed, Florie brushed her tears with the back of her hand. "I'm worried about Mr. Baker," she lied.

"English Baker is a mighty hunter," Basheet droned. "With the *Jenna al Mootfah*, he will kill all of the elephants."

A rifle shot bellowed from the glade, followed by a general din of crashing branches and wild trumpeting.

"See? English Baker even now opens the mouth of the Child of the Cannon," Basheet screeched excitedly. "Do not worry, *Sitt*. He has placed us into the wind. No elephants will come this way."

Florie tore blades of grass and tossed them in the air. They drifted to the north. So, Sam *had* placed her out of harm's way. Was it that he didn't trust her anymore?

"You're right," she said, craning her neck toward the forest. "Elephants will smell us first and then turn away." She patted the boy on his head. "I wish I had Mr. Baker's telescope. Then perhaps we could see what's happening."

Florie's horse unexpectedly snorted, rearing against its reins tied loosely to a small shrub. Basheet gathered the tethers and vainly tried to calm the steed. As if on cue, the donkey began braying, its hind legs lashing out, narrowly missing the lad.

Through the underbrush fringing the *nabbuk*, the dark bulk of a buffalo, its head lowered, churned toward them. Strands of vegetation clung to the great sweep of horns hooking over its massive boss. Muscles bunched and gathered under its black hide. Clods of earth flew through the air. She heard it snort once, mucous blowing from its nostrils.

"Dear God," Florie yelped as she swung the Fletcher to her shoulder and cocked its right hammer. "Please, sweet Jesus, let me be steady now." The rifle's sights bounced over the thundering bovine's head. What had Sam said about buffalo? A shoulder shot only? The horny boss of its skull was too thick?

In the fraction of a second it took to make her decision, the sights slid past her initial point of aim between the buffalo's eyes and rested on its shoulder. Her finger squeezed. Fire and thunder erupted. The big bull faltered as the slug passed through muscle and shattered the shoulder joint. The donkey jerked free from its tether and careered at an odd angle away from Florie and the boy. Basheet sped after the animal, lunging at its reins. Distracted, the bull veered to gore him as its legs buckled. Florie saw her chance as the monster wheeled to her left, offering a broadside shot. She fired her remaining barrel just behind its shoulder. The bull collapsed, grunting and bawling, legs thrashing.

"Please, let that be all," she pleaded, her belly rolling queasily. Her hands shook.

The buffalo, even in its death throes, still struggled to reach its feet and wreak destruction on its puny slayer. Florie spat the acid taste from her mouth and quickly reloaded the Fletcher, driving the charges home with the ramrod and setting the percussion caps on the nipples with quivering fingers. In four deliberate strides, she approached the bull. The rifle bellowed again as she delivered a shot into its spine. At last the great beast was still, blood pooling under its black carcass.

Sitting down heavily in the grass, her legs suddenly too rubbery to remain standing, she covered her head with her arms. Basheet perched quietly behind her, but did not touch her. She was still sitting with her head down when Sam and the Hamrans rode up.

Sam gently helped Florie to her feet, and was surprised when she buried her head in his chest and hugged him tightly. There were no tears, but nor would she relinquish her embrace. He wasn't sure if he should comfort her or praise her.

The *aggageers* gathered about the dark bulk of the buffalo. They prodded the still form with their swords. Abou Do uttered an oath as he examined the infected wound from the snare. Then he inserted his finger into the channels carved by Florie's bullets.

"The *sitt* is a mighty hunter," he said softly, a round-eyed look of wonder on his face. "She shall feast with the men in our village tonight."

***

Joyful voices echoed through the air, an atmosphere redolent with wood smoke and broiling meat. Hamran ponies and camels loaded with dripping slabs of elephant and buffalo steaks had been arriving for hours. The village had never seen such a wealth of protein as far back as the eldest of the elders could remember. Abou Do, the Sherrif brothers, and little Jali were smothered with praise and good wishes. The villagers sang a joyous ode to the Englishman. Others paraded about with the elephants' tusks perched on their shoulders. One Hamran lifted the buffalo horns and shook them triumphantly.

But it was Florie who garnered the most attention. Her praises were not sung aloud; after all, the Hamrans agreed, how does one praise a woman? But, as the killer of the black buffalo, there was a muted respect and admiration from the men who simply stopped whatever they were doing to stare at her. The women, however, crowded about to touch her clothing and hair. Several of the older women jabbered excitedly and pointed toward the center of the village. A bevy of younger ladies surrounded Florie and whisked her off to a large tent. She attempted to speak to them, to disengage from the gentle prodding of their hands, but they swirled about her, chattering and gesturing. *Is this part of the same dream in which that black nightmare charged me? Or is this a new dream?* Her limbs felt leaden, her head heavy. Hamran women tugged at her garments. She couldn't stop them.

Florie, standing naked, was aware that the older women were scolding younger girls who were giggling at the sight of her white skin, pink nipples, and auburn pubes. A hole about a foot deep and as much across had been dug into the floor. Hot embers glowed in its bowl. An ancient, toothless female guided her to stand over the hole, feet apart. The crone produced a bag cut from antelope hide and carefully sifted a measure of its powdery contents onto the embers. The powders hissed as they burned, sending thin tendrils of smoke roiling between Florie's legs, curling over her torso and arms. Her nostrils flared as she sniffed the aroma of sandalwood, cinnamon, oil of roses, and other fragrances she could not identify. Then the Hamran women lifted a linen shroud over Florie and gathered it loosely about her neck, leaving her head free. They arranged the shroud, or robe—she wasn't sure which—to fall like a tent to her feet, its long cone trapping the smoky incense and heat about her body. Her muscles relaxed as the captured heat built. Driblets of sweat trickled between her breasts, down her ribs and thighs. If this was part of the dream, it was the best part.

When the women finally removed the shroud, the smoke had dissipated. Outside the tent, it had grown dark. The air was deliciously cool, or so it felt as two younger women rubbed the perspiration from her skin with soft cloths. Her flesh tingled. The perfumes released from the powders lingered as the women dressed her in clean linen.

The evening meal passed in a blur. Florie sat next to Sam near a roaring fire while Abou Do related to all how the elephants had been bagged, and how she had killed the mighty black buffalo. His audience murmured its appreciation, then begged for a re-telling. She watched Sam pantomime his stalk of the elephant. He raised the Fletcher aloft so all could see her rifle. Then, to her surprise, he clasped her hand and led her in a circle around the roaring fire. She felt disembodied, as if she were perched in the branches of a tree and watching from above. Her fingers were interlaced with his. Sweat dappled her brow and lips.

Sizzling slices of meat were carved from the mass broiling over cooking fires. The Hamrans gorged themselves. Sam ate voraciously, but Florie only picked at her food. She felt his nearness, their legs sometimes touching as they ate. When the heart of the buffalo was served, she only tasted a sliver. Her appetite had fled.

In the late evening, long after the Hamrans had retired and the fires crumbled to pulsing coals, Florie wrapped herself in a blanket and went to Sam's tent. There had been no inner argument, no hideous reflection on what had happened in the wheat field in Mehadia, only her need for him. He was sitting on the edge of his cot, ready to turn in. She let the blanket slip from her shoulders and stood naked before him.

"Florie ... I—"

Touching her fingertip to his lips, she quietly shushed him. She placed his hands on her breasts and felt her nipples harden. As she dropped her hands from his, he continued his exploration, his fingers gliding across her ribs to the small of her back, then over the curving swell of her hips. She moaned. Her skin grew hot. Passions long submerged began to stir. He tilted her face to his and kissed her deeply.

"My bed is a poor one," he whispered.

Florie smiled as she led him to the covers. Their coupling was desperate, almost as if the dangers they had faced were manifested in their contact. When they finished, she lay on his bed, gazing at the full moon through a gap in the entrance flaps. A lion roared in the distance, reminding her they were in Africa. Inside the safety of the tent, the spicy essence of her steam bath lingered.

Just before dawn, she awakened. For a moment, she thought she had been dreaming. She touched Sam's cheek. He shifted, slowly blinking awake. He ran his fingers through her hair.

"If I had panicked or missed my shots, Basheet would be dead and so would I," she said softly.

"But you didn't miss," Sam murmured sleepily. "Basheet is fine, and so are you."

"I was lucky." She curled her fingers in his beard. "If your life depended on me, I don't know that I'm strong enough."

Sam raised himself on an elbow. "Tonight, I … we—"

She placed her fingers over his lips. "It was mine to give."

"I can't take you home."

Florie shivered slightly, the air in the tent suddenly chill. "I am home," she whispered. She touched him again and felt his manhood stir.

Chapter Thirteen

Sam added the finishing touches to his sketch of the landscape. In the foreground, he drew rows of dhurra plants and groves of tamarind trees, while a dark shading of mountains soaring above the plains filled in the distance. He turned the page of his journal and penciled a new entry:

1 September 1861

Abou Do and his sword hunters have guided us through their lands to survey the rivers feeding the Nile. But these tributaries do nothing more than flow into the Atbara and Setit, filling their bellies with seasonal rainwater. They are unremarkable streams and I feel as if I am wasting my time tracing their courses.

We need to reach the Angreb and Salaam, but to do so means crossing into the lands of Mek Nimmur, the Abyssinian bandit that has scourged this region for two decades. If he will let us pass, then it's on to investigate the Rohan and Dinder Rivers. I don't expect to find anything more but the same: highland rains swell the rivers, then they dry up. At some point, with luck, we'll find a dahabeah to transport us to Khartoum where the Blue and White Niles meet. Khartoum! That's my goal. From there I can truly explore, if the Leopard King will let us through.

His drawing and entry complete, Sam stood in his stirrups to survey the progress of the caravan. As it drew abreast of him, he waved to Hadji Achmet to tighten the line of camels and donkeys. When two of the latter animals lagged behind, an animated Basheet slapped their hindquarters with a stick to drive them along. Three *aggageers* acting as scouts flanked the caravan. Jali trotted a half-mile ahead.

Florie rode her familiar dromedary, its *makloufa* ornamented with bits of fragrant wood and colored cloth offered as gifts by the Hamran women. She warmed as she thought of the women and their cone of incense.

"Stay close now," Sam called to her. "Don't drift behind the caravan."

Tapping her camel lightly on the flank with a stick, she directed the animal toward him. She saw the look of concern on his face. "What is it?"

"We're nine days out of the Hamran camp," he replied, worried. His eyes searched the craggy hills. "Our Bishareens are too quiet. The *aggageers* have their shields on their arms, not hooked on their saddles. I'd say we're near the lands of Mek Nimmur, the killer of leopards."

"The slaver of women," Florie added in a hushed voice.

"There," Sam cried. "By those bluffs to the north. Riders." He extended his telescope and turned its lens until images came into focus, then began counting. "About thirty horsemen. They don't look too friendly."

Abou Do and his sword hunters galloped toward Sam, dust swirling in a cloud about them. "That is Mek Nimmur leading them," Abou Do said nervously. "I don't think it would be wise to travel through his lands, even though it would make our journey shorter."

Florie's mouth tightened apprehensively. "How much shorter?"

Abou Do lifted his hands and spread his fingers. "This many days, Sitt."

"We'll be low on supplies by then, but it will be the safer route," Sam replied uneasily. He turned in his saddle and spoke to his men. "All of you. Take a musket from our stores and keep it in plain view. Let's hope those lads notice we're heavily armed and just leave us alone.

"Florie, pull your hat over your hair and tie it down. I don't want them getting too curious."

Florie tugged her hat over her ears firmly. She looped a leather string over the hat's crown, folding the brim down, and knotted it under her chin.

Sam nodded approvingly. "No one will be interested in you now. You look like one of the men."

"Thanks. You know how to make a lady's day."

Mek Nimmur and his soldiers drew closer, then paralleled the caravan. Sam tried not to make eye contact, but he glimpsed the Leopard King's short, black beard, and scarred forehead. A crescent shaped gorget like those worn by medieval knights hung about his neck. Protruding from his sash were a pistol and a curved sword. The rest of his men were armed with matchlock muskets, thin tendrils of smoke drifting from the fuse-like matches. They *looked* like a tough lot.

For an hour, Mek Nimmur and his soldiers kept pace, eyeing the broad-shouldered *feringhi* and his diminutive companion. The sight of the caravan's muskets and the long swords of the Hamrans seemed to keep them at a distance. If they were searching for someone, Sam wondered, would they risk trying to stop the travelers? He glanced at Florie. Her hand rested on the butt of her pistol. He hoped they wouldn't. With the sun setting, Mek Nimmur and his band finally broke away and galloped toward the rugged hills.

Sam whistled with relief as he watched the cloud of dust diminish. He was glad Florie had tied her hat down so tightly. "We keep moving. I don't want us to be anywhere near those blokes. They were awfully curious. We'll go on all night long if we have to."

***

Florie paced expectantly along the banks of the River Dinder. She cast a cautious glance over her shoulder toward the Abyssinian highlands. No dust, nothing to indicate pursuit. It had been nearly ten days since they had passed the Leopard King's domain. Twice earlier, dust clouds had been spotted in the distance, but did that mean horsemen were on their trail? For the last four days, however, they had traveled more easily as the bluffs and cliffs of Mek Nimmur's territory gave way to the softer contours and banks of the river valley.

Perhaps the Leopard King would not show up, but she knew Sam wasn't certain. Sam was hunkered in one of the mud huts at the river's edge, haggling with a dahabeah's captain over the price of passage from the Dinder to the Blue Nile, and then on to Khartoum. If he were successful, the dahabeah would cut many days of hard walking to reach the city—and leave any enemies behind them.

Florie continued to pace. A soft breeze stirred the fronds of a small grove of date palms. The singsong language of trade echoed from the bazaar of the river town of Bellumin. Dates, dhurra, mangos, charcoal; all were items of barter. What held her attention, however, was the riverboat beached a short distance away. Its rudder was nearly tall as she was, and a furled sail hung from a slanting yardarm.

Reaching Khartoum was a bittersweet goal for her. On one hand, Sam would be closer to his dream of exploring for the true source of the White Nile. She didn't truly understand why he was driven to locate the river's birthplace. His talk of carving a place for himself in history made little impression on her. Perhaps such a notion was peculiar to the English race. Her own history was hazy and insecure, but she noticed how he champed at the bit to be on the second leg of his adventure. He was definitely happiest when he spoke of finding the Nile's headwaters.

Khartoum, on the other hand, offered a refuge of sorts for both Sam and her from the long arms of Emile Zeb and Ohmed Pasha. According to Sam, the British consul in Khartoum was an old friend named Petherick. Once there, Petherick would not only offer them protection, but Sam was sure he would keep her safe while he continued his exploration. She had tried to argue that she didn't want to be kept safe, that she wanted to stay with him. Sam didn't seem to listen, not even when she vowed that she would not be abandoned again. There were times when she just wanted to box his ears.

Hadji Achmet approached her from the cluster of Bishareens lounging in the shade of the palms. "Perhaps the *sitt* should not wait for

Baker Pasha in the burning heat. We would be glad to give up our shade to you."

Florie smiled and shook her head. "My thanks to you and your men, but I'm too nervous to sit."

"Allah smiles on those with patience."

"Then Allah has not been smiling on Baker Pasha," she replied absently. Confused, Hadji Achmet returned to his men.

If only Sam had more patience. So much had changed in the days since they fled the Leopard King's lands. The Hamrans had returned to their homeland, taking Basheet with them. Sam had grown distant, and drove the caravan at a harsh pace. The tributaries they had crossed since the Hamrans left were a blur. Now, here at Bellumin, the delays in procuring a boat left him crackling with anger. If only he were as happy and carefree as when they had started their journey together.

Sam suddenly appeared from one of the huts. Even from that distance, she saw his lips pinned in a tight scowl, the muscles bunching on his forearms as he knotted his hands into fists.

"Will we have a boat ride?" she bubbled, feigning gaiety.

Sam frowned and scanned the desert reaches beyond the village, half expecting Mek Nimmur's soldiers to come riding over a dune. "It took forever to find the damned captain," he grumbled. "I paid more than I should have, but at least we'll get to Khartoum more quickly." He barked orders at the Bishareens to begin loading the baggage on the dahabeah, cursing them as they rose tardily from their sanctuary in the shade.

Florie skipped into his path. "What's wrong with you? You've been acting like there's a thorn stuck in your backside since we left Mek Nimmur's country. You've explored every branch that feeds the Blue Nile. You should be happy."

"I haven't really discovered a damned thing yet," he said angrily. "I've mapped the Angreb, Salaam, Rohan, Dinder, and a half dozen other rivers I can't even remember. I've no real time to explore. Who will ever remember what Sam Baker discovered?"

Florie searched his face, but he avoided eye contact. "You're wrong. Don't *erniedrigen*—what's your English word—*demean* what you've done. You have your notebooks and maps and specimens. You've accomplished so much." She laid her hand on his forearm. "Sometimes I'm sorry you bought me at that auction in Vidin and all the anguish it has caused you. Please be at peace."

"It's not enough," he replied brusquely as he brushed her hand away. "You're a woman. You wouldn't understand."

"I understand that you want me to stay in Khartoum," she retorted, perplexed by his behavior. "Is that truly what you want?" She spun on her heel before he could answer, and stalked toward the ship.

Sam watched her ascend the ramp to the dahabeah's deck. He bit the inside of his lip to keep from calling her back. The dahabeah's captain had revealed that a man wearing a chain mail shirt had stopped at Bellumin to enquire about a yellow-haired boy or woman who might have passed through. That was a few days earlier. When he didn't find what he was looking for, the man headed east.

With a snort of exasperation, Sam squinted toward the west. In the gray mist of distance, lay Khartoum. He didn't tell Florie that someone was searching for a yellow-hair. Perhaps he should have, but that was an issue he could take on when the time came. It was the distant future that muddied his thinking the most.

The Nile is my destiny, but it's not my greatest concern. It's when I go home to England, my dear Florie, and you can't go with me. And I don't want to go back to England without you, and so here we are. We can only stay together if the journey continues. But what dangers await us?

Chapter Fourteen

Florie shaded her eyes with the brim of her hat against the glare of the Nile sun. "Khartoum," she whispered with dread.

A puff of warm wind bulged the lateen sail of the dahabeah, speeding the boat carrying her and Sam through the glistening water. Ahead, lofty palm trees bent above whitewashed houses and larger buildings. The thin spire of a minaret thrust upwards from the center of the city. Crowded along the shore were a myriad of sailing craft, their canvas drawn, masts silhouetted against the deep-blue mantle of Sudanese sky.

The captain of the dahabeah, an Egyptian with a green bandana wrapped around his head, slowly eased his craft toward the long strand of beach. The keel brushed sand at the bottom, then cut a furrow as it drew to a stop. Three of his sailors muscled a long boarding plank over the side. Two men on shore anchored the plank in the sand.

Florie shook her head in disbelief. Had it been a year since she had embarked on her journey with Sam into the African bush to chart the Blue Nile? Yes, the happiest year of her life! And now, from this city, he meant to plunge back into a world of unthinkable dangers, with or without her.

Sam descended the plank, the wood quivering at each of his heavy steps, his pistol holstered at his belt. With much gesturing, he spoke to the two men who had secured the plank. Florie leaned over the boat's railing to listen as the men haggled and waved their arms toward several brown-skinned men wearing dhotis and turbans clustered under a palm tree. To her surprise, the turbaned men jumped to their feet and jogged to the dahabeah. Sam directed them to carry boxes and bundles of journal notes, floral and faunal samples, sketches, trophies, and guns—all to the British consulate. At first, the porters were sullen and not interested in the Turkish liras he waved. When he flourished a bag of silver coins in addition to the liras, they grinned and hefted the crates.

"Seems like the price of labor has gone up," Sam muttered as he helped Florie off the boat's ramp. His arm around her waist did not linger. Together they climbed the steep bank to a winding street that led into the bowels of the city. The romantic image of Khartoum as a backdrop to the glistening Nile was quickly dispelled by the ripe effluvia of animal shit and rotting food that permeated the streets.

Garbage had been swept or scraped against the low buildings. An open ditch acting as a sewer was abuzz with insect life.

"Isn't there anyone to clean up this filth?" Florie asked as she pinched her nose. To their left was a wider avenue, its roadway pitted but cleared of trash. They followed that street until they discovered a series of dwellings with whitewashed walls and mud-brick fences. Many of the walls were in decrepit condition with loose scabs of paint, chipped mortar, and broken bricks.

Sam proudly pointed to a symbol painted on an archway. "See this? That's the lion and unicorn. This is the consulate of Her Majesty, Queen Victoria."

Florie squinted at the decoration. She could barely make out the badly faded lion, while the unicorn's body was flaking away.

Below the archway, the wrought iron gate was not only unlocked, but was open. Dome palms shaded the consulate's courtyard. Sam dropped his bag and shouted for recognition. A servant with a thin, hooked nose scuttled from one of the second story rooms and leaned over the balustrade. A white fez covered his head, and he wore a dark blue vest with brass buttons.

"I'm here to see Her Majesty's Consul Petherick," Sam bellowed. "Who are you?"

"I am Hallal el-Shami," the servant replied in a quavering voice. "I am Consul Petherick's agent. I'm afraid the consul is not in Khartoum."

"What do you mean Petherick is not in Khartoum?" Sam's voice boomed loudly in the courtyard. "Where is he? I've been up river for a year and I expected to meet him here."

Hallal el-Shami wrung his hands nervously. He did not like the way the vein bulged in the forehead of this new Englishman. "You must be Mr. Baker. Be assured, Consul Petherick has reserved rooms for you in his absence, though he did not mention you were traveling with another." His eyes drifted to Florie as she removed her hat, and he caught his breath. It was the yellow-haired woman described in the rumors circulating through the city. "As for the consul, he had no sooner returned from London when he was ordered to march to Gondokoro to meet the explorers Speke and Grant, your countrymen, I believe. He and his wife have been gone some three months."

"Speke and Grant haven't returned yet?" Sam asked in wonderment. "Why, they left England more than two years ago."

A new plan was forming in his mind as he and Florie followed Hallal el-Shami to a spacious room on the second story. If the two explorers were missing, it was his duty as an Englishman to level what assistance he could, even if that meant mounting an expedition to aid in the search. A flying column perhaps—a dozen camels, a few good men, his rifles—all of it heading up the White Nile in search of Speke and Grant. His destiny would be fulfilled. He'd have more than a mere footnote in history books.

And what of Florie? He turned toward her, but she had already left his side and was standing in a corner of the room, her hands clasped together, a smile curving her lips. She gazed with longing at a large, contoured basin with deep sides.

"Sam, look. A *true, copper bathtub*," she said in a hushed voice, although she emphasized the last three words.

"Yes," Hallal el-Shami said. "Mrs. Petherick had it delivered here. I'm sure she wouldn't mind you using it. I will order women to bring hot water."

Sam nodded his head absently. His vision of a camel column, with him in the lead, was growing more attractive by the moment.

"And Mr. Baker, sir, Consul Petherick brought letters for you from England, and I believe he left several newspapers as well," Hallal el-Shami said, bowing as he backed from the room.

Later, while Florie lounged in the steaming bath, Sam sat with coffee and devoured the newspapers, all copies of *The Times*, all several months old. The first issue, soiled and edge-tattered, revealed that civil war had torn apart the United States. Numerous sympathizers for the Confederacy in Parliament, fearing the Birmingham mills would grow silent with the loss of the cotton import from America's Deep South, were calling for intervention. That, of course, would mean war with the Lincoln government. Sheer idiocy!

Florie stopped sloshing when Sam unexpectedly groaned aloud. "Oh, the poor queen," he said in a hushed voice. "Prince Albert died from typhus at Windsor Castle last December. His voice was always the moderating one. You could count on him to keep us out of some damnable foreign war. Victoria and the entire nation are in mourning."

A square envelope nearly lost among the newspapers bore his sister Min's handwriting. Her note inside said that all was well with his children, and contained local gossip as well as some family matters. A smaller letter written on fine-weave paper was also in the envelope. On the outside fold was the simple word, Father.

Sam opened the note with trembling hands and read the careful lettering.

Dearest Father,
We have just returned from a holiday in Cornwall. You

should have seen the lovely horses we got to ride! I had Ethel on my lap so she wouldn't fall off the saddle.

We are all well. Agnes and Constance are doing nicely at school, and I received a certificate for excellence in composition. I have also been studying my Scriptures.

Aunt Min speaks of you every day. She says that is important for my younger sisters so they do not forget you. I have your portrait with Mother to show them. They ask questions and I do my best to answer them.

I have read of the explorations of Captain Speke and Captain Grant, but nothing has appeared in the newspapers of your discoveries. Please keep us informed so that we may tell all we meet of our famous father.

I miss Mother very much. I miss you very much.

With love,

Edith

How old was Edith now? Fourteen? Fifteen? He glanced at the woman in the tub. Florie was perhaps twenty, he thought, and his own daughter was barely her junior. Yet Florie, with yellow curls plastered against her forehead, her bronzed arms white where her shirt sleeves ended just below the shoulder — who had endured more hardship and danger than any other woman he knew — was playing with a bar of soap, slipping it through her fingers, then catching it before it fell into the suds. He was instantly reminded of how truly young she was.

"All is well at home?" she asked.

"Yes, all is well at home," replied Sam as he carefully refolded the letters and placed them with his journals. He wondered what Edith would say about Florie.

That evening, after they had finished a light supper of salted cucumbers and melons, Hallal el-Shami knocked on their door. "A visitor is here to see you, sir," he said, handing Sam an elegantly printed calling card. It read *Georges Thibaut.*

Just inside the gate of the consulate, an outlandishly garbed figure waited. Dressed in the Turkish style, the man sported an embroidered crimson jacket, crimson cummerbund, billowing blue pantaloons, and soft leather shoes with upturned toes.

"My greetings to you, Mr. Baker," the visitor said in accented English, bowing slightly at the waist. "I am Georges Thibaut, and I welcome you to Khartoum. I am the French consul here. There are only forty or so Europeans in this city of thirty thousand souls. It is wise that we know who comes and goes." He paused for an instant, appraising Sam's thick arms and hard gaze. "Your reputation has preceded you. Bishareens and Jalyns come to Khartoum from time to time, so the story of English Baker and Madamoiselle Florence, his beautiful *sitt,* has been related to all who would listen. That the two of you survived a year in the African bush is most impressive. But first, let me tell you of myself."

Thibaut was perhaps sixty, Sam guessed. Slender and slightly stooped, his crafty blue eyes glinted from a weathered face framed by a thin white beard. He explained that he was a native of Paris and had been in the Sudan for decades, amassing a small fortune in trading sticky gum arabic used in the making of adhesives, ivory, and live wild animals. Earlier in his career, he had personally delivered a pair of giraffes to London, the first ever in Britain.

Sam and the consul entered a small room adjacent to Petherick's locked office. Hallal el-Shami had already placed a bottle of brandy and two glasses on the table.

"You wouldn't have any absinthe, would you?" Thibaut sniffed.

Sam shook his head and offered the brandy. "Sorry, old man, but this is all Mr. Petherick had left here."

"Pity. He probably took everything else with him," the Frenchman moaned. "Let me begin by telling you, a newcomer, that there are parts of Khartoum Europeans do not venture to after dark unless well attended by guards. Secondly, besides your wife, there are two other white women here: Mrs. Harriet Tinne and her daughter Alexine. The late Mr. Tinne was a British merchant, though his wife is Dutch and quite wealthy. The daughter is rather spoiled and is intent on sailing up the Nile to explore its monuments and bring religion to the natives, no matter what the cost. They fling their money about recklessly." Thibaut paused to sip his drink before continuing. "The price of renting boats, buying camels, and even hiring laborers has jumped considerably since they arrived."

"So I noticed," Sam muttered.

Thibaut shrugged. "Perhaps your wife would enjoy the companionship of fellow European women. Three white women in the city at one time is a great rarity. I have invited Madame Tinne and her daughter to my consulate tonight for refreshments. It would be most wonderful if Mademoiselle Florence and you attend."

Sam smiled politely, although he secretly worried how two cosmopolitan women would treat Florie. "She's indisposed at the moment, but I'm sure she will welcome your invitation." He quickly changed the topic. "Have you heard from Petherick since he left Khartoum?"

"Ah, your consul is a brave and foolish man," Thibaut said,

finishing his drink. "He left several months ago to go to Gondokoro upriver. But he did not have the north wind with him so he was forced to have his men drag the boats by hand from shore, backbreaking work. Then he took an alternate route further to the west, I believe to shoot elephant and collect ivory, probably to augment the paltry salary your government pays him. My sources say that he and his party are now mired in the swamps. If they are not dead from the fever or the natives, they soon will be. And Mrs. Petherick, his new wife, must be suffering horribly."

Sam refilled the Frenchman's glass. "Has there been any news of Speke and Grant?"

Thibaut sipped his brandy, rolled the liquor in his mouth, then swallowed. "Your fellow Englishmen were thought to be in the kingdom of the treacherous King Kamrasi in Unyoro far to the south." He lifted his glass in a toast. "May God watch over any more madmen who venture up the Nile, because if he doesn't, *le diable* surely will."

"Then, if God is willing, I will be the one who finds Speke and Grant if Petherick cannot," Sam said before draining his drink.

Thibaut leaned closer to Sam, resting both elbows on the table, his chin cupped in his hands, a look of boredom crossing his face. "Don't be foolish, Mr. Baker. You have come from the Blue Nile and know something of Africa. Yet, for everything you have learned, there's always tenfold more you don't know.

"If you sail south, then you will reach Gondokoro, a holding tank for all the slavers who dredge up their victims from among the southern tribes. You have black tribe fighting black tribe, with a nasty trade in guns to boot. The only ones who reap a profit from slaves and guns are the Arabs and white men. And no one around here— how do you English say—gives a shit."

Thibaut reached into an inner pocket of his jacket and ostentatiously produced a finely made watch attached to a glittering gold fob. "*Damnation*," he said as he glanced at the timepiece. "I had only planned to stay a moment to introduce myself. As it is, I must go now as Madame and Mademoiselle Tinne are expecting me tonight. Please excuse me."

With a slight bow, he extended his warm, moist hand to Sam. "Remember, to venture up the White Nile is folly. If it isn't tribal warfare, then there's malaria or a dozen other diseases that will rot your guts or burn you up with fever," he warned. "With Petherick gone, there is no one else here to help you should you need it, and you undoubtedly would need it. Besides, it might be weeks before the wind changes to blow you south. You will come to your senses by then. If not for your sake, then for the sake of Mademoiselle Florence."

"I'll go on alone if I have to," Sam said quietly.

Florie, wrapped in a blanket and still dripping from her tub, had crept silently through the corridor adjacent to the room where Sam and Thibaut shared a drink. She heard the Frenchman's dire warning. Sam's reply left her shivering.

***

Alexine Tinne, a slender woman with pale complexion and reddish hair, batted her eyes coyly as she greeted Thibaut and his guests. Long, flat, elaborately plaited braids looped under her ears and were gathered at the back of her head with a bow of emerald silk. Bright, greenish eyes were set above a slightly pointed nose. When she smiled, her lips pulled back to reveal small, even teeth.

She grins like a fox, Florie thought. She is sizing up her prey. When she talks to her mother, her gestures are compact. But when she speaks to men, her hands touch lightly upon her upper bosom, and as she relaxes, she lets them drift ever so slyly across her pointy little breasts. She wants men to devour her with their eyes.

Florie had begged Sam not to take her to Monsieur Thibaut's soirée, but he had been adamant that it was proper to put their best foot forward as representatives of the British government in the absence of Consul Petherick. So she had reluctantly agreed.

In her scanty wardrobe was the dress that Sam had bought for her in Bucharest. She worried it might be badly out of fashion, or that it would not fit properly. But when she fastened the last button, she found it a trifle large, yet so confining after a year spent in short-sleeved shirts and loose-fitting trousers snugged about her waist by a simple drawstring or belt. How she longed for that freedom now.

Georges Thibaut introduced her as Mrs. Baker when she and Sam arrived at the French consulate. She was conscious of the furtive smile on Thibaut's face, and that Mrs. Tinne and daughter had both glanced at her hands and undoubtedly noticed the absence of a wedding ring. After introductions, she smiled politely, but rarely joined in their conversation. She tried to stay near Sam, but Alexine Tinne managed to draw him into a discussion on his Abyssinian travels and her own planned expedition to the land of the Dinkas. Soon, Thibaut and a Maltese trader named Andrea de Bono joined them.

Florie excused herself and walked away. A sly, vixen smile curved Alexine's lips.

"Miss Tinne is an engaging woman, no?" The speaker was a man of medium height with pleasing, angular features and reddish-blond hair and beard.

"Forgive me, Frau Baker," he said in German. "I am Johann Schmidt, Bavarian carpenter by trade, African hunter by choice. I heard you speak briefly before. You are not English."

Florie smiled and answered him in the same language. "No, I am Hungarian, but I learned German as a child. It is pleasant to speak in that tongue again."

"I saw you watching *Fraulein* Tinne," he said, his voice serious but his blue eyes twinkling. "You are worried about her trying to bed your husband. She's leaving in a week to go up the Nile and visit the Dinkas. Do you know that both men and women go perfectly naked there? She says she wants to bring Christianity to them."

"Indeed, Herr Schmidt, Miss Tinne has a way of captivating men," Florie replied quietly as she watched Sam laugh and kiss Alexine's hand. Worry momentarily creased her brow. "I will not be sorry to see her leave."

Schmidt chuckled. "Please call me Johann. I understand Herr Baker is planning an expedition toward Gondokoro. It's an evil place, one that de Bono knows well. I would like to offer my services as a guide to your husband. I've hunted elephant in that region, and I own a dahabeah and a few smaller vessels he could use to take him upriver."

"And Miss Tinne did not make you an offer for them?"

"She offered, but I refused what she was offering," Schmidt replied mischievously. "It wasn't money."

Florie returned his smile. "Are you implying something about Miss Tinne?"

"Why, of course not. How could I … how could …, " Schmidt's voice trailed off weakly. His face grew pale. Small beads of perspiration dotted his forehead. "Please excuse me, Frau Baker, I must sit." With a shaking hand he dabbed his brow with a handkerchief and stumbled to a chair. "Damned malaria," he whispered painfully. "It comes on so quickly."

Florie assisted the German to a chair. Shivers shook him. She waved to Sam to attract his attention.

Across the room and standing next to Sam, Alexine Tinne spoke softly as her fingertips subtly strayed across her breasts. Florie saw Sam's eyes follow that movement. When he looked up and saw that she was watching, he blushed. His coloring surprised her. What surprised her more was that it irritated her. That he had even noticed Alexine's delicate flirtations made her jealous.

Sam pried himself from his group. Had Florie been watching at that moment, she would have noticed the smile fade from Alexine Tinne's lips.

"This is Johann Schmidt," Florie said as Sam touched the man's brow. "He's quite ill."

"Malaria," Sam said, mirroring her concern. "Perhaps quinine will help. Herr Schmidt, we will assist you to your rooms if you will allow."

Georges Thibaut fluttered like an awkward bird around the German. "Johann, you should have stayed in bed," he scolded. "I warned you that the fever returns often. It would not be proper etiquette for a German to die in a French consulate. Think of the mountain of paperwork that I would have to do."

"Yes, and you'd have to arrange for burial details, too, you scoundrel," Schmidt replied, smiling weakly. "Who would you get to go hunting to fill your supper table?"

Florie forced her shoulder under Schmidt's left arm as Sam lifted him to his feet, supporting him on the right. She bid the Frenchman and his guests good evening. As they passed through the door, she caught Alexine's attention with a nod of her head and a knowing smile curving her lips as if to say, *Sam is mine and you can't have him.*

Alexine, her cheeks flushed red, glanced away. Florie smiled broadly as she and Sam, with Johann Schmidt wedged between them, exited into the warm Sudanese night.

***

Alexine Tinne, her mother, and their attendants left Khartoum a week later. Camels bawled and goats bleated as they were roughly urged into position by snapping whips and prodding sticks. For the space of a thousand heartbeats, chaos ruled. The caravan slowly took shape, and, with the Tinnes mounted on fine dromedaries at its head, it crept like a many-legged caterpillar into the desert.

Georges Thibaut was the only European to see them off. He waved his hand, ruefully realizing that he had probably experienced his last sex with a white woman for some time to come. Strange woman that Alexine, he mused, part evangelizing Christian concerned for the welfare of the black African, part delectable flirt. He hoped he would see her again.

And as for the Bakers? The Frenchman shrugged. Or should he call them Mr. Baker and companion? He didn't remember Sam ever referring to her as his wife or Mrs. Baker. Mademoiselle Florence, after all, was a lovely young thing, many years Baker's junior. She was something to be cherished and kept in the boudoir. He hated the thought that she would probably end up as a pile of bones bleaching somewhere under the African sun.

***

Pale gray light filtered into the bedroom through partially closed shutters. Florie rubbed the sleep from her eyes and stretched. Pushing the mosquito netting aside, she padded barefoot to the window and glanced through its slats.

The sun had risen, but clouds had marched in through the night. This sky was overcast, so different from the dazzling, empty sky when Alexine Tinne had trooped away nearly a month earlier. On the broad face of the Nile, she saw dahabeahs gliding through the water, their angled, lateen sails giving them the appearance of great gulls sweeping over the waves. She had grown used to the sight of fishermen plying the river's waters after the call to the Dawn Prayer by the muezzins. But this felt different. Was it the muted colors caused by the clouds that caught her attention?

Throwing the shutters wide, she stepped out onto the small balcony. Boats continued to glide silently. That was it. No creaking of taut cordage or the snap of sailcloth. Sailors pantomimed shouts. It was the wind! Every morning since she and Sam had arrived in Khartoum, the wind had blown in from the Nile, carrying the myriad noises of a busy river port into the city. But now it blew to the south, away from Khartoum. It was the wind Sam had been waiting for.

Florie rushed into the drawing room where Sam usually slept. The divan was empty. She discovered him sleeping soundly at his desk, head cradled on his crossed arms. She paused, studying his face in the pale light. There were circles under his eyes, a suggestion of hollowness at his cheeks, and a hint of grey at his temples.

"You work too hard, my love," she whispered. "I sometimes wish I were the Nile and the full center of your attention." As she leaned over him to shake him awake, she spied a listing of goods partially hidden under his face: gunpowder; 400 pounds of corn; saddles; 10 crates of colored beads …. The list went on. At the bottom of the paper, she read: Florie's bath basin.

That meant Sam had finally relented and planned on taking her with him. She had argued that it was safer to be on the trail with him then to wait a year in Khartoum with the likes of the oily Georges Thibaut. Sam had grimaced when she made that point.

"Thank you," she said, gently kissing his cheek. Then she shook his arm vigorously. "Wake up, old man. The wind has changed."

***

A rider on camelback approaching Khartoum from the direction of the Blue Nile, reined to a halt, and turned his face downriver. The wind Magram Bur felt on his cheek blew from the north. He had followed the Nile for weeks, stopping wherever villagers congregated along its banks. His question to them was always the same: had they seen a white man accompanied by a yellow-haired boy or girl on the river? Too often, they had not. That damnable Mek Nimmur had let them slip past his lands without even investigating. Since then, Bur had followed their trail and gone in the wrong direction for a week before realizing his error. Now everything pointed to the Englishman and yellow-hair being in Khartoum. With the changing wind, they could sail upriver and soon be lost in the vast unknown of the White Nile's headwaters. He had to move quickly.

An hour later, Bur flung himself from the saddle of his mangy camel. He flitted through Khartoum's reeking, garbage-strewn alleys, and over sluggishly flowing open sewers. In his threadbare, soiled burnoose, he blended easily into the landscape of the city's slums.

The man he sought was sipping coffee at a small table outside of a rundown café. Dressed in a burnoose of alternating black and white stripes, the man was in his middle years, his bearded jaw showing strong strains of silver. His eyes darted about, studying the throng that shuffled past him.

A shadow fell across his table. He glanced up, his hand closing on the hilt of a dagger hidden on his lap.

"May the blessings of the Prophet be upon you, Mahomet el-Nar," Magram Bur said. "Emile Zeb of Vidin has sent a message to you."

Mahomet, the man in the striped burnoose, relaxed his grip on his blade. He reached for the rolled bit of paper the slave catcher offered. The message was written in a familiar hand.

"So, Emile Zeb has need of my services. Probably desires more slave women from Gondokoro," he said as he finished his coffee and dropped a coin next to his cup. His brow furrowed as he continued to study the missive. "This is odd. He's after a certain woman, a yellow-hair, it says. I have found him many fine slaves, but never a yellow-hair."

Magram Bur smothered a curse. "She travels with a white man, a big fellow from England."

"Word has it that such a foreigner and his younger friend arrived here several weeks ago. I have heard they will be heading to Gondokoro to secure porters for a journey up the Nile."

"Beware of the yellow-haired bitch," Magram Bur said. "She has a bite to her." He jabbed his finger at the scars on his cheek.

"Then you were clumsy," Mahomet said with a shrug. "But, more importantly, what of this white man?"

"He is an English dog. If you can, leave his body to rot."

A thin smile curved Mahomet's lips. "Emile Zeb knows that my fee will be high?"

"Of course. But I cannot go with you. The yellow-hair knows me too well."

"Then I will leave for Gondokoro tonight," Mahomet said. "There are too many Europeans in Khartoum to do this properly. If the Englishman is headed to Gondokoro to hire porters, then I must be there before he arrives. He will find no white faces to protect him."

***

"Aunt Min! Aunt Min! It's snowing outside."

Edith Baker pressed her fingers and nose against the windowpane, watching her breath cloud the glass. Constance dashed to the window and quickly smeared the outline her older sister had left there.

"Just watch. I can make a better picture than you," she squealed with glee.

Min clapped her hands together to gain the attention of the four boisterous girls. "Now, ladies, it will be Christmas in a few days," she said, a hint of scolding in her voice. "Your Uncle James will be bringing a great spruce by and by. If you behave yourselves, you can all help decorate it. Edith, you can put the candles on."

"I want to help, too," Agnes whined.

"You all can help," Min said soothingly. "But you have to take turns watching Ethel, too. Remember last year? Now, what do you want Father Christmas to bring?"

"I want a hobby horse with a pink saddle," Constance cried as she spanked her hips in nervous anticipation.

"And I want a doll with a glass face and real hair," Agnes chimed. "Edith, what do you want Father Christmas to bring?"

"I want him to bring Papa home," she said quietly.

Min placed her hand over her mouth to hide her surprise. She quickly ushered the sisters toward the playroom. As the girls disappeared up the staircase, she glanced out the window. Large flakes were falling heavily, blanketing the fence and shrubs with a powdery, white mantle.

"Where are you now, brother of mine? How many more Christmases will you miss?"

Chapter Fifteen

Faint breezes puffed Florie's hair as Sam's tiny flotilla of dahabeah and transport lugger glided smoothly up the Nile, sailing past great fans of papyrus. A brightly crested hoopoe, its monotonous *hoop-hoop-hoop* cry echoing along the banks, thrust its down-curving beak into a hole in the trunk of a mimosa tree in search of insects. Crocodiles sunned on the muddy banks. She wrinkled her nose is disgust as she remembered the crocodile that almost gobbled Basheet. How she hated those monsters.

Seated on a folding chair on the aft deck of the dahabeah, Florie watched Sam while he worked its sweep, the sinews in his arms standing in iron ridges as he fought the river's current. His eyes were bright, his face intense. What a change had come over him since they left Khartoum. He had been so sullen waiting for the winds to change that he often went days without speaking to her. Now he was the explorer again, full of passion and energy, on a mission to find his lost fellow explorers.

Her eyes narrowed as she stared at the Nile, loving it and hating it at the same time. The river kept them together, but it also kept them apart. She felt like a member of the crew with duties and tasks to perform, not his confidante or his partner. I don't need orders, she thought as she watched the sweat drip from his face and the muscles ripple across his chest as he controlled the boat. *I need you to make love to me again.* Biting her lip, she wondered why a distance as wide as the Nile seemed to have come between them.

By late afternoon, the northerly breeze they had enjoyed snuffed out completely, leaving the air thick and stifling. The Nile's flow slowed to a sluggish meander, its surface green and greasy with algae. Rotting trunks of broken trees thrust like crooked fangs through the ooze. Floating water plants, their stems and fronds intertwined, formed miniature islands that broke loose from the greater mass and scudded against the sides of the boats.

Sam sniffed the fetid air as he watched Marabou storks stalking among the stumps in the shallows, dining on decaying fishes and other offal. The hum of countless mosquitoes reminded him of the danger of time too long spent in such a bog, especially as the sun slid toward the murky horizon.

"I'd advise anchoring in the deeper waters where even the lightest of winds will keep those damnable little assassins away," Johann Schmidt called from the deck of the lugger as he slapped a mosquito dining on his arm. He and Richarn, his Nubian servant, manned the transport boat with the help of a few Bishareens.

"Good idea," Sam agreed. "Once we're anchored, will you join me for a drink?"

"I will, and I'd like to see this *Jenna el Mootfah* of yours. All the Bishareens have spoken of it."

"Just don't ask me to shoot the damned thing."

An hour later, after supper dishes had been cleared, the two men retreated to the raised deck at the rear of the boat. Sam poured a measure of brandy in Johann Schmidt's cup and offered a cushion on the deck. Florie slept in her bed below deck. She had turned in after eating, mentioning a slight fever. He hoped it wasn't malaria.

The two men spoke of guns, hunting big game, and the habits of animals. Sam uncased the massive Holland four-bore and handed it to the German. "Good Lord," Schmidt said in awe. "If I fired this, I'd be walking sideways the rest of my life."

They toasted each other's homelands, both noting that it had been years since they had last seen their families. Schmidt leaned back against the gunwale, his fingers laced together behind his head. He studied the subtle shifting and blending of colors as the warm gleam of a crimson sunset blossomed against low hanging clouds in the west. A pod of hippopotami grunted and splashed in the distance. The throaty chorus of countless bullfrogs boomed a serenade from the banks.

"I've been on the Nile many times and its beauty never gets old," he said. "Africa is like a mistress, tantalizing you with her delights, more so than any woman can. I love her smells, her sounds, the adventure she offers. She's fickle, though. One mistake and you *will* feel the pain."

"If one needs a mistress," Sam countered.

"It's been a long time since I've thought of a woman," Schmidt replied, a crooked smile curving his lips. "I was going to be wed back in Bavaria, but I hadn't a *pfennig* to my name. You need money to get into the guild, and itinerant carpenters make little. I told my betrothed that I would be an ivory hunter in Africa and bring back a fortune within a year. I could enter the guild then, and our lives would be set. That was ten years ago. I still do not have the *pfennig*. Now you know why I say this land is a powerful mistress."

"Then we all have our mistresses," Sam remarked. He forced Florie out of his thoughts.

"That's an odd thing to say, what with a wife and all."

It was Sam's turn to shrug. "My first wife died some time ago," he said, his gaze growing distant. "She left me with four daughters. I simply couldn't see myself raising a family alone, growing old as a clerk in my father's sugar company, and then retiring to die as an old man in bed. Not when there's so much to see in the world, so much to discover. I want to be remembered as someone of importance, damn it."

"Is that why you go there?" Schmidt gestured upriver with his chin.

Sam was silent, seemingly preoccupied with running his forefinger around the rim of his cup.

"And what of Florence?" Schmidt asked. "She's not really your wife, is she? You had separate rooms at the consulate in Khartoum. You have separate cabins here."

Sam pursed his lips and stared at the river. "I've shot elephants in the jungles of Ceylon," he said at last. "I've coasted down the icy Danube, and built a railroad in Bulgaria. I've been to a slave market and bought a slave. No, Florie and I aren't married. Nor is she my mistress, but she is part of my life." He paused, imagining the woman sleeping below. "We're just … together. I only know that if I quit my journey now and return to England, she can't go with me. Yet if I continue, I put her in harm's way. So we go on as if there is no tomorrow. I don't really know what else to do."

Silently they watched the last thin arc of the sun dip below the horizon. Soft bands of copper and vermilion shaded the remaining shreds of clouds. Below deck, Florie moaned in her sleep.

Schmidt's gaze drifted from the sunset to the man sitting across from him. "You haven't told her any of this yet, have you? Can your journey last forever, Sam? And what happens to her if you die out here?"

Sam drained his cup and did not answer. Later, after Johann Schmidt returned to his vessel, he waited outside of Florie's cabin, listening to her soft, even breathing through the thin carpet that hung as a primitive door. He cautiously peeled back the edge of the carpet and peered in. She was sound asleep, hair curled on her pillow, her bared leg pale as ivory against the dark blanket. He sighed and rested his head against the doorframe. Their lovemaking in the camp of the *aggageers* had become a memory he had shoved away deep in his mind. Although the sight of her naked leg stirred him, he turned away.

***

For two more days, the boats glided on the river without detecting human presence. Antelopes and other animals came to the water's edge to drink. Once, a lioness appeared, but snarled and sprang back into the bushes. On the third day, Florie spied movement on the eastern bank. A number of warriors were gathered, leaning on their spears as they watched the boats sail by. Their naked, ebony skins glistened with moisture.

"Are those men dangerous?" she asked, shading her eyes.

"I think they're Dinkas," Sam said. "Perhaps Alexine Tinne has visited them."

Florie was glad he had responded to her question. They had spoken little since Johann Schmidt had visited with Sam. "They certainly aren't bashful, are they?" she said. "I'm sure Miss Tinne is enjoying herself."

Sam tried not to smile. "I bet you and Alexine would have grown to be fast friends if you could have spent more time together."

With her fists on her hips, Florie turned on him. "Indeed. I'd rather cultivate a better understanding with Mek Nimmur. I bet that Alexine Tinne, Monsieur Thibaut, and you would have formed an interesting threesome."

Sam backed away with mock surprise. "That's a viper's tongue you wag on occasion. Peace, woman. Especially since I have a gift for you."

From a wicker box, he produced a large waxed, waterproof envelope. He handed it to Florie. She accepted it questioningly.

"There's money in it, and a letter I've written to the manager of Shepheard's Hotel in Cairo," he said soberly. "Should anything happen to me, I want you to return to Cairo. There will be more money and a room waiting for you at the hotel. He'll make sure you receive it. After that, you can travel to wherever you want."

With her heart thumping, she gingerly pinched the envelope, not wanting to open its flap. "Why are you doing this?" she asked with dread. "I don't want to go any place else. You should know that if you die out here, I die with you."

Sam paused, unsure how to answer. "Why that's nonsense," he finally sputtered. "I only want to protect you should I not make it back."

"I don't need protection," she said softly. "I only need—"

A gun suddenly boomed a warning from Johann Schmidt's lugger. Florie started at the sound. She was sure Sam had not heard her say *you*.

Richarn frantically waved a smoking rifle from the boat's bow. "Baker Pasha! Baker Pasha! Herr Schmidt has fallen ill! He's not moving!"

Sam bounded toward their little rowboat stored on the deck. "Florie, get the medicine chest. I'll unlimber the boat."

A few minutes later, he and Florie clambered aboard the lugger. Johann Schmidt lay on the deck next to his bed, a thin blanket soaked with perspiration partly wrapped around him. His skin burned with fever and his eyes were closed. Sam gently laid him on the bed. Florie covered him with a clean blanket.

"The quinine we've given him doesn't seem to be helping," Florie said, holding Schmidt's limp hand. "This must be more than malaria."

Sam shook his head helplessly. "I've heard of something called blackwater fever. It walks hand in hand with malaria, but it's more dangerous. I don't like how his chest rattles as he breathes. Richarn said that when Johann made his water, it was dark as sin. All we can do now is make him as comfortable as possible."

***

Florie sat next to Johann Schmidt's cot, sponging the sweat from his face. For over three hours she had been sitting next to him. *Is this what awaits us?* She pushed a wisp of hair from her eyes and straightened her back. *Malaria? Blackwater fever? What if Sam got sick? I'd never leave his side.*

Johann suddenly gripped her arm with surprising strength, his eyes wide and milky.

"Sam, he's awake!"

Sam knelt beside the cot and held Schmidt's wrist, feeling for his pulse. He shook his head sadly. "It's racing faster than I can count."

Schmidt jerked upright, the blankets falling from him. "Have you seen Margarethe?"

"Yes, Johann, she's right here."

Florie exchanged knowing glances with Sam and sat on the edge of the bed. She held the dying man's hand, but his empty gaze had drifted far away.

"Yes, beloved, I am here," she whispered softly, caressing his hair.

"Margarethe, I should never have left you. I thought I could sell ivory that would make us rich. But Africa," he tugged feebly at her sleeve, his last reserve of strength dwindling, "it sucks you dry and spits you out like a wrinkled seed."

"Yes, rest now, Johann."

Schmidt tried to lift himself on his elbows, but fell back with a gasp. *"Ich liebe dich, Margarethe!"* His eyes cleared for an instant, and he recognized Sam and Florie. *"Ich bin sehr dankbar .... "*

Sam gently closed his friend's eyes and covered him with the blanket. Florie held Schmidt's hand against her cheek for a moment before turning away. A tear rolled down her cheek. She thought of the envelope Sam had handed her and she shivered.

***

Later that day, a small burial ceremony was held on the banks of the White Nile on the edge of Dinka territory. Sam wrapped Johann Schmidt in a clean sheet, sewing it shut with fishing line. Richarn and several porters dug a grave. Weeping, the Nubian laid his master's body in the earth and covered it. After Florie offered a quiet prayer, Sam hefted several ponderous stones over the mound to keep jackals and hyenas away.

***

Muskets bellowed thunderously. Florie bounded from her berth to the short ladder leading to the main deck, heart racing, her pistol clutched in her hand. Since Johann Schmidt's death, it had been a week of tortuous navigating on the Nile, leaving everyone bone-tired. She heard Sam's feet clump on the deck. "What's happening?" she called.

"Stay down," he yelled from above. "We left the bogs during the night and have been in open water since then. I don't know what we're coming into now."

Florie crept slowly up the few stairs and crouched beside him behind the gunwale. "Are we under attack?" she asked anxiously.

Sam squinted against the light. He detected many men gathering on the bank ahead of them. "I don't think so. There aren't any musket balls whistling about our heads or striking the boat."

"Do not fear, Baker Pasha," Richarn shouted from the lugger. "This is Gondokoro. They always fire their guns to let everyone know a new ship has arrived. If we would have had Egyptian soldiers aboard, they would have fired at us."

"Just the same, we'll take no chances when we go ashore." Sam released the tension on the hammers of his rifle as he turned toward Florie. "I think you should take care of yourself, if you know what I mean."

With a quick nod of her head, she disappeared down the ladder and into her cabin. Inside her traveling trunk were a bulky shirt, a floppy hat, and a familiar tin of saddle cream. Once before she had used them to hide her identity.

Sam frowned as he surveyed the town. A few ramshackle buildings formed Gondokoro's center. Beyond those were several rambling structures of logs and clapboard, partly surrounded by stockades. A brick church, roofless, lay at one end of the town, but from its dilapidated look and brush-choked grounds, it had not seen parishioners in some time. Most of the remaining structures were tents of various sizes and hues arranged in irregular clusters around multicolored banners and flags.

If the town looked moribund and uninviting, the greeting he received as they moored near the bank was distinctly frigid. As he crossed the boarding plank to the shore, Sam felt rather than saw hundreds of pairs of eyes turned upon him. There were no salutations from any of the traders gathered there. He heard a hushed whisper of "English" and "spy" from more than one mouth among that throng.

At last one of the traders, a thin fellow with a series of circular tattoos etching both cheeks, stepped forward and pressed his fingers to his lips in greeting. "I am Khurshid Aga, agent of Andrea de Bono," he said in clipped Arabic as he fingered the butt of a pistol stuck in his sash. "I speak for all of the trading clans in Gondokoro."

"I met de Bono in Khartoum," Sam replied flatly. He tried to count the number of guns and swords among the crowd. There were many.

"My master did not inform me that visitors were arriving," Khurshid Aga said as he furtively studied the Englishman, noting the breadth of his shoulders and the long-bladed knife at his hip. "I should warn you that Europeans are not welcome. Many people in Gondokoro would believe that you are here to interrupt their commerce." His attention was distracted to another European of smaller stature and build, with almost effeminate features and downcast eyes, descending from the dahabeah, yellow strands of hair peeking from under a floppy-brimmed cap. The newcomer cradled a light, sporting rifle in his arms, and a pistol tucked into his belt.

"I'm not interested in your commerce," Sam said. "I'm here to search for two of my countrymen, John Speke and James Grant. Have you heard of their whereabouts?"

Khurshid Aga pursed his lips and shrugged. "We have heard of two Englishmen held prisoner by a king far to the south, but that was some time ago. They may be dead, or they may be on their way down the Nile. I do not know."

"Then perhaps we shall have to wait a bit for them to show up, or maybe we'll head upriver to find them," Sam replied crisply.

"It would be far better to look for your friends than to stay here," Aga warned. "Two Englishmen and a handful of Khartoum blacks do not make a strong force should the others in Gondokoro take a disliking to your presence."

Sam leaned close to the trader until their noses nearly touched. His hand rested meaningfully on his knife handle. He knew that Aga was warning him of the town's ages-old slave trade. "Be assured, my friend, should trouble arise, I will come looking for Khurshid Aga first," he said in a quiet, even voice. "In the meantime, we'll camp on that little flatland to the south and be out of everyone's way."

***

Sam surveyed the efforts of the porters as they layered palm fronds to form a roof over the crudely constructed supply hut. He stepped back a few paces, his hands on his hips, to better study the camp's layout. The supply hut had been built near his tent at the camp's center. Florie's tent lay next to his. The smaller ones for the porters were spread in a circle as a buffer to any unwanted traffic from Gondokoro. A makeshift corral of palm trunks surrounded the camels and donkeys.

Just before the noon meal, a visitor arrived in the camp and demanded to see the white pasha. Richarn, somewhat intimidated by the visitor's hard voice and iron gaze, brought him to Sam's tent.

"Baker Pasha, this man has asked to see you," Richarn announced.

Sam glanced up from his notebook. The visitor had the high cheekbones of a desert tribesman, a black beard flecked with silver, and dark eyes glittering under hooded lids. The man wore a simple burnoose striped in black. He raised his fingers to his lips in greeting and bowed.

"Honorable and esteemed Baker Pasha," he said in heavily accented English. "I am Mahomet el-Nar of the Dongolowan people. We have heard you need workers to carry your supplies. I have twenty men to serve you."

"Twenty?" Sam rose halfway out of his camp chair. "You did say twenty?"

"Yes, Baker Pasha," Mahomet el-Nar replied, nodding his head. "They are all seasoned men."

Sam scratched his head in disbelief. Twenty experienced porters were more than he might have hoped for. His handful of Jalyns and Bishareens were too few to mount a vigorous expedition.

"Wages?"

"Standard payment in salt and silver," the Dongolowan replied as he stroked his beard.

"Done!"

"And I must be named the *vakeel*, the headman of your caravan. All of the men must answer to me, and I answer to you."

"Still done." Flabbergasted at this stroke of good fortune, Sam beamed.

Mahomet bowed, and then cleared his throat. "Begging your pardon, Baker Pasha, but this humble son of the desert has one more request. He begs the honor of a glimpse of the fabulous *sitt* who gave water to your men before herself, and who slew the mighty buffalo with her own hands. Word of her has reached far."

"I'll ask her," Sam said with a grin.

Whistling happily, he left the tent. To be offered twenty men at standard rates was beyond good luck—and to pay in salt, a little silver, and a glimpse of Florie was challenging all good fortune. Things were certainly starting to look up.

A few moments later, he returned to the room with his fingers entwined with Florie's. "This is Mahomet el-Nar of the desert Dongolowans," Sam explained. "I've just hired him to be *vakeel*. He wished to see you."

Mahomet smiled deeply and bowed again, his hands offered palms up to her. "I bask in your glow," he said simply.

"Baker Pasha told me you are bringing many of your people to help us," Florie replied hesitantly. Something about the way Mahomet's eyes had narrowed when she entered the room made her feel uneasy. "As he has thanked you, so I also thank you."

"May the blessings of the Prophet be upon you both," Mahomet said, flashing a great smile. "I promise to serve you well."

Touching his fingers to his lips, he dismissed himself, and, with a swirl of his burnoose, disappeared out the door. Once away from the foreigner's camp, he went directly to a small grove of banana palms where his men waited.

"You made the arrangement with the Englishman?" one of them asked.

"Yes," Mahomet replied. "But we will have to be careful how we get rid of him. He has a dozen porters with him, all armed."

"And is the yellow-hair here?"

A smirk curled Mahomet's lips. "The boy that arrived with Baker was no boy at all. Baker was so happy to hire us that he willingly paraded the yellow-hair in front of me. When the time comes, we kill him, snatch her, and be back in Khartoum in a fortnight."

Chapter Sixteen

Florie whimpered as she turned over in her bed, her dreams a confused jumble of images. A man in a dark-colored burnoose stalked her from the ragged wheat fields of Mehadia to the steaming banks of the Nile, a pitted, rusty curve of sickle blade covering the stump of his right hand. She tried to hide, crouching first in the wheat stubble, then among the rotting stems of papyrus. He always tracked her down, sniffing the air, howling like a dog when he discovered her. She awoke once, bathed in sweat, straining to hear sounds of her pursuer. Finally, she fell into a deep sleep as the sun crested the horizon.

Rifle shots erupted upriver, south of the camp. She sprang to her feet, her breath exploding in quick gasps, and dashed out of her tent, visions of the sickle-handed man still throbbing in her head. Sam was already outside, one of his loaded rifles cradled in his arms. Two more shots rang out. More shouting.

"What's happening?" Florie demanded as she rammed lead bullets down the barrels of the Fletcher.

"I can't tell," he replied, staring into the distance. He cautiously walked toward the river. "It could be some slave hunting party letting everyone know they've returned, or maybe Petherick has finally arrived. If hostiles were attacking, there'd be more yelling and shooting."

A hundred yards away, a group of perhaps thirty people were trudging along the narrow beach. In their lead were two white men with rifles slung over their shoulders. The taller of the two had a thick, reddish-brown beard.

Sam stopped and squinted. Florie watched in surprise when he began sprinting toward the newcomers, waving his hat as he ran.

"Speke," Sam cried. "John Hanning Speke!"

Florie stood rooted in the sand, her fingers covering her lips. Speke? Was this the same man Sam was going to look for? She glanced at her nightclothes that were more revealing than hiding. How could she face Sam's friends dressed like this? Without waiting, she ducked back into the tent.

***

Sam charged red-beard, sweeping him up in an enormous bear hug and pirouetting boisterously, his feet kicking up spurts of sand. The newcomer blinked in astonishment, an embarrassed smile curving his lips. He didn't quite know how to react to the ebullient, hairy lunatic hugging him. "Why, you're not Petherick," he finally gasped.

Sam put the man down and held him at arm's length so they could mutually inspect each other. "Speke, you don't recognize me? Why, of course you wouldn't. I only had a mustache the last time we met. I'm Samuel White Baker."

"Baker? Sam Baker? The hunter from Ceylon?" Speke's eyes widened as recognition slowly dawned. "Yes, of course. We met aboard the *Dathia* in the Mediterranean, what, seven or eight years ago? But I was expecting John Petherick. What the deuces are you doing here? Where the hell is Petherick?"

Sam studied his old acquaintance. Speke's skin was weathered and browned like worn leather. His hair hung below the edges of a battered hat, his thick beard thrusting from his jaw. Although he was gaunt and his clothing threadbare, his pale blue eyes burned with passion.

"I'm sorry I can't properly answer your question, my friend," Sam replied. "I was told in Khartoum that Consul Petherick is upcountry somewhere, probably searching for you."

Speke's brow furrowed in anger. "That ill-bred scoundrel was supposed to meet me here and have a boat waiting to take me to Khartoum. I bet he's hunting ivory or gathering slaves. The Foreign Office will hear about this."

At first taken back by Speke's outburst, Sam quickly grasped the man's fist in a firm handshake. Stress and fatigue could easily make the most courageous of explorers edgy.

"I'm quite sorry," Speke said lightly. "It's been a long, hard journey." He turned toward his fellow traveler and introduced him. "This is Jim Grant, a true Scotsman, though I haven't held that against him. We've been through a lot together."

Grant's eyes were reddened with fever, his knees poking through holes in his trousers. His handshake, however, was strong and vibrant.

"You wouldn't have a bit of *haggis*, would you?" Grant asked hopefully. "Of all the things in the world to crave, that's what sticks in my mind the most: damned boiled sheep guts! God knows it must be the fever."

Sam laughed and clapped both men on the back. "I came thinking I would have to walk all the way to the Equator to find you, and here you show up in my very camp. Come back to my boat and you can tell me about your discoveries."

The three men crossed the boarding plank to the dahabeah and retreated to the quarterdeck where a canvas awning protected them from the sun. Richarn was waiting for them. Sam whispered instructions to the Nubian.

Sam offered a hand toward a small table and several chairs. "Gentlemen, please have a seat. I've sent one of my men to bring refreshments. Now tell me, please, what did you find?"

"Well, Baker, we've indeed identified the great lake I named Victoria Nyanza as the true source of the Nile," Speke began, his eyes burning brightly. "We trekked from Zanzibar, following the old slaving routes. Once we reached the lake, we followed it north and found a great falls dropping its flood into a river. I named it Ripon Falls after Lord Ripon who helped sponsor my expedition. Our measurements of altitude are precise. There's no doubt that Lake Victoria is the mother of the Nile. But it was a hard trek. Of our caravan, the twenty or so porters you saw with us on the beach are all that remain of sixty. But now it's done. The Nile's source has been verified!"

"Is there no laurel leaf in Africa left for me to earn?" Sam asked wistfully.

Speke glanced at Grant. The Scotsman smiled and delved into a well-worn bag that had been strapped over his shoulder. After a moment's search, he offered Sam a tubular case sealed with straps on both ends. He unbuckled the straps and opened the tube. Several maps were rolled inside.

"Here, this one," Speke said, indicating the largest of the sheets.

The map spread across the table represented Speke's sketch of the flow of the Nile from Lake Victoria. Notes were scrawled within the boundaries of the lake, while unfamiliar names dotted parts of the river and sections of the neighboring countryside.

"This is Ripon Falls," Speke said, his excitement increasing as if the map conjured visions of their adventure. He pointed to a mark on the north end of Lake Victoria. "Lord save us, but what a flow of water dropping down those falls, truly the spring of the Nile. From there, we left the flow of the river and departed cross country to the northwest." His finger traced a thin red line drawn on the paper. "We once more contacted the Nile here, but then it bent to flow due west. We named that flow Somerset Nile."

"Our guides said there is a waterfall called Karuma a march or two beyond, but we didn't explore in that direction," Grant said, continuing Speke's story. "Jack and I had been held for months as virtual prisoners in the kingdom of Kamrasi, and by the time we finally left, we were physically spent. Our calendars were useless, but we knew we were far behind schedule. We only wanted to reach Gondokoro and meet with Petherick. So we decided to abandon the river and head overland directly north, the shortest route to where we now stand."

"The local peoples spoke of a great lake to the west of where we were," Speke added. "They called the pool the *Luta N'zige*—the Dead

Locust Lake. We believe that beyond the Karuma Falls the Somerset Nile flows west to empty into this lake." To emphasize his point, he tapped a blank space on the map with a dirty forefinger. "From there, the Nile exits somewhere on its north end to resume its course to Khartoum. We, of course, have no proof of this, but if what the natives say is true, the *Luta N'zige* could well be part of the Nile sources. It has yet to be discovered and identified. Find that and you will have your laurel leaf."

Sam brightened visibly at the mention of the unseen lake. He didn't notice Florie's quiet approach across the boarding plank and onto the deck until Grant discreetly cleared his throat.

"Gentlemen, I'm ... I'm truly sorry," Sam stumbled over his words, his face flushed with embarrassment. "This is my ... my *chère amie*, Florence von Sass."

Florie, her hair plaited and pinned on her head, wore the blue dress from Madame Kopecky's shop. "You are the missing explorers," she exclaimed excitedly as she set a bottle of wine and three glasses on the table. "Richarn came running into camp and said we had English visitors. I ... I thought you might like some refreshment." Of a sudden, she wondered how her accent must sound to the newcomers.

Speke and Grant glanced at each other in amazement. It was wonderfully fortuitous to meet with Sam Baker on the Nile, but to also meet a beautiful young woman was beyond belief.

"Yes, quite so," Speke said, his eyebrows arching. "Damn it all, Baker, I thought you already had a wife. Surely this isn't her?" He winced when Grant kicked him lightly in the shin.

"We've been a long time in the bush country, Miss von Sass," Grant said. "My partner and I are both very honored to meet you."

Florie blushed. In spite of Speke's rudeness, her heart was singing. These were the lost explorers Sam had been so determined to find. What a heavenly stroke of good luck that they had walked right into camp. Now there was no need for another dangerous expedition. Perhaps she and Sam could return to England with them.

"I'd like to talk to you if I could," she said happily, her hand curling around his arm. "It's very important."

But Sam was oblivious to her touch and words, his mind already charging full bore into the logistical problem of marching to the *Luta N'zige*. He would need as much information from the two men as he could get.

"Later," he muttered tersely as he bent over the map. "I have much to do to plan for our trip upriver."

Florie's hand dropped numbly from his arm. It was not what she wanted—or expected—to hear. "Yes, I suppose you do," she said as she walked dejectedly toward the gangplank. Behind her, Sam continued to study the map.

***

On the third day after the arrival of Speke and Grant, a new fusillade of gunfire erupted from the direction of Gondokoro. Speke emerged from his tent with a revolver in hand, while Sam and Jim Grant quickly loaded their rifles.

"It's just their way of welcoming newcomers," Sam said, shading his eyes with his hand as he glanced down the river. "Another boat must have arrived."

Minutes later several of Speke's porters jogged into the camp. "Petherick Pasha has come," one porter yelled. "He and his wife have beached their dahabeah. They have much ivory on their deck."

"That fool was supposed to be waiting here for me, not hunting elephants," growled Speke.

Within the hour, John Petherick, his wife, and a small band of followers emerged from the brush separating Sam's encampment from Gondokoro. Petherick, a barrel-chested fellow with a thick bush of coarse whiskers, wore a sweat-stained shirt, equally filthy trousers, and had a double-barreled, eight-bore rifle slung over his shoulder. As he drew near, he studied his countrymen, bewilderment written on his face.

"Speke? Grant?" Petherick's gaze shifted from one man to the other. "We thought you were both dead, no word from you in months. Why it's absolutely wonderful that you are both safe. And who the hell are you?" He cocked his head as his eyes widened in recognition. "Sam Baker? Can it be you? I haven't seen you since the highland games at Atholl's."

Sam grasped the Welshman's beefy fist in greeting, although he noticed the other two explorers had not accepted the consul's extended hand.

"Captain Speke," Petherick began, his eyes flitting to Speke and Grant. "I'm truly sorry—"

"I don't want your damned apology," Speke blurted, his face reddening with anger. "Your orders were that you were to be waiting for us. Good God, man. We've just come from the jaws of Hell itself!"

"Please, sir, your language," Petherick said, bristling. "My wife is present."

Katherine Petherick was a wan ghost of a woman wearing a man's gray shirt and a tattered, stained skirt of red calico. In spite of the tropical heat, a woolen shawl covered her shoulders. Gray smudges of exhaustion shadowed her eyes and the hollows of her cheeks. Strands of white streaked her brown hair bound in a thick bun. She smiled a greeting, if the stretching of gaunt skin over gums and teeth could be called a smile.

"Gentlemen, I understand you have scientific issues to discuss," she said softly, sensing the tension between her husband and the explorers. "If I could beg your pardon, I shall retire to the town and rest for a while."

"I am sorry, Mrs. Petherick, but I won't allow you to take up residence in that cesspool," Sam said, shaking his head firmly. "Please, my … my wife is in the large tent and she would be most happy if you rested there for a bit." He did not make eye contact with Speke or Grant when he referred to Florie as his wife. He waited until the woman had headed toward the tent before he continued. "In the meantime, gentlemen, let's retire to the deck of my dahabeah where we can discuss the matter undisturbed."

"I have nothing to say to this … this rogue," Speke raged. "He abandoned us. He can go to blazes for all I care."

"But I hunted elephants only to add to the funds needed to get you back to civilization," sputtered the consul as he confronted Speke. Drops of spittle clung to his thick beard. "Surely you didn't think my government allotment would cover everything. Besides, nobody knew where you were or when you would arrive here."

Speke scowled. He had never cared for the arrangements the Geographical Society had made with this Welsh adventurer parading as a diplomat. "There is no excuse," he countered. "If Mr. Baker had not been here, Captain Grant and I would have been at a total loss. You made things very inconvenient, and I guarantee that the authorities in London will hear of it."

Petherick's eyes bulged as his anger grew. "But this is such a trivial matter. My wife almost died out there."

Speke, contemptuous of the fuming consul, ostentatiously examined his fingernails. Without another word, he pivoted on his heel and stalked to his own tent. Grant shrugged helplessly and followed his comrade. Sam, left alone with Petherick, tried to defuse the situation.

"John, both of those men have been under extreme stress, half-starved and nearly lame," he said. "Join me on my boat for a brandy. I have a keg yet untapped."

Petherick snorted his disgust, but, not having to face Speke's antagonism, he decided to accept Sam's offer. "It's been a while since I've had a hard drink," he said. "But what of my wife? I just can't leave her here."

"She'll be fine with Florence," Sam assured him. "Besides, after months in the jungle with a bushy-faced rascal like you, I should think she'd enjoy a little feminine company."

"Agreed," Petherick thundered, slapping Sam on the back. "Now where's that drink?"

***

Florie was resting on her cot when the commotion outside awakened her. A feeling of dizziness and nausea had gripped her, and she'd hoped a nap would help her combat the cold clutch of fever. She heard footsteps approach the tent, but they were not the heavy tread of any of the men.

"Mrs. Baker," called a thin voice from outside. "Your husband said I might rest a while out of the sun."

Florie opened the flap and was startled to find a white woman standing there.

"I'm Katherine Petherick ... Kate ... wife of Her Majesty's consul to Khartoum."

"Please, come and sit, Kate," Florie said, extending her hand to the tent's interior. "I'll have one of our men brew some tea."

The two women sat at a small, folding table at the center of the tent. Florie wasn't sure if she should open the conversation. For the moment, Kate Petherick seemed content to knot her fingers together. Then she stopped fumbling and stared at Florie through narrowed eyes.

"I'm truly amazed to see such a young woman as your self in the dark heart of Africa," Kate said in a husky whisper. "What brings you and your husband here?"

"Mr. Baker heard that Captains Speke and Grant were missing," Florie replied. The older woman's haunted gaze made her feel uncomfortable. "We had just finished exploring the sources of the Blue Nile when he decided we might be able to offer some assistance. So here we are."

"Good Lord," Kate said, startled. "You mean to tell me you've traveled with your husband among the savages of the east? For how long?"

Florie chewed on the inside of her lip. *Why should this woman be questioning me? Should I tell her that Sam and I are not married? No. Better to let that bit of information pass.* "For over a year," she replied. "He would like to explore the White Nile as well."

"And you mean to go with him?"

Florie felt her pulse quicken as she nodded her head slowly.

"Child, you mustn't go into the Nile swamps. I've just come from there," Kate blurted, her hand clamping around the younger woman's wrist. "We were lost for months in the Sudd, the great bog of floating grasslands. Our food gave out, and then our powder got wet. Fever claimed our *vakeel* and several of our porters. It struck me weeks ago and almost killed me. Look at me. How old do you think I am?"

Florie recoiled from Kate's intensity. "I ... I ... don't know," she stammered. "Perhaps forty ... forty-five."

Kate's grip suddenly released and her face crumpled. She slumped wearily against the back of her chair. "I'm truly sorry for my behavior, Mrs. Baker," she mumbled. The circles under her eyes seemed darker.

"I'm just trying to warn you. I'm only twenty-six years old."

A shiver coursed through Florie. Was it the fever, she wondered, or this woman's story?

"Please lie down, Kate. I'll see what's taking the tea so long."

Kate Petherick sighed and bit her lip. Suddenly, she felt incredibly tired.

***

Sam saw little of the Pethericks over the next few days. The consul and his wife withdrew to their own boat, preferring to distance themselves from the explosive John Hanning Speke. The last straw had been when Speke refused John Petherick's offer of his dahabeah to transport both him and Grant to Khartoum.

With Speke sulking and the consul in self-imposed isolation, Sam sought the company of the dour Grant. The Scotsman was more than happy to find a kindred spirit interested in geography and the wonder of discovery. He sketched a rough map showing where he and Speke had left the course of the Nile, and the estimated location of the fabled Dead Locust Lake. Although he apologized for the crudeness of the map, he urged Sam to follow the route that he and Speke had used; it would carry him a bit further to the east and he wouldn't have to travel through the country of the Nyam-Nyams, who were known for their grisly rituals and cannibalism.

"Do not leave the trail if at all possible," Grant warned. "We have no idea what the tribes are like, or how difficult the terrain is in that direction. Here is where you will enter Kamrasi's kingdom of Unyoro." He stabbed the map with his forefinger.

Speke sauntered to where the two men were huddled. He eyed Grant's sketch.

"Be sure you have plenty of trade goods to bribe Kamrasi," he said. "He's a thief and scoundrel of the highest magnitude. Had we more men and guns, I might have waged war on him."

"Yes, but, Jack, we were explorers on this mission, not soldiers," Grant countered.

"Indeed," Speke sniffed, rolling his eyes in exasperation. "Anyway, my dear Samuel Baker, we can't thank you enough for making your dahabeah available to take us to Khartoum. I wouldn't touch anything offered by that renegade Petherick. The Foreign Office shall hear about him. Be that as it may, now that we've rested a bit, the thought of a boat voyage rather than walking does sound wonderfully inviting."

"Miss von Sass will be accompanying us then?" Grant asked.

Startled, Sam looked up from the map. "Why no, gentleman. She and

I will go together to find the *Luta N'zige*."

"Are you feverish, man?" Speke said. "That country we traveled through is no picnic or walk in Hyde Park. The trail's not only brutal, but the natives are totally uncivilized. Both Jim and I suffered from enough fevers and sicknesses to make our todgers shrivel and fall off. It's no place for a lady."

"Please reconsider, Sam," Grant begged.

Speke shook his head in disbelief. "Are you even married to her? Should something happen to you, there will be no protection for her from Her Majesty's government. Why, Sam, she's not even English. From her accent maybe she's Hungarian or Slovak. There isn't an Englishman who would look twice to make sure she's taken care of."

Agitated by Speke's tone, Sam bit the inside of his lip to keep calm. "She *is* going with me, Jack. Florence wouldn't have it any other way. She's quite extraordinary, you know. All I ask, gentlemen, is that you won't mention her once you return to England."

Grant firmly pumped Sam's hand. "Marry her before you get to England," he advised. "It'll be better for both of you."

Sam smiled and clapped the Scotsman on the shoulder. "Make sure the boat returns to Gondokoro for us," he said. "We'll take the lugger upstream as far as we can. If we're lucky, we'll have discovered the lost lake and be back in time to catch the winds blowing from the south. I hate the thought of marching all the way to Khartoum."

Speke and Grant crossed the boarding plank to the dahabeah. With a singsong chant from their African porters, the boat was poled into deeper water and the sail hung. Sam waved until the vessel rounded the curve of shore.

Florie joined him at the river's edge. Kate Petherick's warning still simmered in her mind, but she had come this far and Sam was going on.

A day later, just after dawn, the Pethericks also sailed north. Florie swallowed hard as their boat disappeared. She realized they no longer had friends in Gondokoro.

***

Mahomet el-Nar watched the British consul's dahabeah disappear down the Nile. The arrival of so many Europeans had delayed his actions. But now Baker and his yellow-haired *sitt* were alone.

"Tomorrow, Baker plans to sail from Gondokoro to explore the southlands," he said to the other Dongolowans squatting near their campfire at the fringe of Sam's encampment. His men had been smoking cannabis. "Once on the trail, we will cut him down and throw his body in the river for the crocodiles. Then we'll sell his blacks to Khurshid Aga.

The yellow-hair will soon be ours, and we will be very rich."

A dozen yards away, Richarn crouched in the bushes. He had gone to the latrine ditch to relieve himself when he saw the Dongolowans converge around the fire. Mahomet's words caused him to tremble with fear. He had to warn the pasha and the *sitt* before these terrible men had a chance to strike, but if he moved now, one of the cutthroats might notice him. Soon it would be sunset; he would wait until dark for all of these terrible men to fall asleep.

Chapter Seventeen

Sam brushed his hands together and surveyed the piles of supplies and trade goods with satisfaction. Behind him, a campfire blazed, helping to dispel the chill air of early evening.

"Tomorrow morning, we'll have the porters load the goods on the lugger, and we'll be off," he said. "Thank God we have enough men now."

Florie smiled hesitantly and wrapped her blanket more tightly about her shoulders. She couldn't rid herself of Kate Petherick's warning, but Sam seemed to have everything under control.

Without warning, Richarn charged toward them, his chest heaving and his eyes wide with terror. It took a moment for him to find his tongue. "It … it's Mahomet el-Nar and his men," he finally spluttered. "They're scheming to kill you and steal the *sitt* away."

Sam seized Richarn by the shoulders. "Mahomet? How can that be?"

"It is true, Baker Pasha," Richarn gibbered, his eyes darting fearfully toward the Dongolowan tents. "I heard them speaking of their plans. Mahomet will tell you he loves you even as he takes a knife to your throat. He even called the *sitt* yellow-hair."

Sam ground his teeth angrily as he glanced at Florie. "Then he must be working for Emile Zeb. That does it. I'll put an end to this mutiny right now."

"You need more men," Florie warned, stepping in front of Sam.

"Not to deal with those dogs," he said, a resolute glint in his eyes. "Wait for me here, and keep that pistol handy." He disappeared into the tent and rummaged about. A few moments later, he emerged with his Ceylon ten-bore and the box of small nails he used to pin specimens to display boards. He rammed powder charges down the barrels, followed by a handful of nails in each tube. "This'll make 'em hop."

Florie remained rooted in her tracks, her mouth half open in horror as Sam stalked away. A vision of Papa leaving to battle the Austrians flashed through her mind. She remembered clinging to his arm, begging him to stay. He promised he would return, but he never did. Then their house exploded and Mama disappeared. In a single day, she had been stripped of her parent's love, her childhood, her security, and left to a fate of fear, deprivation, and loneliness. Until Sam came. And now he was walking away to war as well.

She scampered after him, grabbed his arm, and spun him about. "Do you think you can fight everyone in the world at once?" she spat angrily. "Do you really believe that I'll calmly stand by while you commit suicide?

Then I might as well join you and die by your side."

"What do you suggest?" he said, a dangerous edge to his voice. "That we wait until their knives are at our throats?"

Her eyes locked on his. She refused to back down. "Let's leave now. Forget the boat. All of Mahomet's men would wake up if we tried to load it. We take what supplies we can and disappear into the night."

Richarn tugged frantically on Sam's sleeve. "We must leave, sir. There are too many bad men. Too many."

Sam grimaced. It wasn't his style to run away from a fight, but Florie's desperate grip on his arm warned him that wisdom walked on her side.

He shook his head in disgust. They would have to move inland in a hurry, to put as much distance between them and Gondokoro as possible. "We only have a dozen men we trust, so we'll need to cut our supplies. Load the animals, but for God's sake do it quietly. We'll leave in an hour. I don't want to be here when Mahomet and his gang awaken."

***

Florie slumped wearily in her saddle. Their desperate flight during the night meant there hadn't been time for sleep or a decent meal. She blinked against the sunlight filtering through a thin haze of clouds. The Nile was nowhere in sight. The jungle-covered terrain near Gondokoro had given way to scrub brush, a smattering of dome palms, and rocky ridges.

Reduced to the pair of horses she and Sam rode, with only a few camels and donkeys remaining for the handful of Bishareens and Jalyns to drive, they had been forced to abandon half of their trade goods in Gondokoro. She gnawed mechanically on a strip of dried antelope meat. It was tasteless and coarse, like old leather. As she watched, one of the Bishareens staggered and nearly fell.

"We have to take a break, Sam," she said. "We're all done in."

"Soon, but we have to make sure we're far enough away from Gondokoro," he replied. A shout from the caravan's tail caused him to turn in his saddle. "What the hell?"

Richarn, waving his rifle wildly, dashed toward the head of the column. He had been trailing behind, acting as a rear lookout of sorts. "Baker Pasha, behind us," he panted. "Behind us!"

Standing in his stirrups, Sam studied the skyline in the direction they had just come from. A dust cloud hung in the distance. On a windless day such as this, it meant a large party of riders followed their trail.

"How long before they're upon us?" he asked as he rummaged in his saddlebag for his telescope.

"They are riding hard by the size of that cloud," Richarn replied, trying to gauge distance in his head. "Less than a half hour."

"Who are they?" Florie questioned as she shaded her eyes with her hand. "Do you think it is Mahomet and his men?"

"If it is, they got horses from someone in Gondokoro, probably Khurshid Aga," Sam said. "Or, if we're lucky, it's just a raiding party going after slaves farther to the south. Whoever they are, we can't outrun them."

Sam opened his telescope, adjusted its lens, and scanned the trail ahead of them.

His glass wandered over a thin fringe of dome palms and scrub brush peeled back to reveal a stony expanse gashed by narrow gorges. Those gorges just might provide a hiding place. He handed the telescope to Florie.

"See those ravines?" he asked, pointing into the distance. "We'll hide among them until they pass."

"Won't they see our trail?"

"Not among the rocks. Quickly now!"

The porters drove the animals into the ravines, pushing westward away from the main trail. Sam lingered to keep an eye on the riders. He didn't have to wait long before he heard the clatter of hooves on stone. He glanced at the gorges. There was no sign of Florie or the caravan. Easing around the curvature of a boulder, he pressed the telescope to his eye and surveyed their pursuers. Perhaps twenty horsemen were strung in a long column. Khurshid Aga's black flag, its silver stitching of Arabic script glinting in the bright rays, flapped above the lead rider. Long-barreled muskets protruded into the air like porcupine quills. If this was a raiding party to collect slaves, it traveled without the supply camels necessary for a prolonged expedition. This had more the appearance of a hit-and-run foray with a definite target in mind.

As Sam swung the telescope over the column, a familiar face appeared. Yes, there was Mahomet el-Nar bouncing in his saddle. Behind him rode the rest of his Dongolowan cutthroats. They galloped past the rocky stretch gouged by ravines where Florie and the caravan had disappeared without taking notice.

Sam collapsed his glass and retreated from the boulder. There was no going back now. Gondokoro would be on alert. Their only hope of escape was into the unknown.

***

The moon had risen, sending angular shadows cutting across the caravan's path. Animals and cameleers disappeared into pools of darkness, re-emerging moments later into the silvery light.

Florie swayed in her saddle; she caught herself dozing. She reached for her water bottle, then pulled her hand back. No, the water would have to last until they found a new source. The extra barrels had been left in Gondokoro. With a bit of soiled cloth, she dabbed at her brow. How many hours had it been since they'd left the trail and entered the tortured land of ravines and rocky escarpments? Eight? Ten?

"Damn," Sam spit the curse as the lead camel balked and refused to go further. "At this rate, we'll be caught in the rainy season. Maybe we shouldn't have left Speke's track."

"Please don't second guess yourself," Florie said, her voice scratchy. "You saw Mahomet leading his men after us. If we hadn't gone in this direction, God only knows what would happen had they caught us."

Sam laughed mirthlessly. "I have to admit I would've liked to have shoved my rifle up Mahomet el-Nar's arse and let fly."

Florie sagged wearily in her saddle. "Another time, maybe. Are we going much further?"

"The camels won't go on, so we might as well camp here," he replied tersely, dismounting. "But no fires tonight. I don't know where Mahomet and his men are, and I don't want them seeing a glow from a campfire."

Florie slid from her *makloufa* and unbuckled its straps. She heaved the saddle to the ground to use as a pillow.

"Go ahead and rest," Sam said. "The men and I will feed the animals and take turns on watch."

"Let me know when it's my turn." She sighed as she wrapped herself in her blanket. She was asleep the moment her head touched the saddle. Sam did not awaken her.

***

From Sam's journal:

March? April? 1863

I'm not sure of the exact date, nor have I had time to keep my diary up to date. We've been in and out of these cursed ravines for a week, heading south-southeast. I haven't allowed campfires or hunting for fresh meat. All are in a foul mood. There have been no other signs of Emile Zeb's slavers, but I don't dare take a chance that they might see smoke or hear the echoes of a rifle shot.

According to Speke's map, I believe we have been traveling roughly parallel to his trail. It's impossible to be exact.

F. is tiring, should have remained in Khartoum. I don't know what I can do. This entry shows my uncertainty.

Nothing is exact. Not the date. Not the map. Not even sure how I feel about F. traveling with me.

Richarn believes there is a village nearby. I hope so. I need to get my bearings.

***

Florie peeked over the rocky summit of a ridge. On the plain below, smoke curled lazily from dozens of cook fires. Wood and mud houses shaped like beehives dotted the landscape. Scores of people were cooking food, tanning hides, repairing roofs, and attending to myriad other chores.

"Latookas," Richarn said with certainty as he peered from his perch on the ridge. "Herr Schmidt said they were friendly, but I've never met them."

"Can you speak their language?" Sam asked.

"Perhaps, perhaps not," Richarn replied with a shrug.

"Well, then let's find out. We need dhurra and water, so we'll bring a few bales of trade goods."

"I'm coming, too," Florie added firmly and checked the cylinder of her pistol.

Smiling, Sam mounted his horse, his Ceylon rifle slung over his shoulder. "And I don't believe that my saying no is an option?"

"Don't even consider it," she said bluntly.

As the tiny caravan approached the village, Latookan sentinels whistled a warning on small bone flutes. Within moments, dozens of warriors brandishing spears and shields sprinted toward the newcomers. Florie held her breath while Sam motioned to his men to remain quiet.

The Latookans wore elaborate headdresses combining their own plaited hair woven through with a fine twine formed from softened tree bark. Braided into the ensemble were pieces of burnished copper and beads of red and blue porcelain. Many of the warriors brandished oval shields of buffalo or giraffe hide, spears, and long-bladed knives. These they shook and waved fiercely, but none made a hostile move toward the newcomers.

Richarn strode forward, his open palms held before him. A Latooka warrior with many layers of beads bound into his hair lowered his spear and also advanced. The two Africans conversed, Richarn motioning several times in the direction of Florie and Sam. At last, both men nodded their heads and returned to their respective groups.

"Their chief, Katchiba, welcomes you as a friend of Schmidt Pasha," Richarn reported, his face glowing with his new importance as *vakeel* and interpreter. "That was his son, Dukuba. He said we could camp outside the town and present ourselves to Katchiba once our tents have been raised. We may bring our trade gifts then."

While Sam attended to camp construction by hammering tent stakes into the earth and spreading the canvas awnings, Florie sorted through the barrels and bundles of goods, examining choice tidbits and shiny ornaments. She selected strands of bright glass beads, gutta-percha hair combs, and small, hard-paper cards decorated with tiny bells. She shook one of the cards; the bells tinkling merrily. It reminded her of the trinkets offered for sale at the harvest fairs in Wallachia. The fairs were held each year in the district capitals after all the crops had been brought in. Thousands of peasant families flocked to the city to eat, drink, dance, and gawk. It was one of the few pleasant memories from that time in her life. She wondered if the people of Mehadia still went to the fair.

"Time to go," Sam called after he had assured himself that everything was ready. The porters wore clean shirts and carried muskets over their shoulders. Several bore trunks of trade goods. Florie brought up the rear, her hat pulled tightly over her hair.

Katchiba was a raisin of a man, dried and shrunken, but with bright, intelligent eyes. A cape of zebra hide embellished with pieces of colored glass and polished bone mantled his withered shoulders. He sat on a stool covered with giraffe hide, with his wives and sons gathered behind him. The women wore aprons of antelope skin around their hips with the tails dangling down their buttocks. Brass bands circled their arms, and wooden plates of varying sizes thrust their lower lips outward in a bizarre fashion. The younger girls in his entourage were clad only with a string of beads around their loins. When Florie approached them, they circled about her, feeling her clothing and her hat, but careful not to touch the ivory skin they were sure would splinter under the slightest pressure.

With a wave of his hand, Katchiba motioned the newcomers closer. He spoke rapidly to Richarn, but his gaze never left Florie and Sam.

"Katchiba says he remembers Schmidt Pasha as a man of fair trade, and is saddened to hear of his death," Richarn interpreted. "He admits he has heard of the *Luta N'zige*, but has never seen the great water. If guides are needed, he can supply them if payment greater than simple glass beads can be arranged."

Florie nodded her head solemnly. From a small, brassbound chest she produced her choicest selections: a folding knife, green-tinted eyeglasses, and a small mirror edged with faux pearls. She handed these to the king who examined each item with great interest before placing them in a small pile at his side. Then he waited as if expecting more gifts. He tilted his head slightly as one of his wives pressed forward to whisper in his ear. Katchiba nodded his head sagely and spoke.

"The king asks the *sitt* to show her teeth," Richarn explained.

With her brows creasing with curiosity, Florie flashed a bright smile at Katchiba and his wives.

"Hah," Katchiba cried. He rose from his stool and leaned toward her to closely inspect her mouth. He giggled when he spoke to Richarn.

"The king says the *sitt* is indeed a beautiful woman," Richarn translated, "but if you knock out her bottom teeth and place an ornament in her lip, she will be even more beautiful."

Sam laughed loudly, then covered his mouth with his hand to stifle a further outburst. Florie pouted. She suddenly swept off her floppy hat. Nimble fingers plucked at the ribbons holding the coils of hair together. Shaking her head vigorously, she released a cascade of golden tresses down her shoulders. From her bag of feminine necessities, she produced one of her small tortoiseshell combs and ran the tines smoothly through her hair. With a tiny scissors, she snipped a thick lock measuring seven or eight inches in length. She offered the hair to Katchiba.

"*Njinyeri*," the king cried as he accepted her gift in wonder, holding it to the sunlight to catch its golden sheen. "*Njinyeri*!"

"The Morning Star," Richarn rendered in a hushed voice. "The *sitt* has captured the Morning Star in her hair. She will always be called *Njinyeri*." The king nodded his head sagaciously and spoke to his sons.

"Katchiba accepts the gift from your wife and has ordered his sons to guide us to the Asua River," Richarn said. Then he smiled at Florie. "The *sitt* has done well."

Florie's face glowed with pride.

By the time their audience with the king ended, only ragged streaks of vermillion remained from the setting sun. Sam smiled proudly as he and Florie strolled to their camp. "Beautifully done," he said to her as they entered the cool interior of their tent. "What possessed you to give a lock of your hair to him to seal our deal?"

"I remembered something Johann Schmidt told me when we first met," she replied as she tried to tie her locks into a tail. "He said I could make more friends with my hair than I could with a bundle of beads or trinkets." Her fingers fumbled with her hair ribbon. "Oops. Could you help me, please?"

Sam eased behind her, his fingers clumsily attempting to twist the ribbon into a knot. "I can't quite see what I'm doing," he mumbled.

Florie bent her head downward, exposing the curves of her neck and the lobes of her ears. She felt his breath fanning her skin. Her pulse pounded. "Is that better?" she whispered.

The ribbon fell from Sam's hand. "I'm not very good at ...."

She turned toward him, her lips parted, those depthless eyes peering into his.

"If I let myself fall in love with you, it will be harder for us in the future," he said, sadness tinging his words.

Florie shook her head slowly. "Future? What about now? We're together in Africa. You know the dangers. There might not be a future."

"What we do in Africa, we do by choice," Sam said. "At some time, when I leave for my home, those choices will be taken away from me. I don't want to hurt you."

"Hurt?" Her brow wrinkled with puzzlement. "Holding yourself away from me is hurt." She tangled her fingers in his shirt and drew him close. Her breathing quickened. "If you won't let yourself love me, then at least let me love you."

"But—"

"Shh. No more." Her hands stole under his shirt and across his chest to his belly, then glided to the drawstring of his trousers. "My future is *now*."

Chapter Eighteen

Sir Roderick Murchison combed his fingers through his thinning thatch of graying hair and groaned inwardly. His mood was as bleak as the early September sleet lashing the windows of the Society's headquarters.

"Now what do we do?" he asked Austen Henry Layard, Undersecretary of the Foreign Office. "Only a few months ago, Captain Speke was the toast of Britain. We fêted his discovery of the Nile's source as the greatest achievement of our century. We not only provided him with funds for his expedition, but even awarded him our gold medal."

"I know, I know," Layard rasped, picking up his friend's lament. "We can't force him to publish a formal paper of his geographical findings. You've heard that his entire memoir is going to be printed by *Blackwood* in Edinburgh, and you—"

"Now, that's a magazine that deserves a spot next to the shitter," Murchison interrupted. "What a slap in our face."

Layard nodded his head in agreement and tugged at his waistcoat, trying to smooth imaginary wrinkles. His thick beard disguised the rugged, ruddy complexion he had earned during his discoveries of the ruins of ancient Babylon and Nineveh more than a decade earlier. But he had given up the mantle of explorer and archeologist in favor of becoming a politician, and now his politician's senses had been aroused. He clucked his tongue apprehensively. "I hear Dick Burton is already challenging Speke's assertion that Lake Victoria is the true source of the Nile. He says that Speke has only cobbled together his assumptions based on mere glimpses of the lake and its streams. Nor does he speak highly of Jim Grant."

"Africa had been the strength of the Society, but at this moment it has become a bit of a bother," Murchison muttered angrily as he shuffled through a stack of papers on his desk, searching for a particular note. "First there was Speke's rampage against Petherick, then the legal mess that followed."

Layard seized upon Murchison's thread of reasoning. "And now you have Speke ready to publish his memoirs with a popular magazine rather than a scholarly journal. As counterpoint, Burton is ready to unleash his vindictive intellect against Speke."

"And to top it off, we've just received news that David Livingstone's expedition to the Zambezi has gone belly up," Murchison snarled as he dramatically waved the note he'd been looking for. "The malaria has killed all of his missionaries and his wife to boot. He's on his way back, a defeated man. It's truly a pity."

"Lord Russell is concerned that the Foreign Office will have to get involved in all of these African activities when we have more important things to worry," Layard said, arching his thick eyebrows for effect. "There's the war in America with thousands killed at some place called Gettysburg. Her Majesty is concerned over that meddlesome nitwit in Paris, Louis Napoleon, and his intrigues in Mexico and Piedmont. And don't forget the Russians. The tsar's Baltic Fleet arrived in New York in the summer, and some of his ships have remained there. The next thing you know, Russia will be allied with the Lincoln government and we'll be hauled into some foolish foreign war again."

"What we need is a new hero to carry the African standard," Murchison thundered, thumping his fist on his desk. "What about that fellow Baker? We've received his report about his discovery of the sources of the Blue Nile, and damned fine work that was. But that was months ago. Didn't Speke say Baker was off to search for another lake as a Nile source further to the south and west? If he's successful, we could put a little polish back on Africa and raise the public's interest in our work."

"The problem with Baker is that he has already exceeded the orders allowed him by the Foreign Office," Layard grumbled. "He was supposed to explore the Blue Nile streams and that's all, not pursue the White Nile. If he does something stupid and incites the natives, then the French or the Prussians might start nosing around. All hell could break loose."

Murchison smiled thinly. "But, according to Speke, Baker only had a small party and was headed into regions even the slave traders don't go," he said, shaking his head. "And there's that business about a mistress. Speke said Baker had a Slavonic woman with him—wouldn't even call her his wife. If that's the truth, I hope the poor fool can be discreet about it. We certainly wouldn't need to have scandal thrown in."

"Heaven only knows if he's even alive," Layard added.

Murchison tugged on his lower lip as he glanced at his friend. "Quite true. And if he is alive, how will he ever make it back home? We haven't given him any help."

***

With his arms folded across his chest, Sam surveyed the oxen skeptically. The great beasts had come at a price: a trunk full of his trinkets was gone as well as an armload of trade muskets, powder, and shot. The oxen could be ridden, Katchiba maintained as he accepted the trade goods, and they needed the beasts since all of the animals brought from Gondokoro had perished from disease. It would be the trio of complacent bovines at the chief's price, or nothing.

"I suppose we don't have much choice in this matter," he said in Florie's general direction. "Which of these creatures would you like to ride? Beef, Steak, or Suet?"

Florie, sensing Sam's souring attitude, pretended to kiss the smallest of the animals. "This is the prettiest one. Suet, you called it. I won't look much like a damsel on its back, or you a knight in shining armor, but if it gets us to the *Luta N'zige,*" she paused, smiling mischievously, "I will adopt it and rename it Baby Sam."

Sam mumbled an inarticulate curse.

"Please quit scowling," she scolded, balling her fist and stamping her foot angrily. "We've been here for weeks and we have to move. You don't expect me to live among the Latookas forever, do you? You know Katchiba still thinks I would look good with my front teeth knocked out. And if we don't get moving soon, my teeth will fall out by themselves."

Sam wiped his hand across his forehead, barely hearing what she said. He tried to calculate how many supplies the oxen could bear in addition to riders, but the numbers swam muddily about. He spat his disgust with himself.

"You know why we've stayed here," he said. "It's because the slave catchers might still be out there, and they have more guns than I do."

Florie glared at him blackly. "So we're here forever?"

"You know what I mean."

"No, I don't. Though I love Katchiba and his people, this has become a prison." She waved her hand toward the lowlands to the south. "What are you scared of, Sam? Are you afraid that once we're out there you can't protect me? I don't need protection."

Sam glanced away, embarrassed by her indictment. "Maybe we should return to Khartoum where it's—"

"Safe?" Florie shook her head, reading his thoughts. "There is no place where it's safe, but I'd rather face the danger head-on than sit here."

"What do you suggest?" Sam asked, his face a picture of exasperation.

"We've come too far to turn back," she replied, pounding her fist into her palm to emphasize her point. "Your *Luta N'zige* is out there somewhere, not in Khartoum. This is what we'll do."

Stooping, she hefted a leather riding-pad and slapped it on the back of the nearest ox. The startled beast snorted. "Come on, you long-horned lovely," she cried, her eyes gleaming with new excitement. "You'll carry us to the Dead Locust Lake, or we'll eat you for supper on the spot!"

***

Rafts of thick white clouds drifted leisurely across an azure sky. As the caravan trekked southward, the lush familiar grasslands of the Latookas quickly gave way to gray-green lowlands thick with scrub brush and thorns. Florie gazed anxiously at the panting men hacking apart the dense, prickly foliage with long, heavy knives. Sam had rotated the porters from carrying supplies and guiding animals to the physically draining task of swinging the knives. Sweat rolled freely from ebony hides and white. Blisters swelled and broke. It didn't seem right that she lounged on the back of an ox while others sweated like dogs.

She slid from the riding pad and stuffed her hat into a supply bag. "Yaseen, take a break," she called to one of the Bishareens.

Yaseen, his grin lacking two front teeth, gladly handed his knife to Florie.

"Leave that for the men," Sam ordered with a frown.

Her mouth formed a thin line of stubbornness. "No. I cut grain and firewood for ten years in Wallachia. I know how to swing a blade."

With deft fingers, she tied her hair back under a broad blue bandana, then rolled up her sleeves.

"It's hot work. You could always take your shirt off." Sam laughed loudly at his joke.

Florie slashed at a branch, severing it with a clean stroke. She waved her machete menacingly. "Be careful you don't get in my way or you'll have to change your name to Samantha."

Hours later the ground became softer and the brush thinned. Pools of stagnant water covered with thick layers of algae dotted the marshland. Scabby stumps of long-dead trees thrust from the ooze like rotten teeth.

Sam examined the terrain through his telescope. The swamp extended as far as he could see. "We'll head east," he finally said. "Maybe there's a way around it."

Someone further back in the caravan shouted something. A Jalyn porter wailed in misery. Several of the Bishareens began pointing to the rear. Sam pivoted about and leveled his telescope. A half-mile behind them, nearly two-dozen horsemen wound their way through the brush that his column had recently cleared. He spied Mahomet el-Nar in his black and white burnoose among them. The Dongolowan chief was urging his men to greater speed.

"Damn," Sam cursed in alarm. "They just don't give up. Emile Zeb must have upped the bounty on us."

"How did they find us?" Florie gasped, trying to hide her fear. She drew her pistol from a leather bag slung over the broad back of an ox and checked its cylinder.

"Found our trail, maybe. Might have even spied us with the Latookas. It doesn't matter now."

"What will we do?"

Sam swung his telescope back over the marshes. "We head into the swamp away from them." He shoved the glass back into his saddlebag and reached for his rifles.

Florie gripped his arm. Worry for him flickered across her face. "Where are you going?"

"I think I'll send a little gift their way," he replied, a grim smile curving his lips.

"No! It's too dangerous."

"Listen, Florie, I need you to lead our people into the swamp," he said, cupping her face in his hand. "The slave catchers won't be able to charge us on horseback once you're in that bog. We'll stand a better chance if I can slow them down a little. I'll be along by and by, but I need you to be strong. Don't look back. Just keep pushing our men on."

Florie's eyes formed a silent plea.

"And loosen your hair," Sam added gruffly. "I want the slave catchers to see you and go after you. I'm planning a little surprise for them."

Then he was off, sprinting toward the distant riders, the massive Holland four-bore bouncing on one shoulder, his old Ceylon double-rifle slung over the other.

Filled with dread, Florie watched him go. She thought about disobeying him, about following him into battle. No. Sam had entrusted the safety of all their men to her. She had to lead them.

With a twist of her wrist, she swept the bandana from her head and released the ribbons that coiled her hair. Golden waves rippled in the sunlight. "Richarn," she cried. "Get the men moving. Into the swamp!"

***

The slave catchers picked their way through the splintered and broken expanses of brush and thorns, a difficult path for men on horseback. Mahomet el-Nar cursed his men to double their efforts. The trail of the Englishman and his woman was hot: a bit of torn cloth hooked on a thorn here, a broken strap from a packet there, even blood on a leaf from someone's scratch. The blood had darkened and looked dried, but when he rubbed it with his thumb, it was still viscous enough to leave a smear.

Rising in his stirrups, he peered through his telescope toward the marshland. Tall reeds swayed without benefit of a wind. Shadows appeared at the base of the reeds, pushing through the dense growth. The *sitt* emerged, straddling the back of an ox, the sun gleaming from her hair as she waved her scarf over her head.

He lowered his glass, his brow puckered with doubt. Where was Baker? He scanned the reeds again. The Englishman must be at the head of the column, he surmised, plunging deeper into the marshlands and lost to view.

"Allah smiles upon us," Mahomet said. "We've caught them at last. They are less than a mile ahead. We'll circle them and cut them to pieces."

A blast like mid-summer thunder suddenly crackled the air, followed by a *whump* of sound and one of the Dongolowan horsemen was swatted from his saddle in a spray of blood.

Mahomet stared at the tangle of guts protruding from the hole in the man's belly. He was sure the fellow was dead before he hit the ground.

"It's Baker," he bellowed, pointing at a stand of thicker foliage. "Over there. See the smoke from his gun? Spread out and surround him. I want his head!"

The raiders fanned right and left, ducking low on their saddles, fearful of the monster gun that roared like a maddened djinn. Another shot whined through the air, but from a smaller rifle. The ten-bore slug clipped branches and plowed into the trunk of a tree. A horse reared in fright and pitched its screaming rider backward from his saddle. Panicking, the other horsemen scattered.

***

Sam glimpsed the riders weaving through the rugged brush. His nose bled from the concussion of the big Holland rifle. He had also fired both barrels of his Ceylon ten-bore. With his rifles empty, he retreated a hundred yards, stumbling over branches his men had cut. The branches gave him a plan. He quickly heaped them into several waist-high mounds. From a small, leather bag belted at his waist, he fished out a hollow metal tube. Inside were the last of his precious matches. He tested the wind. What little there was blew lightly against his back. Striking a match, he touched its greedy fire to the pile of dry leaves and tiny sticks he had shaped into a cone under one stack. Tendrils of smoke snaked through the network of branches. Flames began to leap. Grabbing a burning branch, he thrust it into another pile, then another. An inferno shot into the air. The thin wind pushed the conflagration into the dry, tangled landscape of brush and thorns. Cries of warning flew among the slave hunters. A horse screamed its terror. Musket balls whistled angrily about. Then the wind shifted, the fire bursting in a different direction, cutting off Sam's retreat. The blaze crackled near him. Smoke curled thickly, stinging his eyes and forcing him to cough.

"He's over here," cried one of the slave catchers. "He cannot escape. I have him." Standing in his stirrups, he raised his musket.

Sam slid his big knife from its sheath. There was no time to reload his guns before the Dongolowan fired.

An ox bellowed mightily as it hurtled obliquely toward the slave catcher. Clots of dirt flew from its hooves. Golden hair flowed from the ox-rider's head. The slave catcher crouched in his saddle, his eyes wide with surprise. His horse reared, legs flailing and nostrils flaring, screaming its fear. The ox veered at the last second, its powerful shoulder colliding with the horse, knocking it to its side and pitching its rider into the flaming brush. Florie howled her anger as she guided the ox away.

Whirling cyclones of flames leapt toward Mahomet el-Nar and his men, greedily devouring the tinder-dry brush. Sam coughed again as smoke swirled around him. His eyes watered. Then he spied an opening in the firewall and dashed through. Florie was waiting for him.

"Damn it, I thought I told you to stay with the men," he shouted angrily as he brushed embers from his shirt and hat. "You could have been killed."

She slid from the back of the ox. Her face was as grimy as his. A tear formed a channel through the dirt. She hugged him, holding him as tightly as she could. And Sam, rather than disengaging her arms, returned the hug, lifting her from the earth as if she were weightless.

**

The oxen bawled their fatigue and refused to move. Florie tried kicking her mount in the ribs, but the beast wouldn't budge. The expedition oozed to a halt in a marsh thick with knee-deep slime. The rotting, gaseous stench of the muck made her stomach churn.

"We won't get anywhere if this keeps up," Sam groaned, dragging a forearm across his sweat-stained face. "We'll have to unload the oxen and carry the supplies by hand to firmer ground. I hope this damned swamp comes to an end soon."

"Do you think Mahomet and his men are still following us?" Florie asked between gasps of weariness.

Sam made a face. "I've gone back on our trail a couple of times and I don't hear any sounds of pursuit, at least from that direction. If they survived the fire, they may have followed the edge of these marshes to try to cut us off somewhere ahead, but that will take them many hours."

Florie nodded in understanding, although it hurt to do so. The back of her neck was aching. Her skull throbbed. She felt cold.

That evening the sun burned a muddy, molten red as it set. In the still air, the whining hums of mosquitoes palpable. The caravan camped on a small, dry island. With no wood for campfires, supper consisted of the last stores of dried antelope meat.

A refreshing sleep was nearly impossible. Florie covered her head to keep the mosquitoes away. She tossed and turned, the sticky heat of the night leaving her damp with sweat. Nightmares followed.

Sam shook her shoulder. "Come on Florie, time to get up. We have to get out of this bog."

"Is it morning already?" she moaned, trying to push him away. "I don't feel like I've slept a wink."

The coppery eye of the sun rose high and seemed to stall as if the weight of the stagnant sky kept it from ascending further. Sweat poured and animals bellowed. No breeze, no clouds. Only the incessant hum of the savage mosquitoes.

Florie's riding ox suddenly jerked to a halt, its thick legs firmly mired in the mud. She slid from the saddle and passed a rope around the bull's horns. Several of the porters grabbed the line with her and pulled it tight. The bull strained against the gluey grip of the muck. One leg pulled free with a sucking sound, then another. Without warning, the taut braiding snapped. Porters and woman floundered in the ooze, arms waving as they struggled to regain their balance. Florie's lurching splattered mud across her face and shirt. The mosquitoes swarmed hungrily.

"For God's sake, let's get out of this place," she cried dejectedly, flinging fistfuls of muck at her ox, which had begun a melancholy bawling. She didn't recall ever being as tired and dirty as she was now. "I could scrub for a week and I don't think I'd feel completely clean again."

"At least your mud mask keeps the mosquitoes from biting," Sam replied, trying to keep a straight face.

Florie suddenly straightened and tilted her head as if listening.

"What do you hear?" Sam asked, puzzled. Nothing seemed out of the ordinary to him.

"Shh," she hissed fiercely. The ox bellowed again. "And get that damned cow to shut up!" Sam reached into the grain sack and produced a double handful of dhurra for the animal.

"There. Do you hear it now?"

A distant rumbling sound was barely audible over the whine of insects.

"Yes. It sounds like water running over rocks," Sam replied with wonder. His eyes widened and his voice rang with new excitement. "That's the sound of a waterfall! It has to be the Karuma Falls Speke and Grant spoke of. All of these swamps must drain toward their Somerset River." His gaze locked on Florie. "My God, do you know what this means? We're in the lands of Kamrasi and the Unyoro people. The *Luta N'zige* must be very near."

The Latookan guides stiffened when they heard him say Kamrasi. Slowly they retreated as if they expected enemies to materialize from the very earth. When they finally felt that none of Kamrasi's warriors would appear, they turned and jogged toward their homeland.

"Wait," Sam cried. "We need you to take us to Kamrasi."

Richarn shook his head. "They will not stay with us, Baker Pasha. The Unyoros are the hereditary enemy of their people."

"Then we keep on going without them," Sam said with agitation. "We haven't come this damned far to be scared off so easily. Let's get moving in the direction of that sound."

Groves of banana and date palms provided cooling pools of shade along the banks of the newly discovered river. The elevation slowly rose and the stagnant breath of the marshland disappeared. Thunder from the gorge rumbled and echoed.

Florie stepped back in awe. The river's flow cascaded over rocky protuberances in a brilliant spume, churning to a white froth where water collided with huge boulders. Below the tumbling confusion of rapids were a series of forested islands. Wisps of smoke drifted from the largest; a sign that people were near. She instantly realized how frightful she must look caked in drying mud with bits of vegetation stuck in her hair. She'd probably frighten any Unyoros away. A flicker of motion caught her attention.

From a small knoll perhaps a hundred yards away, an African with a headdress fitted with corkscrew antelope horns was watching them. A broad-bladed spear rested over one shoulder. He unexpectedly raised his hand to his mouth and shrilled a piercing, ululating cry that echoed from rocks and trees. More cries rang out, seemingly from every direction.

"My God," Sam said as he pivoted on his heel. "Unyoros. Hundreds of them. They're all around us."

Florie gulped. Warriors in leopard skins appeared from among the trees, banging long spears against their shields of zebra hide. With fearsome howls, they leaped and sprang and hooked their horned headdresses from side to side as if goring an enemy. There were so many of them she stopped counting. It was like a great storm about to break.

"Florie, grab your rifle," Sam roared frantically. "Richarn, form the men in a circle behind the baggage. Be ready! They're coming near. Don't fire until I do!"

Florie stared at the rifle clutched in her hands. Two shots would not stop that horde. She stood next to Sam, her hip touching his, praying they would die swiftly together.

Sam raised the fearsome Holland four-bore to his shoulder, letting its sights center on the leading Unyoro chieftain. Behind the chief raced scores of warriors, all shouting loudly and beating their spears against shields.

"Damn," Sam cursed under his breath as he mentally figured the odds. More tribesmen were flooding in from left and right. "The rats in the bottle now!"

He had failed Florie—couldn't protect her. Let the end be fast and merciful, he silently prayed. His finger curled around the trigger.

Chapter Nineteen

A diminutive Unyoro laughed and jumped over a fallen tree. Another Unyoro leapt over the same tree, naked, female breasts bouncing.

"Don't shoot," Florie cried, lowering her rifle. "They're not attacking. Those are women and children running with them."

Sam swallowed hard as he peered above the Holland's sights. She was right. Nude children were singing as they ran, holding the hands of women who loped behind the men. No, it wasn't really running, he thought as he studied their movements, rather more a series of long, gliding steps and hops mixed with brief sprints. Not a charge at all, but simply a fast-paced dance pattern.

The Unyoros circled around them, forming two parallel rings. Chanting at the top of their lungs, the men continued to shake their weapons while the ululations of the women added to the cacophony. A dozen tall, lithe Unyoro warriors strode among the members of the caravan. They showed no surprise at seeing white-skinned visitors, although they did stare wonderingly at Florie's golden hair. One of the Unyoros briefly conferred with Richarn.

"I don't understand their tongue other than a few words," the Nubian said to Sam. "They say they have a slave woman named Bachita who knows Arabic. We can speak to them through her."

Two Unyoro men led a slave woman forward, their hands gripping her arms as she cringed in fear. Concentric rings of scars decorated her cheeks. Elaborate cicatrices circled each bare breast. She shook her head from side to side.

"I think I understand her anxiety," Florie said as she approached the slave girl. She reached into a box of trade goods and lifted a string of brightly colored beads. With a smile, she draped the beads around the slave's neck.

"We are looking for the *Luta N'zige*," Sam said in careful Arabic. "I am the brother of Speke and request a meeting with King Kamrasi. Surely your wise king can show us where the great lake lies?"

Bachita preened as her fingers rubbed the string of colorful beads the white *sitt* had given her as a present. As property, she had few rights in the lands of Kamrasi. "The king has sent these people as your escort," she said in a high-pitched voice.

"Just what we need," Sam spat, his hands on his hips as he surveyed the screaming, gesticulating mob. "What with those antelope horns, leopard skins, and that infernal screeching, it's more like an escort from

Hell." He turned his attention back to Bachita and pointed to several of the Unyoro warriors. "Tell them I am Speke's brother."

Bachita looked vacantly at Sam, then at the warriors.

Florie reached into her dilapidated canvas bag and produced one of the tortoiseshell combs Sam had bought for her in Bucharest in what seemed a lifetime ago. She offered the comb to the slave woman. "Here, my dear, take this."

Bachita, her mouth forming a perfect O, snatched the comb. She turned to one of the warriors and spoke to him. The man's eyes grew wide when she mentioned Speke's name, and he quickly relayed the information to several of his fellow warriors.

Sam grinned at Florie. "You have a way with the locals no matter where we travel."

"It takes a slave to know a slave," she replied curtly as she refastened her bag.Bachita nodded her head vigorously as the warrior spoke to her in a burst of words. "These men will take you to see King Kamrasi, O Brother of *Mollegge*," she said. "*Mollegge* is the one you call Speke."

Florie clung to Sam's arm as the Unyoro escort led the caravan through groves of plantain. Shadows blotted the ground as the sun dipped toward the horizon. Flickering torches cast an eerie, wavering light. As they entered a village consisting of perhaps thirty sturdy huts with conical roofs of brush and reeds, naked children, curiosity warring with their fear, ran up to them. Without hesitation, they touched Florie's hands, face, and hair. Women looked up from their cooking fires and grain-grinding stones, but did not speak. One girl, her nubbin breasts outlined with circles of white paint, filled a basket with bananas and joined the procession.

"Bachita, what is this?" Sam demanded when the escort stopped. They had entered a clearing hacked from the waving papyrus stalks. The ground was spongy. Mosquitoes whined voraciously. The hut facing them had holes in the roof and looked particularly dirty.

"The chieftains have told me that Kamrasi is not in Atada, this village, but in his main city at M'rooli," she replied, her eyes darting nervously about. "You will visit him shortly. He asks that you stay in the house the great lords Speke and Grant stayed in. Since you are Speke's brother, he knows you will understand."

A woman appeared with a load of firewood and deposited it in a ring of stones. One of the men laid his torch to the bundle until it ignited. The little girl carrying the basket of bananas placed the food inside the hut.

Sam's face grew dark with apprehension. "And when exactly will we meet Kamrasi?"

"A slave cannot know the thoughts of a great king," Bachita whined. "Perhaps in the morning."

Sam shook his head in disgust as the Unyoros departed. At least the fire and smoke from the camp blaze had diminished the cloud of mosquitoes.

Florie emerged from the hut. "It smells of mold and wetness, and I didn't want to look too closely at the vermin crawling on the ground. Do you think we could sleep next to the fire instead?"

"We have our blankets," he said, smiling thinly. "I'll cut some of the papyrus and lay it on the fire. It's wet enough to make smoke to keep the mosquitoes away."

With his heavy bush knife in hand, Sam waded into the moist fringe of the swamp and hacked an armful of papyrus fronds. He coughed as he laid a green sheaf on the fire, a backdraft of smoke momentarily stinging his eyes. With the blaze finally under control, he lay next to Florie and wrapped her in his arms. As she quickly drifted off to sleep, he gently moved a lock of hair that covered her eyes and kissed her forehead. She shivered against the warmth of his flesh and the woolen blanket. Fever was setting in.

"Now I know why Speke wanted to leave Africa so badly," he murmured.

***

Florie shaded her eyes against the glare of sun, then rubbed her temples to drive away the lingering ache in her head. M'rooli, the capital of the Unyoros, didn't look like much of a city, she decided. A crude palisade flanked equally crude gates. A dozen Unyoro warriors had gathered outside the gates, spears over their shoulders. Some of the men balanced on one leg, the soles of the opposite feet planted obliquely against their knees. She wasn't sure if they were guards or a welcoming party.

Sam whistled tunelessly as he rested the Fletcher rifle in the crook of his arm. Buckled over his shoulder was a leather baldric with his sword attached.

"I wish I had a highland bagpipe," he said as he worked an imaginary pipe with wiggling fingers and lifting elbow. "That'd put the fear of God in this savage king."

"I've heard one of those *baggypipes* before, when I was growing up in Hungary. It was before Christmas, Saint Micholás Day, I think." Florie tried to sound serious, but her voice broke with a giggle. "I just remember it screeched like someone had poked a cat in the eye."

"I do wish our clothes were in better shape," Sam commented as he inspected the frayed cuffs of his trousers. "Everything is in rags. Maybe we'll have to dress in bark cloth. Then you could show off your womanly charms like Bachita."

"I don't think I have any womanly charms left," Florie said sadly. She unlaced the top of her shirt and peered down her front. "Oh, no, they're gone," she blubbered in mock anguish. "All I have down there are two dried up prunes."

"Well, if you're a prune, then I'm an onion." Sam smiled, trying to cheer her up. "My layers are simply being peeled away. Pretty soon there'll be nothing left of me except a worthless core. I wonder if my daughters would even recognize me looking like this."

"What are they like?" Florie asked hesitantly. "You told me once you have a daughter a little younger than me."

Sam was startled to silence. In the time he and Florie had been together, he had rarely spoken of his daughters, or of Henrietta. It was part of the barrier he had erected to fence off his English life from Africa. He sifted through his memories. "Edith is fifteen now," he finally said. "She is much like me: stubborn and never quite accepting things the way they are. She's a good shot, too, and wanted to come with me to Africa, you know. And Agnes is so serious, so much like her mother. Constance finds humor in everything. I remember trying to punish her for taking rock candy when she was told not to. She made such a funny face that I let her off the hook. And Ethel," his voice faded, "was little more than a baby when I left. I wonder how much she has changed."

"I should like to meet them some day."

"Perhaps," he said softly, half to himself. "Perhaps."

"Thank you, Sam," Florie said.

She swept her hat from her head and handed it to Richarn, then undid her thick braid. The freed locks drifted like golden waves over her shoulders. Her hair, she decided, had had a striking effect on other Africans, so why not the Unyoros as well? And while it might well be a more soothing savior than Sam's guns, she welcomed the cold bulge of her revolver against her belly.

"Are you ready?" Sam asked.

"Yes," she replied firmly.

***

"Miss Baker, I presume?"

Min extended her hand, which was accepted gracefully by Sir Roderick Murchison.

"So good of you to see us, sir," she said quietly. She placed her hand on the shoulder of the young woman standing next to her. "This is my niece, Edith Baker. She is Samuel Baker's eldest daughter." Edith curtsied politely.

Murchison offered chairs to his visitors and directed his secretary to bring tea. As he settled into the hard chair he preferred, he paused and studied the women. Miss Baker the Elder was definitely maiden aunt material, he decided. She looked stalwart and thickish, and was probably a real bulldog in an argument. As for the niece, clear blue eyes gleamed with an inner strength far exceeding her adolescent years.

"And what can I do for you today?" he asked.

"My brother Samuel left for Africa nearly four years ago," Min began. "We know he completed his journey to Abyssinia, but the last letter we received from him was when he was in Khartoum. Now we've read Captain Speke's book and discovered how the two men met in a place called Gondokoro. That was the last news we had concerning my brother, and that's well over a year ago. Certainly the Royal Geographical Society must have heard something by now."

"I would like to know if my papa is dead," Edith blurted fearlessly. Her gaze locked into Murchison's as if to read his very thoughts.

"I'm truly sorry, ladies, but I have not received any recent information," Murchison replied, carefully choosing his words. "Be assured the Foreign Office and the Society are doing everything in their power to find out what has happened to him, but, quite honestly, the last information we have is the same information you have."

"I am not afraid if you tell me he has died," Edith said.

Min patted her niece's arm comfortingly. "Why don't you step outside, my dear," she said. "I would like to speak to this gentleman alone."

Dutifully, Edith rose and left the room. As she exited, she left the door open a crack and paused just beyond to listen.

Min wrung her hands. "Is it true? You honestly don't know if he is dead?"

"We've heard nothing," Murchison replied bluntly.

"Then have you heard anything about my brother traveling with a foreign woman? There has been some word about that, too. If so, it's that kind of information I must keep from his children."

Roderick Murchison hesitated before answering. For a moment he wished he had followed his boisterous early life as an avid foxhunter rather than turning to geology and geography. "No, Miss Baker. I've heard nothing of that sort of vile rumor," he lied.

Min looked relieved. "Thank you," she said, accepting the hand he offered in parting.

Min and Edith clambered into the cab waiting outside the Society's offices. The older woman gave her niece a reassuring hug, but Edith was strangely quiet for the remainder of the day.

Chapter Twenty

Kamrasi, King of the Unyoro, perched atop a copper stool centered in a broad carpeting of zebra skins. A long, elegantly folded garment of bark cloth hung from his right shoulder to his ankles. A single copper bracelet adorned his left arm. He impatiently tapped one carefully manicured finger to remind the slender slave girl standing behind him to keep her ostrich feather fan waving to drive away the flies. These white visitors should not see a king brushing away common pests.

"Where is this brother of *Mollegge*?" Kamrasi demanded, a touch of impatience tingeing his voice. "Is he bearing so many gifts for me that he keeps me waiting?"

"We do not know," replied one of the chieftains. "I gave the white man your invitation. You remember from the time that *Mollegge* spent with us that these whites are strange creatures."

"That is true," Kamrasi agreed. "*Mollegge* acted as if his wits had deserted him, talking to no one but himself, even refusing the gift of our women. But this brother has brought his own woman, you say?"

"A wondrous being with hair like the sun and skin the color of an elephant's tusk," the chieftain answered. "I have seen so myself."

The king rolled his slightly protuberant eyes in anticipation. "Then perhaps he is preparing this female as a gift. *Mollegge* and his friend came to us like beggars, offering us few presents of mention. I believe they tried to cheat us. This new white man, this brother, he will have to give us much finer presents."

A trumpet suddenly blared strident and discordant notes from outside the city.

"What was that?" the king asked, cringing slightly. "It is more horrible than the cry of a maddened elephant."

"I believe the brother of *Mollegge* has arrived," the chieftain replied. "And he does not come like a beggar."

***

Sam coolly surveyed the meeting area in M'rooli. He had entered through the city gates seated on an *angarep* covered with giraffe hide and borne on the shoulders of four of his strongest men. Florie walked boldly behind him, her hair shimmering on her shoulders. Richarn led his little column of porters, proudly carrying an unfurled Union Jack in one hand and the noisy trumpet in the other, blasting away on the instrument as he saw fit. The porters were strung out in single file to make the visitors appear in greater numbers than they actually were. Balanced on their shoulders were the remnants of the trade goods.

As Sam was set down before the king, he noted that besides the little girl with the ostrich feather fan, Kamrasi had stationed ten heavily armed warriors near his stool. Hundreds of curious Unyoro men and women formed a semicircle to partially ring the meeting grounds. Sam curled his finger, motioning Bachita forward to act as interpreter.

Kamrasi scowled. This foreigner was obviously quite used to giving orders.

"I am the brother of Speke," Sam said, his voice rolling like quiet thunder. "Do you recognize the emblem of Speke that we carry?" He motioned to Richarn to lift the flag high and let it wave in the breeze.

"I, who am the light of the Unyoro, recognize the emblem of Speke," Kamrasi said to his lieutenant who, in turn, relayed the acknowledgement to Bachita. "You have entered my lands as he did, as a friend. What is it you want in my country?"

"We seek a great lake called the *Luta N'zige*," Sam replied. "My queen and many of our learned men would have knowledge of its location. They would know if the great river Nile descends from its belly. We have brought you many gifts to show that we have come in good will."

Sam waved to his men who trotted forward to display the presents. There were strings of beads, a fistful of iron knives, several razors, a pair of pocket watches that ticked loudly when wound, and a small carpet of intricate Persian-style design. Florie had added a hand mirror, another of her precious combs, and a bolt of brightly colored calico to the cache. Beads and bangles and buttons glinted and glimmered in the bright sunlight.

Kamrasi's expression did not change. He eyed the wonders of the white man with seeming indifference although these gifts were better than those *Mollegge* had given. Still, the visitors must have more to offer. The flapping Union Jack seemed to hold some kind of magic, and certainly the fine rifle the stranger cradled in his arm would make an excellent present. But what of this white woman? Kabuta was right. She had hair like the sun and skin the shade of ivory. Yes, she would be the ultimate gift. But what did the white man value most: the woman, the magical emblem, or the fine rifle? He would have to negotiate carefully with *Mollegge's* brother to get exactly what he wanted.

Bachita listened to what the chieftain said, making sure she understood the king's message correctly. "Kamrasi says that he will have his men guide you to the Dead Locust Lake. But he will need further proof of your friendship. The magical cloth your servant waves would indeed make a fine gift. And the beautiful rifle you carry."

Sam smiled and shook his head. "Tell the king that the cloth only has magic for people of my country. My rifle is my companion and knows my spirit. Together we have taken many heads of game and have fed our followers well. My spirit would wail in sorrow should the rifle be given away."

Kamrasi remained expressionless. Inwardly, however, he was gloating. The white visitor valued the cloth on the stick and the rifle. Perhaps the female would be obtainable, not as a pure gift, but with a trade.

The Unyoro chieftain relayed new orders to Bachita. The slave woman's brow knit with uncertainty as she spoke to Sam. "Kamrasi says that if you are unwilling to part with your magic cloth and gun, then you must be willing to get rid of something less desirable. He offers you two of his wives for your white woman."

"What?" Sam stared at Bachita in amazement.

Kamrasi rose from his copper stool and strutted toward Florie. She squeezed her fists tighter as the king's narrow gaze traveled from her face to her feet. When he spoke, his voice was imperious and commanding.

"You will be guided to the great water, but your woman will remain with me," Bachita interpreted. "I desire the woman with the hair of gold. You may take three of my wives in exchange."

The king lifted Florie's arms and inspected them. He poked her breasts and grinned. She swatted his hand away.

Growling his anger, Sam took a single step toward Kamrasi. Spears were instantly leveled at his chest.

Florie angrily planted her hand on the king's chest and pushed him backward. Kamrasi gasped at the sacrilege. He ordered a spearmen toward her. Before the warrior could strike, she slammed her shoulder into the king and he collapsed onto his chair. In a moment, her revolver was pressed against Kamrasi's cheek.

For a dozen heartbeats, there was absolute silence in M'rooli. Kamrasi's protruding eyes screwed down toward the muzzle of the pistol and the terrible white woman whose lips snarled furiously and whose cheeks were flushed crimson. He knew what the weapon could do; he had received such a gift from *Mollegge* and had shot one of his own slaves with it to prove his power. But this dangerous, wild woman was another matter.

Sam broke the silence first. "One of these days, my dear, you're going to create an awful mess with that toy of yours," he said quietly, his eyes focused on her tightened trigger finger.

"All of my percussion caps were ruined in the swamp," Florie said, her voice beginning to tremble. "This damned thing won't fire anymore, but I'll wager the King of Kings doesn't know that."

Sam grinned. "Then, my little Medusa, lower the hammer and slowly back away. I will give the king his gift."

As Florie stepped back from Kamrasi, Sam raised his hands, palms outward, toward the king. "Bachita, tell Kamrasi that in our country my queen forbids that wives be exchanged. Tell him I would rather give him a gift close to my heart."

The Unyoro monarch blinked rapidly, afraid that the crazy woman with the sun in her hair would attack him again. He listened to the slave and nodded his head tactfully. Better to let the brother of *Mollegge* speak, he reasoned, than have him release that pale-skinned fury once more.

Sam lifted the baldric over his head and offered his sword to one of the chieftains. The man bowed as he presented the weapon to his sovereign.

Kamrasi, still blinking, swished the sword from its scabbard, admiring its heft and the gleam of its long, curving blade. Yes, this indeed was a gift worthy of a king and was by far better than a mad, unwilling wife, no matter what her appeal. He could still have the last laugh, however.

"The brother of *Mollegge* has presented me with many fine gifts," Kamrasi said through his slave. "I did not mean any insult to him or to his woman. I would have been happy to give him five wives for his, truly a great bargain. But their ways are not our ways. In the morning, I'll send warriors to escort him to the *Luta N'zige*, but it lays many, many marches away, perhaps the passing of two full moons or more."

One of the chieftains suddenly bent toward the king and mumbled some words. Kamrasi's eyes flared angrily and the warrior hurriedly stepped away. The king smirked inwardly in satisfaction even as he scolded his lieutenant. He had seen the white man's face grow bitter at the news. They were fools like *Mollegge* and his partner in seeking the birthplace of the great river, he thought. And for what? To scratch-scratch markings with their tiny sticks on the white tablets so thin you could practically see through them? To make little drawings they called maps? It would be different if they had found great treasure, or vast herds of cattle at the fountains of the river, but theirs was a peculiar madness.

The king of Unyoro beckoned to his chieftains, his fan girl, and the slave appointed to carry his stool, pivoted on his heel and left the compound still swinging his sword. The audience was over. But for weeks afterward, the gossip in Kamrasi's villages swirled around how the white *sitt* had challenged the mighty king.

***

Sam's heart sank as his little band left M'rooli. If the lake was indeed two or more months' march away, as the king said, it would be late April or May before they arrived. The rainy season would again be a threat, and by the time they returned to Gondokoro, the winds would be blowing from the wrong direction. Did they have enough strength to continue such a long journey?

His shoulders bowed as if he carried a ponderous load. "Two months to go yet, I'm afraid."

Florie forced a smile. The desolate sound in Sam's voice weighed upon her. "Don't worry," she said, trying to sound cheerful. "We'll see this through to the end."

"No, no," Bachita exclaimed excitedly. Since King Kamrasi had not beckoned her, she had followed Sam and Florie out of the city, hoping to receive more gifts. "The *Luta N'zige* is only a few days from here, not the passing of two full moons."

"What do you mean?" Sam's brows furrowed in confusion. "Didn't Kamrasi say it was many days' march?"

The slave girl rubbed her hands nervously over her breasts.

"Say it again, child," Florie said softly as she lay a calming hand on Sam's forearm. Bachita was probably older than she was, but behaved more like a young girl.

The slave's eyes darted toward the comb blended among Florie's blond tresses. It was a twin to the one she had received earlier. Florie removed the item and presented it to her.

"When Kamrasi said that the lake was two full moons away, one of his chieftains tried to correct him by saying it was only this many marches," Bachita explained as she held up a hand to display three digits. "He said that the lake lies beyond the river in the direction of the setting sun. The king was very angry with him."

Florie glanced quizzically from Bachita to Sam. "What does she mean?"

"Perhaps Kamrasi plans mischief," Sam replied as he rubbed his chin thoughtfully. "I wouldn't doubt that his spies saw that we've been ill with the fever. If he keeps us on the trail long enough, maybe he figures we'll perish and then all we own would be his."

"And his so-called guides would be there to pick up what they and the king want," Florie added.

"Speke and Grant warned me about Kamrasi," Sam said. "That bug-eyed creature practically robbed them of everything they owned. When he finally let them leave his country, they looked more like a pair of wayward scarecrows. He even grabbed their medicine chest. I hope Speke had left plenty of laxatives in it, if you know what I mean."

"Don't be vindictive," Florie scolded with mock indignation.

"Vindictive? Hell, Bachita says that if we go with the guides south for a day, we'll reach a river I think Speke called the Kafoor. If we cut due west from there, we'll find the lake in a day or two. Let's move out within the hour."

***

A sweltering sun hung high in a cloudless sky overlooking the trail leading from M'rooli. Florie lifted her face to note the sun's position, but the movement made her dizzy. She closed her eyes and swayed on the saddled ox. She squared her shoulders and gritted her teeth. Sam mustn't notice her weakness.

A short distance ahead, Sam rode with Kamrasi's promised guides. The two Unyoros were young warriors armed with lances ornamented with brass wire. The taller one, named Rabonga, had crisscrossing decorative scars on his chest. The younger lad, Nagomo, had no marks on his skin and had not yet achieved distinction as a hunter or warrior. A third figure stumbled dejectedly after them. Bachita had been ordered by her master to continue as interpreter, or perhaps as punishment for showing off the gifts the white travelers had given her.

Florie dragged her forearm across her sweaty brow. The moist air filled her lungs, making breathing difficult. She swayed again. Hour plodded into hour. By the time they camped for the night, she could barely walk. She made sure Sam wasn't watching her when she slid from the saddle, but the moment her feet touched the ground, her knees buckled. With her back to the ox for support, she waited until her head quit spinning. It took a long time.

"You're hardly eating anything," Sam observed as he sat next to her at the campfire. He reached over and touched her forehead. "Fever."

"I'll be fine," she said hoarsely. "There's no quinine left so I'd better fight through this here and now. If you don't mind, I'm turning in."

As she retreated to her *angarep,* her legs wobbled. She closed her eyes tightly as the fever seized her in a grip that clamped her ribs like a vise. Shivers twitched her body, despite her blankets. Yellow suns appeared to drift behind her eyelids. Sharp spasms knotted her muscles. Sweat poured as her breathing became shallow and labored. Her brief snatches of sleep were punctuated with horrible hallucinations; the images were mercifully unclear, but left her with an awful sense of dread.

In the middle of the night, she started awake, wide-eyed and shaking, looking for Sam. But he was taking his turn on guard duty. A hyena cackled obscenely in the distance. The undertaker of Africa, she thought to herself. She fought to stay awake, but once more drifted into an agitated sleep.

Just before dawn, she awoke with lances of pain darting through her skull. The motion of pushing back her blanket and swinging her legs left her feeling dizzy and nauseous. Sitting on the edge of the *angarep*, she cupped her head in her hands. Mosquitoes hummed threateningly as the seething blister of sun creased the horizon. It would be another long, hard day in the stifling heat and humidity.

Sam rattled the flap of the tent. "Florie, time to get up. We have to get moving."

"I'll be right out," she croaked, hoping her voice sounded stronger than she felt. She waited for Sam to leave, then padded to a shallow basin of water. The liquid felt deliciously cool as she splashed it on her face, across her neck, down the front of her shirt, but then caused her to shiver violently. A convulsion wracked her belly and she vomited into the basin. Outside, she heard the men packing supplies. One of the oxen bawled. Soon the tent would be taken down. Hurriedly, she cleaned away her purge and dressed. "He won't find me weak, not with the lake so near," she pronounced woozily. "Please, God, don't let it be far."

***

Three miserable, steaming hours dragged by. To Florie, it felt like three years. She tried to remain alert, to listen to Sam explain to their two Unyoro guides that he did not want to follow the Kafoor River to the south, but that he wanted to cross it and head directly west. Her glassy-eyed stare fixed on the blue-green haze of distance. The lake was supposedly in that direction, perhaps at the foot of a line of hills that appeared more apparition than reality through the quivering lines of heat.

"Bachita," Sam snapped. "Tell them that King Kamrasi has ordered them to guide us, no matter which direction we take. If they are ever questioned which way we went, all they need say is that we followed our feet."

After Bachita's translation, a puzzled look creased Rabonga's face. Then he suddenly clamped his hand on Nagomo's shoulder and erupted with laughter. The younger Unyoro winced.

"Rabonga says that is a stupid thing to say, but funny," Bachita said. "He thinks Kamrasi would enjoy the joke. He is, after all, one of Kamrasi's sons. He says he will guide you directly to the lake."

Sam grinned. "Good. Now that that's settled, we should get going. Bachita, tell the guides to take the lead. Richarn, get the men up and moving. Florie, are you all set to go?"

Florie, slumping in her saddle, snapped erect when Sam called. For a moment she thought she saw Mahomet el-Nar and his henchmen lurking in the bushes, then realized it was a hallucination brought on by the fever. "Ready," she rasped weakly.

Within an hour, the caravan reached the banks of the Kafoor where it bent to the south. Sam surveyed the stream critically. "Looks like the River Styx, if you ask me."

Through her fever, Florie gazed at the river with dread. It meandered sluggishly amidst chunks of floating vegetation, a morass of branches, and an undulating scum of green algae. It reeked of decay, heat, and sickness.

"This deep here?" Sam asked Rabonga as he held his hand at waist level. The tall guide glanced at the river, and then placed his hand just below his breastbone.

"Too deep for the oxen to swim with all that debris floating on the surface," Sam said, concern etching his face. "We'll leave the animals here and have three of our men take them back to the Karuma Falls where we first met the Unyoros. Send Nagomo with them so they don't get lost. I'm afraid we're going to be on foot for us the rest of the way."

Rabonga ordered Nagomo to lead the oxen and porters away. When they were out of sight, he scrambled down the dusty slope to the river and stepped tentatively into the matting of algae. The algae shifted with a peculiar greasy motion. Raising his spear above his head, Rabonga waded deeper into the flow. The morass reached his chest, staining his flesh a sickly green. Then he was across the river and waving to the others to follow. Next came the porters and Bachita, threading their way across the Kafoor, bearing little more than a few guns, ammunition, and several bales of necessary supplies. The tent and *angareps* were left with the oxen.

"Come on, Florie, we're next," Sam said. "Yaseen will bring up the rear. Now hang on to my hand and step lively."

Florie reached out her hand, sensing rather than feeling his strong, reassuring grip. But even though Sam was in front of her, she couldn't see him. Day suddenly turned to night. The heat and stink of the air poured into her, through her. A furnace seemed to consume her body; a maul of fire hammered at the back of her brain. The mud sucked at her feet. Two steps. Three. Four more steps. This had to end!

Sam involuntarily released her hand as he windmilled his arms to maintain his balance. As he found secure footing, he reached back for her. But to his horror, Florie's face contorted in agony. He stretched toward her, but she crumpled and slid beneath the surface.

"Florie," Sam cried as he plunged toward her. Black water showed through a gap in the algae where she had been standing, then disappeared as the green scum closed back. "Florie!" He sloshed mightily against the river's turgid current, desperately searching for her. Yaseen struggled toward him from the east bank. More of the men splashed into the stream to help.

Spitting water and algae, Sam fought his way toward where Florie had vanished. He swung about frantically, crying her name. Then his foot contacted a solid form. His fingers groped through the morass, touched her arm, lost contact, then found it again. In a surge of water and greasy scum, he pulled her to the surface and squeezed her tightly against his breast. A glance at her pale, breathless face chilled him to the bone. With legs churning and breath exploding in ragged gasps, he carried her toward shore. Yaseen and Rabonga reached him and helped lift Florie's body above the river's surface.

An eternity seemed to pass before Sam felt his feet scrabble on firmer ground. He collapsed, coughing, and tore frantically at the laces of Florie's shirt. Linking his fingers under the small of her back, he pulled upward, forcing her to arch. Her mouth gaped. He pulled again and again, then released his hold and pushed against her ribs with the heels of his hands, pumping up and down. Water spewed from between her lips as he rolled her to her side. With his heart in his throat, he felt for her pulse. "Good Jesus, Florie, please breathe," he pleaded as he massaged her breast and arms. "Richarn, bring me brandy!"

Richarn stared for an instant, then sprang toward a water-soaked bundle lying on the bank. He rummaged through its contents before finding the corked brown jug.

Sam trickled a little of the spirits into Florie's mouth. She choked and sputtered in reaction. Her chest heaved as she sucked in a raw breath.

"That's the way," he whispered, cradling her head against his chest. "Just breathe and sleep. We'll get you well again."

"What is wrong with her, Baker Pasha?" Bachita asked in a frightened voice. In her nervous excitement she had scratched her breasts until bright beads of blood dappled her dark skin.

"It's the sun stroke or the fever," Sam said as he scraped away the scum that scabbed Florie's arms and neck. "We have to find a village where she can rest. Ask Rabonga where we should go. Hurry!"

Several of the porters cut saplings and bound them together to form a crude stretcher. Sam wrapped Florie in a blanket and gently laid her on the framework. Against the dark fabric, her skin seemed startlingly white. The gray circles under her eyes heightened her pallor. Her breath rattled horribly. He poured water into a cloth and bathed her face.

Rabonga stooped over Florie's recumbent form and shook his head. He straightened, jabbered at Bachita, and pointed westward.

"He says there is a village a day's march, but he doesn't think the *sitt* will make it," Bachita said fearfully.

Sam closed his eyes and touched his forehead to Florie's. It didn't matter what Rabonga thought, only that he find a place where she could rest.

"Time's wasting," he said and motioned to his men. Together they lifted the stretcher and followed Rabonga away from the river. An animal trail twisted through the dense vegetation and around mosquito-infested swamps. A herd of waterbuck splashed through the shallows, their ribbed horns bobbing. In the distance, a lion coughed.

Sam felt like an automaton walking mechanically at Florie's side as they wandered through a little valley filled with tall papyrus rushes. To him, the rushes looked like the black plumes of a hearse waving over her limp, pallid body.

Just before sunset, the little party trudged into a village. It was empty.

"Sickness drove everyone from here," Rabonga said. "We must not stay. There are bad spirits here."

"You can go if you like," Sam replied dazedly. "The *sitt* and I will sleep here tonight."

The porters placed Florie in a hut where dark shadows gathered. Sam dug in his pack and unwrapped a ball of animal fat from its layer of waxen cloth. He discovered the bottom half of a broken water jug inside the hut and plopped the fat into it, then tore an old, threadbare towel into strips to serve as wicks. Once lit, the flames spit and sputtered. The stinking glimmer of light drove the shadows back.

Gently touching Florie's face, he outlined her cheekbones and jaw. His fingers brushed against her still lips. Her skin felt waxen and warm. The golden hair, plastered by sweat to her skull, only accentuated her paleness. She looked incredibly fragile, as if the slightest pressure of his hands on her skin would leave bruises.

Florie suddenly gasped. Her body convulsed as her legs kicked spasmodically.

Sam threw his body over hers to hold her still, cradling her head in his arms protectively. She thrashed for a few more moments, then went lax. Her chest sagged, barely moving.

Richarn and Bachita, wide-eyed with fright, stood frozen by the violence of her seizure. Sam placed his ear over her heart, then rose, his face ashen. He arranged the blanket over the dying woman. His eyes were deep pools of misery as be rested his hand on the young Nubian's shoulder.

"Go, my friend, and look for the pick," he mumbled. "We will start digging a grave for the *sitt*."

Richarn bolted from the hut, tears streaming down his cheeks.,

Chapter Twenty-one

In the dim light of the false dawn, Sam slumped against the rough, outer walls of the abandoned Unyoro hut, his exhaustion complete. The cool air smelled of moist earth recently disturbed and the dank mold of rotting vegetation. His hands and clothes were caked with dirt from the grave dug at the edge of the village. With demoniacal fury, he had attacked the ground with the pickax, as if the exertion would cleanse him of the hopeless feeling chilling his heart. The broken blisters on his palms stung with sweat and blood.

Florie's grave was ready.

The last of the animal fat candles guttered low, its rancid, burnt odor mixing queasily with the raw, earthy smells. Silence, like a funereal shroud, descended on the cluster of huts, muting the constant drone of insect and arboreal life. But he was aware of only one sound drifting through the night air: Florie's shallow, painful breathing.

It's only a matter of time now, he thought wearily. She is in God's hands.

Sam fought to stay awake, to listen for her, but his head bobbed with fatigue and his eyes drooped shut. He was sure he could still hear her, but there were other noises too. Indistinct scrapings. Voices. Darkened, blurred images that did not belong in Africa.

"Sam, you really shouldn't be with this woman," came a whisper from the night.

He blinked as a shadow loomed in the darkness. He knew that voice.

"Your vows were with me, Sam."

"Henrietta?"

"Yes, Sam. Why did you forsake my memory and leave home?"

"But ... but you died." He squinted into the shadows, but in the pale pre-dawn it was like peering through smoky gauze. "The girls ... I couldn't care for them by myself."

"Did you even try?"

"Yes. Yes, I did. They were with me wherever I traveled."

"Always to be watched by someone else." The shadow seemed to glide at the edge of his vision. *"Tell me, Sam, what are the names of our daughters?"*

"Why ... why there's Edith, and Agnes, and Constance ... and ... and ..."

"You don't even remember our baby, Ethel."

"But I do," he groaned.

"And now you're here in Africa, in the most God forsaken area of the world

where the bounty of our Lord Jesus Christ hasn't even reached. And with a woman who has usurped my place in your life. You should be with your children. This foreign woman is not part of our family."

"She's right, Sam," whispered another wraith.

Sam felt a prickle of fear creep down his spine. "Who the hell are you?"

"Why Sam, I'm disappointed. I'm Mollegge."

"Speke?"

"Sam, let the wench die. Honors will be heaped on you when you return to England, like they were heaped on me. After all, isn't that what men like you and me want? To be idolized? To be remembered for our great deeds? Everyone will want to wine and dine you. You'll be famous, but not with that woman at your side. You're not really married to her, are you? What will people say?"

"Papa?"

Sam gulped, struggling to peer through the shadows.

"Papa?"

"Edith?"

"Yes, Papa, we're all here, the four of us."

Sam reached out, his fingers clutching through the darkness. "But I can't see you."

"No Papa. We've all changed. We're older and more grown. Even little Ethel has become quite the young lady. You should see her, but, of course, you can't. You've missed so much of us. Leave the woman and come home. She's not our mother."

"Edith? Agnes?"

"Come home, Papa."

The voices were lost among the tendrils of mist seeping from the jungle. In his deep slumber, Sam twitched and moaned as he listened for other dark shadows. But the gathering silence was like that of a tomb.

A little later, a hyena laughed its banshee laugh. Perhaps it smelled death in the air, the promise of a carrion feast.

Shuddering, Sam blinked groggily awake. His thoughts were muddled, haunted by his nightmare visitations. Damned hyena. His poor, dear Florie would be laid to rest in this lonely, tragic place, and that filthy beast would come pawing at the grave to disturb her remains. He must not let that happen.

Florie? Lord God, he'd fallen asleep! His arms thrashed as he struggled to his feet, straining to detect her raspy breathing from within the hut. There should be some kind of sound; instead it was grimly silent. He staggered to the doorway and paused, fearing to enter its darkness.

The sun was peeking over the horizon, its first pure rays streaming through the layers of dripping palm fronds. With his shoulders drooping with despair, he entered the hut. He could just distinguish the outline of

Florie's still body lying on the stretcher. He stumbled to her, sank to his knees, and lifted her hand to his lips.

"Sam?"

The voice was barely a whisper. Did it come from the thin bundle on the cot or was it another wraith from his dreams?

"Sam? I can't see you."

"I'm here." His voice quavered, unsure if he was still wrapped in his nightmare. The flesh of her arm felt cool to his touch, almost too cool.

"I owe you so much." Her words were faint.

He rubbed her hand against his cheek, then kissed her palm. "You owe me nothing. It's I who owe you."

A shadow of a smile curved her lips. Then she sighed and was quiet.

"Florie?" Sam shook her gently. "Florie?"

Her eyelids fluttered. Her gasp was long and thin. Her strength was ebbing. "Find the lake, Sam. I'm only a burden. Please let me die."

"What?" He blinked in shock. "Die? No."

"When you return home, remember me please," she whispered. "I love you."

"Florie, you can't quit now." He cradled her head in his arms. "You're coming to England with me. I promise."

Her breath rattled ominously.

"Florie, I love you. Don't leave." Sam's lips brushed hers. She murmured something indistinct, shivered once, and closed her eyes

Sam lost track of time as he held Florie, stroking her hair, outlining her face with his fingers. Sometime during the mid-morning, he drifted asleep again. He had tried to fight it, to stay awake and watch over the pale shadow dying in his arms, but his fatigue was overwhelming.

Dreams again filled his sleep. Henrietta was with him, but she was not the indicting wraith that had visited him earlier. This Henrietta was vague, as if she was partly made of fog, but she clutched his hand firmly as he lifted her to a narrow, rocky shelf. Palm fronds, moist with morning dew, dappled their clothes. The rising sun cast lances of liquid light through the heavy vegetation. Nearly eight thousand feet below stretched the Ceylonese valley and their homestead at Newera Eleya. Thick forests bordered the painstakingly cleared land. In the distance, a silver thread of river snaked through the trees. Rice paddies in the riverine valley glistened like tiny jewels. Nearer the base of the mountain, rows of coffee plants swelled in the growing heat. Henrietta laughed and pointed at a herd of elephants crossing the river far below. But her features were becoming more distinct, no longer Henrietta, replaced by a face that had become even more dear and precious to him. As she turned, her straw hat fell back on her shoulders. Soft mountain breezes caressed her golden waves of hair. Blue eyes gleamed. Never noticing the elephants, he crushed her to him and covered her lips with kisses. A moment later she was gone, a ghost evaporating in his embrace.

When he finally stirred several hours later, he thought he was awakened by voices. Then something soft touched his lips. Blue eyes and a wan smile greeted him.

"I'm so hungry," Florie whispered.

Sam laughed with delight. "Yes, of course you are," he cried joyously. "Your fever has broken. I'll find you something to eat. Richarn! Bachita! The *sitt* is awake!"

***

Bachita stepped carefully over a moss-covered log and cocked her head to listen. The guinea fowl clucked again, then burst into the open, a bundle of black-white spangled feathers running frantically about, cackling wildly as it tried to lure her away from its nest. Bachita lunged, but the hen darted away. She shook her head in disgust. It was too hard to bag the fast running bird. Instead, she studied the vegetation where the bird had come from. There! She eased through the tall grass and found a shallow bowl scratched into the dirt. Nestled within were a dozen brown eggs.

"God bless you, Bachita," Sam said as she handed him a basket filled with the eggs. She didn't understand his English words, but the smile on his face clearly conveyed his gratitude.

Florie dozed while Sam cooked. Richarn watched over her and smiled when Sam entered the hut. "She was talking in her sleep, Baker Pasha. Her dreams seem to be good dreams."

"And her color is much better," Sam said, placing his hand on her forehead. "The fever has fled."

Florie opened her eyes at his touch. Familiar, smiling faces ringed her. They jabbered and it took a few seconds to make sense of their words. Even Sam seemed to be talking in a strange tongue. Why did she feel so weak, so dizzy? She hazily recalled getting ready to cross a river with him, but after that there was nothing, as if time had slipped away.

"I have some food for you." Sam propped a pillow behind her shoulders and carefully spooned the liquid into her mouth. "It's not quite the kind of chicken soup grandmother would make," he apologized.

"I don't remember my grandmother," Florie said, "but it's perfectly delicious." A droplet of broth trickled down her chin, but before she could raise her hand to wipe it away, Sam had dabbed the offending soup with a cloth. "Please, you're treating me like a child," she said in mock irritation.

"You nearly died and now you're reborn. If I have to feed you like a baby to make you stronger, then so be it."

"What about the lake?" Florie asked, struggling to sit more upright. "Are we at the lake?"

Sam smiled grimly. "No, I'm afraid we haven't found it yet. Tomorrow, after you've had another day's rest, we'll start back for Gondokoro. If we're lucky, we can still catch the south wind to take us to Khartoum."

Florie pushed away the next spoonful of soup. "Without finding the *Luta N'zige*? No, Sam. We go on until we've seen and mapped the lake."

"My fixation on that damnable lake has nearly killed you," he said gently. "Nothing in the world is that important."

Florie's face suddenly flushed. She couldn't believe what she was hearing. Sam had driven himself, her, and all the others, to the breaking point and now he wanted to limp away. Astounding. Ridiculous. "That's the most blockheaded thing I've heard! No, it's not the fever," she grumped as she pushed his hand away from her cheek. "We've gone through so much, and I know we're very near."

"But it's not worth your life. Tomorrow we'll start back."

"Then you go back without me," she said, shaking her finger, scolding. "Once upon a time you gave me my freedom. It's been my choice to be with you ever since. I swore to myself I'd never leave you, but if you continue with this insanity, then I'll find the lake without you if I have to crawl to it on my belly." She glanced searchingly around the hut. "Where's my pistol?"

"You said all the percussion caps were ruined," Sam replied meekly, taken aback by her show of determination. "The gun is worthless."

"I don't care if it shoots or not. It'll make a dandy club I can use to beat some sense into you. Now help me stand up. I've got to get dressed."

Wisps of morning fog still drifted through the lowland forests as Sam assisted Florie to her feet and guided her outside the hut. She tried to walk on her own, but her legs wobbled and she sat down.

"I can do it, just give me a moment to gain my strength," she said.

"No, the men will carry you," Sam ordered. "Now lie down."

Gritting her teeth, she pushed herself to her feet and tried to take normal strides. She nearly collapsed again. "Fine, fine," she said, throwing her arms up in exasperation. "I'll ride, but we're still going to find the lake."

***

With Florie firmly ensconced on a stretcher of branches and palm leaves, Rabonga led the caravan through the forest. They trekked along the north ridge of a broad valley choked with swamps and thick jungles that stretched to the west. By staying on the high ground, they avoided most of the heavy vegetation and moisture. But ravines choked with stands of tall papyrus also gouged the ridges. The angles of descent and ascent became too severe for the porters to carry the sick woman on her litter.

"I can walk," she protested.

Sam made a face. "How far?"

Florie tilted her head back to view the next ridge they had to climb. The effort made her dizzy.

"On my back," he ordered, jerking his thumb to his shoulder.

Dutifully locking her arms about his neck, she hooked her feet around his hips. As they climbed, she pressed her cheek happily against his broad back. He had told her he loved her when she lay sick, she remembered, and had promised to take her back to England. And now they were climbing this hill as if they were a single entity. She wondered if the sun in England shone as deliciously warm as the sun in Africa.

Rabonga approached Sam after they cleared the ridge. Florie stood next to him, leaning on his arm. Bachita, panting with exertion, bent over with her hands on her knees.

"He says there is a village called Parkani just ahead," Bachita translated between gasps for air. "He has spoken to the village elders and told them of your coming. You will be made welcome. They don't have much food to feed such a party as ours, but they are willing to share."

Parkani was a cluster of perhaps twenty huts ringing several cooking fires. The ubiquitous horde of children greeted the caravan as it tramped to the edge of the village. They howled with delight as they glimpsed white skins and fair hair.

Sam raised his hand in friendship as three wrinkled old men with bark-cloth robes over their shoulders approached. He offered them the last few strings of beads, a folding knife, and the pickax as gifts. "I don't think we'll need that damned thing again," he said under his breath, jabbing his finger at the pick.

"Sam, look," Florie exclaimed as she pointed toward the cooking fires. Several naked girls tending the flames giggled and ran toward the huts.

"Indeed," he said, his brow wrinkling. "We've all seen naked girls before, my dear, or has the fever knocked you on the head again?"

"No, you *balfasz*!" She said the expletive in Hungarian. "Look what's cooking on the fire."

Sam's gaze focused on the circles of flames. Jabbed onto sharpened poles and baking slowly in the heat were several large fish with coarse, pink-orange scales. "Fish," he cried, rubbing his eyes in disbelief. "Those are fish. We must be very near the lake. Bachita, ask the elders how far to the *Luta N'zige*."

The elders conferred with each other, then pointed to the west where a range of mountains, blue in the distance, stood etched against the horizon. "The Old Ones say those mountains are on the far side of the lake," Bachita interpreted. "We are only a little way from the *Luta N'zige*, but it will be dark soon. They say if we start early in the morning, we will be there before the sun has climbed its highest."

Florie hobbled to Sam's side and threw her arms about him. "We're almost there," she said happily. She imagined walking hand in hand with him through a golden English wheat field. "We're almost done."

***

Thin wisps of night mist still clung to the bushes when Florie awoke. While the heavens above were still bathed in darkness, soft lemon and coral pastels brightened the eastern horizon. Sam was already preparing for the trip to the *Luta N'zige*. She watched in wide-eyed wonder at his frantic burst of energy as he finished gathering his equipment and notebooks.

"I need to sketch the route we've taken, perhaps do a watercolor of the lake. I do hope there are some paints left," he said to himself, unaware that she had awakened. "Then, to determine elevation, I have to use my thermometer to measure the change in the boiling temperature of water. After that, I'll have to find boats to take us on the lake so I can study its linkage to Lake Victoria that Speke and Grant discovered. I should get my instruments ready and—"

"You're tiring me out just listening to you," Florie interrupted as she levered herself on an elbow.

Sam's eyes burned brightly. "So much to do. I still have to arrange for a Parkani guide."

"Then leave me here," she pleaded as he finished packing the thermometer. "The men will have to carry me and I'll only slow you down. Your eyes will be my eyes. I'll follow you later."

He wheeled toward her, and, with a great sweep of arms and legs, plucked her from her blankets as if she were a child, then lifted her high so she had to look down at him. She tried to catch her breath and push him away, but she was helpless in his grasp.

He gazed deeply into her eyes. "You told me that we started this together and we'd finish together, even if you have to crawl to the lake on your belly."

"I wish you wouldn't quote me." She laughed as she finally disengaged from him. Her heart sang. She was Sam's partner; they had done this together. God, how she loved him!

When they went outside the hut, the Jalyn and Bishareen porters were waiting with the stretcher. "No, Sam, I don't need that," Florie said with determination.

Richarn chuckled. "*Sitt*, the men will not leave until you lie down."

"But—"

"They know how sick you were," Sam interrupted. "Now be a good patient so we can visit the lake."

The Parkani elders ordered a boy of about twelve years to guide the tiny caravan. With a wide grin at his new-found importance, the boy led Florie and Sam westward over a small grassy hill and into a deep valley thick with brush and papyrus. The sun slowly ascended, lighting the thick stands of jungle. Although it was early in the morning, the air felt hot and sticky. They struggled across the dank valley floor and toiled up the opposite slope. As they neared the summit, the Parkani abruptly turned and motioned to the crest.

"*Luta N'zige*," he said, his head bobbing up and down.

Florie turned toward Sam. She'd heard the guide's words, but somehow could not comprehend their full meaning. Rabonga gripped Sam's arm and gestured toward the summit. Only then did she realize the end of his journey was at hand. She expected Sam to yell at the top of his lungs and dash wildly toward his goal. Instead, he directed the porters to put the litter down.

"Remember, we do this together," he murmured as he placed his arm about her waist, lifted her to her feet, and half-carried her the remaining steps to the top of the hill.

The grassy scalp of the summit gave way to a sharp granite cliff revealing a vast panorama stretching below them for as far as they could see. "God in heaven," Sam said in a hushed voice.

Florie blinked in disbelief. Like a sea of quicksilver, the *Luta N'zige* sparkled with a billion motes of brilliance under the morning sun. Its motion was endless, its farthest boundaries wrapped in the mystery of distance. To the west, across the water many miles away, the great bluish range of mountains loomed like brooding sentinels unwilling to relinquish the lake's secrets.

"*Albert*," Sam declared loudly. "I name this lake Albert Nyanza after England's late prince consort. Somewhere to our south and east lies the Victoria Nyanza, so named after our illustrious queen by Captain John Hanning Speke. Together, Albert and Victoria give birth to the mighty Nile."

Florie bit her lip. She watched the Parkani trot down a zigzagging trail. Could this really be happening? Why didn't Sam just run down to the lake? Was he waiting for her?

"Come on," he said. "Let's find our way to the water." Before she could react, he swept her into his arms, and followed the Parkani down the hill and across a sand meadow dotted with palm trees, more palm trees, and then through a phalanx of papyrus.

Waves rolled onto a white, pebbly beach in an endless procession of liquid motion. Sam set her down in the sparkling shallows of Lake Albert. Luxurious, cool water lapped about her ankles. He dipped his cupped hands into the lake and tasted its waters. Then he raised a second cupping to her lips. Her eyes met his as she drank deeply.

***

From Sam's journal:

16 March (tentative)
We have procured three canoes from villagers on the lake and rowed to the north for two days. Precipitous cliffs surround us, the Albert Nyanza being a huge depression in the general landscape. Great mountain ranges border the lake on the west and southwest. There can be little doubt that other rivers feed this lake. Similarly, heavy rainfalls in the surrounding mountains must also contribute to the lake's posterity.

No European foot has ever trod the lake's sands before us, nor have the eyes of a white man ever scanned its vast expanse of water! I thank God for this opportunity.

19 March
We continued to paddle near the eastern shore. At times we passed beaches of white sand extending for hundreds of yards to the base of sheer cliffs. At other times the cliffs plunged directly into the lake so we could row directly up to them and push against them with the paddles. These great masses of rock are mostly granite and gneiss, but mixed with red porphyry. Giant euphorbia and feathery date palms project from clefts in the stone. Rivulets like liquid jewels formed tiny waterfalls that sprinkled us as we passed below them.

I have cut a mast and rudder for our canoe, and tied my blanket to the yardarm as a sail. I'm sure it is the first sailing vessel ever seen on the surface of this lake. It gives me benefit to explore more of Albert.

30 March
The lake has narrowed noticeably. The water has become quite dead, hardly stirring as we paddle on, yet when I concentrate on a bit of floating leaf, I can tell the current slowly moves to the north.

To our east is a vast cut of water flowing into this lake, Speke's Somerset Nile I am certain. Somewhere in that direction is Karuma Falls. But what should we do to get home? Should we follow the Albert Nyanza north into the unknown, or go east and take the longer, familiar, debilitating path that had brought us to this great wonder?

***

"Damn and damn," Sam cursed again as he read the tubes of the Casella thermometer. "How can this be?"

"I don't understand," Florie said, peering over his shoulder. "What is Mr. Casella telling you today?"

Sam scratched his head in wonder. "Speke told me he had calculated the elevation of Lake Victoria at thirty-seven hundred feet above sea level. Yet here, my thermometer reads two hundred seven point eight degrees Fahrenheit, which means Lake Albert is over a hundred feet lower than Victoria."

"And?" Florie tried to stay interested, but the calculation of the boiling point of water in relation to elevation eluded her.

"It means that Victoria feeds Albert and Albert feeds the Nile. Here, look at the map Jim Grant gave me." With a grimy forefinger, he pointed out the relative location of the Victoria Nyanza and the Somerset Nile flowing northwesterly out of it.

"And this is just about where we are," he said, stabbing with his finger at a vacant area on the map. "That's too short a distance between the two lakes for the elevation to drop that much. Unless .... " He studied the map again. "There has to be a greater waterfall between Karuma Falls and here, which would explain the drop between Victoria and Albert."

"Then the proof is in the seeing," Florie declared flatly, although she didn't quite know why finding another waterfall was so important. But Sam was happy and excited, and so she felt happy and excited for him. So much had changed since she had fallen ill, and then the wonder of finding the great lake. He was animated and full of energy. And he included her in everything. It was beyond wonderful.

"But I'm worried about fevers," Sam said.

She touched her fingers to his lips to silence him. "It's something both you and I have to contend with. We've been at death's door before. What's another knock? Besides, you know full well that your Geographical Society will question you about all your findings. I think it's best if we follow your hunch and find this new waterfall."

"I'm beginning to think you're tougher than I am," he said, kissing her lightly on the forehead. Before he could move away, she seized his arm and dragged him back. Her lips met his.

***

Florie shivered, despite the warm air, as moisture glistened on exposed flesh. Was it the coolness of the mists drifting lazily over the river causing her chill, or the mysterious roar growing in volume as their canoe proceeded upriver? She had heard muted thunder from the moment they had embarked at dawn's first light. Sam had noticed it, too. Now every stroke from the paddles drove them nearer the pulsing cacophony.

"The waters are getting too rough to paddle further upstream," Sam shouted above the din to his oarsmen. He crouched slightly at the midpoint of the canoe and pointed at a ribbon of sand bordered by thick rushes. "Swing around and land on that beach. We'll walk from there."

As the canoe crept near the thick stand of reeds, it suddenly swept in a violent half circle, its bow caught by whirlpools swirling among submerged rocks. The canoe's stern crackled into the vegetation. A loud snorting erupted at the intrusion, and a great bulk thrashed through the rushes.

"Hippo," Florie screamed, clutching the sides of the canoe as the bull hippopotamus crashed through the reeds and plunged into deeper water, waves swirling ominously. Then the river roiled as the huge animal heaved itself upwards, striking the bottom of the canoe with its powerful head, half lifting the craft from the river, then dropping it. The rowers screeched their fear as they clung desperately to the gunwales.

Sam, on his knees, lifted his Ceylon ten-bore and leaned over the side where the hippo had once more submerged. In the clear water, he saw its dark mass gliding below them, then turning in a short circle. He thumbed a hammer back and fired as the beast broke the surface. The shot missed, but the water foamed where it struck. Whether it was the report of the gun that scared the behemoth, or simply its satisfaction that it had frightened the puny creatures that had invaded its domain, the hippo broke off the attack and moved away.

"I'm glad he's gone, Sam," Florie said, her voice shaking with excitement. "Look!"

Monstrous crocodiles lurched into the water from the banks where they had been sunning. Great jaws gaped.

"Had we fallen in, you would have made a tasty morsel," Sam quipped as he reloaded his right barrel. "A quick snap-snap and that would have been it."

"And you would have given them a bellyache and the shits," Florie said wryly. "Don't you think we should head for shore?"

Sam nodded and directed the rowers toward the shingle of sand. With powerful strokes, they drove the canoe onto the beach, only too happy to be on dry land.

With the canoe beached, Sam lifted Florie to the sun-warmed sand. Hand in hand, they followed an animal trail that led upward through the jungle. A thin spray of moisture dappled the air with color as the sun burst over the edge of the eastern cliffs. Multicolored flycatchers and brown babblers flew around them, plucking insects from the air, while yellow-fronted tinker-birds chirped loudly as they hopped among the acacias fringing the cliffs.

Florie gasped in amazement when she and Sam emerged on a small crest of rock above the flood. Heavily wooded cliffs jutted into view, the deep emerald color of the vegetation standing in stark contrast to the pulsating spumes of brilliant white water billowing from the river's plunge down the dark stones of the gorge. A rainbow arched across the falls, its spangled ends disappearing into the froth.

"It must fall over a hundred and fifty feet," Sam said, shaking his head in disbelief. "It's simply magnificent. The force of the water means there is declining elevation the entire length. It explains the drop in the landscape between the two lakes and the two falls."

Florie tugged at his shirtsleeve. "Sam, you should name it after yourself," she said as he leaned close to hear her. "You've earned it."

With a smile, he shook his head. "No, my dear, not after me. This will be named after Roderick Murchison, president of the Geographical Society. He might be a pompous skinflint, but without his blessing, none of this would have been possible."

Squeezing his hand, she tried to shape the unfamiliar name with her mouth. She wasn't quite sure why Sam would honor another man and not take credit for himself after all he'd been through. It didn't really matter, though. Their journey was coming to an end.

"Does this mean we can go home now?" she asked hopefully.

Home. The word hammered deep into Sam's soul. He looked at her, his brow creased. Yes, he had promised to take her home. Part of him flushed with the warmth of Florie standing next to him, their arms touching. Another part recoiled in doubt and shame, wondering how England and his family would accept them. How would his daughters view her? What if word got out that he and she had been living together in Africa without marriage? Although he disliked the phrase *living in sin*, he knew in his heart that society would hang that chastising label about their necks without so much as a second thought. He had put the whole idea out of his mind for so long that mention of returning home was like a hard rap on his forehead.

"We'll worry about home once we get back to Khartoum," he replied carefully.

Chapter Twenty-two

The village of Kisoona burned. Mahomet el-Nar mentally calculated the wealth he would receive from Khurshid Aga as thick clouds of smoke boiled from a dozen houses set on fire by the slave raiders. Musket shots continued to crackle as the few Unyoros who had not been captured or killed fled into the forest.

This was the third—no, fourth village he and his men had raided since the fire the Englishman had started in the brush lands beyond Latooka territory, and Kisoona held a cache of ivory as well. He smiled grimly as he strutted around his prisoners, enjoying their shock and humiliation. A few of the women wailed and rattled their chains, their breasts quivering. Downcast, the young Unyoro men endured their captivity in silence. A vivid image of newly captured slaves bearing that horde of tusks northward paraded through his thoughts. Slaves and ivory! Yes, it had been a most prosperous trip. There was no reason to find the troublesome Englishman and his equally troublesome yellow-hair.

"We're done with this village," Mahomet growled to one of his henchmen. "Most of it has burned, and we captured as many slaves as we could. We'll stay here for the night, slaughter a cow or two for supper, and then leave for Gondokoro in the morning."

Stroking his beard, Mahomet wandered among the chained women. A young Unyoro woman shuffled back from him as he approached. With a chuckle, he fondled her breasts. "This one will do," he said meaningfully. "Put her in one of the huts."

As the sun slid murkily toward the horizon, flames flickered and shadows danced in the heart of ravaged Kisoona. Haunches of broiling beef hung over a cooking fire, fat dripping and hissing among the white-hot coals. The slave catchers had discovered several jugs of native beer and consumed those with the same gusto as the fire-seared roasts. They joked and relived their adventures, drinking and eating until their bellies were distended. Now liquor slurred their words, and their heads nodded in fatigue as the darkness in the jungle deepened. A single guard, his shoulders hunched against the chill air, dozed at the edge of the camp while the pale sliver of moon peeked from behind lazily drifting clouds.

***

Florie covered her mouth with her hand in horror as she stared at the wounded Unyoros. One man had his cheek and chin laid open by a sword cut, his blood crusted black on his face. Another pressed his bullet-shattered forearm tightly against his abdomen. Two more men, bloodied from slash marks, kept glancing fearfully over their shoulders. She tried to listen to what they were explaining to Sam and Rabonga while Bachita interpreted.

"There are slave catchers somewhere ahead of us," Sam finally said to her. "Can you smell the smoke? They've burned some of Kamrasi's villages and taken dozens of his people as slaves. Kamrasi has fled into the forest."

"I thought I smelled smoke," she said as she sniffed the air, her nose wrinkling. "Do you think Mahomet and his men are responsible?"

Sam ran his fingers through his hair and frowned. "Mahomet? Maybe, but I swear we gave them the slip a long time ago. Now I don't know what to expect."

"Can't we go around these slave catchers?"

"Rabonga says he is going to free his people. Apparently the slavers are camped in the ruins of Kisoona."

Although the wounded, pathetic Unyoro survivors clutched at her soul, the notion of facing slave raiders sent a ripple of apprehension down Florie's spine. "What are we going to do, Sam?"

He bared his teeth in an uncertain grin. "Rabonga and his few men won't have a chance against their guns. He needs our help and our rifles, so we go to war with him. If we're lucky, we'll catch the slavers unaware and free their prisoners."

"Then give me a gun," she demanded, her eyes narrowing with determination. "If it is the Dongolowans, I want to help get rid of them."

"Too dangerous," Sam replied, shaking his head. "If things go badly, you shouldn't be there. This is a fight I think you'd better stay out of."

As Sam pivoted toward his men, Florie grabbed his arm, her eyes blazing. "Don't turn away from me. If I have to, I'll follow you with my pistol even if it doesn't work. And if things do go badly, God forbid, what am I supposed to do alone in this jungle? We've been in this together from the start!"

Richarn and several of the porters shifted nervously. They had never seen the *sitt* challenge Baker Pasha so.

"Please," she said through gritted teeth.

Sam cast a helpless glance skyward. He had seen that look on her face before and knew it did little good to argue. He retrieved the Fletcher rifle and tried to look past her grin. "Here's your buffalo gun, freshly cleaned, mind you. I want you to keep out of mischief when we meet these slave catchers. None of that dashing about you like to do; that'll only get us in trouble. And don't fire unless I tell you to."

Florie tried to control the thumping of her heart. Sam was going into battle and taking her with him. She watched him scrub the nipples of his rifles with a brass brush before threading them back into their apertures near the breech and tightening them with an ebony-handled key. He peeled open a new tin of percussion caps and inserted one over each nipple. It was a methodical activity she had seen him perform many times.

"It's too bad those caps won't fit my revolver," she said.

"I think I feel safer with your little pistol useless," Sam returned with a chuckle.

Rabonga, his mouth tight with anger, spoke rapidly to Sam and Bachita.

"It seems the captives are chained around palm trees," Sam said as he doled out rifles and ammunition to his men. "The slave catchers are at the center of the village and they've been drinking. That's good. We need surprise on our side."

Florie tied her hair back with a strip torn from the plaid blanket that had served them so well. Its weave of reds, blues and greens imparted a barbaric dash of color against her blond hair. She tucked her useless revolver under her belt. "For good luck," she muttered in response to Sam's dubious glance. With her weapons, powder belt slung over one shoulder, loose fitting shirt, and skin tanned by the African sun, Florie looked more like a Barbary pirate than a Hungarian refugee.

""The slave catchers have more men and guns than we do," Sam said. "I don't want to get into a shooting war with them if I can help it. I just have to make sure that our people can get close before they're discovered.

"If things go badly, find Kamrasi," he continued softly, his eyes searching Florie's face. "Barter whatever you need. You must make your way back to Cairo. Shepheard's Hotel. Remember it."

"No," she protested. "I can't—"

"No time," he said as he hefted his ten-bore. "It'll be quite dark soon. Follow me, and be very quiet."

Florie laid the Fletcher over her shoulder, drew a deep breath, and crept into the brush after Sam.

An hour later, with a crescent moon shining overhead, the handful of porters led by Sam and Rabonga approached the silent village. Most of the huts had been torched earlier in the day, but a few dwellings just ahead of them still remained intact, silhouetted against the firelight. From his vantage point between two of the huts, Sam noticed the cook fire burning low. The drift of conversation and laughter from the slave catchers had run its course. Snores rumbled from the village center. A careful survey of its perimeter showed that the foolish Dongolowans had posted only a single, sleepy sentry. The soft trilling of a birdcall from the forest on the far side of Kisoona signaled that Rabonga and all of the porters were in place.

"Stay by these huts," Sam ordered Florie in a hushed voice. "Rabonga is heading toward where his people are chained to warn them to stay quiet. Richarn will take out the sentry. We're under-gunned, so I'll walk into the village and fire into the air to draw Mahomet's attention. Keep your piece ready, but don't shoot unless the slavers come your way." He squeezed her arm and turned toward the village. Before he could march away, she threw her arms about his neck. Her lips sought his in a hard, hungry kiss.

"Be careful," she whispered in his ear. He held her tightly for a moment, then gently disengaged her arms.

"Remember to stay put," he whispered. "You're watching our backs."

Pivoting on his heel, he strode boldly into the village straight toward the cluster of men slumbering around the cook fire. As he neared the Dongolowans, he tried to pinpoint Mahomet el-Nar. With only glowing coals in the fire pit, it was too dark to be certain where the chieftain slept. The best way to find out was to get right to it. He pointed his ten-bore at the night sky and squeezed the trigger. A blast of thunder and flame erupted into the heavens. Monkeys slumbering in the trees shrieked. Birds cawed raucously. Groggy slave catchers squealed in fear and confusion.

"Hold where you are," Sam commanded, the twin muzzles of his rifle sweeping over the cringing crew.

"English Baker," cried one of the Dongolowans in disbelief. "How did you get here?"

"I walked," Sam growled. He kicked a log into the fire. Sparks exploded upward and yellow flame leapt brightly.

From out of the shadows, Richarn led the band of porters, their muskets trained on the slave catchers, the cocking of the hammers clicking loudly. "The first of you reaching for a gun will have his face blown off," he warned.

"Where is the key to the chains?" Sam demanded.

"Mahomet has the keys," the Dongolowan said. "But he is not among us."

Sam searched the faces of the slave catchers. "Then you'd better tell me where to find him."

***

Mahomet el-Nar, startled from a deep sleep by the explosion from Sam's rifle, sat up on the bedding of straw inside one of the huts and clamped his hand over the mouth of the naked Unyoro girl at his side.

When she struggled, his fingers closed tightly on her windpipe, squeezing until she was still.

Slowly he eased toward the door. A savage scowl curled his mouth as he peeked outside. The light cast by the cooking fire silhouetted the broad back of that English dog, Baker. No one was looking toward the huts. He could retreat if he chose to, but then he'd lose a fortune in slaves and ivory. Eliminate the white man, he was sure, and the rest of the porters would panic and flee into the forest.

Mahomet drew his curve-bladed knife and edged from the hut. He crouched, measuring the distance to his enemy. A dozen steps, a leap, in a moment it would be over. His muscles tensed as he leaned forward.

"It would be wise not to move," Florie grated as she shoved the barrels of the Fletcher rifle into the small of Mahomet's back. She had glimpsed the reflection of firelight from his knife as he emerged from the hut.

Mahomet cursed as he pivoted, his arm smashing down on the barrels of the gun before she could pull the trigger. He grunted loudly as he jammed his elbow into her belly, slamming her hard against the wall of a hut. The rifle spun out of her grasp. With knife raised, he sprang toward her.

Florie, stunned by the blow, struggled to stay on her feet although her knees threatened to buckle. Sobbing for breath, she tried to cry Sam's name, but only croaked incoherently. Firelight glimmered liquidly on Mahomet's descending blade. She raised an arm in a futile attempt to block his stroke. Her forearm went numb as it collided with his. Something like bitter fire burned across her chest as the knife sheared through the strap of the powder belt covering her shoulder, then sliced through shirt fabric and flesh. The strap deflected his blow just enough to save her life.

Mahomet shot a glance over his shoulder at the confrontation around the campfire. His men were being disarmed, too stupefied to even put up a fight. His wealth in slaves and ivory was drifting away like wood smoke. Only the *sitt* remained. He'd find a way to get her to Emile Zeb and collect the reward.

Florie felt the hot wetness of blood flowing down her arm. Her shoulder and chest ached. She tried jamming her feet into the ground as he curled his arm under her chin, but he manhandled her like a rag doll into the jungle. She squirmed and fought his iron grip.

"Be still or I'll slit your throat," Mahomet said as he cuffed her on the head.

With her face tingling from the blow, Florie clamped her teeth hard on his forearm. Blood welled. He cursed, released her, then tangled his fist into her hair and yanked her to her feet.

"Bitch," he screamed, his knife flashing frostily.

Florie swept her pistol from her belt. The *click-clack* of its hammer cocking froze the big man before he could strike. His eyes widened with uncertainty. Then his fear was gone. With a cry of blind rage, he lifted the blade high.

The revolver's hammer fell on its useless cylinder.

***

Sam kicked away a slave catcher's musket as a Dongolowan foolishly reached for it. He swung the butt of his rifle and shattered the man's jaw.

"No more stupid moves," he bellowed.

Richarn stepped into the flickering campfire light. "I will watch them, Baker Pasha."

"No. Get the *sitt*," Sam ordered. "She's waiting beyond those huts."

Richarn nodded his head and trotted off. Moments later his howl penetrated the night. "The *sitt* is gone! I've found her gun!"

Sam froze for a moment as he digested the news. Florie would never have abandoned her rifle. That meant more slave catchers were about. Mahomet el-Nar! Smothering a curse, he grabbed the weapon from Richarn and sprinted toward the huts. Fearfully, he dashed from one hut to another. A dead Unyoro girl lay in one of the dwellings, but Florie was nowhere to be seen. He called her, his voice echoing. No answer.

"Here, Baker Pasha," Richarn cried as he held a torch aloft. "Tracks into the forest."

Sam crouched in the pool of light cast by the torch. Crimson droplets speckled the trail. More blood dripped from a broad leaf. A severed powder strap lay on the ground. Footprints pressed in the sand led into the shadows. The small ones were hers, the larger ones ....

"Florie?" he cried into the darkness.

No answer. She could be anywhere.

Leaves slapped his arms and thighs as he dashed into the jungle. He skidded to a halt and listened. Desperate voices, suddenly louder, sounded just ahead. Smashing through a barrier of fronds and vines, Sam nearly stumbled into the small clearing. The light from Richarn's torch glinted from Mahomet's knife. Florie was bent backward, trying to fend him off with that silly, futile pistol.

"Drop!" Sam roared.

Florie instinctively sagged to her knees. Mahomet's glare of hatred flickered from the woman to the Englishman.

In the space of a heartbeat, the Fletcher rifle was at Sam's shoulder, his eye aligning along the length of its barrels, its sights worthless in the night. His finger tightened. The gun bellowed, its flash of fire blinding and the haze of smoke a darker blackness. Then Rabonga dashed through the underbrush, running past Sam, stabbing at the dying slave catcher with his spear. The Unyoro's wild cry of vengeance ululated eerily.

Sam swallowed and stumbled toward Florie. He lifted her in his arms and clutched her tightly to him. His hands were slippery with her blood. Peeling her shirt down over her shoulders, he examined the cut in the poor light. Although blood welled freely, he shook his head in wonder that the knife had not bit more deeply. The thought of losing her left him feeling drained, almost weak-kneed.

"For God's sake, take me away from here," Florie moaned, her head pressed against his chest. She didn't want to look at the dead man sprawled on the ground. "Please take me home."

And Sam, not quite knowing what she meant by home, held her tightly and whispered, "Aye."

***

Kamrasi sat on his copper stool, his only remaining leopard skin cloaking his shoulders. The stool and cloak were all he had been able to save from the raiders. Even the young girl fanning him was using a makeshift palm leaf rather than the royal ostrich feather fan. That had been abandoned during the flight from M'rooli. He tried to look stern.

"King Kamrasi," Sam said in a loud voice. "The men who enslaved your people are your prisoners. Do with them as you will. In return, I ask for guides to help us get back to Khartoum."

The king nodded his head gratefully at Sam. Perhaps he could squeeze one more gift from *Mollegge's* brother. His gaze swept greedily over Florie, but came to rest firmly on the Fletcher rifle nestled in the crook of her arm.

"Surely you will not need such a fine weapon in your homeland," he said.

"The rifle is mine now, King Kamrasi," Florie replied, smiling slyly. "But I do have a parting gift for you." She plucked the revolver from her belt and handed it to the monarch.

Kamrasi's features lit with pleasure as he accepted the useless weapon, balancing it in his slender hand. *Hah!* he thought happily. *I have finally gained a treasure and the whites are leaving my kingdom as well. My ancestors have indeed smiled upon me.*

Richarn waited for the king of the Unyoro to depart before speaking. "Baker Pasha, the men have loaded the supplies and guns on the oxen we sent ahead to the falls. Rabonga has chosen guides to travel with us. We're ready to leave."

Sam's face darkened with concern as he turned to Florie. Bandages looped over her shoulder and across her breast. He had stitched her wound shut with a remnant of fishing line. Tears had started from her eyes, but she never groaned or cried out.

"It'll be a dangerous journey back to Khartoum," he said as they strolled back to their camp.

"Aren't we living on borrowed time anyway?" she asked quietly. "Can God put any more obstacles in our path than he already has?"

Sam shrugged. "God is God, and this is Africa."

But in his mind, he knew one great obstacle still remained: England. His thoughts were bitter. *That name fills me with both joy and dread. On the one hand, I'll be able to see my daughters again. But on the other, my journey with Florie has ended. What becomes of us now? I must make a choice, but which is it? My indecision eats at my gut.*

Chapter Twenty-three

"Well, I suppose we'll have to do something," Sir Roderick Murchison mumbled, half to himself and half to the bearded man seated in the overstuffed chair opposite him. "Africa has become such a fiasco."

Austen Henry Layard tapped his knee impatiently with a stubby forefinger. "Lord Russell would appreciate if the Geographical Society would put something about Africa in a good light. Dick Burton won't visit you, and that dolt Speke had to go and shoot himself dead in a silly hunting accident. Livingstone is still out of vogue, and besides, that dried up old prune plans to return to the Zambezi if it kills him, which it probably will. Now Petherick has been accused of dealing in the slave trade. The next thing you know, we'll have to close the consulate in Khartoum."

"Maybe the RGS really should do something for Sam Baker," Murchison said. "I hate to say it, but he's our one remaining champion to wipe away some of the tarnish."

"Baker? You didn't even want him to go to Africa in the first place," Layard said as he stared out the window at the deepening gloom of early evening. "Why, we don't know where he is, or if he's even alive. The last news of him was that he had headed south from Gondokoro shortly after his meeting with Speke and Grant. That was nearly two years ago. If he is dead, then what?"

"My dear Autie," Murchison said slowly, a plan formulating in his brain, "the Society will award Samuel White Baker its Victoria Gold Medal—posthumously, of course. He must certainly have perished somewhere in central Africa or we would have heard something by now. But his efforts in exploring the Setit, Atbara, and other tributaries will not go unnoticed. He will be a hero to the people of this nation."

Layard grimaced and cleared his throat. "You do realize that by granting him the Gold Medal in absentia, you will be admitting to his family that he has died. And there's the matter of that foreign woman as well. What of her?"

"His sister and daughters will bask in his glow," Murchison replied stubbornly. "As for *that woman*, if he has died, then surely she'll be gone as well."

"You're swimming in deep waters on this one, Roddy. Recognition of Baker is one thing, but the Gold Medal will open up all he has done to scrutiny. If news of his woman becomes public, it's my duty to remind you not to let it sully the Queen or Crown in any way. The British Empire doesn't tolerate soiled heroes.

"But be that as it may, I'm sending Seth Graham-Gordon, one of my best men, to Khartoum to close the consulate before Petherick puts us at war with Egypt. He can do a little snooping into Mr. Baker's past while he's there. If there's anything about a foreign woman, he'll ferret it out."

The president of the Royal Geographical Society wasn't really listening to Layard's lecture. He was too busy searching for a clean sheet of stationary and his calendar. Better to honor Baker quickly, he thought, and shed glory on the Society to boot.

***

Plague scourged Khartoum. Vultures, like black Harpies, wheeled in wide spirals above the burial pits east of the city. The brass eye of the late afternoon sun cast a baleful glare over the city streets, withering the tottering inhabitants of the overcrowded poorest sections of the town.

"Remember when I wondered if God could put any more obstacles in our path?" Florie asked Sam in a hushed, shocked tone as the felucca they had rented near Gondokoro approached the wharf. A bloated human body floated in the water near the skeletal remains of a partially sunk dahabeah. Debris and dead fish washed against the wharf's pilings. "Well, I think He has."

A gaggle of scarecrows gathered at the shore, hoping the rare incoming vessel bore food or medicine. They howled their disappointment and tugged at their beards when it disgorged a dozen or more people as gaunt as themselves. They paid only passing interest in two of the passengers: a European man and woman, wearing ragged clothing, their skin browned by the sun.

Florie's face paled as she stepped from the boat. "Sam, I'm afraid of this place. It stinks of death." She reached into her bag and produced a pair of handkerchiefs. "Here, place this over your mouth," she said, handing him a dainty square. "The air near the river could be foul with fever."

"Well, we're here now and shan't be leaving over a little stink," he replied gruffly. He scowled as he stuffed the handkerchief into his pocket.

Florie glanced away from him, feeling tightness in her throat. Over the past week, he'd become sullen, finding fault with every little thing she did: the soup she made was too cold; she had misplaced his notebook; a box of his drawing pencils was missing. And on every count, she was to blame. As they neared Khartoum, he'd become even more cross, as if the end of their journey had left him floundering, strangely directionless for the first time since they had arrived in Africa.

With his fists bunched, his long strides forced her to run to keep up as they moved past vacant buildings, trash-littered streets, and clouds of black flies feasting on carrion. A brief puff of breeze carried the sickly stench of a crematory fire. The authorities were at work burning the dead.

"There's the consulate," he said curtly.

Curled scabs of paint still marked the outline of the British lion on the stucco wall, but no vestige of the white unicorn remained. It was as if the symbol of British power had been all but forgotten in this remote outpost.

Sam pounded on the heavy wooden gates with his fist. When there was no answer, he used the pommel of his knife. He was about to turn away when the gate opened with a screech from protesting hinges. A nervous and pale Hallal el-Shami poked his head out. His eyes widened with surprise.

"I am pleased to see you, Baker Effendi," said the factotum as he bowed. Then he frowned with concern. "But also not so pleased to see you."

"What the hell does that mean?" Sam growled. "Have you got the plague, or is England at war with someone?"

"Monsieur Thibaut is here with one of your countrymen," el-Shami replied.

"Petherick is here?"

The factotum wrung his hands anxiously. "No, Effendi, it is a man from your government. He is not a happy man."

As the door swung open further to let them in, Florie tugged at Sam's sleeve. "What is it? What is this all about?"

"Damned if I know," Sam said darkly as he hefted his bag and strolled onto the consulate grounds, "but I'm sure as hell going to find out." Ignoring decorum, he banged open the door to the main office and dropped his baggage on the floor.

A man with a sallow face and drooping mustachios rose from his chair with a scowl. "So who are you to come bursting in here unannounced?" he demanded. The man's eyes slowly widened in recognition as he surveyed Sam from head to feet. Then he stared at Florie. "*Mon dieu!* Samuel Baker? Can that be you? Alive? Here in Khartoum? And Mademoiselle Florence, too? But you are both dead!"

"Not quite," Sam replied. "And who are you?"

"*C'est mois* ... Georges Thibaut! I must apologize for my rude welcome, but since the plague hit Khartoum, everything has gone to—how do you English say—hell in a hand basket. But, please, there is a man from your country here asking about you."

Florie stared in shock at the French consul's appearance. His comic Turkish attire was gone, replaced by a rumpled suit a bit more dignified in style but almost equally comic in its loose fit. What shocked her more, however, was his emaciated state. Not a big man in the best of times, Thibaut had shrunk to little more than an animated skeleton.

"It's the plague," Thibaut explained when he saw Florie's expression. "A local woman brings produce and a little meat for me later in the afternoon. Everything has become very expensive so I try to eat only once a day. Perhaps that's why you didn't recognize me right away. I've lost considerable weight." He exhaled deeply before continuing. "The plague has killed over a thousand. It starts with a heavy bleeding at the nose, followed by a burning fever, and, after a few days, the afflicted is dead. Even my servants have died.

"But you are both here now. You must have an incredible story to tell. And you, Mademoiselle Florence, you must—"

"Who's this Englishman you babbled about?" Sam interrupted.

"*I'm* that Englishman," boomed a voice from behind them.

Sam pivoted in surprise. The newcomer had entered the room so quietly that even his danger-tuned ears had failed to pick him up. The mustachioed man was dressed stylishly in a cotton twill jacket, the grip of his revolver protruding menacingly from the holster strapped across his chest. His cold blue eyes surveyed them with indifference.

Military, Sam thought as his mouth formed a thin line. And from his bearing, he's probably an aristocrat as well. This fellow likes to be in control.

"So you're Samuel White Baker." That was more statement than question. "My name is Graham-Gordon, of Her Majesty's Foreign Office. I'm pleased to meet you."

His handshake was firm.

"And you are in Khartoum for what reason, if I might ask?" Sam said. "I doubt you're here for the climate."

A shadow of a smile flitted across Graham-Gordon's lips. "I'm afraid not. It's quite a sad story, really. Consul Petherick returned here about a year ago. He and the governor of the city got into a terrible argument, something about how Petherick was trying to recover his ivory from the Egyptian government. When he didn't get satisfaction, he tried to sue the Khedive of Egypt. The governor then accused him of slave trading. Finally, the Foreign Office recalled him. I'm here to close the consulate. You've made the other part of my job much easier by showing up when you did." He paused, his eyes shifting from Sam to Florie and back to Sam. "And that's the problem."

Thibaut leaned forward and whispered to Sam, "*Votre amie parle français?*"

Puzzled, Sam made a face as he glanced at Florie. "No, she doesn't understand your language," he replied in French. He hadn't spoken that tongue in years and it tasted rusty. Then he asked in English, "Why should that matter?"

"*C'est meilleur que nous parlons français,*" Thibaut answered as he nervously twisted the ends of his mustachios. "It is better we speak in French," he said knowingly at Graham-Gordon.

"Unless Miss Florence can be excused from our conversation," added the British agent.

Sam glared at both men. "What's this all about? I'd as soon we speak English so she can understand as well."

Florie felt a bitter taint in her mouth. She had heard her name used, but with the French language she didn't know what Sam and the other men were talking about. The tone of their voices, however, was unmistakable. She was at the center of their conversation.

"I'd as soon speak English, too, so let's be blunt," Graham-Gordon said. "The sooner I get this over with, the faster I can leave this dunghill of a city. Is Florence your friend, your wife, or what? Or is she simply your mistress?"

Florie blinked in surprise. No one seemed to notice her. She felt like a ghost in the room, present, but without substance.

Sam felt a hot flush of anger creep up his neck as he took a step toward Graham-Gordon. "And why should that be of any concern of yours?"

"Because, my dear Baker, you are about to become a hero to the English people," the agent answered with a smirk. "You've been awarded the Geographical Society's Gold Medal. Your discoveries in Africa will place you on a pedestal; however, the Foreign Office wants to know if there is anything that would cause embarrassment to Her Majesty."

Sam looked confused. "Gold Medal? A hero?"

"Yes, a hero," Graham-Gordon replied with a roll of his eyes. "Your daughters and siblings have all been informed that you are alive and well, and are about to return to England as a hero."

"My daughters? But how did you know?"

"My good man, England has its own spies in some flyshit speck of a place called Gondokoro. You were reported arriving from the interior several weeks ago. So, let me ask you again: are you and Florence legally married or does she just warm your bed?"

"That is not your business," Florie said, her hands curling into fists. Anger seethed through her. What would these men know about real marriage? She and Sam had been through more than any man and woman could expect to face in a lifetime together. There was no need for churchy things, not in the African jungle. Sam would tell them.

But Sam was silent.

"The Foreign Office notes that both Speke and Petherick spoke of your relationship," Graham-Gordon continued. "Monsieur Thibaut has also described your first arrival in Khartoum, what, three years ago? I doubt that you found a priest in the African bush the past three years to dispense the necessary sacrament, and I'm sure you weren't as pious as a monk when you were with her."

Surely Sam will speak up after that insult, Florie thought wildly. Why won't he look at me?

"You see, it wasn't a problem when everyone thought you were dead," Graham-Gordon explained. "But we simply can't allow you to return in glory with scandal dogging your footsteps. Even your sister has made inquiries to my superiors."

"My sister?"

"Yes, and she had your daughter with her, too. Edith, yes, that's her name."

"Sam, tell them we are like man and wife," Florie said, trying to smother her growing fear. "We've been through so much together."

Sam didn't reply.

Florie closed her eyes so no one could read her pain. His silence was a cruel cut. Could it be that he'd forgotten his promise to her? Could it be that when he said he loved her it was only out of pity? Where was the man who rescued her from slavery, who saved her life from fever, who shared the wonders of the Albert Nyanza with her? Who made love to her? The man she thought she knew—she thought loved her—simply stood with his head bowed, staring at his feet.

"What do my children know?" Sam finally said, without words in her defense, as she hoped and expected.

"Nothing, as far as I've been told," Graham-Gordon replied smoothly. "But the sooner you walk away from this little tryst, the better off they'll be."

Sam rubbed his hand over his brow. He imagined his discoveries mocked, his daughters snubbed by society, his family the object of ridicule. This was his fault. He should have thought things out more clearly. His findings would center him in great public attention, and that attention would focus on those closest to him as well. Then how would he explain Florie?

"I've thought much about it, but I don't know what to do. I can't sort it out," he said wearily. He turned toward Florie but refused to meet her gaze. "The only thing I do know is that our journey together is over. I can't take you with me, and I'm empty."

Florie sensed her world crumbling and felt helpless to prevent it. Her fate was being decided without anyone asking her. In the empty canyon of silence that followed, she choked back a sob, leaned against Sam, and covered her face. Emotions and memories collided. "How can our journey together be over?" She thumped her fist futilely against his chest. "I love you so!"

Sam squeezed her shoulders and pushed her away. "We've been through this before. It would ruin my family. All of England will be watching."

Florie swiped the back of her hand across her face, smearing away the wetness. "Aren't I part of your family, too?" she cried, her voice breaking, and hating that it had. "You have your lake and your discoveries. Is that all you ever wanted? You told me you loved me, that you'd take me home with you."

"I ... I can't," he said gruffly. "But I'll make sure you're taken care of."

Florie backed away from him, shaking her head. A sneer curled her mouth. "I don't want your help. I'm not afraid of England, and I don't want you to be ashamed of me anymore. Some day you'll have to find out what's most important to you!" She plucked her bag from the floor and ran to the consulate's door. Her hand twisted the knob.

"Where will you go?" Sam demanded.

Florie steeled herself against the ache biting into her heart and turned toward him. "I'm leaving. Please don't follow me." Throwing open the door, she plunged into the growing gloom of a Khartoum evening.

Stunned, Sam stared at the open door, shocked by her flight. He hesitated, torn between two guilts churning in his mind: his family and Florie. But the misery in her eyes, misery he had caused, began knifing deeper into his soul. She had given herself to him body and spirit, and he had given her nothing in return. Every promise he had made to her had been broken. He had become a man of lies. The wonderful woman who had stood by him for so long was gone. He suddenly felt strangely unbalanced, as if part of him had been carved away.

"It's best you forget about her," Graham-Gordon chided. "If you play your cards right, there'll be a knighthood in this for you. Think about the Queen and the honors she will bestow on you. For Christ's sake, think of what this means to your family."

Sam squinted at Graham-Gordon. The agent's sardonic tone irked him.

"Baker, you must admit, this ... this Florence was an entertaining trifle for you these past years—a tramp in the bushes, if you know what I mean. But we men of the world—"

Graham-Gordon never saw Sam's fist collide with his jaw.

"I'll find her and get this squared with her," Sam promised as he headed toward the door. "When I return, make sure our friend from the Foreign Office is gone."

"Mon dieu!" Georges Thibaut said under his breath as he bent and peered at the unconscious agent. "The man must love her. What a fool!"

Chapter Twenty-four

Florie ran down the street away from the British consulate, her shoes clacking loudly on the cobblestones of the deserted road. Turning right at an intersection, she ducked into a small grove of dome palms and hunkered against the trunk of one. A dog barked a warning from a nearby alley. She didn't care.

"Dear Jesus in Heaven, what just happened?" she said softly, trying not to whimper. "Sam said he didn't want me, that he was empty."

Hugging her knees, she fought back the flow of tears that threatened to engulf her. Where would she go? Her immediate future yawned like a dark hole. To stay in Khartoum was out of the question. Cairo perhaps? But sailing to Cairo would require money. Of course! Sam had given her money and a letter the day Johann Schmidt had died.

Digging into her bag, she uncovered the waterproof pocket containing folded currency. She opened Sam's letter and tried to decipher the message. Although her English had improved, her ability to read fluidly lagged behind. She recognized the words Shepheard's Hotel.

If she were lucky, the *felucca* she and Sam had hired in Gondokoro would still be anchored near Khartoum's ramshackle wharf. With the cache of money, she could charter the boat to take her north. Sam's letter would introduce her to Shepheard's. Once there, she would decide her own destiny. Perhaps Sam would follow, but most likely not. But if he did … her thoughts drifted away uneasily.

Florie slowly rose to her feet, brushed debris from her trousers, and wiped her face with her sleeve. In the bottom of her bag was her hunting knife. Trying to keep her head as still as possible, she sawed through thick locks of hair. When she was done, she stared bitterly at the golden tangle on the ground. She had done this before so Sam couldn't find her. Now it was truly time to go on alone.

***

Sam rubbed a shaking hand over his face to help clear his thoughts. How long had it been since Florie left him? Two days? Three? He had scarcely slept in three days. Although he had followed her outside the consulate, he was unable to determine where she had gone. Alleys and streets converged like runs in a rat's nest. It seemed that the city, in its darkness, had swallowed her.

How asinine you are, taunted his subconscious. *You'd be dead on some forgotten African trail if it wasn't for her, and your Nile discoveries would be lost. You've never truly given a shit about what people thought in the past. Henrietta was your responsibility and she died. You've been running from that same responsibility—for your daughters, for Florie—ever since.*

The gleam of excitement in Florie's eyes, her hair cascading like a fountain of gold, the thrill he felt when she held him, the love she gave him without question. All gone. His fear for her safety bit into him like a rancorous cancer. How stupid, cowardly, and shallow he was.

Khartoum's reeking alleys and disease-ridden slums had revealed no trace of her. The few inns still open offered no clue. What little law enforcement that existed in the city knew nothing of the whereabouts of a white woman with sun-colored hair. And it took money to rent a boat. It was as if she had evaporated like a pool of moisture in the seething heat. How could she have disappeared so quickly?

Dejectedly, Sam returned to the consulate. The gates were locked. Graham-Gordon had evidently finished his job and left Khartoum. Once he arrived in England and reported to the Foreign Office—well, so much for the Baker reputation.

Battling fatigue, Sam stumbled toward the French consulate. He hammered on the door with his fist. Georges Thibaut let him enter.

"You won't strike me, too, will you?" Thibaut said with a feigned grimace of fright. "Monsieur Graham-Gordon was laid out for an hour."

"I guess I did hit him pretty hard," Sam said. "But he deserved it."

"I take it you had no luck in finding Mademoiselle Florence?"

"None. I couldn't have been more than a few minutes behind her, and that was three days ago. Where could she have gone?"

Thibaut clucked his tongue ruefully. "You look terrible. You may stay here and rest if you'd like. I have my contacts searching for her, too."

"Thank you," Sam said wearily.

"She stirs your heart?"

Sam's gaze met the Frenchman's. "Yes, but I didn't realize it until she ran out the door. I've left her before, but this is the first time she has left me. I think I've hurt her very badly."

"And if you found Mademoiselle Florence, what would you do?"

Sam thought of the last time he'd seen her, standing at the door of the consulate, her cheeks streaked with tears, her devastation over his betrayal complete.

"Make it right with her … if she'll let me."

***

Sam twisted in his sheets, his body clammy with sweat. The blankets clung to him like a grotesque second skin.

"Father?" called one of the dream wraiths. *"Why haven't you come home to us yet? I so want you to be here. Why did you leave us so long ago?"*

"My sweet Edith, I'm coming home to you with Mother," he answered.

"But Mother is here with us. How can you bring us Mother?"

"I am coming, sweet one."

"Is that other woman with you, Father?"

Sam did not reply.

"Father!" The Edith voice shrieked in rage. *"Is that her with you?"*

Edith's anger seethed poisonously around him. He was aware of other phantoms. A grimacing Henrietta stooped to retrieve a rock. Agnes ran toward him, a pile of stones gathered in her apron. He felt Florie push past him, crying out the names of his daughters. He tried to pull her back, but her substance flowed through his fingers like mist. Then their stones were arcing toward her, tearing into her flesh with deadly velocity as they called her whore and slut in a Biblical vignette of judgment and execution. The faces of his daughters were those of frenzied demons. Henrietta laughed as she cast stone after stone. He stumbled to Florie's side, trying to cradle her limp, bloody form in his arms, but, to his horror, she dissolved and trickled away.

"Monsieur Baker! Sam, wake up!" Thibaut continued to shake the slumbering man's shoulder.

Sam finally blinked, his sleep-deprived mind still reeling from his dream.

"What is it?" he croaked groggily.

"It is Mademoiselle Florence—at least we think it is," Thibaut said as he held out his hands. "See."

"What?" Sam was instantly alert. He stared at the long strands of golden hair lying in the consul's palms.

"There is no one else in Khartoum that would have hair such as this," Thibaut said. "It was found under a tree not far from here."

"She's cut her hair and dressed as a boy," Sam said in wonder as he held a lock against the light. He remembered the first time he'd seen her like that: on the breakwater in Kostendje after she'd saved his life and he'd saved hers.

"My contacts report that a boy rented a *felucca* two days ago, the same boat you arrived in," Thibaut added. "He paid with Turkish lira. Raggedy-ass boys don't have that kind of money."

"Lira?" Sam's puzzled expression instantly cleared as he recalled the gift he had given Florie back on the Nile.

"And the report says the *felucca* is headed for—"

"Cairo," Sam finished the sentence. "She's going to Cairo. And that's where I'm going, too. I pray to God that I'm not too late. I pray that she remains there."

***

Waves lapped the sides of the *felucca*. Its lateen sail billowed in the warm breeze. Overhead, fish eagles soared, then glided at fierce angles toward the Nile's surface, splashing into the water, emerging with wriggling fish grasped in their talons.

Florie watched as another eagle sped toward its prey. She closed her eyes against the glare of the sun. She had seen predators do their work plenty of times before.

So it begins, she thought, a new life without him. Don't think about it. It will only drive you crazy.

With a shake of her head, she opened her eyes. The eagle was flapping away, a large perch squirming in its talons. She felt like one of those fish. She wanted to feel like the soaring eagle.

"Mademoiselle, your pardon. We'll soon be passing the cataracts."

Florie dipped her chin at the boat's captain, the same sailor who had navigated the *felucca* from near Gondokoro. She bit her lip. Riding the very boat that she and Sam had been on only a few days earlier re-awakened the heartbreak she desperately fought.

Staring into the distance, she forced herself not to picture his face. It was better to enjoy the fields of purple-white lupias interspersed with groves of palms that stretched to the Nile's edge. Beyond, in the sand, rose the colossal stone pharaohs of Abou Simbel, dunes creeping against their serene, fatal faces.

"How long until we reach Cairo?" she asked.

"The river is deep at this time of year, and flows strong," the captain replied. He was happy to have a passenger who paid so well as the *sitt*. But she had appeared at his boat as a boy traveler, not as the beautiful woman with the flowing hair. What had happened to her and Baker Pasha? It didn't matter. "Ten days, perhaps a little more."

Ten days to sort things out, Florie thought bleakly. Ten days in this land of eternity.

As the temple of Abou Simbel receded, she wondered if the stone pharaohs were mocking her.

***

The sullen globe of sun had burned away a thin fog and sent rippling waves of heat across the Nile. Sam shaded his eyes with his hat as the domes and spires of Cairo's mosques and minarets materialized. At the city's outskirts, the great pyramids soared above a mirage of liquid movement.

Brisk winds and the powerful flow of the river had pushed the dahabeah he'd rented from Khartoum to Cairo in little more than ten days. They had sailed past the great stone pharaohs of Abou Simbel and the columned ruins of ancient Philae, past the broken glory that was Luxor and Karnak. But the wonders of ancient Egypt were lost on him; the voyage down the Nile had weighed on him like a prison sentence.

Ten days. That meant Florie would have reached Cairo three, maybe four days earlier. What if she'd decided to cross the Mediterranean and go back to Romania? She could be anywhere by now.

From the waterfront, Sam flagged a carriage that bore him down elegant Shubra Street to the European quarter of Cairo. The city was alive with farmers carting their goods to market, merchants plying their wares in loud voices, and beggars keening for alms. Handsome carriages vied for travel space with donkey-drawn wagons filled with melons or manure. A platoon of Egyptian cavalry bedecked in red fezzes and bright blue jackets scattered pedestrian traffic as they trotted by in a loose formation. He frowned. Civilization. He already hated it.

A quarter-hour later, Sam arrived at the British consulate. Alfred Walne had been Her Majesty's Consul General in Cairo when he and Florie had first landed in Egypt years earlier. Perhaps he would know of a young blond woman with short hair recently arrived. At best, he knew, it was a long shot.

The Queen's consulate in Cairo was an imposing building compared to the decaying quarters of the one in Khartoum. Strong granite columns supported the arched entrance as if to say "Britain stands firmly in Egypt." Sam entered and cornered a fellow with a round, boyish face, sandy-colored hair, and a pince-nez perched on his nose. He introduced himself.

"I'm only a secretary, sir, but I know the Consul General is not here today," the young man explained. "He's in Alexandria and shan't return for three days. Are ... are you *the* Samuel Baker of the Nile?"

"Yes, I suppose I am," Sam replied. "Why do you say that?"

"Truly, sir, all of the British community in Cairo knows of you by now. It's been in the newspaper that you have received the Victoria Gold Medal from the Royal Geographical Society."

Sam plucked at his beard. "Then I suppose all of the Empire knows of that as well."

"Yes, sir, I'd wager so. But the details are sketchy. I'm sure that when the Consul General returns in a few days, he would love to hear your story. After all, we'd thought you dead."

"I've heard that before," Sam said.

"As a matter of fact, we received a telegram yesterday addressed to you," the secretary continued. "We had no way of contacting you, so we simply kept it in hopes you'd turn up. Please follow me."

He opened the door to a small office. Mumbling something under his breath, he shuffled through several folded sheets of paper rescued from a pigeonhole on his desk, twitched one free, and handed it to Sam.

Sam quickly read through the message, swallowed hard, and read it again. It was from his sister Min.

> Dearest Brother,
> Have received word that you are alive and well in Khartoum. Foreign Office had reported you dead months ago, but kept that news from your daughters. You have received RGS Gold Medal. Girls are very proud of you.

His daughters were proud of him. He read those words over and over. So they hadn't forgotten him. He had to think for a moment how old they were. Ethel would be ten, while Constance would be twelve years old, and Agnes fourteen. That made Edith seventeen, nearly eighteen.

He read on.

> Foreign Office has finally told me you have a companion. Details sketchy but you court scandal. Beg you consider the station of your family. Trust your good judgment.
> Min

He reread the paragraph concerning the Foreign Office. There was no mistaking what Min meant. Mr. Graham-Gordon must have telegraphed the news to London. So this, then, was the ultimatum: return to England alone and in glory, or risk certain dishonor and humiliation. Sam shook his head sadly and walked toward the door.

"Mr. Baker, sir," the secretary cried. He clattered down the hallway waving a small rectangle of paper. "Mr. Baker! I nearly forgot to give you this. A young man delivered it several days ago. I'm sorry, but I didn't get his name. But it is addressed to you."

Samuel Baker, Esq. was scrawled across the envelope. Sam felt his heart skip a beat. It was Florie's handwriting! He tore open the sleeve and found a folded paper. Written in German, her childish letters covered one side:

> Dear Sam,
> I arrived in Cairo on Oct. 12. Should you get this, know that I am safe, but will be leaving soon. I thank God for our time together. May He watch over you and yours.
> Florence

Sam blinked as he read the message again. She had arrived on October 12. "What is today?" he nearly shouted as he spun on the hapless diplomat.

"Why … why, it's Thursday, sir," the secretary stammered as he backed a step and readjusted his pince-nez.

"No, the date! What's today's date?"

"It's the fifteenth. October fifteenth."

Sam stared at the note. Could she still be in the city? But where? It would take days to make inquiries, to scour the streets. He glanced at the note again. It was written on Shepheard's Hotel stationery. Of course. Shepheard's. The waxed envelope he'd given her during the trip to Gondokoro not only included money, but also instructions directing her to Shepheard's. With luck, she might still be at the hotel.

"Can you send a telegram to London?" he barked.

"Why, yes, sir. But it will take time to get a response."

"Damn the response!" Sam's eyes burned fiercely. "Here's what I want you to send."

With a pencil snatched from a nearby desk, he jotted a message on a sheet of consular stationary and stuffed it into the secretary's palm. "Now, how far to the Shepheard's?"

"The hotel?"

"Of course, you fool. How far?"

"A half mile, perhaps a bit more," the secretary replied in a quavering voice. "Shall I flag a cab for you, sir?"

"No time. Send that message immediately and give me a copy." The urgency in Sam's voice sent the younger man scurrying to do as he was bid.

A few minutes later, Sam dashed through the consulate doors and into Cairo's busy streets. His hat flew from his head and landed on a dusty curb. He ignored it.

I have to finish this business now, he thought grimly as he ran toward the hotel. For better or worse, this has to be over!

Chapter Twenty-five

Florie drew her arms in tighter, wishing she could shrink in size. She sagged more deeply into the chair, glad she had chosen to sit in a corner of the Shepheard's Hotel's open terrace where tropical plants and small potted trees had been placed in profusion. The chair, nearly hidden among the lush vegetation, provided a hideout of sorts.

At first, she had tried to sit inside the hotel, but the huge, arched doorways bordered in multicolored tiles and swirling arabesques seemed to loom menacingly over her. A fog of tobacco smoke clogged her nostrils, and the cacophony of voices rang in her ears. She felt closed in. Outside, at least, there was the open sky.

A constant flow of European women passed by, their voices chirping merrily in a language she barely understood. Clothed in the latest of fashions, they wore tight-fitting blouses with loose sleeves of a light and airy material colored as delicately as if created by nature. Their hair was pinned under dainty bonnets with tucked nettings to let down if insects buzzed about. But most remarkable was their skin, of a miraculous paleness like washed ivory. To her, they were like seraphim released from Heaven. It was difficult not to stare at them as they drifted by.

Florie was suddenly conscious of her own hands and face, bronzed by years under the African sun, making her look more Egyptian than European. Once she had reached the hotel, she'd given up her trousers and shirt for her dress, the one that Sam had bought for her in Bucharest so long ago. The poor thing, however, was not only threadbare, but badly out of style as well. She tried to keep her feet tucked under the chair so no one would see her scuffed shoes, their buttons long since gone and replaced with antelope-hide laces. Her battered, floppy-brimmed hat covered her close-shaven skull. What if one of those wonderful English ladies turned and noticed her?

With a sigh, she wondered if she shouldn't go to her room to spare herself this agony. But she had spent two days there already, and its closed confines were more than she could stand. She needed space, and sunlight, and the greenery of the African plain. But she felt Africa was closed to her. What was left? Bucharest? Perhaps she should return to Kostendje and the ox-wagon of old Vidar Dubrin. Maybe she'd find another man like Tamas Comanasti back in Wallachia.

Her eyes rimmed with tears. Goddamned Sam. She clamped her jaws tightly, fighting her anger and disappointment. He had treated her not like a *sitt*—a woman of importance and his most intimate partner—but as a piece of baggage to be discarded when no longer needed. The message she left for him at the British consulate was only meant to tell him that she was alive and ready to move on with her life. And that was if he even came to Cairo to look for her.

Across the open court, partially hidden by a number of dwarf palms planted in bronze vases shaped like elephant legs, was the hotel's cocktail bar. Several men in British army uniforms had gathered there to drink and socialize. Cigar smoke wreathed their heads before dissipating in the midday breeze. One of the men, a blond officer with sweeping mustachios, noticed the woman crouched in her chair and hiding her feet. He motioned toward her with his cheroot. His companions peered at her for a moment, a ripple of laughter shaking their shoulders. The officer tugged at the hem of his tunic as if preparing for an inspection. One of his chums clapped him on the back. He stepped deliberately toward the woman, a smirk curling his lips.

Florie had seen that kind of look in a man's eyes before and she dreaded it. It reminded her of the Pasha of Vidin. Please don't come this way, she pleaded silently. I know what you want. Turn away! Please!

The officer was half way across the court when a flurry of activity stopped him in his tracks. A tall, broad-shouldered man with a thick beard and wearing a plain, much-worn coat had burst from the main entrance to the hotel. The man surveyed the tables on the terrace, boldly pushing past people who stood in his way. He strode directly toward the officer. The soldier glanced at the newcomer's eyes and retreated. Disappointment twisted his face as he returned to the bar and the jeers of his comrades.

The newcomer stopped in front of Florie, his chest rising and falling rapidly. His hands dangled at his sides, a sheet of paper crumpled in one fist.

"Sam?" His sudden appearance almost dazed her.

Sam's face was grim. He tried to control his breathing. It had been a blood-pounding run from the legation, and now he needed his courage. His lips formed into a hard line. The paper gripped in his fist crinkled loudly as his fingers tightened.

Florie swallowed hard. She rose to her feet, her anger rising to the surface.

"I don't want to see you again," she blurted. "Please leave!"

He loomed over her, aware that her hands had curled into fists. Did she mean to strike him? It didn't matter. "A wise man once asked if my heart was stirred by a certain woman. It took a long time for me to figure that out. Too long."

Florie felt a betraying trickle of moisture on her cheek. She tried to read his eyes, but couldn't. Be strong now!

"I've made *my* decision," she said firmly. "Why you are here is *your* business."

Sam drew a deep breath and shook his head. "No, it's *our* business. I'm truly sorry for what I've done. I betrayed you. But now I don't care what my family or society thinks about us."

Florie's gaze locked on his. Was this the same man who had rescued her in Vidin, lived with her in Africa, yet who had denied her in Khartoum? "Sam, what are you saying?"

Sam's brow creased as he glanced at the paper crumpled in his fist. He dropped to one knee and placed her hand in his. "I'm begging your forgiveness. And if you will, I have this." He smoothed the paper against his thigh and handed it to her.

It was a telegram. It took her a moment to decipher the unfamiliar words.

> Mr. James Baker, Esquire
> London
> Dear Brother James,
> As you know by now, I am returning from Africa. Stop. Am hoping Florence will be with me. Stop. If all works out, will meet you in Paris to make wedding arrangements. Stop. Will arrive by train at 2 p.m. on October 25. Stop.
> Samuel Baker, Esquire

Florie looked at Sam in confusion. "What does this mean?"
It means nothing unless you answer my question," he replied.
"Question?"
"Florence Maria von Sass, will you marry me?"

Florie's senses reeled. Had her ears betrayed her? Why was Sam kneeling in front of her? Why was there moisture wetting her cheeks?

For a long moment she stared at the paper, then let the note fall to the floor. Slowly she withdrew her hand from his. "I can't," she said tonelessly.

Some of the ethereal English women were staring now, she knew, seemingly bemused by the ragged man kneeling in front of the dowdy woman in the floppy hat. She grabbed her bag and held it as a barrier between them as she stepped back.

Bewildered, Sam retrieved the message and rose unsteadily to his feet. "I've made mistakes," he said. "Damnably bad mistakes. I'm so sorry."

"Are you?" She wanted her fury with him to boil over, to make him feel the same lost emptiness she had felt. But that anger had fled, melting away as she gazed at the bedraggled man fumbling with the rumpled telegram. Some of Sam's confidence had eroded. Lines of fatigue etched his face. His shoulders were more bowed.

Florie's lips pressed in a hard, firm line. "I'm sorry, too, Sam, but the pain goes too deep."

"Before, in Khartoum, I said I didn't want you," he said, a wan, tired smile curving his lips. "I was very wrong. I do love you, more than I thought possible. All I ask is for another chance."

With a shake of her head, she turned from him and began walking away, past the fluttering, gilded patrons, past the bar with its platoon of inebriated officers.

"I've know I've hurt you, Florie, and for that I'm truly sorry," he called after her. "But now you must decide what's most important to you."

If she heard him, she did not stop.

***

The sun had set beyond a bend in the Nile, its dwindling flush of crimson and purple melting into blackness. Florie rubbed her hands over the rough surface of a bench overlooking the river. The Nile's beauty at dusk normally haunted her, leaving her wishing that the palette of colors would last all evening. But in the past weeks, the numbness left by her flight from Khartoum had washed away the magic of the African night. The Nile reminded her of the shame Sam felt.

The tint had gone from the sky when she finally rose from the bench. It was dangerous for a lone woman to walk along the river at night, but she didn't care. Sweeping her hat from her head, she ran her fingers through the bristle on her skull. Just as well she couldn't see what she looked like in the river's reflection. What had old Katchiba called her? *Njinyeri?* Morning Star, because of her golden hair. She smiled at the thought.

Then suddenly she realized that every memory of Africa—of Katchiba and Basheet, of the buffalo she shot, and the *Luta N'zige*—were bound with the man she had walked away from at the hotel. And that man was a living part of those memories: the joys of discovery, the constant dangers, the passion they shared. He was not just the man who had bought her at a slave auction, not just the one who had saved her countless times. He was like she was, filled with fears and doubts, sometimes stumbling, sometimes striding boldly forward. She was like he was. And they were both in desperate need of each other's strength and love.

Her hands smoothed the worn, blue dress over her breasts. Why had she worn it into Shepheard's? Wouldn't it have made more sense to remain in disguise and blend in with the city's population if she truly didn't want Sam to find her? And the note she left at the British Consulate after she arrived in Cairo. Why would she want him to know that she was here? And the hair she left behind in Khartoum for someone to find.

Florie clutched her hat tightly. She knew why she had left clues. Once, she had told Sam to decide what was most important to him, and on the hotel's terrace he had asked the same of her. Now she knew what it was that was most important. This was to be *her* decision.

With a little cry, she spun her hat into the river. There was no more shame. She wasn't the boy trying to hide an identity. She wasn't the lonely girl who had followed Sam to the depths of Africa just to find security. She was a woman capable of making her own choices, a woman who had found the man she loved and wanted to be with him.

Be careful, warned her inner self as she turned toward the hotel. *Don't be a fool.*

Above, the moon had risen in the dark Egyptian night. She prayed Sam was still waiting.

***

Torches on the Shepheard's terrace had been lit, their flames snapping eerily in the night wind. A few hotel patrons had enjoyed after dinner drinks in the warm hours of early evening, but had departed at the chill air of moonrise.

Sam sat in the chair Florie had vacated. After she'd left, he found himself enervated, as if a pump had lost its prime. He had ordered a brandy, but its taste was disagreeable and he had drunk less than half. He had closed his eyes, trying to sort out the jumble of thoughts flying through his mind. The hours had flitted by.

"Sam?"

His eyelids fluttered open. Blue eyes bored into his.

"Your brother will be waiting for us," Florie said. Her eyes sparkled. "Perhaps we should go meet him."

***

James Baker paced nervously on the platform of the railway station in Paris. He glanced at the large, brass-framed clock with its distinctive Florentine-style numerals for the fifth time in as many minutes. The train from Marseilles was running late.

Paris. He didn't like the city, or the ferry crossing at Calais, or French food, or even the language. As a former military man who had seen service abroad, he much preferred the slower pace of life and the constant hint of danger in the far-flung backwaters of the British Empire to the bustle and din of cities like Paris.

But Sam had asked him to come, and the telegram spoke of a bride, something he had never expected from his widower older brother. So the rumors were true, he mused. There had been a woman with him in Africa. He wondered how this would sit with Min and his other sisters. Did Sam's daughters even know? What if she was some type of tramp or gold digger?

James caught himself physically shaking his head as people meandered by. No, Sam would know what kind of woman she was. They had survived five years in Africa together, after all.

The whistle on the Marseilles locomotive sounded in the distance.

Well, he thought, in a few minutes we will know what Mr. Samuel White Baker has brought home.

***

Austen Layard puffed on his pipe and glanced absently at his pocket watch. He had been waiting in Sir Roderick Murchison's office for nearly ten minutes and the president of the Royal Geographical Society had not yet turned up. He would wait a little while longer, but then would have to be off to government business.

The door latch suddenly turned and Murchison entered. Tucked under one arm was a folded sheaf of papers. Thin beads of sweat covered his brow.

Layard chuckled. "Say now, have you been on the athletic field with the college boys?"

Murchison inhaled a great breath to restore his calm. "Sam Baker has returned from Africa."

"Quite so," Layard agreed. "We received a report from Cairo nearly a week ago. Baker damn near broke Seth Graham-Gordon's jaw."

"Yes, all part of the dangers of the service, I guess," Murchison said. "But look what I received by steam packet this morning." He tapped his fingers on the papers. "It's Baker's preliminary report. Bloody hell, the man has discovered another source of the Nile. He's even included maps. And to top it off, he has named the greatest of the Nile waterfalls after me!"

Layard whistled as he peered over Murchison's shoulder at a map. "So now your name is set in geography, Roddy. You have a falls near to where the Queen has a lake."

"I wonder how she'll take that news." Murchison smiled.

"You'd *better* worry about the Queen, my friend," Layard chided, taking a deep drag on his pipe. "The other part of Graham-Gordon's report from Cairo is just what we feared. Baker was with his woman. My people tell me she registered under her own name at Shepheard's, but the two of them have stayed in her room. And why not? They've spent the last five years together. It's simply scandalous. Should this news reach Her Majesty, I'm not quite sure what we'll be able to do with him."

Murchison's face went white. "My God!"

Layard tapped his pipe into a cut glass dish. "Murchison Falls, eh? I know what I would do if I were you."

"And what is that, pray tell?" Sir Roderick asked, squinting at his friend.

"Assuming Baker will soon be in London, downplay his arrival. Give him a couple of weeks to meet with his family. Then invite him to Burlington House to present his findings to the Society. By then we should have a pretty frank appraisal of both the man *and* the woman."

"Jolly good," Murchison agreed with a nod. "But this will have to be done delicately. Baker, for whatever character flaws he may have, still has provided us with a great discovery."

"And the Queen can accept the discovery," Layard said, stuffing the pipe into his waistcoat pocket, "and reject the man."

But Murchison no longer listened. He had unfolded another of Sam's maps and was seeking the X that marked his waterfall.

***

A cold wind fluttered Emile Zeb's robes as he hurried down a wharf along the Danube. Behind him, Vidin's citadel of Baba Vida loomed gray and forbidding. He stumbled on uneven stones and almost pitched to his knees.

Calm yourself! He shook his robes nervously as he tried to restore his dignity. *There! The boat is waiting just as I ordered.*

A small skiff with a canopy on its deck and furled sail was moored to the wharf. One of his trusted men was busy onboard.

He must remain calm. In a few days he'd be safely in Constantinople and away from that brute Zast Ohmed Pasha. It was too bad the governor had found out that Baker and the slave girl were on their way to France and permanently out of reach, but he'd tried everything he could to bring her back.

Emile Zeb sucked a deep breath. The money stuffed in his belt under his robes was reassuring. Once away from Vidin, he would be able to start business anew.

The ladder leading to the boat was slippery. The craft bobbed when he finally stood upright on its deck. A long, cloth-swathed bundle lay a few feet from him. Curious, he peeled open one end of the bundle.

Magram Bur's eyeless, earless face leered at him. His throat had been slashed.

Zeb gibbered, retreated a few steps, and bumped into someone. He turned, his tongue thick in his mouth, and staggered back. The dark-robed assassin clutching a curved dagger in his fist followed him toward the boat's narrow bow.

"The Pasha wishes you Godspeed," the assassin hissed. His dagger flashed icily. Emile Zeb did not have time to scream.

***

James Baker waved at Sam as he stepped off the train. There was no mistaking his older brother, still broad-shouldered and fiercely bearded. But his face, darkened by the sun, was seamed with the hardships he had endured.

With a tight-lipped grimace, James waited for the woman to make her appearance. In his mind's eye, he had pictured an un-groomed, half-caste, wire-haired Arab. After all, what European woman could survive five years in dangerous Africa? Besides, Sam had written him that she spoke Arabic better than English. But the girl who descended from the car and placed her hand on his brother's arm was not the half-wild savage he had imagined. Short, tight curls of golden hair peeked from under her dark toque hat, its netting pulled back to frame a bronzed face set with flashing blue eyes. She wore small onyx and gold earrings, a satiny blouse of alternating dark and light blue stripes with a white collar, and elegant shoes just visible below the hem of her medium gray skirt—all the latest fashions purchased in Marseilles, he was sure. Her first words to him thanked him for coming at Sam's request. She did speak English, he was surprised to hear, if with an accent.

James barely broke his gaze from her as the threesome strolled from the train station. She moved with an elegant, fluid grace, her arms swinging freely, unencumbered by bracelets, or rings, or other feminine gewgaws. He could well imagine her striding down a jungle trail, a rifle over her shoulder. Her lips were set in a determined, if slightly sensuous, mold. And her piercing blue eyes brimmed with quiet confidence.

What sights they must have seen, he thought. This is not some common woman Sam has found.

Declining a cab, they walked to a nearby portrait studio and sat for a photograph.

"I sketched a picture of us when we were in Abyssinia, but I'm afraid it doesn't do Florie justice," Sam quipped as the photographer readied his camera. She squirmed on her chair, glancing at Sam over her shoulder.

"What's the matter with you?" he asked as she repositioned herself for the third time.

A momentary look of exasperation clouded her face. "It's all of these clothes, Sam. And these shoes! I'm not used to this much covering."

James nudged his brother and winked.

Later, after a modest meal shared at a small café, the brothers discussed wedding arrangements while Florie listened quietly. Yes, James believed, the church on Arlington Street could be reserved at short notice. Yes, November 4 would fit nicely. And yes! Both he and his wife Louisa would be honored to act as witnesses. But how many guests should be invited? Certainly the daughters.

Florie and Sam exchanged glances. He placed his hand on hers.

"James, you well know that Florie and I have been together some time. Under God's great heaven we've been as husband and wife, though no church would recognize that."

Florie digested his words, smiling as she nodded her head in agreement.

"We will be married as to the laws of England, but the ceremony will include only us," he continued soberly. "I would bring no discomfort to my family to have them attend. Those laws bind them more strongly than they bind us. Afterwards, we'll go to Richmond to introduce my daughters to their new mother."

James cleared his throat nervously, unsure what he should say in front of Florie. "Uh ... Sam, you're forgetting Min. I suspect she already knows about you two. She has been strong with the church, you know, to make sure your girls were raised correctly while you were gone."

Sam leaned on his elbows, tapping his lips with the tip of his forefinger. "Min is my sister, not my wife," he said finally. He felt the gentle pressure of Florie's hand on his arm. "If this church thing is a scandal for her, it'll be her scandal, not ours."

"Well said." James grinned. "Louisa and I will be behind you."

***

Florie bit her lip and flashed a nervous smile at Sam as the Reverend John Oakley read the marriage vows. She felt the moisture on her palms increase as the minister spoke of love, commitment, and sacrifice. A thrill coursed through her as the I do's were pronounced. For a bare moment she thought of his family's reaction. Then Sam tipped back the veil of her cream-colored hat and peered into her tear-filled eyes.

"Was it worth the wait?" he whispered.

"Worth the wait," she said huskily.

Their lips met, and she clung to him, suddenly afraid that it might all disappear in a dream.

"God bless you both," said the curate.

"Hurrah, you two," James Baker cried, a broad smile splitting his massive beard. Louisa rushed forward, pried Florie away from Sam, and hugged her. "Welcome, dear sister," she said between sobs.

The ceremony had been a private one, held in a wing chapel just off the nave of St. James Parish on London's Arlington Street. Only five people were in attendance: the bride and groom, the minister, and James and Louisa as witnesses. When it came time to sign the marriage register, Sam scrawled his name boldly across the ledger. Florie held the pen awkwardly. She tried to write her name but the letters were distorted and her spelling wrong.

"I've shot a buffalo and fought the slaver catchers," she mumbled apologetically, scratching out her first attempt, "but I think I've forgotten how to write. Let me try again."

With her hand shaking with nervousness, she finally wrote Florence M. Baker.

Sam lifted the same hand and kissed it. "'Til death do us part," he said quietly. "And now it's time to meet my children."

Florie's brow wrinkled. She tried to imagine four girls calling her mother. It was easier to imagine facing a charging buffalo.

Chapter Twenty-six

Frost covered the grounds around Lochgarry House. A thin, rimy layer coated lampposts, fence rails, and the branches of nearby ash and fir trees. Smoke curled from the main chimney. Faded rays of sun tried to pierce the pewter-colored November clouds.

"I should suspect everyone will be waiting for us," Sam said, adjusting his coat as he peered from the window of the carriage.

Florie fanned herself despite the cool air seeping into the coach. "Sam, I'm so nervous. I think we should go somewhere so I can change clothes. I think I've soaked these through."

With a chuckle, he patted his wife on the arm. "You'll do fine. The children will love you."

But Florie continued to wave her fan while softly saying a prayer in Hungarian.

A maid greeted them at the door, taking Sam's hat and coat in one arm, and draping Florie's shawl over the other. They heard the ticking of a massive clock in the next room. After the maid left, it was the only sound they heard. A long, cumbersome minute ticked by.

"Is there life in this house?" Sam roared. Florie giggled and tried to shush him.

Min appeared through the arched doorway. She wore a severe blue dress and her hair was pinned tightly against her skull. It was just like Sam to go hooting about indoors, she thought. Such behavior was for the stable or hunting field.

"Welcome back, brother," she said, her tone cold and distant. She approached him quickly, raising herself on toes to plant an austere kiss on his cheek. This was the moment she so dreaded, the moment Sam returned to take her family away.

He, in turn, briefly embraced her. "Minerva. We have much to discuss, dear sister. But first there's a more important matter." He stepped away from his sibling and grasped his companion's hand in his. "This is Florence, my wife."

Min had tried to ignore the young woman with the ridiculously short haircut when she first entered the room. A glimpse confirmed what she had heard. This Florence was indeed a handsome girl, but she was so absurdly young. How could this mere child take *her* place as a mother? Still, she was the woman of this house and would welcome her guests, including this foreign upstart.

"Florence," Min said in acknowledgement, a hint of frostiness in her voice. Their embrace was a mere suggestion of contact.

"Sister Min, thank you for welcoming us," Florie responded hesitantly. She wanted Min to like her, but sensed the barrier between them. Awkward seconds of silence dragged by.

"Now, where are my girls?" Sam asked impatiently. He tried to peek into the next room, waiting for Min to invite them into her house.

"Of course, of course," Min said, flushing with embarrassment. "They're in the parlor waiting for you."

Sam took a step toward the room and paused. He looked back at Florie.

She smiled and waved him on. "Go ahead. Meet your daughters first."

Florie watched Sam open the doors to the parlor and disappear within. She heard youthful cries of happiness and the sound of running feet. Even though she couldn't see them, she imagined the girls hugging and kissing him, tears of joy plastering their faces, and Sam hugging and kissing them in return. She wanted to laugh, and cry, and laugh again for them. But Min's cold gaze kept her joy in check.

"I understand you have known Sam for some time," Min said, a faint quiver in her voice as she listened to the celebration in the next room. She hated the sounds.

"Five, almost six years," Florie replied.

"What are you? German?"

Florie swallowed, wondering at the older woman's bluntness. "No, Hungarian."

"You two were married in Hungary then?"

Florie was sure that Min already knew otherwise. "No."

"Africa, perhaps?"

So, Sam's sister was like a lioness stalking her prey, Florie decided. It was time to get to the point.

"Actually, no. We were married in London a week ago."

A shocked look crossed Min's face, and her hand went to her cheek in distress.

"Does Sam think I'll turn my girls over to a German who has knowingly lived in sin?" She glared angrily at Florie, but forced her voice low lest it carry to the parlor. "I have given my heart and soul to those children for seven years! I will not stand for this!"

"Sister Min—"

"I am not your sister."

Florie felt an incredible calmness settle over her. She, too, could be like a lioness defending her territory. "You're right. But I *am* Sam's wife. And those are *his* children. They will decide if they want me as a mother.

And be assured, Min, I will do everything I can to make a loving family. I had hoped you would be part of that household."

"And what if they don't want you as a mother?" Min clutched greedily, desperately at the thought.

A faint smile curved Florie's lips. "I will still be Sam's wife."

Sam appeared under the archway. His hair was disheveled, his shirt collar open. His cheeks gleamed wetly with both his daughters' tears and his. Smiling broadly, he glanced from Min to his wife.

"The girls would like to meet you."

Florie inhaled a deep, calming breath, and smiled at him. "I'm ready," she said softly.

With her hand in his, he led her into the parlor. Four girls clustered together on a sea-green divan, their faces still wet with their happiness, but their lips drawn together in tight, sober lines.

"Ladies," Sam said, his voice booming, "this is Florence, your new mother."

Silence. Florie bit her lip and shifted her feet nervously.

"Mother?" asked Ethel, the smallest of the four.

"Not really Mother." That was Edith, the eldest. Calm blue eyes locked with Florie's.

"You are Edith," Florie said quietly. "You are as beautiful as your father said."

Edith did not reply.

"Did you really shoot a buffalo?" Constance blurted.

"Papa said you almost died from a terrible fever," Agnes added. "He said you fought evil slave traders, too. Why is your hair so short?"

"Can you tell us stories?" Constance had taken a step away from her sisters. "I miss it when Mama told stories."

"But she's not really Mama." Edith's gaze shifted to Sam. "Is she?"

Flustered, Sam was about to reply when Florie touched his arm.

"No, Edith," she said. "I'm certainly not your real mother, nor can I ever be. But what I can give you and your sisters is the love I feel for your father. I hope that is enough."

Smiling broadly, Sam tilted Florie's face back and kissed her. His daughters gasped in astonishment.

"Will you let me be your mother?"

Ethel ran forward and threw her arms around Florie's waist. Agnes and Constance followed. Florie hugged and kissed them all, her tears mixing with theirs. Only Edith held back.

"I ... I know Papa loves you," she said hesitantly, "but, I ... I .... " Her voice ebbed as she bit on her lip.

"You should take your time, dear Edith," Florie said gently. "I only ask that you give me a chance."

Edith saw the joy lighting her father's face. When was the last time she had seen him so happy? This beautiful young woman, barely older than herself, had transformed him, had restored the loving father she remembered. Her sisters seemed to accept her.

But what of Aunt Min, who had guided and cared for them since Mother died? She had always urged the girls to be respectful, yet loving. Edith glanced beyond the parlor door, but the older woman was not in sight.

Florie held her hands out to her. "All I ask for is a chance."

"I … I'll try." Edith politely joined her sisters. When she finally gave Florie a hug, tears rolled down her cheeks.

***

"Hurry, you two!" James pounded on his brother's bedroom door. "I don't think the Royal Geographical Society would like their keynote speaker to arrive late."

Sam glanced at Florie and shook his head in mock indignation. "I'd forgotten how everything runs on a time schedule," he grumbled. "A time to eat, a time to take the train, a time to sleep. Next I'll have to have a time just to piss."

"Or make love," Florie chimed happily. "But James is right. This is your big night. All of your geographer friends will be there, and you can tell them about your wonderful adventures on the Nile. And in a week we'll meet the Queen. I think I'm more nervous about that. What if they all reject us?"

"It really doesn't matter anymore," he assured her. "We are who we are, and I wouldn't change that for the world, though I do admit that sometimes I wish we were still on the Nile. We didn't have clocks there, did we?"

Florie smiled. She held up the last of the tortoiseshell combs Sam had given her, admiring it against the glow of a lamp. "I wonder if Bachita still has the others? I so miss our old friends from Africa."

"I bet you miss the malaria, too," he teased.

More thumping rattled their bedroom door. "Father! Florie! Please hurry!"

It was Edith's turn to urge them to make speed. It had been a teary, joyous night in her Aunt Min's home when her father had returned with his new wife. At first she had been stunned that the lovely woman with the strange accent had become her stepmother. But after her younger sisters had been packed to bed with stories of African adventures, she and Florie had stayed up and talked until the wee hours of the morning. They spoke of love and loss, of determination, of sacrifice, then of love again. When she finally went to bed, after the clock in the great room stroked three, some of the hollowness she felt when she thought of Mama was gone. A new kind of warmth was beginning to seep in.

When the bedroom door finally opened, Edith rushed to give her parents a hug. She stopped short, however, her hand covering her mouth in wonder. Her father, clad in a dark suit, looked confident if a trifle menacing. But it was Florie, gowned in satiny material, her golden hair slowly growing back and partly hidden by a stylish hat and veil, who almost whisked her breath away.

"They will love you both tonight," she pronounced. Seconds later, she escorted them out of the apartment to the coach where her uncle James waited.

***

At Burlington House, the home of the Royal Geographical Society, the Duke of Wellington was speaking to Rear Admiral Murray and several guests from India, while a few steps away the Comte de Paris punctuated his conversation with the smoking end of a cigar. Sir Roderick Murchison stood by the entrance way to the meeting hall and beamed as he accepted accolades from the membership; after all, it wasn't often one had a great waterfall named after him.

"The Bakers have arrived," Austen Layard panted. It had taken him several minutes to work his way through the throng to reach Murchison. "You've met the woman, haven't you?"

"Yes, I have," Murchison replied airily as he smoothed out imaginary wrinkles on his coat sleeves. "She and Baker stopped by the other day so we could arrange his presentation."

"And?" Layard's cheeks puffed with aggravation. He knew his friend was playing him along.

"She's quite charming, but very shy." Murchison sniffed. "Here, come and look at some of his watercolors. It's unbelievable they made it back from Africa with him. He'll be ready to give his speech in a few minutes and tell us all about it. I say, there they are over there. Let's greet them."

Florie clung to Sam's arm as they entered the building. After a momentary hush, admirers swept toward them in a cacophony of sound. She squeezed his hand. "This place is not for me. I will not be able to speak so much English. Please, could you excuse me?"

"But, Florie, I wanted you to sit by me on the stage," he objected, his brows furrowing with concern. "You are part of this story."

She felt panic surging through her as learned and wealthy men converged. "No, please. I'll stand off to the side. Edith and James will be with me. I'm very proud of you." She let go of his hand and melted away before the first surge of guests surrounded him.

After ten minutes of near chaos, the gavel banged the meeting to order. Members flocked to their seats in expectation as Sir Roderick Murchison stood at the podium to deliver his introduction. His gaze swept regally over the audience. This was his moment, too.

"It is my great pleasure to call you all together for the inaugural Autumn Address of the Royal Geographical Society. Let me call your attention to two issues regarding the conduct of the man seated on the stage. His devotion to geography has provided us with an incredible storehouse of discovery and information regarding the sources of the Blue Nile, and this he accomplished entirely at his own cost."

The audience responded with applause and cheers.

"Secondly, his noble conduct ensured that Captains Speke and Grant, in their grave and exhausted condition, would safely return from Africa, preserving and sharing their findings of the great inland lake now known as Victoria." More cheers. "As said, at his expense he continued the journey on the White Nile and confirmed the existence of another source now named after our late beloved Prince Albert. His is a story of sacrifice and resolve, and we are all beneficiaries of his great determination. I give you Samuel White Baker."

As Sam stepped to the podium, Burlington House rocked to a standing ovation. He glanced quickly to his left. He spied Florie behind a curtain in the wings, her arm linked with Edith's. She smiled and nodded at him.

"Thank you, Mr. President," Sam began. "Esteemed members of the Royal Geographical Society and guests of the Society, it is with significant pleasure and relief," a chuckle rippled among the listeners, "to report that the great mystery of the Nile sources has been solved. Please, save your applause until I have finished. My story has two parts. The first is of the Eastern or Blue Nile. Its great treasure house of rain rises in the highlands of Abyssinia. It is here .... "

For the next hour, the audience sat mesmerized by Sam's report on his travels first up the Blue Nile, then the White. Virtually the only sounds other than his voice were the faint rasping of newspaper correspondents' pencils on their tablets. And even those stalwart reporters paused in awe as he described his adventures and discoveries.

"And so, smitten with disease and barely alive, we made our way back to Khartoum." Sam paused, holding up his hand to once more allay applause. His gaze swept over the guests. Many were sitting on the edge of their seats.

"There is one whom I must thank and it honors me to do so in your august presence. This person has the heart of a lion, and a courage that transcends both youth and gender. Without her strength and devotion, I wouldn't be alive to address you tonight. Mr. President, my Lords and Ladies, Gentlemen, allow me to present my wife."

Sam turned and strode toward the curtain at the wings. He bowed to a figure standing there.

"Oh, no, Sam." Florie's eyes were wide. "No." She shook her head as he gripped her hand and led her to the podium. She felt her face flushing as the audience rose to its feet and exploded with applause. Finally, she flashed a great smile at them. Pandemonium reigned. She leaned toward her husband and whispered in his ear, "I wish I had my pistol. I'd use it on you."

"I'm sure you would, my dear," he said, waving at the crowd. "I'm sure you would."

She tilted her face to his. "And what if the Queen doesn't like us?"

With a gentle smile, he pressed his lips lightly to hers. "Then we'll go back to Africa," he said. "We still have the slave trade to destroy."

***

Later, outside Burlington House, Sam stamped his feet as he and Florie watched their brougham pull to curbside. "Winter is coming," he said, his breath a frosty cloud in the chill night air. "Makes one wish for the Nile, doesn't it?"

Florie smiled and nodded her head. She waited for the coach driver to open the door. The clouds suddenly parted and lit the street with a ghostly glow. She glanced into the heavens at the cold, clean face of the full moon. For a moment her memories swept her to her home in Hungary and Mama's lap. How did that old song go? She hummed a few notes and the words came tumbling back to her:

Hail Mother Moon o'er autumn night,
Thy pale caress of heavenly light
Wakes lovers' hearts under dusky sky,
With a solemn promise that winter's nigh.

Sam lifted her toward the seat. Her hands rested on his shoulders as she gazed deeply into his eyes. Then she remembered what she had asked herself that night so long ago; now she knew her answer. She had found the man whose heart beat with hers as one.

Historical Note

Sam and Florie Baker's explorations of the Blue Nile and White Nile were real events. My story is based on Sam's books describing his adventures. His two-volume epic *The Albert N'yanza, Great Basin of the Nile* was published in 1866 and covered the journey to the *Luta N'zige* (Lake Albert). A year later, he published *The Nile Tributaries of Abyssinia* that detailed his earlier journey up the Blue Nile. Both titles went through numerous printings well into the twentieth-century. I also consulted two modern biographies of Sam Baker: Richard Hall's *Lovers on the Nile* (1980), and Michael Brander's *One Perfect Victorian Hero: the life and times of Sir Samuel White Baker* (1982). Interestingly, a 357-mile-long hiker's trail from Gondokoro, near the modern day city of Juba in southern Sudan, to Lake Albert was opened in 2014 to follow Florie and Sam's footsteps.

While I have attempted to maintain the chronology of events as described by Sam, I had to fill in various gaps with fictional episodes. Elephant hunting with the Hamrans, for instance, remains essentially true to Sam's description, as does meeting Speke, Grant, and Petherick at Gondokoro. Similarly, Alexine Tinne (later murdered by Tuaregs in the Sahara), Johann Schmidt, Georges Thibaut, and Kamrasi are real. Emile Zeb, Magram Bur, and Mahomet el-Nar, on the other hand, are fictional, as is their pursuit of Florie. Khurshid Aga and Andrea de Bono, however, were slave traders who actually operated in the region.

Florie received only cursory note in either of Sam's books. She was clearly with him during these adventures, and appeared in several illustrations, but he referred to her simply as F. Typical of the male hubris of the era, he dwells neither on their physical or emotional relationship, elements that I have tried to build upon. The story of Sam buying Florie in a slave market has been part of the Baker mythos for generations. Although Sam does not mention this important event in his writings, Michael Brander notes that Florie only told the story in her later years.

In 1866, Queen Victoria knighted Sam, although she disapproved of his marriage and declined to meet Florie. In 1869, Sam traveled with the Prince of Wales on a voyage up the Nile as far as Aswan; Florie stayed in England to help Edith (now married to a country vicar) with her newborn daughter. It was the first time that Florie and Sam had been separated for more than a few days at a time. Sam's trip to Egypt was a harbinger of things to come. A year later, he was hired by the Khedive of Egypt to mount a military expedition to march to the Nile lakes and quell the slave trade. This time, Florie refused to stay behind. It was their last great adventure together.

But that is a story that remains to be told.

About the Author

Ken Czech is a recognized authority on the historical literature of exploration and big game hunting. His studies and bibliographies on those subjects are widely quoted by book collectors, rare book dealers, and well-established auction houses. A retired history professor, Ken and his wife live in the Upper Midwest on an abandoned granite quarry. Visit the author's website at www.kenczech.com

ALL THINGS THAT MATTER PRESS

FOR MORE INFORMATION ON TITLES AVAILABLE FROM
ALL THINGS THAT MATTER PRESS, GO TO
http://allthingsthatmatterpress.com
or contact us at
allthingsthatmatterpress@gmail.com

Made in the USA
Columbia, SC
05 October 2017